For Leonore,
With very kind
many good wishes,

Freddy
(B. Scharf)

MASKENBUSCH

CW00516904

MASKENBUSCH

by

B. SCHARF

WINDSOR PUBLICATIONS

© B. Scharf 1994

To Lottchen

The author wishes to thank all those who contributed to the development of this novel, and in particular Mr Malcolm Gesthuysen, without whose valiant help and encouragement it might never have been completed

British Library Cataloguing in Publication Data
Scharf, B
  Maskenbusch
  1. Fiction

  Paperback   ISBN 1 870417 10 0
  Hardback   ISBN 1 870417 09 7

Published by Windsor Publications, Windsor, England

Printed by Antony Rowe Ltd, Chippenham, England

CHAPTER ONE

M, OR MORUS Maskenbusch, to give him his full name, was badly in need of a job. His current position with Eurotrip, the well-known travel people, did not offer any scope whatsoever for the creative use of his talents, nor could he discern the slightest prospect of advancement, in spite of the glowing promises lavished upon him only two months ago. Surely, he felt, a person such as he should be able to do better than be confined to the tedious vetting of substantially identical forms? 'You will meet any number of fascinating people and there is not the slightest doubt whatsoever that you will make your mark in hardly any time at all. And if you do really well (as I am quite certain you will), you may even become a Eurotrip courier and see the world as very few people are fortunate enough to see it.' That is what he had been told in the interview, and at the time these words had made a deep impression upon him, in spite of the fact that he had already seen a fair bit of the world and that at the present juncture in his life his principal aspiration was to settle down, get married, and start a family perhaps. Still, in the reassuring embrace of Eurotrip his future had promised to be both secure and rosy, and he had been happy to accept the job on offer. In the event, however, the people he met were by no means fascinating (at any rate, he did not find them so in the least), and as for making his mark, the less said about that the better. Nor was he very popular with his colleagues, who regarded him with considerable and barely concealed suspicion. When, therefore, his section supervisor intimated, not without obvious irony, that he would be wise to consider a change, to look for other employment in which his talents might make a greater and more worthwhile impact, M heaved a sigh of relief, tendered his resignation, which was accepted with some alacrity, and stepped out into the wide world to join the ranks of the unemployed.

Being out of work was not a novel experience for M, not by any means. Not that he was running short of money, nothing like that, for having only recently returned from two stints as a court interpreter in Germany he still had quite a substantial nest-egg to cushion his descent into penury, enough even to buy the very house in which he was lodging, though he seemed to be doing his utmost to squander his savings as if there were no tomorrow. How else was one to explain the maniacal zest with which he insisted on exchanging his perfectly good scrip dollars, honestly earned at Nuremberg, for pounds sterling only two days before a major devaluation of the British currency, ignoring the unquestionably sound advice of his friend Silversmith, a student at the London School of Economics and avid reader of the *Financial Times*, who understood these things, and in spite of the strained, almost frightened glances of the finance people at the American Embassy, who clearly thought him as mad as a hatter? And what indeed was one to make of the way in which he put all his money into a current account at the Westminster Bank, where it would be quite certain not to attract any interest whatsoever?

But although he was all right financially, he was not happy. For, apart from his first glorious year as a refugee in England, when the Home Office, a kindly but restrictive guardian, would not allow him to earn a living at all – a situation over which he had mercifully no control of any kind and for which he therefore also bore no responsibility – he had never enjoyed being out of work. Faced with such a predicament he would accept the most menial, the most poorly remunerated position, rather than become a burden to the State – in his book the ultimate failure. To derive any kind of satisfaction from being unemployed – in fact even to be able to tolerate the state of being superfluous to anyone's commercial requirements – you have to be tough or insensitive or philosophically perverse, at the very least. M, being none of these, suffered from a deep sense of inadequacy and a rock-like conviction that he would never be able to find work again, not in a million years.

As a prisoner of war in Japan – he spent altogether three years in captivity there – he even went so far as to consider seriously whether he would be able to manage in England on just three bowls of rice a day while living in a tin shack. On the other hand, not being allowed to work was a different matter altogether, a fate that could be shared happily with several thousand other people, all of them relying on such weekly and adequate payments as the Czech Refugee Trust Fund in its generosity and wisdom bestowed on them.

At 28 years of age, M was lanky and almost tall. A great if aimless walker and extremely short-sighted, he – peering through round, wire-framed spectacles – was inclined to keep his eyes firmly on the ground in front of his feet rather than on the environment, however splendid, through which he happened to be passing. His hair, only a year or so ago abundant to the point of being a nuisance, was beginning to recede, and he worried a lot about being excessively long and thin, just as in his middle years he would worry increasingly about being fat and unable to bring his weight down, try as he would.

Together with his friend Löwenzahn, who had radical plans for a solution of the Palestinian problem and had, on a secret mission in Jerusalem (as he claimed), acquired a most dramatic knife-scar which both paralysed and enhanced one side of his face, M used to criss-cross London in all directions, much as during his school years in Vienna he had traversed that city in the company of his friend Josef Brunner, in either case without the slightest idea where he was or where he was going. M, incidentally, rather envied Löwenzahn for having such a fine scar, according to the latter a great asset in dealing with women, of whom, as he was never loth to explain, there were two types: his mother and all the others.

In spite of the fact that his life so far had been relatively varied – both relatives

2

and friends would shake their heads in utter, chuckling disbelief – M, a latter-day Candide, had not as yet acquired much worldly wisdom or maturity of judgment. This, on the whole, proved not to be a bad thing, for it gained him many friends, since almost anyone could easily feel superior to him. Nor did his lack of maturity worry M unduly, for in the inner recesses of his mind he realised full well that maturity in any respect signified the end of the road and could be followed only by decay. Whenever maturity came up for discussion, he would argue that if wine were poured, at an equal rate, both into a small glass and into a large barrel, the glass would fill up in an instant whereas it would take a long time to fill the barrel, which in the end however would contain far more of the precious liquid.

Although M was undoubtedly immature and quite frequently naïve, there was nothing wrong with his sense of humour. During his school years in Vienna, he had been friendly with a waiter at the Kaffee Weimar who used to supply him with numerous back-numbers of such publications as *Fliegende Blätter* and *Gartenlaube*, as a result of which he suffered an overdose of feeble jokes. Reading all this unfunny dross eventually made him hate virtually all jokes – only a few select Jewish jokes were exempt – and he developed an almost pathological dislike of funny men and buttonholing party bores with their fatuous anticipatory grins and self-satisfied laughter, whom he regarded as positively anti-humorous. In his opinion, humour, rather like a pearl in an oyster, had to be the result of mild irritation, of not being quite in tune, the hallmark of the true humorist being that he was ever prepared to throw the pearls of his wit into champagne, allowing them to dissolve freely.

For as long as he could remember, M had been a voracious reader, ever on the lookout for 'good' books by 'great' writers that would stimulate his imagination without at the same time making excessive demands on his powers of concentration. Progressing from a small but choice diet of books recommended as suitable for children – *Robinson Crusoe*, Grimms' *Fairy Tales* and *Gulliver's Travels* come readily to mind – he had, in the course of time, sampled a wide and stimulating variety of other literary delights as well, ranging from classical novels to poetry and plays. After a period of several months, during which he indulged freely in 'novels for the educated woman', he again reverted to more respectable fare, gradually extending his range in line with the circumstances of his life. The availability of reading-matter being, at various stages of his 'career', severely restricted, he was, time and again, compelled to venture onto unfamiliar and less conventional ground, which contributed greatly to the breadth of his literary experience.

From time to time, whenever he felt the need for spreading the wings of his intellect, M also read works presenting a panoramic, readily comprehensible and preferably dramatised view of some large subject such as mathematics or the history of the world, and he frequently enjoyed browsing through more specialised texts on art, philosophy, and in particular psychology, which offered, as he hoped, the means of influencing and even dominating others, for he was firmly convinced that knowledge and insight were reliable sources of power. M never managed or, when it came to the point, actually even wanted to dominate anybody but was himself often a welcome and opportune object for other people's egocentric aspirations. He liked to think of himself as a potentially great mathematician and was never happier than when in the process of solving some mathematical problem, however humble. He also 'knew' a number of languages and had, while serving on a Norwegian ship, written a very sentimental play in which the characters addressed each other in English, German, Norwegian and Czech, each according to his mother tongue. The action, which was based squarely on his experiences at the time, also took place on a Norwegian ship, but M had long ago forgotten what the play was actually about. It did, however, demonstrate one thing quite clearly: a common language understandable to all would be most desirable. Since he wrote that play, M had forgotten his Czech, so even he might have had difficulty in understanding this work, had it not been lost.

In the past few weeks M had written several letters of application without any more signal success than a reply from Messrs. Thomas Cook explaining that he was unfortunately overqualified for any of the positions just then available. He happened to be sitting in the kitchen of No. 12 Westlake Crescent, his abode for the past two years, enjoying his evening repast of goulash and noodles and scanning the pages of his local paper, *The Bayswater and District Gazette*, when he suddenly thrilled to the following advertisement:

LINGUISTS (ALL TONGUES) !!!
Are you forward-looking, dynamic and aware?
If your answer is in the affirmative, join the tutorial team of
Britain's leading language institute for students of all ages.
This may be the chance you have been waiting for.
PREVIOUS EXPERIENCE NOT ESSENTIAL.
All applications to Box No....

He felt that fate itself was taking him by the hand, setting his feet on the right path. This, at last, promised to be a position for which he might well be admirably qualified. No-one could, after all, deny that he was a most capable linguist or that he was – potentially, at least – forward-looking, dynamic and aware. Teaching was sure to be fun, and he certainly had no reason to doubt that he would be really good at it, although to be really first-rate he might have to do some revision – tidy up some points of grammar, perhaps. Anyhow, he had always been able to cope, and the greater the challenge the better he liked it. The possibilities were simply staggering. With his flair for languages and his natural teaching ability – an ability not merely imagined but proven – he might well become head of modern languages... a professor at London University even, in due course. Changing abruptly to a rather different track, he then considered the possibility of meeting, in his lofty capacity as a moulder of young minds, a really lovely girl student. She would be slender and at the same time lusciously plump, wild, submissive and demure, with long, long, really lovely legs, but not too tall. Thoroughly ready for his various fatherly ministrations, she would be eager to please him, Morus, in the most exotic ways. When this little dream had faded – as, alas, dreams are prone to do – the practical side of his personality took over. Trembling with eagerness he stacked his dirty dishes in the sink (other dirty dishes were there already to welcome them) and cleared the table. From his stock of unused paper he selected the most presentable sheet and began to write:

'Dear Sir or Madam,

With reference to your advertisement in *The Bayswater and District Gazette* of today's date' (he struck out 'advertisement' and substituted 'interesting advertisement'. This too did not entirely satisfy him, so he added 'most' to make it 'most interesting advertisement') 'I wish to apply for the position offered, my principal languages being French' (which was sure to be in demand) 'and German.'

'Too stiff altogether,' he reflected. Then, with obvious satisfaction, he withdrew his first draft from the typewriter, threw it into the waste-paper basket and started on another sheet – again the best he could find – for he knew that in matters such as this no expense must be spared. This is what he wrote:

'Dear future employer,

When may I come to see you? I am convinced that I can be of real help to your esteemed organisation and am very eager to star' (noticing his slip he added a 't' to 'star') 'in your service, seeing that at present my talents are entirely wasted. My principal languages are French and German, which I studied' (feeling that one or even two universities might not come amiss at this point, preferably on the good old Continent, he continued) 'at Bordeaux and Heidelberg, respectively, and even though I say so myself, my knowledge, both practical and theoretical, of these languages is impressive, although I did not complete my studies owing to circumstances entirely beyond my control. I also have a good working knowledge of certain other languages,' (these he listed, together with one or two others of which he had no knowledge whatsoever) 'but would not venture to offer them to an institute as prestigious as yours without further study.

I look forward to your positive reply.

Yours most keenly,

Morus Maskenbusch'

'That should do the trick,' thought M with eminent satisfaction as he extracted the letter from his typewriter in order to read it again in its now postable state. Although he did not write many letters – arguing that his enjoyment of this, in his opinion, largely lost art was so intense that it might easily take him over entirely – he regarded those he did write in much the same way in which a burglar might regard the tools of his trade, that is to say, as the means essential for gaining access to what was jealously guarded or ordinarily inaccessible. He made it a rule, therefore, to hone every word, every last comma, to perfection, while never permitting himself to lose sight of any relevant factors, however apparently trivial, or of his ultimate purpose.

M's latest creation pleased him to such an extent as to arouse in him, which was not unusual, the need for an audience. Accordingly, he went to call on his friend Silversmith, who lived in the room across the hall. Silversmith was habitually short of money, provisions and other material goods. Although a great borrower, he was by no means a great lender. On the other hand, he was a superb debater of obscure points, a fellow with a great sense of fun and a vicarious connoisseur of 'the good life'. M found him sitting on his bed, with a large dictionary on his knees, trying to extract all the words the letters of which were to be found in the sentence 'Exobrill spells better value.' He had been at this task for the past three weeks, ever confident that his systematic approach (which he modified at least once every other day) would yield rich rewards in the Exobrill Christmas Competition. Silversmith, in the still eye of the long vacation, as it were, had in any case nothing better to do and, besides, he liked to keep his mind active and his responses sharp. As for his systematic approaches, he normally reserved them for special projects such as the present one, which seemed to offer prospects of making money, but when it came to studying and other more mundane activities he, very much like M, tended to rely on sheer genius.

When M burst in upon him, Silversmith was extremely glad to see him, for the evening had been on the point of becoming tedious and a conversation with M was at this juncture preferable by far. Nevertheless, to begin with he did not respond to his friend's entry but simply continued with his self-selected task. Only his longish nose twitched slightly in pleasurable anticipation of intellectual fireworks to come, a familiar reaction which did not escape M's attention.

'I have just written a truly brilliant letter, do you want to hear it?' Wasting no time on unnecessary preliminaries, M came straight to the point. Silversmith, however, who had what in his opinion were far weightier news, chose to ignore M's announcement, at least for the moment, reporting in turn that he, Silversmith, had now perfected a method which would ensure that he won all the major prizes – first, second and third – in the Exobrill competition. In future he would be using not merely one but three leading dictionaries of the English language – the Shorter Oxford, Webster's and Nuttall's – to make certain of a really comprehensive haul and he could no doubt rely on Rosabelle (his on-and-off girl friend) to type his list three times, in different order and on three different machines, although he had not as yet, put this to her. Such a strategy was indeed beyond criticism – a point which M conceded most readily, adding that plans as brilliant as this were, in his personal experience, rare indeed. His somewhat excessive praise – deliberately over-the-top and received by Silversmith with suitable if disingenuous modesty – gave M the chance he had been waiting for, and now, at last, it was his turn to occupy the limelight.

M proceeded to read his composition, commenting about its background, the reasons for his approach and other aspects which he considered noteworthy. Silversmith, for his part, cheered him on, offering both valuable and not so valuable suggestions, and was in turn treated to some good-natured banter, which he savoured, as always, to the full. They had some tea, engaged in sundry hilarious reminiscences and speculations and generally put the world to rights. When M finally left at about 2 o'clock in the morning in order to copy his masterpiece and prepare it for posting they both agreed that this had been a most memorable evening, as indeed it had.

Another memorable evening of a rather different kind ensued, a get-together in M's room to celebrate M's liberation from the thraldom of Eurotrip, with two bottles of wine, several bottles of beer, as well as some bags of peanuts and other produce left over from the previous year's Christmas party.

M and Silversmith were the hosts, and then there were Rosabelle and Lipkin, who did not live at No. 12 but were frequent visitors. Lipkin, unemployed and, owing to a real talent for clumsiness and an imperious sense of justice, virtually unemployable, thought of himself as a Communist, although, possibly to their mutual benefit he had always lacked the resolution to join the Party. Rosabelle, dark and heavy-featured, with an abundance of unkempt black hair, usually scowling but renowned for her heart of gold, worked as a typist and general factotum at a local solicitor's.

Rosabelle, now coyly perched on Silversmith's knee, pretended not to notice the rather crude way in which he handled her admittedly somewhat excessive bosom as if about to squeeze it into a more appealing state. Having no illusions about her effect on men, she was quite ready to indulge him in this and other ways, for she was firmly convinced that in this life everything had to be paid for, and besides, she quite enjoyed the present proceedings.

Although unattractive to most men, Rosabelle had one ardent admirer – Lipkin of the prematurely balding, skull-like head, who was wiry and short and far too shy to open his heart to her and tell her that he loved her. As for Rosabelle, on the other hand, it had never entered her head to think of him as a potential boyfriend or, as it eventually came to pass, the man in her life. Silversmith for his part regarded Rosabelle and her golden heart as a bit of a joke, but being a realist through and through and far from choosy, he was ever prepared to make do with what happened to be on offer.

Lipkin and Silversmith, both having had a little more alcohol than was perhaps good for them, were arguing the pros and cons of boxing versus ju-jitsu as methods of self-defence. Lipkin, a flyweight, had done a bit of boxing in his time and knew, as he kept telling them over and over again, how to take care of himself. M, who had skimmed through a number of books on ju-jitsu and even practised this art on brooms and chairs, naturally favoured the Japanese system. As for Rosabelle, she did not join in, preferring, as she usually did, a more passive role. Lipkin – a truly gentle person totally averse to violence when he was sober (unless, of course, his sense of justice had been outraged), but who could not, after a drink or two, be relied upon to restrain his temper – was getting increasingly annoyed with Silversmith as the latter continued mauling 'his' Rosabelle, and Silversmith in turn reacted by descending into a snooty and tiresome routine of 'you don't say's and 'really's.

Feeling that some radical change of direction was needed in order to prevent the party from getting out of hand, M offered to tell them about Port Darwin, Australia, where, as he claimed, he had had an experience highly relevant to the topic of self-defence. The others acquiesced (although they had heard this story before on more than one occasion), as it seemed to offer a way out of the present unpleasantness and partly in order to humour M, who started immediately in his usual, well-tried fashion:

'I do not suppose that any of you have ever been to Port Darwin – very few people, relatively speaking of course, have. In any case, you didn't miss much. Port Darwin in December 1942 was above all hot, dry and dusty. Imagine, if you will, twenty thousand thirsty Australian soldiers and heaps and heaps of empty beer bottles as far as the eye could see. A few withering palm trees, lots of desert, and the sea, blindingly blue in the burning sun. A hotel and a plateau at the very edge of the sea. Soldiers in small groups here and there drinking their beer. Some of the seamen from our ship, the good old *Bergano* – more often referred to as "that floating coffin *Bergano*" – and, of course yours truly, were also there, intent on some serious drinking.

8

As for me, I was there to prove a point. It had been put to me in none too polite a manner that I didn't care for drinking because I was scared, afraid to make a fool of myself, a bit of a coward really. A challenge like this could not be ignored, obviously.

So, there we were, five or six of us, with lots and lots of beer, whiskey and – I can see it now – a squat, light-blue tin of Libby's pork sausages. I don't know why, but in those days nobody's drinking party seemed to be complete without Libby's sausages. Having said, somewhat rashly, that I could drink any one of the others under the table – mind you, there was no table under which to drink anybody – I made a point of downing my share of the booze as rapidly as I could. Soon I was as drunk as a lord (although I really cannot comprehend why lords should be more given to drunkenness than the rest of us) and simply passed out. When I came to again, there was that veritable giant of an Australian policeman – he seemed to be at least eight foot tall – and being drunk I naturally felt obliged to challenge him to a fight. In fact, it turned out that it wasn't a policeman at all but my friend Odda, the one who died later in an accident, poor fellow, but that is a different story. He may have been my friend, but that did not stop him from hitting me fairly and squarely between the eyes, thus bringing my drinking extravaganza to a sudden end. Fortunately I wasn't wearing my glasses at the time, but for a week or more I was walking about with not one but two real shiners, with everybody telling me that I looked like a horrible old monkey.'

M, whose throat had gone dry with so much talking, took a pensive sip of wine before proceeding with his story.

'When I woke up again several hours later – it was now the middle of the afternoon and hotter than ever – everyone had gone except Trondhjem, who seemed to have trouble getting to his feet. Incidentally, Trondhjem was, of course, not his real name but that of the town he came from. I felt, rather surprisingly no doubt, like having a glass of milk, and so I asked Trondhjem to give me some money, to which he responded by telling me to go to hell and pelting me with the remains of the sausages. But to cut this long story short,' (Lipkin seemed to be falling asleep) 'I eventually did get my milk at a downtown milk bar, was nearly arrested as a Japanese spy by a real policeman in shirtsleeves and with a tropical helmet, and eventually returned to the plateau, where I saw Odda arguing hotly with a group of soldiers whom he had joined. Understandably elated by my achievement – I had, after all, proved my point that I was not afraid of a drop or two of alcohol – I felt in need of company, so I went over to join in their discussion.'

At this point M noticed that Lipkin had left the room, but there was Rosabelle listening with gratifyingly rapt attention. M, who did not care who was listening to his tales as long as somebody was, went on as follows:

'One of the soldiers, a wide-shouldered, stocky bloke, almost cuboid in shape he seemed, asked me, quite politely, if I would like to see a corpse, to which I answered,

"Why not, anything for a laugh". The fact that I agreed so readily is, of course, a measure of the state I was in, for had I been my normal self I would rather have run a mile than look at a corpse. The soldier who had asked me then got up, as did a friend of his, a tall, lanky fellow, and they took me with them. So off we wandered to the very edge of the plateau, from where a kind of track led down to the sea, the lanky soldier with his arm about my shoulder and the stocky one right behind. "Where is the corpse?" I wanted to know, as I couldn't see anything of the kind. "Here, you Pommy bastard," said the stocky one and hit me squarely in the face. As I collapsed I instinctively put my arms about his knees, whereupon the three of us tumbled down into the sea, which met us with sundry debris, masses of bottles and various products of nature, some of them not at all pleasant. To cut a long story short,' (having got past the climax of his tale, M was himself beginning to be bored with it) 'in falling, the stocky bloke seemed to have hurt his wrist, and his mate didn't look very happy either. As for me, I now felt as sober as a judge, so when they asked me to lend them some money I knew that this was the one thing I must not do, for it might have given them the idea that I was afraid of them, whereas I was merely apprehensive. So I muttered something about "ju-jitsu blackbelt" and similar rubbish. This did the trick, for they did not insist. We simply returned to the plateau, where they told me to "scram", and that is exactly what I did.'

'You were a bit lucky, weren't you?' commented Lipkin, who had returned. 'After all, you don't know anything about ju-jitsu.'

'So what? They were not to know this, and when I grabbed the short fellow's knees, that might very well have been a most skilfully executed throw, which clearly proves my point.'

They now put on a gramophone record of dance music, which inspired Silversmith to drag Rosabelle about the room, much to the distress of Lipkin, who was looking on with a very sombre stare. Lipkin himself did not dance, nor did M. However, having read a book on ballroom dancing by Victor Silvester, he was able to discourse at great length on how to place the feet correctly and how to tell whether the tune being played was a tango or a waltz. In his seafaring days, during an exceedingly agreeable spell in Melbourne, Australia, he had in fact attended a dancing class in Collins or Flinders Street, where he used to go carrying an iron rod wrapped in a copy of *Truth* to protect himself against attackers on the dark and lonesome road leading from the Victoria Docks to the bright lights of the city. Although he failed in his primary objective, which was to master yet another art leading to conquest of the gentle sex, he did wind up with certain experiences which he, if nobody else, thought hilarious. He also realised that to become an expert dancer he would have to follow other, possibly more theoretical paths of study – hence the book.

Having tired of strutting about with Rosabelle, Silversmith went to his own room, where he put on his wine-red dressing gown in order to make himself more comfortable. He returned with two towels, which he wrapped about his fists and started to shadow-box in the general direction of Lipkin, while leaping about madly and congratulating himself on being the 'Champ'.

This brought the party to a somewhat abrupt end. Lipkin, already most irritated by the way in which Silversmith had been treating his adored Rosabelle, agreed to see whether he could stand up to Silversmith for three rounds. This was quite untypical of him, for he was really a very gentle soul, quite averse to fighting anything but genuine dragons. At any rate, he too had his fists wrapped in towels and, with M acting as referee, the 'fight' commenced. Indeed, it proved to be a fight in which the beginning and the end virtually coincided, for Lipkin's very first blow, a left to the mouth, brought his opponent down, causing his lip to swell up. At this point M, like any referee worth his salt, had no alternative but to stop the fight (an opinion clearly shared by the tenant below, who protested against the noise by pounding on the ceiling with a long-handled broom specially acquired by him for just such occasions). And so, since nearly all the wine had been drunk and all the nuts eaten, they decided to call it a day. Rosabelle helped M to clear away the debris and to restore the furniture to its proper setting. Lipkin, weighed down with guilt and a sense of profound failure, slunk away, and Silversmith went to bed to take care of his lip and a very unpleasant headache.

CHAPTER TWO

ALTHOUGH M had almost given up hope of ever hearing from TTTW Ltd again, several weeks later a letter arrived. Seeing that it was a very thin letter sent in an envelope apparently used before and with the stamp upside down, he decided that it must be a rejection note and, accordingly, threw it into the waste-paper basket unopened. However, he changed his mind – after all, you never could tell – and having retrieved and opened the letter, this is what he read:

'Dear Dr. Maskenpusch,

Thanking you for your letter of the 3rd ult., which we perused with considerable interest, we have great pleasure in advising you that you, dear Dr. Mashenbush, have been selected for inclusion in the TTTW shortlist of SUITABLE APPLICANTS. We would, accordingly, suggest that you attend at these premises on 27th inst. at 1 pm precisely, when the Undersigned will be happy to make your acquaintance.
I trust that this arrangement is agreeable.

Yours most sincerely,

Adolphus R. Pendlebloom,
Managing Director and Chief Executive.'

Further details could be gleaned from the heading of the letter, namely, that the company's head office was in Frith Street, Soho, that the Board, apart from A. R. Pendlebloom, Ph.D. (British), included various illustrious and aristocratic persons and that the company's motto was *'Per Ardua ad Astra'*. This M interpreted, with considerable relish, as meaning 'Through hardship to the stars'. In doing so, he felt as if he were renewing an old and agreeable acquaintance. Had he not, after all, been one of the leading Latin scholars, second only to the great Geiger himself, in Form 7c of the Klappenhorn Gymnasium in Vienna, and had not his talent for Latin, that ancient and venerable language, been one of the keys – Mathematics was the other – to the attention, however fleeting, of Gretl Navratil, who sat at the front of the class?

Alas, Gretl had not always been kind to him, making it sadly obvious that his dumb, dog-like devotion would never be returned, but the very thought of her sufficed to fill his heart with longing and to inspire his dreams, and for this he was profoundly grateful. Of course, in the shadow of the events which eventually led to Austria being swallowed whole by Hitler's greedy Reich (not, it would seem, a wholly unwilling morsel), M's quite properly unreciprocated desire for Gretl Navratil stood absolutely no chance and was bound to come to grief, sooner or later. Indeed, the end came when, standing behind a pillar, M – breathless with joy because Gretl, his Gretl of the radiant blue eyes, trim, doll-like figure and long, straw-coloured pigtails, the Gretl of his most intimate dreams, had actually smiled at him, Morus, her truest but, alas, least regarded champion – happened to hear her say to Hubricht, who in the seven years in which they had shared the same class had never once spoken to him directly, 'Of course, I know that Maskenbusch is a Jew and, to tell you the truth, I simply can't stand the sight of him, but he is jolly good at Latin, and what with the exam next week, what choice have I got?' M did not wait to hear more but simply slunk away, swallowing bitter tears. Severely disillusioned and somehow diminished in his own eyes, he never forgave Gretl for what he regarded as her treachery, and it profoundly affected the way in which he eventually came to think of his native country. In later years he had the impression, whenever he remembered this incident, that he never helped her again, but in fact he was never quite certain whether he did or he didn't.

Having lovingly considered his new if spurious title, there for all to see in black and white (Dr. Maskenbusch sounded simply marvellous), and refusing to be discouraged by the fact that most of the letter, including Dr. Pendlebloom's signature, was duplicated, with only variable information such as the date and approximations to his name inserted separately by hand, M immediately rushed off to inform Silversmith of his good luck. The latter, however, still firmly in the embrace of Morpheus, one of his favourite deities, and consequently less enthusiastic than M had hoped, limited himself to a series of defensive growls and unhelpful suggestions.

The Frith Street offices of Tutors to the World Limited were on the third floor of a rather dilapidated, elderly building near Old Compton Street. Although its appearance was distinctly discouraging, the area in which it was situated greatly appealed to M, for whom all things sleazy and potentially permissive had an irresistible attraction. He welcomed the profusion of bookshops, Italian delicatessens and restaurants, strip-joints, cinemas and theatres. He liked the look of the people hurrying along, strolling or simply standing and arguing at street corners, and even the dirt in the roads, the mysterious paper parcels in doorways, which occasionally turned out to be drunks sleeping off their intoxication, and the overflowing dustbins added to his enjoyment. He felt that this was an area perfectly suited to his aspirations, where he would not be bored out of his mind and where there was every chance of interesting – and possibly romantic – encounters.

It was therefore with considerable optimism that he climbed the winding stairs, their stone steps smooth with age. Breathless and aching all over, he at last reached the parrot-green top landing with its brown, peeling doors. On one of the doors there was a sheet of headed TTTW letterpaper crudely attached with sellotape, which instructed visitors to 'KNOCK PRIOR TO ENTRY'. Somebody had changed the TTTW motto, which now read '*Per Ardua ad Aspro*', and had drawn two semi-circles, each with a dot above it, to which he had added the humorous legend '*Mama mia*'.

Behind the door they were arguing. M, fearing that this might not be a good time for him to make his entry, waited for a minute or two until the noise had subsided and then knocked cautiously. However, there was no reply. So he knocked again, this time more firmly. The door opened slightly, and, having for a few long seconds stared at him disapprovingly through the gap, a woman with mauve butterfly spectacles and straight, grey hair caught up in a bun snapped:

'Yes, what is it?'

'I am to see Dr. Pendlebloom at 1 o'clock. My name is Morus Maskenbusch.'

'Morris Who?'

'Maskenbusch. Dr. Pendlebloom wrote to me suggesting that I see him today.'

He held out his letter of appointment, which she brushed aside without as much as a glance, but then she allowed him to enter and sit down at an old utility desk heavily laden with papers and supporting a black Remington which might well have been a valuable antique.

'Dr. Pendlebloom is a very busy man. Still, now you are here, you might as well complete this.' She pushed a form at him and left him, disdainfully, to his own devices and the taciturn companionship of a young typist in a state of obvious distress, ferociously banging away at her machine as if she held it responsible for her present trouble and meant to punish it good and proper.

Having tried to engage her in conversation and failed miserably, M gave up the struggle and looked around the room instead. It was small, with very pink walls and a disproportionately tall, unbelievably grimy window. All the woodwork had been painted dark brown, but the office furniture – various desks, cupboards and chairs – was extremely varied, both in colour and style. In one corner there was a large roll-top desk, the special domain, no doubt, of the lady with the mauve spectacles. The walls were covered in charts, notices and travel posters, and on the filing cabinet stood two empty vases, a bust of Beethoven and a Christmas card. Paper in various stages of decay dominated the scene, imparting to it a certain homeliness.

As for the form, it was long and intricate, but M did find that the answers to several questions lent themselves well to improvisation, which came as a great relief. Nevertheless, there were two questions which clearly required a more subtle technique, since they related to information volunteered by him in his original letter of application but now forgotten. Try as he would, he could not remember at which universities he had claimed to have studied nor what languages he had listed in addition to French and German. Having given these matters much anguished thought (the state of his fingernails eventually bore witness to this), he decided simply to circumvent them by boldly asserting that, though his studies had been extensive and conducted both privately and at universities abroad, he rated his practical linguistic experience far more highly and was prepared, nay eager, to undergo any test reasonably likely to substantiate his suitability.

He had hardly finished with the form when the lady with the spectacles came in again and sat down at the roll-top desk. Without as much as a glance at him she said, 'Dr. Pendlebloom will see you now. Don't keep him waiting.' M, thinking that he merely had to pass through the door by which the lady had entered, went out, only to find himself in a dark corridor with several doors on either side but without any indication where they might lead. Not at all eager to return to the reception office, where he would have had to admit failure, and indeed unable to recall where it was, he meandered, with increasing desperation, from door to door trying to fathom where he might find the Principal. Only the doors of the toilets, one for male and one for female staff, were marked, and he was beginning to fear the worst when out rushed the bespectacled lady, waving his form at him and screeching, 'You're keeping him waiting, you know, I told you he was busy, we are all busy here.' Having pushed the form into his hands, she was on the point of darting back into her space, but before she could do so M managed to elicit the vital information from her.

This time M's knock was answered after only a short delay.

'Ah, come in, come in, my dear friend! So you have already met Miss Gomberg, our Managing Secretary, a most invaluable member of our organisation, please believe me. She can of course be difficult, most women of her age are, but you and I, being men of the world, must look under the surface, as it were. We must make certain allowances. However, when the chips are down – an odd phrase that, I wonder where it originated, but perhaps you can tell me ... Where was I? Ah yes – whenever a problem arises, whatever its nature, it is always Miss Gomberg to whom we turn for assistance, and she never lets us down.'

During this peroration, in the course of which he was pumping M's hand in a display of total sincerity and goodwill, Dr. Pendlebloom's bird-like dark brown eyes darted all over M, who, for his part, had entered into a state of passive receptivity, a sort of suspended animation, prepared for whatever might befall.

Dr. Pendlebloom – although not an academic man in the conventional sense, indubitably a graduate of the University of Life –was not a tall man. He was dapper, delicately perfumed – perhaps to erase from his memory the all-pervasive stench of fish which had haunted his childhood – and his fingernails were exquisitely manicured. He was as bald as an egg, but had, by way of partial compensation, a black moustache, neatly trimmed to the shape of a perfect rectangle. His English was meticulous and only slightly foreign, and he was sincerely proud of the fact that he had entirely forgotten his mother tongue. A man of boundless energy, unflagging determination and virtually perfect freedom from self-doubt and any sense of humour, however rudimentary, he had, as he was ever ready to explain to anyone in need of advice and encouragement, achieved considerable worldly success entirely by his own efforts, but, according to certain malicious persons, by virtue of an astonishing ability to twist and turn his way through and out of any situation, especially in matters of business. Whatever the problem, he was firmly convinced that he and he alone knew how to resolve it. He did, however, respect the opinions of others, provided that in matters of 'business' they were manifestly successful, and, up to a point, even deferred to them. His self-assurance and his authoritarian views made him a difficult person to live with, and when his first marriage broke up, no-one who knew him had been at all surprised.

Although generally and automatically opposed to any improvement or progressive idea of which he himself was not the originator, Dr Pendlebloom could be influenced with relative ease by anyone whom he regarded as naturally inferior, such as women except in their most traditional roles or the members of his staff. So easy, indeed, was it to affect his decisions by making him believe that one was merely helping him to formulate his thoughts that he sometimes appeared to be putty in the hands of his own minions, but nothing could have been further from the truth. In spite of numerous failings Dr. Pendlebloom had many devoted friends and admirers, not least among the female members of the staff, quite a few of whom felt that it was their bounden duty to serve and protect him in whatever way they could. Nor could one help being impressed by the missionary zeal with which he regarded languages, in his eyes the very pinnacle of human achievement.

The introductory phase successfully completed, Dr. Pendlebloom ascended a kind of rostrum on which stood an enormous, shiny mahogany desk, while, at his invitation, M subsided into a very low, billowing armchair from which he could barely see the great man, who presently intoned:

'However, to come to the point, to get to the business we are here to discuss, let me, to begin with, tell you how extremely impressed we have all been with your most remarkable qualifications. Such a young man, and already such knowledge and drive.... May I have your form?' He studied the form for a minute or two, adding to it, in red ink, comments of his own, and then continued: 'Your practical turn of mind does you great credit. Take my word, as a much older man ...'

'Not at all ... , by no means ...'

'Oh yes, much, much older. How old would you say, I am?'

'Well ...'

'No matter. To come to the point – but first let me tell you about our organisation, one of the leading language organisations in the world – and by this I mean in the entire world, not just in London or even Britain but also in Paris, Rome, Damascus and other famous cities too numerous to mention. You are, of course, far too intelligent to judge us by what you see.' He was looking down on M like a benevolent, elderly weasel. 'These premises, modest as they must seem to you, are but a convenience, a temporary stepping-stone to much bigger, much better things. Tutors to the World Limited, the organisation of which I have the honour to be the Managing Director, is an enterprise on the very threshold of the future, entirely in line with what the future demands. Its policy is based on three principles: one – determination of demand; two – determination of the way in which a particular demand can best be met; and three – determination to meet the demand unflinchingly, in the most positive manner. Take, for instance, the case of the Chairman of one of our leading international corporations.' Dr. Pendlebloom lowered his head in a gesture of reverence. 'You would be astonished if I revealed its name, but suffice it to say that only last week this important company was entrusted with a giant contract worth millions of pounds in Finland.'

M, who had forgotten that Finnish (of which he did not know a single, solitary word) was one of the languages mentioned in his letter of application, was at this stage only mildly interested, but his detachment changed to alarm when, after a short pause, Dr. Pendlebloom continued: 'This important company' (these words seemed to fill him with considerable, lip-smacking pleasure) 'will, as you no doubt realise, require all sorts of Finnish language services such as tuition, interpreting and guiding, and so I put it to the Chairman' (another pleasurable term this) 'that we were the right people for this job. He was, I am proud to say, absolutely delighted to hear that such a service was available, and he immediately decided on booking a course of intensive Finnish tuition, according to the very latest methods, for over one hundred leading members of his staff. It will be our task to design a properly programmed course and to supply the necessary tutors. Thanks to our comprehensive experience in the planning of language courses for commerce and industry, it will all work like clockwork.' Dr. Pendlebloom rubbed his hands with glee. 'And, of course, this is also your great opportunity. For you, my dear Maskenbusch, being expert in this rare but important language, have been selected to organise this important project on behalf of TTTW'.

It is a matter of record that in the 18th century, in the wake of Peter the Great's westernising reforms, certain Russian noblemen employed coachmen and similarly lowly persons from Finland to teach their children French. However, since the tutors did not know any French, nor, for that matter, how to read or write, they taught their charges a kind of vernacular Finnish instead, and nobody was any the wiser. Now M found himself in a comparable though reversed position. Blushing furiously and cursing his luck, he made deprecating remarks about the quality of his Finnish (not yet of the standard intended … still requiring some minor polish … would not venture to claim … etc.), but Dr. Pendlebloom would have none of this. 'Believe me, a very much older and in one or two respects possibly more experienced man,' he explained, 'these people would not know the difference if you taught them Chinese. Whom, after all, are we kidding? You know and I know that none of them will ever learn anything. And, come to that, why should they? When it comes to the point, they will get along perfectly well without Finnish. And if communication problems were to arise, the Finns could always try to learn English, also, of course, at TTTW. This, of course, does not mean that any but the very highest standard would be acceptable, but I am convinced that you, a perfectionist – please correct me if I am wrong – would not have it otherwise.'

Dr. Pendlebloom now blew his nose at some length and very melodiously. His respiratory tract thus cleared, he continued: 'The important thing is to think in positive terms at all times. Why, do you think, do so many brainy professors and highly qualified civil servants and scientists get nowhere at all in this world? Let me tell you why. It is because they think, quite wrongly, I assure you, that they know all the answers, that they know what matters, and, of course, they don't. Not by any means. But we, I mean you and I, we know that what really matters are our students, for they are our bread and butter.' Dr. Pendlebloom smacked his lips appreciatively. 'Still, if they are happy, why should we be otherwise?'

Even though the logic of this argument seemed to be somewhat untidy, M, at last on the inside of the magic circle, felt himself suffused with a glow of forward-looking, dynamic and aware optimism.

However, far from bringing out the champagne to celebrate this newly formed partnership, Dr. Pendlebloom now quickly terminated the interview by calling Miss Gomberg, to whom he introduced M with great and complex courtesy. She in turn conveyed M to her own office, where she recorded such particulars as were required and advised him of his conditions of employment and remuneration. This done, he left, a fully-fledged member of TTTW.

Pendlebloom, incidentally, was not the original name of the Head of TTTW but had been chosen by him when he joined the British Army at the beginning of the war, in order to avoid any special treatment in case of capture. At the time this was common practice among volunteers from countries under German occupation and a most reasonable measure for their protection. As for his new name, he had chosen it in preference to a long list of possible alternatives because it seemed to him both refined and exquisitely English. Having worked his way up from very inauspicious beginnings, he naturally set great store by refinement, respectability and culture: in short by those characteristics which he regarded as quintessentially 'English'.

As a prisoner of war in Japan M had come across a similarly anglophile person, Lieutenant Takahashi, who was in charge of the camp. Before the war Lieutenant Takahashi had been a student at Oxford, where he had acquired an almost unshakable admiration for all things British. In particular, he had come to believe that every Englishman was a 'gentleman', and every Englishwoman a 'lady'. It apparently never occurred to him that, being engaged in a battle for survival, these particular 'Englishmen' simply could not afford to 'play the game' according to rules such as those to which he had once been accustomed. But as for kindness and generosity, intelligence and wit, loyalty and steadfastness, or any of the other qualities of genuine value of which there was no lack among the inmates, these never entered the orbit of his awareness and would perhaps not have been appreciated by him if they had.

However, when, after an evening roll-call, in the course of which the Lieutenant, as was his custom, had gone from room to room concluding every inspection with a formal 'goodu nightu', Jack Crawley, an ex-marine from Glasgow and – thanks, no doubt, to valuable experience gained at Borstal – a most successful camp entrepreneur, saw fit to call after him cheerily the very same greeting, skilfully imitating his pronunciation, he finally 'saw the light' and, a man of extreme opinions, arrived at the conclusion that he had been mistaken all along and that there was, after all, no such thing as an English gentleman. So, after judoing Jack Crawley all over the camp yard for about ten minutes – just to give vent to his disappointment and restore the balance – he decreed a series of measures ranging from roll-call in the yard to searches of working parties returning to the camp. He also restricted the distribution of Red Cross parcels to the prisoners, and rumour had it that he was selling them on the black market. In other words, having been a most creditable 'clown', he became a real 'bastard', much to everybody's relief. He was, after all, 'the enemy', and at least one could now hate him freely without feeling that this was somehow unfair.

CHAPTER THREE

ON THE evening of M's appointment to the TTTW panel of tutors there was great celebration at No. 12. Sandwiches were eaten and wine was drunk, and the tenant in the room below repeatedly had occasion to knock for silence with his broom, an activity which resulted in his bringing down a goodly part of the ceiling. Naturally, Mrs. Bingley, the no-nonsense landlady of the establishment, was not prepared to put up with such rowdy behaviour and promptly gave him his marching orders. This, incidentally, was Lipkin's first visit since the 'party' at which he had flattened Silversmith, and he would not have been surprised if he had been shown the door there and then and told never to show his miserable face again. By his standards this would have been an act of pure justice. After all, had he not stooped to knocking down a man unacquainted with even the rudiments of the manly art and, worst of all, a friend? On a number of occasions since, he had got as far as the front door of No. 12, only to go away again without even knocking, convinced that he would no longer be welcome. Today, however, he had at last overcome his misgivings and taken the decisive step, but had been received in very much the usual manner, Silversmith having long since persuaded himself that he could have won the contest easily if he had been sober and if Lipkin had not been so unbelievably lucky. He certainly bore him no grudge and proved it by offering him a Marmite sandwich, an offer that was eagerly accepted.

M's new job with TTTW was not going to be his first experience of teaching, not by any means. In his later years at the Klappenhorn Gymnasium he had been earning some small amounts of money, which he required mainly to buy his favourite coconut sweets (sweets so delicious that he could hardly bear to eat them and would confine himself to nibbling them, crumb by satisfying crumb), by preparing some unfortunates, victims of excessive parental ambition, for various exams well beyond their meagre capacities. After leaving Vienna in 1938, while M and his family lived in the Czechoslovak town of Moravská Ostrava, a fine and thriving place with trams and cars and bright lights galore and with many coffee-houses in which to read newspapers and magazines, play chess or admire the billiard players, he and his friend Maslov had started the 'Language Institute BA-MA (short for Maskenbusch-Maslov and by courtesy of the printer) by advertising in a local newspaper (which exhausted their entire capital), and had eventually wound up with two students, one for Arabic and the other for Swedish. They threw dice in order to decide who should teach what, and M, who always managed to lose in any contest of chance, wound up with Arabic.

For a variety of reasons, this venture had not been a success, and the less said about it the better, for M did not know a word of Arabic and had to rely on keeping a page or two ahead of his student as they ploughed through somebody's incredibly complex 'Arabic Conversation Grammar', the only book on this difficult language obtainable in any of the local bookshops, while Maslov, a baker's apprentice of real talent, had similar problems with Swedish. His most substantial experience, however, M had gained in a small, snow-bound village in Slovakia, where he was employed to teach English to a group of would-be emigrants. This being January 1939 – only a few months before the ever rapacious Reich and its fellow travellers at the time, Poland and Hungary, helped themselves to various slices of what had until then been a good country to live in – the time available for studying ran out too soon, and, in fact, none of M's students, not even the most gifted, ever made the grade or, indeed, any grade at all.

As a child at his grandparents' home in Klimkovice, a tiny village near Moravská Ostrava, M had often had occasion to observe women sitting on their doorsteps, relentlessly filling the gullets of vehemently protesting geese. More recently, reme-dial tutoring had given him an insight into the probable emotional state of a goose in the process of being stuffed, but as for his time in Slovakia it taught him how to cope with uncomfortable questioners and their questions. He never forgot, and, indeed, always recalled with much relish his very first lesson, when he was confronted by a formidable Hungarian lady who wanted to know the English equivalent of whatever it was, which was a bit mean, for she had only just looked up the word in her dictionary. M, who had no idea – after all, he himself had had English at school for less than two years, although school had not by any means been the only place where he came into contact with this noble language – simply made up a word (no matter that an expert linguist might have taken it for Chinese or Swahili rather than English). When, as yet unimpressed, the lady challenged him, saying that according to her dictionary it was such and such, he first explained that the correct pronunciation was so and so (thus proving that he was indeed a born teacher) and that her dictionary was obviously quite out of date, whereas his was the modern term in general use. Besides, he pointed out, her term denoted a small and inferior one such as common people of low standards might be expected to have, whereas a something or other (again he used the invented term, which had, however, changed slightly since he used it the first time – a circumstance which fortunately escaped her attention, although not that of the bright boy in the front, who looked vastly amused but made no comment) was considerably larger and preferable in every way. M also advised her, for good measure, not to use any dictionary whatsoever until she had reached a much higher level of knowledge, all dictionaries being prone to mislead the uninitiated.

The crisis thus dealt with and the troublesome lady crushed, at least for the time being, he proceeded to analyse, from both the linguistic and philosophical points of view, the sentence 'a hungry man is an angry man', in which he acquitted himself most creditably.

This incident did not pass him by entirely without trace. For when, after the lesson, he happened to look into a mirror, he discovered that his face was white with chalk, applied, no doubt, during those anxious moments when he had had to cope with cross-examination by his tormentress and establish, once and for all, his authority. It appeared that during that exchange he had inadvertently wiped his hot, perspiring brow with the cloth for cleaning the blackboard. If his nose had been red, he would have resembled a clown in a circus, and he now understood what had made the two boys at the back of the class so happy and why some of the other students seemed unable to refrain from giggling.

Nothing happened for about three weeks, but then Miss Gomberg did get in touch and asked, or rather commanded, him to attend for his first lesson. The student, a valuable client of several years standing, M was told, would be requiring elementary German tuition. The choice of textbook being apparently up to him, before setting out on this his very first assignment, M had equipped himself with *Guten Tag*, a German primer which he had found on Silversmith's bookshelf.

Upon his arrival he was informed, not on this occasion by Miss Gomberg but by Catty, the typist whom he had met already on the occasion of his previous visit and whose mood, incidentally, did not seem to have improved since then, that the student was already waiting for him in room 23A, the second room on the left, next to the Gents. M, already a quarter of an hour late, went there immediately and found a small, fat boy about ten years of age, who after much embarrassed twisting and turning accepted (without even the slightest enthusiasm) his tutorial ministrations. It was plain as a pikestaff that the boy knew not a word of German, and M accordingly decided to start him on the alphabet. This proved to be extremely difficult since the boy was totally unacquainted not only with German but also with English, French or, apparently, any other civilised language.

When, at long last, the bell rang, hesitantly announcing the end of the lesson, M was in a state of paralysing boredom, and the boy too looked pretty exhausted. Back in the office Catty explained that M had been sent to the wrong classroom by mistake and that the student he should have taught, an elderly gentleman, name of Allbright, had been waiting for him until about five minutes ago, when he had decided to call it a day. The boy should in fact have had a Romanian lesson, but since Madame Tartagliu, his usual teacher, had not turned up and M was apparently doing fine anyway, it did seem rather pointless to take any action at so late a stage.

'I didn't know you knew Romanian as well … it doesn't say so on your form,' said Catty reproachfully, adding 'I'll get the blame, of course, when the old cow finds out. As if she never made a mistake, the silly old bitch.'

Catty's indignation appeared to be profound. The corners of her disdainful mouth were turned down, and her face with its powerful, succulent nose looked blotchy and puffed about the eyes as if she had been crying or was perhaps on the point of it. M, soft as putty when confronted with an attractive girl in need of consolation (provided, of course, that he did not regard himself as the cause of her misery), felt drawn to her immediately and was quite prepared to accept that if a mistake had been made, this could not have been her fault, not in any way whatsoever. In any case, he was able to reassure her that no harm had been done, for everything had gone very well and he would not, of course, dream of betraying her secret. Of this, he promised, she could be quite, quite certain. Carried away with a mad excess of chivalry, M even went so far as to declare that in the circumstances he would not dream of accepting a single penny for the lesson. Catty, most favourably impressed with his attitude, agreed that this might offer a way out and, by way of reward, volunteered the information that, far from being a Miss, that dried up old so-and-so had blackmailed old Pendelpig into marrying her, and by all accounts he now hated her guts.

Later, on his way home, M, mulling over the events of the afternoon, felt that he had every reason to be satisfied. He had had his baptism of fire as a language teacher and had acquitted himself with some practical distinction. True, at the back of his mind certain rudimentary doubts were beginning to form, but Catty was a distinct improvement on Miss Gomberg and a 'relationship' with her was by no means an impossible dream. M foresaw the most enticing possibilities. And, besides, he had earned his first fee – not perhaps a very large fee and not one he was now likely ever to receive – but who would deny that it was a step in the right direction?

Close to Marble Arch it suddenly occurred to him that he would need to obtain a more suitable German textbook. Perhaps, he thought, it would be a good idea to try Foyle's. Not having anything better to do in any case, M retraced his steps along Oxford Street, and, following a circuitous road, made for 'the largest bookstore in the world'. Before reaching it, however, he passed a small, untidy second-hand bookstall, where absent-mindedly browsing he suddenly caught sight of a slim volume entitled *The Linguist's Primer of Modern Romanian*. Considering the afternoon's events, M felt that his find was somehow significant. And since the book was also quite cheap, he bought it without further ado, having decided that his intended purchase of a German textbook could, after all, wait for a day or two. Although later, at home, he discovered that his '*Modern Romanian*' had in fact been published in the year of Queen Victoria's Jubilee and was not so much modern as of historical interest, he was entirely content with his acquisition. Clutching his treasure under his arm, he passed through the backstreets of Soho, looking in shop windows, reading such advertisements as were of special interest to him and generally enjoying the sights and sounds of this, his favourite area. In a delicatessen he bought some Italian cheese and noodles for his supper, and finally went home via Bayswater Road and Queensway.

Once at home M, quite peckish by now, immediately headed for the tiny kitchen – not only the place where food was prepared and normally consumed but also the main focus of social activity – and found Lipkin and Silversmith arguing whether or not it was morally defensible to take money for services. Lipkin, an idealist to the core with dreams of the dignifying and civilising mission of manual labour and of workers' co-operatives in which all helped together as brothers and sisters to advance the common good, without even a hint of 'I'm all right Jack' or 'My home is my castle', said it wasn't. Given his deep distrust of money, which he regarded as the cause and effect of much evil, his attitude was, of course, entirely predictable.

Silversmith, for his part, argued persuasively and with fine rhetorical fervour that to treat money as a kind of universal scapegoat was both silly and untenable. He pointed out that in the real world, 'and we know no other', choices had to be made, and that a system such as that advocated by Lipkin was, in fact, totally impractical. 'All very well,' he exclaimed, 'to be going on about "To everyone according to his needs" etc., but such sentiments, however noble they may sound, have no place in real life.' To illustrate his thesis, he compared a drunken layabout who beat his wife and abused his children with a brilliant constructor of bridges, while Lipkin pointed out that a speculator who was of no use to anybody might well be indecently rich and living in the lap of luxury, whereas an honest miner toiling away in the bowels of the earth so that all of us might enjoy heat and light was most unlikely to own, in his probably all too brief life, much more than the clothes he stood up in. Lipkin, whose formal education, such as it was, had come to an abrupt end at a very early age, had garnered much of his philosophy from odds and ends of Marxist literature and could, in any argument, be relied upon to resort to its most hackneyed phrases. As for M, he might have pointed out that all this was far too simplistic but decided not to bother, for his news of the day's activities were far too important to wait until the subject was well and truly exhausted. Besides, he knew from experience that his chances of getting something to eat might be seriously impaired if he allowed himself to get drawn into the discussion.

It would be difficult to imagine two people more dissimilar in background and temperament than Silversmith and Lipkin, and at certain times one could not help feeling that their friendship was founded on nothing more substantial than mutual incomprehension. Whereas Lipkin was inward-looking, shy and frequently tongue-tied, Silversmith made friends easily and never had the slightest difficulty in formulating or expressing an opinion. While Silversmith prided himself on approaching all matters in a clinically logical manner, Lipkin was a romantic at heart, with leanings towards mysticism. Although Lipkin believed firmly in the inherent goodness of man, he was basically a pessimist, who expected little and frequently got less, but Silversmith, a cynic to the core, was ever convinced that all things would turn out just right for him – a conviction that was hardly ever disappointed. Even in appearance they differed greatly, Lipkin being insect-like and wiry, while Silversmith was tall, of pinkish complexion and somewhat overweight.

Lipkin grew up in a small town in Poland where his father had been a Jewish tailor who during the war, like so many others, became a victim of *Einsatzgruppe D*, Hitler's most infamous death squad in the occupied Eastern territories. His childhood had been marred both by extreme poverty and by the rampant anti-semitism that surrounded him on all sides. That he, his family and indeed all Jews were responsible for the crucifixion of Christ was something he recognised as merely ridiculous, but certain other accusations which seemed to him less fantastic – about Jews tending to exploit the poor while being physically inept and afraid of hard work, for instance – hurt him deeply, as did the incessant jibes and threats to which he and his family were exposed. He felt that any Jew who by his attitudes or conduct lent credibility to any of the accusations levelled at Jews in general was a traitor to his people, and it irked him that so many of the most respected and influential members of his community fell short of the standards he set for them. He thought of himself as a communist and dreamed of a brotherhood of man unstained by inequality, injustice or exploitation – a kind of messianic utopia in which the lion would truly lie down with the lamb. Although opposed to Zionism, a movement he regarded as elitist and oppressive but, above all, unjust to the non-Jewish Palestinian population, he was fiercely proud of the state of Israel, which he perceived as having restored dignity to the Jewish people throughout the world and to himself personally. Indeed, it was his fervent hope that one day he might be able to go to Israel, where he would live in a kibbutz and by humble and devoted work make a small but acceptable contribution to the life of his nation. With this end in view, he spent much time (and being generally out of work he had a lot of it to spend) studying modern Hebrew from a textbook. A convinced atheist, he still made a point of taking part in all the main Jewish festivals, claiming that they were purely cultural events without any religious significance whatsoever. A fundamentally solitary person, he had no real contact with anyone, apart from his mother, his friends at No. 12 and Rosabelle. As for his mother, whom he had somehow managed to bring over from Poland and who now looked after him, she was a taciturn, grey-faced woman with a weak heart. She knew hardly any English, which made shopping and similarly mundane activities very difficult, and she never ventured out of the house without her black headscarf.

Silversmith, on the other hand, the only son of elderly parents – his father was a greengrocer in the Midlands and a pillar of the local Church – was quite free of any prejudices such as those to which Lipkin was subject. A handsome, intelligent and good-natured child with a lot of charm, he had always been treated with great indulgence and even spoiled by all and sundry. This had nurtured in him not only a quite inordinate self-esteem (not always justified by his performance) and a thoroughly pragmatic attitude to life but also very high expectations. It never occurred to him to doubt that all good things in life were his by right and he firmly believed that it was within his power to achieve them. Oddly enough, on the rare occasions when Silversmith had worked alongside real working people, during the war for instance, he had always been accepted readily by his mates, in spite of the fact that he was a born 'lead-swinger' and not averse to taking advantage whenever he could. Lipkin, on the other hand, was generally regarded with great suspicion and distrust – something he could never understand or get used to.

'I taught my first lesson today,' M announced, 'and it was great.' This statement was perhaps not as accurate as it might have been, seeing that he had not actually imparted any useful knowledge to his student, and whereas all manner of things that had occurred might fairly have been described as 'great', the actual lesson was not of their number. Lipkin merely muttered something about capitalist exploitation but Silversmith was more enthusiastic. He wanted, in particular, to hear all about Catty and, having given free rein to his rather overheated imagination, considered M's prospects on the amatory front, explicitly and with great zest. At this, Lipkin, who was none too keen on this kind of banter, which he regarded as degrading to women, turned sulky, but M would have been the first to admit that, where women were concerned, Silversmith, who had already enjoyed intimacy with numerous girlfriends and was known, occasionally and provided that he could afford to do so, to frequent prostitutes, was certainly streets ahead, at any rate of himself. To celebrate M's inauguration into the 'academic world', they shared the remains of an elderly Swiss roll, while M, having prepared his supper, made short shrift of it.

CHAPTER FOUR

TWO days later M discovered that most of the work at TTTW did not, in fact, take place at Frith Street, where, apart from the office and Dr. Pendlebloom's inner sanctum, there were only three classrooms – Nos. 1, 17 and 23A – but at a disused warehouse in a nearby *cul-de-sac* cunningly converted for the purposes of instruction. Hoping to see Catty, who had already taken to haunting his dreams by day and night, he had arrived early, but this time it was Miss Gomberg he had to deal with.

Even on her good days no-one would have been likely to describe Miss Gomberg as pleasant, but on that particular day nothing had gone right for her since she had woken up in the morning with a splitting headache (she was very prone to this affliction) and she was accordingly even more offhand with M, even more snappy than when he met her the first time. In her most peremptory manner she made him sign the TTTW AGREEMENT before telling him where to go and what to do. By this simple act M, who never bothered to read legal documents before signing them (as if he were afraid that trying to understand legal language was bad for the brain and likely to cause it grievous injury) managed to waive all rights enshrined on his behalf in English Law, agreeing to all manner of duties (voluntary and without remuneration) and obligations. He promised, for instance, to forego various slices of his income in the event of lateness, failure to appear for a lesson, refusal of a student for whatever reason, and so on and so forth, and was threatened with INSTANT DISMISSAL and other dire consequences 'without prejudice to the Company's rights ...' if he were guilty of any major misdemeanour/infringement such as using the office telephone for private calls or – perish the thought – 'entering into a private/clandestine arrangement with one or several of the Company's students' while the Agreement was in force or 'during a period not exceeding three years following the termination of said Agreement'.

In the course of his career with TTTW M became increasingly aware of its mythology of grand betrayals, scandalous happenings and their wretched sequels, which could only be hinted at in whispers, on special occasions and among the initiated faithful. There was, for instance, the cautionary tale of Simbim Grobachevsky, one-time head of the English department, who, blind with ambition, had decided to set up on his own in some God-forsaken, rat-infested hovel and actually had the temerity to try to entice some of the students mistakenly entrusted to his care by TTTW, by approaching them on dark winter evenings in the street and uttering blasphemy against the Administration which had been so good to him. Even Dr. Pendlebloom did not escape his vile slanders. Nobody, of course, fell for his blandishments, and so it was small wonder that he eventually went mad, joined the Foreign Legion and married an illiterate native wench years older than he, with whom – and this was the crowning irony – he never managed to exchange a single word, since they did not understand each other's languages. Very sad also was the story of one Casparios, who was caught *in flagrante* making highly disparaging remarks about the general appearance and effect of Dr. Pendlebloom's moustache, speculating *inter alia* whether it was a real moustache, home-grown as it were, or made of one of those new-fangled materials – plastics he thought they were called – which were just coming into vogue. The ingrate was caught by none other than the good Dr. Pendlebloom himself on one of his regular 'non-intrusive' inspection prowls, that is to say while he was listening at the classroom door. Dr. Pendlebloom, deeply shocked by such duplicity, had instructed Miss Gomberg to discharge Casparios forthwith, dismissing him to a life of penury and degradation.

Having snatched the now valid Agreement, Miss Gomberg explained, not without considerable impatience, that the student, a Miss Pratt, registered for French conversation, was in all probability already waiting in Classroom 49 of the Annexe, so would he kindly stop wasting everybody's time and get on with it without further delay. Miss Gomberg's exasperation knew no bounds when M explained, very apologetically indeed, that he had no idea where to find the Annexe, but she eventually divulged the address and even told him how to get there.

M's experience of spoken French was exceedingly limited. Uttering simple statements of the *ah oui, mon petit chou* and *mais non, pas du tout* variety was never a problem, and he was quite good at latching onto the odd word in a conversation (*...ah, les revolvers, c'est bien méchant! ...*) but he could never make out what people were saying to him, a circumstance which on one occasion nearly caused him to be arrested when he was trying to convey a set of Frank Harris's Memoirs across the Belgian border. (These valuable works were in fact confiscated – a major loss from M's point of view.) It was hardly surprising, therefore, that on his way to the Annexe certain serious misgivings arose in his mind, and he even considered giving this particular lesson a miss, rather than face such indignities as might so readily result from it. Eventually, however, wiser counsels prevailed, and he arrived at Classroom 49 only a quarter of an hour late.

Miss Pratt was already there, waiting for him. She was a grey-haired lady of imperious looks and advanced years, slim and with aquiline features. She was dressed entirely in black and wore a black hat, which she never seemed to remove. Her slim, almost emaciated appearance and the fact that she wore shoes with stiletto heels made her seem uncommonly tall. When M arrived she had been on the point of going to the office in order to lodge an appropriately forceful complaint, but in the event accepted M's breathless, somewhat incoherent apology and decided to go on with the lesson. However, it did not take long before it became obvious to both of them that whatever other benefits Miss Pratt might derive from her lessons any improvement in her knowledge of French was not going to be one of them.

Miss Pratt, it turned out, spoke French with far greater ease than M – the very thing he had been afraid of. The conversation continuing in English, their acquaintance made rapid progress, Miss Pratt asking both agreeable and searching questions about M's past, present and future, and M, never loath to unveil selected areas of his experience, responding in a manner both apt and informative. He told Miss Pratt all about how he liked people, how he had always wanted to be a teacher and how TTTW, if not quite as ideal an opportunity as he had hoped, might well have a lot to offer. Miss Pratt, in turn, told him that her name was really Pratt-Lausewitz and that she was – now blushing blotchy-pink and with an apologetic giggle – a kind of crazy, mixed-up kid, inasmuch as on her mother's side – the Pratts that was – she derived from a long line of ever-so-English financial juggernauts (in passing, she even mentioned Edward Lloyd's coffee-house, explaining that one of her ancestors used to take tea there regularly towards the end of the eighteenth century), whereas the Lausewitzes were ancient Prussian nobility, albeit impoverished. M, not to be outdone, explained about his own family's patrician roots, inventing to this end two main branches – the Hamburgers and the Frankfurters. He himself, of course, came from Vienna (he did indeed), although by now he really considered himself more of a Londoner. Nor did he forget to mention Veit Maskenbusch, an entirely fictitious ancestor, whom he described as one of the principal leaders in the 'Peasant Wars', who in 1521 had been executed in Frankfurt by boiling over a slow fire. He even told Miss Pratt, who was listening with rapt attention, about his infancy, when Papa caught uncle Max doing naughty things with the governess – in those days when they could still afford a governess – and generally about life in pre-war Vienna.

Vienna! To most people a city of romance – moustache-twirling junior lieutenants and pretty young shop-girls eager for love – imperial splendour and the blue Danube. St. Stephen's Cathedral (affectionately known as the 'Steffel') and window-shopping in the Kärntnerstrasse. *Gemütlichkeit*, coffee-houses and a band in the park playing waltzes by Strauss. *Die Fledermaus* on New Year's Eve. Wine of the season's vintage at Grinzing and Sievering and outings to the Wienerwald. But this was only part of the story. Vienna was also a city of great poverty and much social deprivation. In 1934 there was a workers' uprising, brutally put down by the Austrian army and fully reported in the popular papers, which at the time seemed to be bursting at the seams with gory accounts of the ringleaders' last hours before they were executed. Trudging wearily through the rain past the Heiligenstädter Hof, the Karl Marx Hof and other endless, dispirited and fortress-like flats (funny how it always seemed to be raining in those outer districts where most of the factory workers lived), M, on his way to visit Frau Marek – an old washerwoman who used to do the family's washing in those halcyon days when they still had a maid and lived at a posh flat in Prinz Eugen Strasse and whom he, a lonely child, regarded as a personal friend – wondered vaguely at the marks of machine-gun bullets defacing the damp but otherwise spotless concrete walls here and there, not as yet fully comprehending their true significance since, after all, he was then only twelve years of age.

This was a time when sentimentality went hand-in-hand with cynical indifference, and a spirit of muddling-through with greedy opportunism. The Austrian state was in its final agony, and when Hitler eventually put an end to what had become a burdensome farce – some people compared Austria to an ailing midget, with Vienna its excessively large head – he was welcomed with great, unforgettable jubilation. M remembered the dense crowds lining both sides of the Mariahilferstrasse to hail the '*Führer*', and how he himself, wearing his enamelled red, white and blue badge signifying Czechoslovak nationality (really pathetic, that was!) and in every sense an outsider, had wished, though with some redeeming sense of shame, that he too might share in the brave new world that was being promised.

'But,' M explained, 'nothing, of course, is ever that simple. Nobility and generosity too had their place in the scheme of things. Take, for instance, Professor Bergenau, my old English teacher. He used to bring his guitar to school every Saturday, and together we would sing *Tipperary, Pack up your troubles in your old kit bag* and other songs which he himself had learned as a prisoner of war in England during World War I. Years before he came to our school he had written a book on English humour, which, I have been told, was both profound and totally unreadable, and – this will make you laugh – he obstinately insisted that the correct spelling of "out of" was "out off", whatever the evidence to the contrary. He hated cigarettes, which he kept calling *"Stinkwürstl"*, and he believed fervently in Greater Germany, Adolf Hitler and the brotherhood of man. In 1945, when the Russians were at the gates of Vienna and virtually all who were Nazis by inclination or opportunism had gone into hiding or reverted to the state of being harmless lovers of wine, women and song, Professor Bergenau volunteered to defend his city and was mortally wounded for his pains. And then there was the long and excessively boring talk that Hilde Habergeiss, one of Hitler's greatest admirers in our class, gave on the superiority of the Aryan race. When Professor Schmitz, our German teacher at the time and eventually our headmaster, called in his usual gruff manner for our comments, I was the only one who responded, suggesting that the talk had been far too short. After a momentary silence – who, after all, would have expected a Jew of all people to dare make such a remark? – there came a general outburst of laughter, perhaps the friendliest reaction I had met with for years. And a few weeks later when I met Hilde in the street – I had left the school by then and she was wearing the full regalia of a BDM *Scharführerin* – she, tall and blond with long pigtails and a face reminiscent of the pale crescent moon as depicted in children's books, actually smiled at me with what I do believe was true friendliness! As for Professor Schmitz, who without any doubt owed his promotion to headship at least partly to years of clandestine membership of the Party, I have reason to believe that it was he who arranged for the marks in my very last school report to be much better than any I had ever received in all of my seven years at the Klappenhorn, so there!

Of course, none of these instances prove anything much about the people concerned, one way or another. Those, for instance, who treated me with kindness may, for all I know, have been guilty of horrific deeds in their dealings with others, and those whom I feared most may have done much that was good. Still, I am sure you will agree that in the final analysis all our judgments are formed both in the light of our own experience and on the basis of generalisations, and although they may not have much to do with objective truth – whatever that may be – they are all we are capable of.'

By the end of her 'lesson', Miss Pratt declared herself well satisfied and offered to take M, whom she insisted on calling *'mon professeur'*, in hand with a view to improving his conversational French. M accepted gratefully and they parted on the friendliest of terms.

On his way out of the classroom M collided with a dapper, exceedingly talkative little man, who after mutual apologies introduced himself as Mr. Daker, formerly of the Foreign Office but now, alas, a mere member of the TTTW team of English tutors. The so-called Common Room, he explained, was out of bounds and likely to remain so, seeing that its only source of light had been broken by a former teacher, who, perhaps in consequence of having drunk an excessive amount of his auntie's home-made rose-petal wine, had gone berserk. Quite in line with TTTW's policy of general bloody-mindedness and penny-pinching parsimony the lamp had never been replaced. Not, he added, that this was any great loss, since at the best of times the Common Room had been a dismal place, cold even at the height of summer, and unspeakably filthy. M formed the distinct impression that his new acquaintance was far from content with his lot at TTTW and thoroughly despised whatever it stood for. Quite naturally, M felt vaguely flattered by Mr. Daker taking him into his confidence, particularly as he was very conscious of his own lowly status as a 'new boy'.

He did not, of course, have the slightest inkling that meeting this new friend might lead to the loss of his most treasured possession, his beige camel-hair coat left to him by his Uncle Moritz, which was so fine and spirited, as it were, that he could never contemplate it without shaking his head in disbelief at his unbelievably good fortune. One day, however, the precious garment simply disappeared without the slightest trace, and M was unable to find it again, try as he would. Having duly mourned the passing of his treasure, M consoled himself with the thought that a coat of such elegance and quality had never been right for a person such as him, to whom duffel coats and similarly commonplace garments were far better suited. When, after a week or two, a coat of identical cloth and cut but in a different colour (navy blue) appeared at the school, worn this time by Mr. Daker, M suspected, and not without good reason, foul play. But unable to prove ownership – his methods of interrogation, though subtle and soundly based on Dostoevsky's *Crime and Punishment*, remaining thoroughly ineffective – he eventually put the matter out of his mind.

When Mr. Daker suggested a visit to The House of Pasta in Burlingham Mews around the corner, a veritable home-from-home and a place where Mr. Maskenbusch would be sure to meet some interesting people, M agreed readily, and they were on their way.

The House of Pasta – HP for short – was indeed a pleasant and homely place. Its dark-brown panelled walls were covered with 'nearly original' reproductions of paintings and posters by Toulouse-Lautrec, the largest one a lovingly executed rear-view of a kneeling lady, and another a fine study of a green-faced gentleman in the process of relieving himself. Mr. Daker explained that according to Ben, the swarthy, barrel-chested owner of the establishment, these noble pictures had been sold to him at a very reasonable price by an itinerant artist who used to earn an honest but stressful living by painting, on his travels through Sussex, Surrey and other affluent parts of Merry England, pretty portraits of cats, dogs, budgerigars and babies – an activity which he abominated, although, according to reliable reports, it did keep the beer flowing. To compensate, he would copy paintings depicting life in the raw, but by no means slavishly as lesser artists might have done. In fact, he omitted such details as were in his opinion inessential, emphasising instead those features which he regarded as particularly significant. He eventually married a rich widow, put away his easel for good and became a most successful interior decorator. It took M quite some time to get accustomed to these pictures and to eat his food at HP without a definite sense of nausea.

In addition to macaroni with cheese or various sauces, The House of Pasta offered cannelloni, green *tagliatelle al burro* and spag-bol, coffee and tea, sandwiches, various salads, mince pies and other fine fare. Ben loved to have people about and did not mind too much if their consumption was minimal, consoling himself, without much confidence and mainly in order to bolster his self-respect (he was, after all, a businessman), with the thought that one day the patrons of his establishment would, perhaps, have lots of money and be eager to spend it on his more profitable delicacies. This would make him very rich, and once he was rich he would be able to sell up at enormous profit and return to his beloved Palermo, where he would then spend the remainder of his days in a manner befitting a gentleman.

The place being virtually empty when M and his new colleague arrived, Ben bore down on them with great and sincere enthusiasm, ushering them to a table which he gave a quick and generous wipe. They ordered black coffee and then settled down to a long chat about various matters of mutual interest concerning TTTW, its staff and the students. It transpired that with three teachers – Mr. Daker, Galbraith and the untrustworthy Dr. McGill, who kept missing lessons and would chase anything in skirts, even the cleaners – the English department was (mainly thanks to the tourist trade) larger and more remunerative than all the other departments put together, also that the office tended to be less than reliable when it came to calculating the teachers' pay, and that old Pendlebloom had acquired his much-vaunted doctorate by paying the appropriate fee to an American 'university' and, as a result, now considered himself an authority on all things British. As for Miss Gomberg ... At his point they were joined by Galbraith, a tall man with receding forehead but hardly any chin at all. He immediately launched himself into a series of complaints about a variety of matters but mainly in relation to a recently acquired gas cooker, asking their honest opinion and – somehow reminiscent of the White Rabbit – hurrying on to yet another grievance without waiting for a reply.

By now M was close to falling asleep, so he made his excuses, paid for his coffee and left, with Daker and Galbraith still engrossed in their conversation.

CHAPTER FIVE

ON HIS way home, which took him all over the place – for he was an inveterate meanderer who would follow any road that looked at all promising, without much concern about its direction and, as a rule, without the slightest idea where he was – M considered his relationship with God.

During his childhood and especially during his years in Vienna, God and M had been on the most cordial of terms, with M forever consulting Him, concluding bargains with Him ('Help me in this exam and I shall say my morning prayers for ten days standing on one foot') and generally dropping in on Him whenever there was nothing better to do and nobody else around. God in turn, still wearing that long, white nightgown which looked as if it could do with a wash, bald-headed and with his quasi-nicotine-stained, off-white cotton-wool beard, took a very special interest in M but was far from satisfactory as a trading partner inasmuch as He tended to ignore the offers of bargains, however generous. He was always there for M both as friend and counsellor. The great thing was, God always understood, always sympathised, never became angry or, having listened to M's reasons, refused His approval. When M's stepmother, in her misguided and ultimately fruitless attempts to improve his ways, insisted that by way of punishment for something or other M learn thirty pages from the Hebrew prayerbook by heart within half an hour and he, relying on her inability to follow, reeled off a medley of blessings, psalms and anything else that came to mind, thus tricking her, who could not even conceive that anyone might sink so low as to trifle with words so sacred and so venerable, God looked remarkably serene and untroubled. Nor did it bother Him greatly when M took to eating ham or even when he broke the odd commandment. This gave M considerable moral leeway, but in a manner of speaking it also set Him free, which suited both of them fine. As long as M did what he believed to be right or good, God was entirely happy, and since M liked to be liked and, a kind of auto-Pygmalion, spent much effort in perfecting his personality to bring it in line with what he expected of himself, their friendship seemed bound to thrive for ever and ever.

During the war, a good deal of which M spent washing dishes and scrubbing floors in ships, things changed, although, to begin with, only very slowly – indeed almost imperceptibly. One day he felt in all honesty bound to admit to himself that he was no longer convinced of God's very existence – after all, how could God possibly exist in a universe of colliding particles, with time as a corollary of change, and M himself equally comparable to a stone and a storm? Then again it occurred to him that if God did exist and was not merely a convenient idea dreamt up to overcome our fear of the anonymity of nature and give both continuity and individual meaning to our lives, He would be as he himself had known Him, in which case He would have very little time for boring adoration, theological nit-picking and, especially, unquestioning faith. Having in former years greatly enjoyed the warmth and splendour of the synagogue, these thoughts did not come easily to M, but he managed to persuade himself that if God did, after all, exist, it would be much more stimulating and therefore gratifying for Him to face a worthy opponent in honest argument than to have to live up eternally to dreary adoration. Nothing in Holy Writ was, after all, more believable than God's friendships with difficult but basically well-meaning individuals.

M was still on his way home, if somewhat off course, walking through the unassuming streets of Elephant and Castle and past mellowing bomb craters, now the habitat of many plants and also places where children played. This was long before the 'developers' came, weaving their evil spells and turning the area into a kind of concrete maze. He was now trying to answer the question whether it was possible to keep up his friendship with God without actually believing in Him, in fact even if He did not exist at all. He arrived, predictably perhaps, at the conclusion that it was, for even if God were merely an idea, merely an aspiration, there was still the reality of his own feelings, ultimately the only reality of which he, Morus Maskenbusch, had reliable proof. Besides, there always remained the faint hope that God was after all still to be found, complete with nightgown and whitish beard, and that He actually cared.

In a doorway in Queensway a man was lying on his side. M asked him if he was all right, whereupon the man rolled over and, offering a bottle, said 'What you need, mate, is a drink.' M, mesmerised, hurried away as quickly as he could.

Number 12 Westlake Crescent seemed deserted. For once M did not stop off at the kitchen, which was one level below his and Silvermith's rooms, but went straight to his own. He immediately sensed that there was something dreadfully amiss. Presently he saw it. Two prints depicting snow scenes in pink, white and baby-blue and with elaborate gilded *papier-mâché* frames were on the wall to the left of the door, defacing the homeliness of his room with garish bad taste. This was the sort of thing that could make his blood boil – an outrage to his privacy, a kind of rape even! His first impulse was to tear down these abominations and to trample them into the remains of wine-red Wilton that covered the floor. But then it occurred to him that this might well lead to his loss of perfectly comfortable lodgings at a week's notice. Mrs. Bingley, in many ways an ideal landlady but definitely hot-tempered – rumour had it that in her youth she had spent several years as a bareback rider on a Peruvian llama ranch – would certainly not put up with rebellious behaviour such as this, so a different way would have to be found. He paced up and down and then, when the main thrust of his anger had died down and, stretched out on his bed, he had reached a more reasonable frame of mind, he considered this and that approach until he eventually felt satisfied that he had hit upon the perfect solution which while being quite incapable of giving the slightest offence, could not fail to succeed.

M went down to the basement, the very nerve-centre of Mrs. Bingley's domain, where she resided with her consort, the severely faded and of-no-account Mr. Bingley. In reply to M's polite knock she herself came to the door, slightly surprised but obviously pleased to see him, her favourite 'boy', while at the same time shrewdly appraising him with just a hint of irony. Mrs. Bingley, a tiny lady in late middle age, upright as a ramrod and wearing her inevitable pinkish turban, had an air of no-nonsense about her – a great help in running the house. She insisted on unfailing politeness and decorum at all times and had been known to get rid of a lodger without further ado merely because he had dared to enquire whether it was really necessary for her to be smoking one cigarette after another and strewing the ashes everywhere while going through the motions of tidying his room, the very room now occupied by M. She had responded to this act of overt indiscipline by there and then requesting him to vacate her premises as soon as he could or even sooner but not later than by the end of the statutory week of notice. Nor would she allow her male lodgers to entertain lady visitors after 10 o'clock in the evening, a restriction that was particularly hard on Mr. Bingley, who enjoyed listening at doors and had, on occasion, even been caught peeping through keyholes. Fortunately Mrs. Bingley had a weakness for viewing houses that were being offered for sale (not that she had the slightest intention of purchasing one) and, whenever she went on one of her house-viewing expeditions, would make a point of taking Mr. Bingley along, thus leaving the house available for such pursuits as could not safely be practised when she was at home. Indeed, in a moment of transient and quite uncharacteristic weakness, for she liked to play her cards close to her chest, she once confided to her unmarried sister Jean that she insisted on Mr. Bingley's company solely in order to keep an eye on him, as there was, after all, no knowing what he might be getting up to if he were left behind. As for the weekly rent, which, incidentally, was by no means excessive, that had to be paid on the dot – this being another area in which Mrs. Bingley would not stand for any prevarication. Not surprisingly, she was a staunch supporter of the Conservative Party, but treated her 'boys' and other lodgers kindly, for she genuinely liked people, especially young people, and, besides, things went more smoothly that way.

Now, following an exchange of civilities and appropriate introductory remarks, Mrs. Bingley – this evening by herself, with Mr. Bingley, as was his wont at this hour, at the local – invited M into her opulently appointed parlour, a room resplendent with Regency stripes and patterned, colourful Axminsters, heavy chintz curtains and fine, traditional furniture in a variety of English styles. The grandfather clock, spotless in shiny mahogany, was ticking away ponderously in a corner, while various Victorian personages, all of them members of the prestigious 'Makers of History in Reproduction' collection and acquired many years ago at a sale in Oxford Street, were smiling down benignly from the walls. But the crowning glories of that agreeable room were undoubtedly the fireplace with its marbled surround and the mirror above in its elaborately moulded gilt frame, a fine example of what might be termed the Neo-Chippendale style. M, however, did not like this mirror, for it reminded him too much of another mirror, one in a film, which reflected a murder past or present – he could not remember which.

At the edge of an armchair as befitted his lowly station, M was waiting for Mrs. Bingley to bring the tea which she had so kindly offered him.

'Milk and sugar, Mr. M?', Mrs. Bingley enquired.

'Yes please, with two lumps if I may.'

Mrs. Bingley poured the tea. She herself used only artificial sweeteners.

'Please help yourself to a biscuit.'

M did as he was told. 'This is very tasty,' he commented, munching with ostensible pleasure.

'Have another one then. Now, what can I do for you?'

Having decided to open his approach with a gambit, M cleared his throat. 'Mrs. Bingley,' he said, 'I am afraid I have an awful confession to make.'

Mrs. Bingley, intrigued (with those boys you never knew what they might come up with), was looking expectant.

'To cut a long story short, my grandfather died when I was only four years of age.' (In fact M was much older when this regrettable event occurred, but for his present purpose a lower age seemed preferable.)

'Poor child,' sympathised Mrs. Bingley, 'What a sad thing to happen when you were still so young.'

'Well, it was in the nature of things and, as I was told later, not entirely unexpected. My grandfather, you see, was more than 90 years old when he died and had grown rather feeble.'

'He had had a good innings then. Still, it must have been quite a shock, seeing that you were only a little lad. Did you know him at all well?'

'Not all that well. I only remember that he was immensely tall and had a long white beard and that he once chased me out of his room with a belt. I was living in his house at the time.' There followed a short pause while they both sipped their tea appreciatively, pensively.

M continued, 'When my grandfather died they covered all the mirrors and pictures in the house with black cloth as a sign of mourning. And being only a small child, this made a deep impression on me – in fact, not to put too fine a point on it, I was terrified.'

'Well, you would be, wouldn't you?'

M now diverging, went on, 'You see, this happened in the country, in an area where people were terribly keen on religion!' Sensing some disapproval (religion being definitely not a suitable subject for flippancy), he hastened to add, 'I myself, of course, have nothing at all against religion – far from it – although I am currently not a believer, as you may know. In fact – and this, Mrs. Bingley, this is something I would never dream of telling anyone but you, as I know that I can rely on you for this not to go any further – I often envy people whose faith is strong and wish that I could be like them. And, besides, where would we be without religion, seeing that our entire civilisation is based on it?' Having thus assuaged any possible concern about his right-mindedness, M took another bite from his by now well-earned biscuit and proceeded to steer the conversation back to its original course. 'As I was saying, the people in that part of Czechoslovakia really enjoyed their religion in a big way.' (This was quite safe, for Mrs. Bingley was staunchly C of E and firmly convinced that anyone following a different persuasion belonged to the lower classes and that all foreigners were peculiar, a fact to which she could, no doubt, have testified from her own experience.) 'But to come to the point, funerals seemed to be a special treat and especially the old folks seemed to regard the cemetery as some kind of social centre. But that was not all. For instance, right opposite the church and overlooking the cemetery, in a small flat on the second floor, there lived Franciska, one of my auntie's friends, an old lady with badly swollen legs, who owned a multitude of wax and plaster saints, some with their heads and other parts missing. And as if this were not enough, all the walls were simply covered with religious paintings, some of them merely sentimental but others positively nightmarish, and – worst of all – walking up the dark spiral staircase I had to pass a niche in which stood a tall wooden crucifix with Christ in his agony, a small candle in front of the crucifix being the only source of light until I reached the top of the stairs. My aunt, who frequently made me go to her friend with messages, samples of home-made cake or simply because she felt that Franciska might enjoy a visit, could never understand why I made such a fuss whenever she asked me to go there. However, you will appreciate that since I did not understand the spiritual significance of the various religious symbols in the house and that they were in fact a great comfort to her, seeing that they took her mind off her own misfortunes, of which there were many, I was really afraid, but, on the other hand, she was very generous with her *Apfelstrudl*.'

Mrs. Bingley, not wishing her own hospitality to compare unfavourably, suggested another biscuit.

'Still, the point of the story is simply that, ever since my grandfather died, pictures tend to terrify me, particularly when I wake up at night. I get nightmares, you see, and keep imagining things.'

'No wonder,' responded Mrs. Bingley, catching on at last. 'If I had known, I would never have bought those pictures for your room in the first place. But they need not be wasted. I'll ask Mr. Bingley to put them up in Mr. Silversmith's room when he comes home, to brighten it up a bit.'

'I rather envy Mr. Silversmith,' M declared, rather disingenuously. 'I really like them a lot, but I know what would happen.'

'Now don't you worry about a thing, no harm has been done. And how are you getting on in your new job?'

The conversation, like the flame of a candle on the point of going out, flickered on for a little and then expired. M, having achieved his objective, thanked Mrs. Bingley warmly for her understanding and helpful attitude and left in a glow of satisfaction at his own cleverness. He did not expect Silversmith to object too strenuously, and, as it turned out, he was quite right in this respect too, for Silversmith actually liked the pictures, once he had become aware of them several days later.

Before returning to his room, M, now ravenous, went to the kitchen to see what he could find, but the proverbial cupboard being quite bare, he went to Nick's café, where he enjoyed a nice, satisfying moussaka.

In his room again, he brought his journal up-to-date and then went to bed, where he browsed through a certain well-thumbed and familiar magazine. Now that a definite term had been set to the presence of the pictures on the wall, they no longer bothered him in the least, and he did in fact have a most restful night free from undesirable dreams of any kind.

I can see her now, on that cold, windy day, with her straw-blonde hair and flimsy frock, selling trinkets in front of the church. She must have been desperate to be offering her wares to a mere schoolboy such as myself, or perhaps she was inexperienced or simply shy, and I, being close to her in age, seemed easier to approach than older, more daunting persons. At the time I was helping a boy in my class with his Latin, and, as I happened to be on my way home from a lesson, I had a little money in my pocket with which I was hoping to buy some crunchy coconut. But there she stood, with her blue eyes imploring and with her pathetic little tray, and suddenly I had no choice but to give her the money, which I did and then quickly walked away. For a few minutes I really felt good, for in helping her I had acted, as it seemed to me, in a truly selfless manner.

After a while, however, I began to wonder whether I would have been equally generous if it had not been a young and, to me, attractive girl but a disgusting old man or woman or even a boy who had approached me. What reminded me of this event was the man in the doorway, whom I would have helped if he had asked me. On the face of it, it might appear that here was the answer to that old, nagging question which has never left me. Yes, I would have given my money to a disgusting old man, but to be perfectly honest, my reactions in these two cases were not really comparable. For with the girl I really wanted to give her the money whereas with the man in Queensway it was more a matter of moral compulsion, as if I wanted to pay some mysterious debt which I owed to society in general.

I now ask myself, am I as a person really a separate, unique and, in the short term at least, stable entity – very much as in the purely physical sense – or simply a core of consciousness with an outer, active set of instincts, drives, needs and propensities, capable of merging, briefly or for long periods of time, with others? Putting it differently, am I the same person whatever my circumstances at the time, irrespective, for instance, of whom I am with, what I happen to be doing, or what is going on around me? If so, this surely means that in every one of my contacts and relationships, not only with people but also with animals and even ideas or objects, a kind of variable, possibly unstable 'extended' or 'super-person' is formed, of which I am only a part – very much as two drops of water flowing together on a table may form a single drop but then separate again as some of the water evaporates – the number of possible combinations of this type being virtually endless. This would explain the possibility of unselfish behaviour, even to the point of sacrificing one's own life for one's family or friends or country, which, like the possibility of an effect without a cause seems, on the face of it, to be inexplicable. However, since the 'super-person' and the person in the narrow sense of the word would not be identical, their real interests too would be bound to differ.

... I think I've got away with it this time, although with L. you can never tell. (M always referred to Mrs. Bingley as L., which was short for 'landlady', in case she ever got hold of his private journal and was tempted to read it. He also made a point of expressing himself obliquely when writing about events in which Mrs. Bingley was, in one way or another, involved.) But it really made me mad to have such aberrations imposed on me. Still, the only way to deal with such a situation is by judicious management of the facts. Which reminds me of my last job at sea, on the *SS Globetrotter*, where I was the mess-boy. The steward, an enormous Dane with a violent temper, hated both Scottie ('Sixteen years at sea and already a mess-boy') and me because he couldn't understand what we were saying and because we were good friends and obviously had a lot of fun in each other's company. One day he caught me eating a *smørrebrød* with about an inch of ham and cheese on a quarter-inch slice of pumpernickel-type bread. This enraged him to such a point that he threatened to give me a 'taste of his fist', which, incidentally, was also unusually large.

Although seething with rage at this insult, I said nothing at the time, but having thought the matter over went to see my friend, the cook, and told him that my honour had been stained by the steward's threat and that according to Czech custom (I was officially a Czechoslovak national) blood must flow to wash it clean again, so would he kindly lend me one of his sharper kitchen knives. He tried to make me change my mind but I remained adamant. And since he would not let me have a knife, I borrowed one from a Finnish deckhand – on the flimsy pretext of wanting to carve a broom-handle – and stuck it under my belt. The cook, a most conscientious man, obviously did exactly what I was hoping he would do and immediately warned the steward, for the latter was nowhere to be seen for an hour or two. When he eventually appeared – I, as ever intent on doing my duty but with the knife tucked ostentatiously into my belt, happened to be washing the dishes – he gave me just one deeply reproachful look (he had, of course, seen the knife) and took off again for the rest of the day. I returned the fearsome weapon in due course, quite certain that the steward would never bother me again.

... Catty not at the office today. God, how I miss her!

Next morning – not by any means at the crack of dawn but with the sun already hot in the sky and Mrs. Bingley's vacuum cleaner buzzing away merrily on the stairs – M, who had gone down to the kitchen to get some breakfast, found Silversmith already there, deeply engrossed in a copy of the previous day's *Financial Times* which he had filched the day before from his uncle, the dentist.

'Gilts were up again last Friday,' Silversmith announced without looking up from his paper, 'But the bullion market is still very shaky.' Silversmith was convinced that reading the *Financial Times* gave him special prestige and put him in touch with the world of business and finance – a world in which he hoped one day to make his mark.

Seeing that M apparently couldn't care less, Silversmith tried another approach. 'You will be happy to learn that my lists are now with Messrs. Exobrill and that I shall shortly be £350 richer.' This was the total for the 1st, 2nd and 3rd prizes. Silversmith was often short of funds but never of self confidence.

'Very glad to hear it. Congratulations!' M responded, 'I shall bear this in mind when I need some cash.'

'Scoff away to your heart's content, but we shall see what we shall see. In the meantime, how about a little side-bet – nothing much, let us say a fiver?'

Although quite prepared to be sceptical, M was not a gambling man. Life with his father in Vienna and good old Uncle Moritz had cured him, most thoroughly, of any desire to get something for nothing. His father, a commercial traveller in picture frames, desk calendars and similarly inoffensive goods, was an incurable optimist quite incapable of living within his declining means, whose budget, based as it was on hopes and dreams, never seemed to balance. This inevitably caused him and his family to slide into poverty and squalor. In later years M still recalled his feelings of shame and humiliation when Papa would entreat him to visit Uncle Max (who owned a shop selling fancy goods in Hernals, one of the poorer districts of Vienna, and was doing all right, thank you) in order to ask him for a small loan which might tide them over for a few days or enable Papa to make a payment on account to the landlord and thus avoid immediate eviction. More often than not these attempts came to nothing, for Uncle Max, an exceedingly thrifty man, would part only with very small and quite insufficient amounts of money, just enough for him to consider that he was entitled to tell his favourite nephew – the only son of his beloved sister Ruth, now, alas, deceased, although with the help of the Almighty and greater care she might have been saved – what a profligate and worthless man his father was, whereas in fact Papa, as M knew very well, was a kind and generous man who had simply fallen upon bad times and whose main fault was that he could not adapt readily to his ever worsening circumstances.

Uncle Max had never forgiven M's father for the death in childbirth of his only sister, nor for betraying – as he saw it – her memory by contracting another marriage. Another thing he – himself basically a mean man – could never forgive was the generosity with which M's father had treated him in the past inasmuch as it diminished him in his own eyes. Morus, on the other hand, was indeed his favourite nephew (there was another nephew, but somehow he did not count), and Uncle Max did his best, according to his own lights, to help and advise him and to mould him in his own image. He had great expectations of his nephew, which nothing could have proved more clearly than the fact that he gave him, on the occasion of his 15th birthday, one of his very own chess sets, Uncle Max being among other things a chess master of international repute. But his uncle's overbearing and authoritative manner as well as the memory of past humiliations eventually made M rebellious, a tendency his uncle tried hard to discourage. However, many years later, when M had married 'out of the faith', in spite of the fact that Uncle Max had done his level best to get him settled with some 'nice Jewish girl' from 'a good family', he finally abandoned him as a lost cause. Not prepared to leave his money to the state or to charity, he took the only road open to him by himself marrying a lady of impeccable background with several children from a previous marriage, who, according to such reports as reached M, fully appreciated the advantages of her new status. M, who valued his independence above all things, did not mind.

Uncle Max's hand-outs and Papa's other sources of income were never sufficient to avoid eviction permanently, although sometimes it did prove possible to put off such an evil event for a few days or even weeks. This process continued until, in due course and after passing through a succession of ever less habitable lodgings, they finally found shelter at the severely overcrowded home of Uncle Georg, the carpenter, who was truly a man with a heart of gold. Incidentally, during all those years of financial hardship Papa never once despaired of winning 'the big prize' in the state lottery, which would make everything all right again and bring back the good old days when money was no problem and the world was a much happier place. However, in spite of all the money he spent playing the lottery, even when that money would have been needed for other, more pressing purposes, he never won anything at all.

And then there was Uncle Moritz. A very rich man in his day, he had evolved a system for winning at roulette which he firmly believed could break the bank of any casino in the world. But, not surprisingly, the casinos broke him instead. M remembered him as a small, thin and extremely pedantic man, unmarried and excessively polite to ladies, who was obsessed with personal hygiene and would wash his hands after shaking the hand of any other person, however clean and wholesome. To M he used to speak in English (by way of acknowledging M's superior education), but mainly about matters of no interest whatsoever, such as M's studies and hotels at which he, Uncle Moritz, had stayed during his travels. Once his fortune had melted away, Uncle Moritz tried, with varying success, to persuade all and sundry – even M's by then chronically impecunious father – to 'invest' in his system. But such money as he managed to get hold of was soon squandered as, once again, the roulette wheel happened to behave in some thoroughly perverse manner, and eventually he vanished out of sight.

After the war M met him again in London – he was staying at a bed-sitter in Kensington – a poor shadow of his former self and spurned by all, but still dreaming ever more fantastic dreams of wealth and grandeur. M, having arrived (by judgment rather than any spontaneous feeling) at the conclusion that his Uncle Moritz was a suitable object for compassion, made it a practice to call on him once a week, every Wednesday afternoon, when he would bring him tins of sausages and other practical gifts and listen, with feigned patience, for he was not a patient person by temperament, to his uncle's often repeated and, in any case, never very enthralling tales and generally do everything a good nephew should. Eventually, however, Uncle Moritz died, leaving a number of elegant suits, a slim gold watch with a heavy gold chain and an exquisite camel-hair coat. Nobody else having come forward to claim any of these items, M kept the watch and the coat, which he considered a fine fit, although it was, in fact, a bit on the short side, but gave away the suits as they were far too small for him and in any case alien to his taste.

CHAPTER SIX

A FEW days later M met Dr. Sombrero-Domingo, originally plain Rudolf Sonntags-hut from Berlin and now Spanish teacher with TTTW. He was a short, elderly man in a dark suit, virtually without any neck and extremely barrel-chested. He wore heavy horn-rimmed spectacles and his badly stained, prominent dentures suggested a surplus of teeth while imparting to his features a kind of permanent grin. His nose, a natural continuation of his forehead, was another dominant characteristic, while the skin on his disproportionately large, entirely hairless egg-shaped head and on his similarly outsize hands was freckled and spotted with age. As he stood there burbling away, waving his hands about in a paroxysm of excitement and quite generally having a whale of a time, he looked to M, at first sight, like a large carp just released from the confinement of an excessively small glass bowl into a spacious pond.

When M entered the office, Sombrero-Domingo was describing, with great gusto and manifestly huge enjoyment, an incident from his life, while Catty, his only public, was listening with rapt attention, her facial expressions reflecting every emotion as the story progressed. Far from being put out by the sudden appearance of a second listener, Sombrero-Domingo raised both arms in a gesture of quandary, which seemed to transform him, momentarily at least, from fish to bird. 'What should I have done?' he bellowed, 'What could anyone have done in such a dilemma? The orchestra was waiting, the public was waiting, but where was Rosinius who was meant to conduct? Rosinius, you see, was sick to his stomach, with his head in the waste-paper basket. But I was a young man in those days. Nothing was too hard for me, for Sombrero-Domingo, you understand, is of the same sturdy stuff as your great English bulldog, bow-wow! I simply sink my teeth into the problem, any problem, and never let go.'

To prove his point he drew back his lips, exposing his dentures further, which made his last statement seem quite plausible. 'In the end, of course, I couldn't always manage, but, believe me, it was not because I was not trying. Where was I? Oh yes, with Rosinius so sick – sick as a dog he was – somebody had to go and direct the concert, and who, my young friends, who do you think it was? Yes, you have guessed it, Yours Truly went, your very own Sombrero-Domingo.' He gave a little bow, as if to acknowledge their applause. 'Of course, I knew nothing about music, never could tell one note from the other, but what did that matter? The orchestra played and played, and I moved my arms about in *Dreivierteltakt* – 'three-quarters beat' as you would say – and everything went just dandy. Nobody noticed, or at least they didn't let on, and so the evening was saved. Who needs a *Dirigent* anyway? But that is the sort of man I was in those days.' Catty twisted her lips into an appreciative smile, while M wanted to know what had become of Rosinius. 'I can tell you that well enough,' thus Sombrero-Domingo with yet another great rib-shaking guffaw. 'The last time I saw Rosinius he was Director of Music in München and did a lot of riding. On horses, you know. I didn't actually see him, because he was riding away on one side of the wall as I was coming up on the other to visit him. So I missed him by seconds. But I saw his *Zylinderhut* – he always wore a *Zylinderhut* when he was riding – and it was bobbing up and down behind the wall. We still send each other Christmas cards, you know.'

'Your story reminds me...' M was trying to make an impact, but Sombrero-Domingo, who was not prepared to let this newcomer steal his limelight, particularly in the presence of a pretty girl, interrupted him summarily before he had the slightest chance of doing a bit of sparkling of his own, saying 'So sorry to cut in, but I do not think we have met. I am Dr. Sombrero-Domingo, but do not come to me with any of your little sicknesses, aw aw, for it is international affairs I used to specialise in, not medicine'. Seeking approval, he glanced towards Catty, who responded with an appreciative giggle and an encouraging 'I bet!'

'I take it you too are one of the toilers in the field of language instruction.' M responded by stating his name and function. 'Ah well, there will be much for us to discuss when we have the time.' Having made this half-promise, Sombrero-Domingo looked at his watch with an air of extreme urgency. 'My God,' he exclaimed, 'what am I doing here talking? I should have started with the lesson twelve minutes ago.' He rushed out of the door, knocking against Catty's desk as he went. M, whose lesson with Mr. Allbright was scheduled for the same time, rushed off in the other direction.

During the following weeks, as summer turned to autumn, M came to see a good deal of Dr. Sombrero-Domingo and they became firm friends. S-D, who had acquired his doctorate *summa cum laude* at the University of Heidelberg, loved beautiful women and beautiful objects (he used to make much of the fact that one of his uncles had been a well-known expressionist painter) and he had deep roots in the German coffee-house society of the years between the wars. In a way he was continuing, however modestly, a noble tradition of elegance, wealth and culture which was already fading into the realm of nostalgic memory when he was still quite a young man. M sensed in him a zest for life and a kind of integrity which found answering chords in his own personality. Sombrero-Domingo on the other hand felt that through M he was somehow in touch again with his own youth. He admired M's wide-ranging mind but sometimes accused him of being way out in his judgments and excessively analytical. The latter characteristic, in particular, he criticised as one of the root causes of anti-semitism in Germany. He also liked to discuss with M political issues of the day, problems of daily life such as regularly beset him since he was almost incapable of taking sound practical decisions or acting in a rational manner, and relationships with students and staff.

An extrovert through and through, generous and endowed with a robust, Rabelaisian sense of humour, Dr. Sombrero Domingo was well-liked by one and all while enjoying the reputation of being a good, highly successful teacher of Spanish, in spite of the fact that, like so many whose roots are deeply buried in their native culture, he was a lousy linguist utterly devoid of feeling for any language but his mother tongue. He thought of himself as a potential journalist both by temperament and inclination and loved to recount how as a student he had interviewed prostitutes in Berlin, who – he had reason to believe – had thought him a splendid fellow. M, too shy to harbour comparable aspirations, saw himself as a kind of original philosopher.

During his years at the Klappenhorn Gymnasium in Vienna M had three friends – Stengel, Birkenfels and Josef Brunner. Strictly speaking, Birkenfels, who was slightly older and a bit of a bully, was more of an enemy than a friend, for M could never trust him or rely on his support in a crisis, even to the modest extent expected of a schoolfriend. Besides, Birkenfels used to throw the chess pieces at M whenever the latter had the temerity to win a game. It was therefore hardly surprising that M was never comfortable in his presence and always on his guard. Not to put too fine a point on it, M disliked and feared Birkenfels, and when, many years later, they met again in London at a function of the Institute of Linguists, where his erstwhile tormentor was held in high regard, he experienced a definite feeling of satisfaction as he saw what had become of him – a boring, excessively fat little man with a perpetual, pompous frown, meant, no doubt, to signify intense mental travail.

On the other hand, M and Stengel – black-haired and cat-like both in stature and bearing – had a lot in common and they genuinely enjoyed each other's company. M and Stengel shared the same schoolbench for many years. They used to borrow each other's books and copy each other's homework, and on occasion they conspired to get the better of Professor Nagel by playing chess under the desk while he was doing his best to instil some knowledge of Hebrew grammar into their resisting minds. They cheated shamelessly during exams and would stare hard at the fly of Professor Nagel's baggy trousers as if there were something seriously wrong with it, causing him to lose the thread, to become very nervous and to leave the class precipitately in order to adjust his clothing.

As for M, he had every reason to be grateful to Professor Nagel for persuading his father, when the latter was trying to be 'practical', not to have him transferred to a vocational school where he might have learned a useful though humble trade, insisting that M was worthy of a proper education and that such an act would be both irresponsible and a heinous offence against the very spirit of Judaism.

Almost every afternoon M would visit Stengel at his parents' hardware shop, and together they would withdraw to the small, window-less room at the back, which stank of cat since the Stengel's moggy had never been fully house-trained. With its square table and packing cases by way of seats, this was a very bare room indeed and downright dirty, which bothered none of them in the slightest degree - not Mr. Stengel with his tattered and grimy flat cap, who looked every bit like a very short walking stick with a curved handle, nor Mrs. Stengel, a haggard woman, who always – be it summer or winter – wore a brown, knitted cap and a pinkish jersey, nor Stengel Junior, nor, for that matter, M. He felt perfectly comfortable, thank you, and more at home there than in his own home, where his peace was always likely to be shattered by his stepmother and where the atmosphere positively reeked of gloom and of fear. At the Stengels' the kerosene lamp on the table shed a warm and homely light, just the right sort of light by which to play chess and solve problems. The two friends spent several months trying to square the circle, with the solution, a kind of cuckoo, apparently always around the corner but always evading them. When it was pointed out to them that according to Professor something or other somewhere or other this was a problem that could not be solved, M, who could never resist a really juicy paradox, replied, 'So much the better, for if it is impossible, we shall do it! – but what he really meant was '*I* shall do it.' They also spent much time delving into the mysteries of '*The Tempest*'. Seeing that neither M nor Stengel knew any English at the time and that their dictionary was almost a hundred years old – there were six tightly packed columns to be read just to discover all the uses of the indefinite article – they never progressed much beyond the 'Dedication' and contemplation of William Shakespeare's balding head, an image destined to remain part of M's intellectual *bric-à-brac* throughout his life.

M spent many happy hours at the Stengels' shop. On occasion Mrs. Stengel, not exactly a paragon of generosity, even invited him to a plateful of soup or gave him some spare bones from which to suck the marrow. M was not at all choosy and quite prepared to accept gratefully anything and everything that would hold body and soul together.

Another place where he felt very much at home was the kitchen behind the pattern shop belonging to Mr. and Mrs. Brunner, the parents of Josef Brunner, his 'best' friend. Strictly speaking, it was not really a shop at all, for there did not seem to be any stock in it and in all the years M went there he never came across anyone who could possibly have been a customer. In any case, it was quite dangerous to enter, for the shop was guarded by a white Persian cat as fierce as it was beautiful.

Whereas with Stengel M shared mostly mystical experiences, Josef was M's main source of worldly wisdom. Josef, fair-haired and tall and with a nose so perfectly straight and so acutely angled that jokes about its potential as a geometric instrument could not be avoided, had a bicycle of his own, which he rode all over town visiting his numerous uncles and aunts, who, always pleased to see him, treated him to *apfelstrudl*, plum dumplings with fried breadcrumbs, poppy-seed noodles and other delicacies, thus laying the foundations of his obsession with fine fare which was to become a characteristic of his later years. Perhaps because of all this excellent food or perhaps because he had inherited some of his father's ability to appreciate all that was truly beautiful, he became enamoured at an early age of the fair sex in general and, ever since he was thirteen, of lovely Gisela, the greengrocer's daughter across the road. This friendship came to a head shortly before his sixteenth birthday, when in the doorway of the house in which she lived – it was simply pouring with rain – he tried to convince her by strong and powerful arguments (these were always his forte) of his desirability as a boyfriend and the practical steps this should entail. Gisela, embarrassed out of her wits, turned this way and that trying to escape on to a more conventional footing and eventually succeeded in getting away from him, but not without having lost three buttons from her overcoat, which Josef in his excitement had twisted off. After this event their relationship became noticeably less cordial.

Josef's father – in his homeland Poland a maker of violins and master carpenter – loved all things English and kept metre-high stacks of old *Manchester Guardians* in the kitchen. He was also a convinced and uncompromising atheist, ascribing most of the great evils besetting the world to the mumbo-jumbo, as he saw it, of religion. A small, wiry man with a slight, rather endearing stammer, he would get hold of the two friends whenever he could in order to read and translate with them passages from the newspapers in his collection. Josef's mother always kept in the background but seemed to shed some mysterious inner light wherever she went. M thought of her mainly as a great and generous purveyor of bread and dripping. Shortly before the end of the war, when her husband had been arrested, she, unlike him not a Jew, went to the Gestapo to obtain his release, thereby bravely saving his life. She herself, sadly, lost her own life when one of the last bombs dropped on Vienna hit the house in which the Brunners lived.

Josef was M's main chess partner and together they would practise English conversation. Initially such conversation tended to be somewhat whimsical (a faithful reflection though of what Dr. Bergenau had taught them) as well as repetitive ('I scratch my head. Yes, do you scratch your head?' etc.), but eventually it became more varied and more of a medium for the exchange of thoughts and observations. At any rate, they had lots of fun as, wandering through the streets, they spoke 'English' as loudly as they could, in order to attract the attention of passers-by to their extraordinary erudition.

Dr. Pendlebloom was cleaning his teeth in the bathroom of his Surbiton home, a splendid example of how the fastidious taste of an interior designer can be most successfully combined with even highly flamboyant leanings towards unfettered luxury. Like many another 'self-made' man, Dr. Pendlebloom felt that both 'good taste' and luxury were necessary for his well-being inasmuch as they confirmed, in their different ways, that having risen, once and for all, above the common herd, he had finally made the grade and could now hold up his head proudly in any company. To protect this happy state of affairs he made much of his married status, joined 'exclusive' clubs of like-minded successful people, never tired of increasing and displaying his wealth and made a great show of general canniness. He also tended to be inordinately concerned with the state of his own health and matters of health in general, rather pathetically trying to resist the inexorable advance of old age. And, of course, he utterly rejected anyone and anything outside his own charmed circle, using to this end an ever-ready armoury of epithets such as 'odd', 'communist' and 'trouble-maker'.

While Dr. Pendlebloom was harmlessly engaged in the bathroom, Mrs. Pendlebloom, alias Miss Gomberg, now in her lace-trimmed nightgown, was sitting in front of the kidney-shaped dressing-table with its top made of genuine Carrara marble, observing herself in the mirror and brushing her long grey hair – still abundant, still hair to be proud of – with admirable persistence. The cares and stresses of the day having drained from her freckled face, now minus spectacles and with a faint smile at one corner of her mouth, she recognised in herself a striking resemblance to Mona Lisa, a resemblance which she cherished and strove to promote in the forlorn hope that her husband too would one day become aware of it. As for her figure, now released from all constraints of clothing, it was devoid of any definable shape, rather as if it had been contrived by Thurber in one of his more extravagant moods.

It took a long time for Dr. Pendlebloom, a most fastidious man, to complete his ablutions, attend to the nails on his fingers and toes, apply *'Troubadour'* to selected areas of his body and change into his silk pyjamas. Eventually, however, he was quite ready and entered the conjugal bedroom, where his lady wife was still in the process of brushing her hair.

In spite of the fact that he was not a passionate man in the romantic sense, Dr. Pendlebloom, far from hating Miss Gomberg's guts as was generally believed at TTTW, was quite happily married to her. Their relationship was firmly based on Miss Gomberg's unquestioning and boundless respect for her lord and master. She saw him as a man of infinite wisdom and ability, but above all as a great businessman, the very pinnacle of human evolution. By comparison, all other men she knew – not in fact all that many – were mere irritating pygmies, and Miss Gomberg made a point of letting them know it. Pendlebloom, on the other hand, basked in the sunshine of her adulation, and, besides, he found her infinitely useful as a thinking-aid and as a source of information such as is not normally within the reach of a managing director.

Entering the bedroom, Dr. Pendlebloom, whose thoughts were never far removed from matters of business, addressed his hair-brushing spouse as follows: 'I am very glad to see that according to our latest set of quarterly accounts TTTW continues to make good progress. At this rate, Ella, we shall soon be able to expand.'

This caused Mona Lisa to turn again into Miss Gomberg, managing director's secretary and principal adviser - a trick which she had learned to perform neatly and efficiently.

'For further good progress at the present rate,' continued Dr. Pendlebloom, 'it will be incumbent upon us to make major changes. We shall, above all, have to get rid of the riff-raff.' He was referring to certain members of the staff who were not pulling their weight – anyone in fact not fit to be associated with TTTW.

Miss Gomberg, entering into the spirit of her husband's comment, remarked with some venom: 'We shall certainly have to do something about that Madame Bellrun-jay before she makes an even bigger fool of herself, the hussy, although at her age you might have thought she would know better. Talk about mutton dressing as lamb – I, for one, call it simply disgusting. Besides, this week alone there have been three letters saying in so many words that she uses the TTTW French classes as an excuse for getting hold of men.' Having unburdened herself of this diatribe she added darkly: 'And, of course, she encourages the others.' Madame Bellrunjay – really plain Lucy Bellringer, after her third or fourth husband – had never even been to France but at TTTW she would have a claim to the courtesy title 'Madame' and the special pronunciation of her name, for as long as she continued teaching French.

Dr. Pendlebloom, a man of uncompromising morality and a staunch upholder of the great British traditions, was deeply shocked. 'But why did you not tell me this before, Ella?' he wanted to know. 'The woman must go at once – tomorrow at the latest.' (His wife was also his chief and favourite executioner.) 'See to it that she does not enter TTTW premises again. And if she gives you any trouble, call the police. Get her ejected by force if necessary...' Dr. Pendlebloom had worked himself into a fine lather of righteous indignation. 'No, Ella, do not try to change my mind.' (She had made no such attempt.) 'For we have a moral duty here, from which we must not flinch. As Sir Ladbroke pointed out the other day, and I concur fully, a single tainted apple...'

I couldn't agree more,' interjected Miss Gomberg, 'that person must not be allowed to get away with it, and she won't, if I have any say in the matter. Of course, she must have known that we were up to her tricks, for quite a few of her students – all men as it happens – have written in to say that they won't continue with TTTW if she goes. Quite a neat little conspiracy this, if you ask me, but we all know who put them up to it.

At this Dr. Pendlebloom grew pensive. 'Perhaps,' he now ventured, 'she is not the one to blame, after all. Perhaps we are dealing here with perverted attempts, possibly inspired by the competition (who will, after all, stop at nothing), to destroy the reputation of a respected and valuable teacher and by so doing damage the reputation of the entire TTTW. Believe me, Ella, you can have no idea what some people will do – to what lengths they will go – in order to gain even the most insignificant advantage. Not that they have the slightest prospect of succeeding with their machinations, not by any means, for I am familiar with all their ruses and shall find ways to foil them. Are the letters signed?'

'They are.'

'And are they from regular students?'

'Some are.'

'I am quite clear about this in my own mind, Ella. We must get rid of the troublemakers.' (Dr. Pendlebloom coming down firmly in favour of the 'Retain Madame' lobby.) 'All said and done, it would, after all, be very wrong for us – morally wrong, as I have said already – not to take a firm stand on behalf of a trusted employee such as Madame.'

'Don't forget though,' responded Miss Gomberg, who felt that another touch on the tiller was required in order to prevent the decision-making process from getting out of control, 'one of those who definitely want to see the back of her is that Miss Almondgreen, who organises the "Clean up Soho" campaign. It's up to you, of course, but that woman could cause us a lot of trouble if she had a mind to.'

Dr. Pendlebloom considered this problem for a long time before pronouncing judgment: 'We must not be too hasty, for this is a matter requiring deep and mature thought. To take sides at this stage would be a great and possibly fatal error. For there are times, Ella, when we must take care to decide only when all the facts are known, but then firmly and without flinching. As Winston Churchill, our great wartime leader, said ...'

After more of the same, the conversation eventually switched to M and his progress within the organisation. Miss Gomberg, who did not like M, for she sensed that he might one day fail to regard Dr. Pendlebloom and the organisation with the undivided respect due to them and, in addition, suspected him of having designs on young Catty, mentioned, not without reluctance, that the course-renewal rate in M's German classes – he now ran two, one for beginners and one at the intermediate level – was 'not bad' and that, strangely enough, his private students too appeared to be satisfied.

'That Miss Pratt has actually changed from one to three French lessons a week,' Miss Gomberg explained, adding sourly, 'Well, she must have her reasons. She is certainly old enough to know what she is doing.'

Dr. Pendlebloom, choosing to ignore her obvious disapproval, suggested that some reward, some form of encouragement, was perhaps indicated. 'It would be failing in our duty,' he said, 'to overlook such promising results from one so young. Of course, we must not go too far too soon, for that would only confuse the young man – cause him to overestimate his value to the organisation. Perhaps,' he specu-lated, 'we ought to make him Head of the German and French departments.'

'In my opinion, for what it is worth, he hasn't got what it takes to be a head. I, for one, do not think TTTW can rely on him one hundred per cent, and to judge by what I've heard such a promotion would not be popular. Besides, you could always offer him more money. Miss Gomberg offered this suggestion very much tongue-in-cheek, well aware that this of all things was not likely to happen.

'No, no, he would not expect it.' Dr. Pendlebloom hastened to put the record straight. 'I can see very well how this might upset the delicate balance of the common room. And where would we be if we had to give a rise to every member of the staff?'

Having reached virtually total agreement, they both went to bed, Miss Gomberg reverting to the state of Mona Lisa, assuming a smile even more enigmatic than before, and Dr. Pendlebloom making himself comfortable with a bank statement, until they felt that it was time to turn off the light.

When, after a particularly unpleasant series of murders not very far from Westlake Crescent, the perpetrator, a mild-mannered, unobtrusive little man, was finally caught, M, who for days on end had felt intensely uncomfortable whenever he saw a policeman (half expecting to be arrested as a suspect), heaved a great sigh of relief. Silversmith and Lipkin admitted to similar feelings when they discussed the event later in the day over a communal dish of macaroni cheese.

CHAPTER SEVEN

ON SHORE-LEAVE in Wellington, New Zealand, M took 49 aspirins within the space of not more than two hours. He was absolutely certain of the number, for the bottle, purchased at Boots at Piccadilly Circus, had originally contained 50 tablets, and he had used only one previously.

M simply adored Wellington, which, with its background of gently undulating hills, reminded him of small coastal towns in England such as he imagined them to be but had in fact never known. He could have sworn and was ever prepared to affirm that the fragrance of succulent, green grass had reached him fully three days before the *Bergano* reached port (whatever the others said), and as she approached her berth, steaming slowly and cautiously through the warm rain, he knew in his innermost heart that Wellington was the place where he wanted to spend the rest of his days – the only place in the whole wide world where he could ever be entirely happy and fulfilled.

Nevertheless M took 49 aspirins, which might well have been the last aspirins he would ever take. His motives for this mad act were complex. Several weeks at sea, with the *Bergano* pitching and rolling endlessly between leaden, mountainous waves as she struggled towards her destination, had left him worn-out and exhausted. He had managed to make an enemy of Einar Olafson, with whom he was compelled to share a cabin (their feud had at that stage reached a point at which M was seriously considering the advisability of killing the hated man with a crowbar or some such implement, and had even gone so far as to select a suitable weapon), and, besides, he was generally tired of the war and all the stresses and privations which it entailed.

But what really prompted him to take such a desperate course was his desire to be with Betty, the dental nurse, with whom he had fallen passionately in love (and who could blame him after all that time at sea?) as soon as he had met her at the YWCA. At the time she was playing draughts with a soldier. M, seeing at a glance that she was not very good at it, advised her what to play, and in due course took the soldier's place, which the latter, completely baffled and apparently unable to grasp what was going on, had vacated without the slightest hesitation. As for Betty, she admired a certain Otto – like M from Central Europe – who, according to her glowing and lengthy account, was ever so handsome, intelligent and brave.

Although M gained the distinct impression that Otto was currently the toast of Wellington and the chief magnet in the town's social calendar, he felt convinced that given half a chance he could get the better of even a competitor as formidable as this and by so doing conquer Betty's affections for ever and ever. They would get married (a simple but tasteful wedding would do, with Betty all in white and with spring flowers in her hair), and they would have lots and lots of simply adorable children and grow old together peacefully among the green hills of Wellington. So, when after the ENSA show, during which the kind-hearted girl had allowed him to hold her hand, they were strolling along in the general direction of the harbour, it was the most natural thing on earth for M to tell her about his iron will, an attribute by which he used to set great store, and how he would be staying in Wellington, in spite of the fact that there were only two ways in which he would be allowed to leave the *Bergano* – feet first to the morgue, or gravely ill by ambulance to the hospital. Betty, deeply impressed, told him how she looked forward to introducing M to Otto and how she was sure that they would become great friends. M was not as sure of that as Betty, but he readily fell in with her plans, for to do otherwise would have been tantamount to haggling about the entrance fee to paradise.

So this is what actually happened: M, having been told upon his return to the *Bergano* that she was due to sail again next morning, decided to act. His plan – a plan guaranteed to prove, once and for all, his absolutely iron will – was to take an overdose of aspirins, just enough to get him into hospital. Ever since he was a little boy in his grandmother's kitchen, where he used to jump up and down on the mattress of his enormous bed in the corner, next to the huge, menacing window, repeating over and over again: '*ácidum ácetylo-salycílicum, ácidum ácetylo-salycílicum*' – words which he had found on a Bayer's triangular pack of aspirins – he had had a special, almost mystical relationship with this drug. Complications with the authorities such as might well ensue could, he felt, be taken care of at a later stage. As for Betty, she would be wonderfully surprised and delighted when she saw him again! Such minor matters as the fact that to get hold of her might prove difficult, seeing that he knew neither her second name nor her address, never even crossed his mind.

M, at the time an engine-greaser on daytime duty, albeit not as yet entrusted with the demanding and responsible task of keeping the engine oiled, got up early in the morning – everybody else in the ship was still fast asleep – and went down to the firemen's mess to make himself a cup of coffee. He then proceeded to dissolve a goodly number of aspirins in the coffee, to which neither milk nor sugar had been added, swallowed the dastardly brew, and, acting on the principle that all evidence must be destroyed, threw the cup out of the porthole into the sea. This accomplished, he descended into the engine-room and started on some polishing task or other, for it seemed to him that his need for hospital treatment would be even more convincing if he were found unconscious while on duty.

To begin with, nothing at all happened – clear proof this, if any had been needed, of M's superior fitness and resistance. However, after a second cup of coffee and more aspirins (the cup was disposed of in the same manner as its predecessor), M experienced a humming sensation in his ears, but it took a third cup and the remainder of the tablets for things to change radically. Bending forward now made M feel as if he were about to faint, thus compelling him to straighten out again. His complexion changed alarmingly (to judge by his reflection in the freshly polished ship's telegraph – an exceedingly handsome device made of shining brass) from green to bluish-purple, and his heart beat as if fit to burst. To complete the dismal scene, he felt indescribably sick. Not to put too fine a point on it, he was sick – repeatedly – thus making such work as he had done previously rather useless. Unable, in spite of his best endeavours, to make himself fall down unconscious, he dragged himself up the ladders to the chief-engineer's cabin, and, after virtually falling through the door – the chief in his none-too-clean underwear happened to be in the process of shaving – asked to be sent to the hospital without delay – a request which his superior regarded as downright hilarious. His laughter reverberated through the entire corridor and brought a number of officers in various stages of undress out of their cabins, inquiring what was the matter, offering ribald comments, curses and suggestions, or simply slamming doors.

Stretched out on the floor of his own cabin, M was again extremely and messily sick. But still he was undefeated. When his friend Tony, the pump-man – about to go ashore for the last time though already the worse for drink – came in, M pointed to some money and begged him to buy some more tablets so that he might finish the job. However, when Tony returned about half an hour later (not that in his current state M was particularly concerned with or aware of time), he was drunk to the point of incoherence. Muttering imprecations, he emptied two bottles of port wine first over M's upturned face and then all over him. It is clearly reasonable to assume that M's lasting aversion to port wine laced with aspirins dated back to this regrettable incident.

The ship's engines were beginning to turn, their massive pistons moving up and down, and the webs of the crankshaft – every one of them half a ton of solid metal – ponderously rotating, when M, slithering and crawling, again got down to the floor of the engine-room. He knew that this was his last chance, for the merest contact between one of his legs and a crankshaft-web would suffice to send him to hospital for a good long spell. His courage was immense, his resolve relentless ... Excluding every thought of what he was about to do, he slowly, ever so slowly, thrust his right leg through the barrier.

With M at the railing, sadly contemplating the shambles of his iron will but with both his legs still intact, the *Bergano*, now gathering speed, made for the open sea.

THANKS to the efforts of a charitable organisation, Rosabelle had been able to come to England shortly before the war, only a month or two after her seventeenth birthday. Originally from a small village in the flatlands of Southern Poland, she had left her home and her family without much if any regret and even with a certain sense of liberation, for the narrowness, as she saw it, of village life did not suit her and she felt unloved not only by her mother, a dour and bitter woman, who regarded her as flighty and reprehensively vain (although God only knew where she had that idea from) but also by her two elder sisters, both of whom were married and had children of their own. As for her father, he had left the village for good when she was still a tiny infant. A faded Daguerrotype of a young, full-faced man in a kind of uniform, which she had found at the bottom of a drawer, was her only clue as to what kind of person he had been, and although she thought about him a lot when she was still a young girl – in one of her favourite fantasies he, now rich and respected, came for her to take her with him to America – as the years passed without the least sign of life from him she eventually came to accept that to all intents and purposes she had no father.

But freedom had proved to be a greatly overrated state, and in some ways indeed she was worse off than at home. True enough, she no longer had to worry about her joyless mother and endless rows about lipsticks and the clothes she wore nor about her general untidiness and even the presence of flowers on the table (an unwelcome source of dirt and unnecessary work according to her mother), but instead she now had to cope with utter indifference and, as a result, profound loneliness. People tended to be put off by her heavy build, her sallow, greasy skin and her frequently scowling appearance. She was regarded by one and all as dull or downright unintelligent, and instead of making friends and leading a life full of interest, beauty and meaning – the kind of life she had dreamed of in her village in Poland – she became ever more isolated. Having come to terms with the erosion of her hopes and the conviction that she would never be a popular person, she tended increasingly to subordinate herself to other people, especially men, accepting exploitation as her proper role. In such circles as she frequented in England, mainly refugee communities of various kinds, people tended to agree that the low regard in which she held herself – probably an inevitable result of her emotionally starved and deprived childhood – was quite justified, and, moreover, she became known as a chaser after good causes, an ever ready volunteer and a 'soft touch'. To please a 'friend' she even took up communism in much the same way in which she might have picked up a pretty blouse or a pair of shoes in the bargain basement of a big store – on impulse and without giving the matter a great deal of thought. Not that men and what they had to offer meant all that much to her, for after some precocious adventures with village boys she discovered that reality never ever came up to her expectations, or, for that matter, those of her partners. There were even some who described her as simply frigid, whereas others, smirking and winking, kept talking about her 'golden heart', an epithet she had still not been able to shake off.

During the war Rosabelle worked at a munitions factory up north, where she met Chloe, who became her closest friend and confidante. Now in the country near

Basingstoke, Chloe was employed at a home for the disabled. Rosabelle and Chloe would write each other interminable letters reporting every smallest detail of their lives. Chloe kept asking Rosabelle to leave London and come to Hampshire, where finding a job as a nanny or lady's companion, or for that matter at the home where she herself was employed, would be no problem. As for Rosabelle, she had not yet given up on London and the freedom of her present life but she felt that there was much to be said in favour of such a step.

Some time after her 'communist period' Rosabelle went to a party where she met Dave, an organiser of a Zionist group on the extreme right of the movement. It took only a few drinks for her resistance, which was never very strong, to become ineffective, so when Dave – a bespectacled, pale-complexioned fellow, who was not exactly a girl's dream but knew what he was about – sidled up to her and asked her the 64,000 dollar question – did she want to help the Jews – there seemed to be only one possible answer. And having, it seemed, quite forgotten how stifling a small community can be, she allowed a new dream to take hold of her – to go to Israel, join a kibbutz and lead 'the good life' for ever more, a life of hard work and dedication, surrounded by like-minded people, far from loneliness and the solitary cares of day-to-day living such as had been her lot since her arrival in England. For the time being she became a conscientious, if undistinguished member of Dave's 'section', went to meetings, listened to speeches, typed letters, addressed envelopes and made herself generally useful. She also allowed Dave to use her in a more personal way whenever he felt inclined to do so, which was not often. This suited her fine, for there was also Silversmith, whom she had met at another party and who was not averse to sharing her favours and services, an arrangement convenient to him in every way. Through Silversmith, however, she came to know M and Lipkin, both of whom, untypically, treated her as a friend and made no demands on her whatsoever.

Now in her tiny bedsitter – unmade bed, various articles of clothing strewn all over the floor and dirty dishes piled high in the washbasin – she was sitting at the table struggling with the rudiments of conversational Hebrew, learning by heart such phrases as 'Whose turn is it to collect the eggs?' and 'I am off to the orange grove' as might one day prove useful in Israel, if she ever got there. To begin with, she had derived great enjoyment from the weekly meetings at which she and her fellow students practised their conversational skills but lately her attendance had become irregular, for once again she felt that she was too slow, that unlike the others she would never succeed and that the other members of the group didn't really like her. Besides, she asked herself, what was the point? Also her other links with the organisation were beginning to weaken, but she still clung to her dream of a happy and fulfilling life in Israel.

Shortly after the war M had been employed in Munich, where he assisted the Americans in administering their sector of the recently shattered Reich. As a member of the 'Allied personnel' he was not as well paid as his American colleagues, nor were his chances of promotion as good as theirs, but he was certainly much better off than the 'indigenous' German personnel. During this period he had spent a night with Ursula, a kind-hearted girl very similar to Rosabelle in appearance and similarly exploitable but quite different in personality and background. Born and brought up in the very heart of rural Kent – her parents were solidly middle-class – Ursula was well educated, a fine painter and an excellent linguist, with a very creditable honours degree in English and History of Art, which she, with well-bred modesty, tended to play down. She was good at puzzles and games, a fair table-tennis player and great fun to be with. She and M greatly enjoyed each other's company and spent much time together, as a result of which it was generally agreed throughout their section – they worked together in the same room – that it would not be long before they were engaged and married.

Engagements and weddings in that close and exclusive circle being much in vogue, it was always difficult to find something really acceptable to give to the happy couple of the day to speed them on their merry way, seeing that prior to the reform of the Mark (which, incidentally, reduced its value to ten per cent) there were hardly any goods for sale at the German shops, while, on the other hand, the choice of articles suitable as wedding gifts such as were on sale at the American PX shops was extremely limited. For instance, when Peter Klauber from England married his Susan from the USA they were given no fewer than five identical napkin sets in unbleached cotton, the only gift available at the very reasonable price of five dollars scrip. As for M, who worked in their section, his contribution consisted of a large marble ashtray – another PX gift thought to be very appropriate, especially for smokers, which the Klaubers were not – as well as his latest poem, which, he claimed, had been inspired by their heart-warming romance. This was perhaps slightly excessive – indeed, just a bit over the top – considering that they were both dry as dust and mean to the point of obsession, and that he could barely stand either of them. Strictly speaking, the poem was also irrelevant, since it purported to celebrate procreation, which was clearly not the point of their union.

With everybody treating them as if they were already married, small wonder that Ursula took it for granted that she was meant for M and he for her. So when at long last M asked her if she would allow him to kiss her, she readily agreed and raised her face to his. One inevitable step led to another, but sadly M's actions owed less to genuine desire than to a compulsive need to prove his manhood. When he asked Ursula – this time against a veritable tide of incipient misgivings – whether she would consent to 'sleeping' with him, she, in an obvious turmoil of emotion, merely nodded and squeezed his arm. And so in due course they found themselves in bed together, where M finally came to realise that, for himself at any rate, there was absolutely no point in what they were doing. This encounter was clearly not a success, but, worst of all, Ursula couldn't understand what was wrong, while M, in a mire of self-disgust and guilt, was quite unable to return again to their easy, pleasant relationship. Conversation between them, even of the most routine kind, became incredibly laboured and eventually impossible. M's trouble was that he was still stuck in the groove of 'handsome prince rescues pure and innocent damsel in distress, they get married and live happily ever after'. No real flesh-and-blood woman could, of course, come up to such a fairy-tale standard, nor, for that matter, could he. Although well aware that he was behaving badly, he found it quite beyond him to do anything about it. Like Goethe's Faust he wanted to love and to be loved, and there was enough of the devil in him to take him part of the way. But Ursula, though possibly as pure and innocent as Margaret, was not as passionate (or if she was, M was not the one to bring out and match her passion), while he, unlike Faust, wasted all feeling in anticipating a variety of horrifying consequences, both for her and for himself. Unable as yet to commit himself and to accept reality or to bear Ursula's silent and questioning reproach whenever they were together, which, in view of the fact that they worked in the same office and shared many tasks, could not be avoided, he resigned his position and went to Nuremberg, where he became a translator and, in due course, a court interpreter.

Faust, incidentally, was really lucky. By signing that contract in blood, and considering both the way in which he treated Margaret and the mess he landed her in, he had really given Mephisto every excuse for conveying him to the most inhospitable region of his dreaded realm. By great good fortune, however, God had bet Mephisto that he would ultimately fail in his attempts at bringing down Faust, although it was hard to fathom why God should have such faith in the incorruptibility of this particular person. Seeing that for power-political reasons God could not possibly lose a bet with the devil – and one is bound to wonder why Mephisto ever imagined that he was in with a chance – Faust was bound to come up smelling of roses, which is exactly what happened.

CHAPTER EIGHT

LIVING in the country at my grandfather's house was great. My grandmother, whom I remember chiefly for her sky-blue dresses and her starched, beautifully white aprons, and Aunt Sali were very kind to me, and provided I turned up for meals I was quite free to come and go as I pleased. Once I went to school I did of course have other obligations as well, but they never became excessively onerous, for when it came to the three R's I was definitely one of the stars in the class, entitled, like any star, to certain privileges. Of course, the hamper complete with two bottles of wine and a choice young goose, which my grandparents were in the habit of bestowing on the headmaster and his family every Christmas, also helped quite a lot.

A great deal of my spare time I spent happily playing on the large heap of dung behind the house, strutting about with my wooden sword (two pieces of wood joined by a single nail) and pretending to be the do-gooding giant Rübezahl, an extraordinary fellow who did the oddest things such as 'reward' a little old woman by turning the bundle of firewood on her back into pure gold (the mind boggles), or the King of the Wolves, an original creation of my own.

In summer the house used to be full of visitors, the most important ones, as far as I was concerned, being my cousins Robert and Hansl. They were not as lucky as I, for they had their mothers, Auntie Rosa and Aunt Ida, to contend with. Robert especially, a fat clumsy boy without much apparent spirit or intelligence, had a hard time of it, for since he was Auntie Rosa's youngest by several years (her five older children were already 'grown up' and formed part of that oppressive collective, the outer family), he was the apple of her eye and she treated him accordingly. She was forever going on at him with 'Don't do this' and 'Don't do that', 'Be careful not to fall', 'Stay with Mummy', 'Give Mummy a big kiss' and 'Don't play with those nasty children', so that at times it seemed as if he were her prisoner or, perhaps more accurately, her pet poodle. Hansl's problems were of a different kind and almost entirely due to his mother's obsession with cleanliness and neatness. Flying in the face of common sense, Aunt Ida kept putting him in white sailor-suits, a type of apparel most unsuitable for him, for at four years of age he was, it seemed, exceptionally dirt-loving and already exceedingly enterprising. Aunt Ida would make a quite unbelievable fuss whenever his hands or his face got dirty, whereas the slightest stain on his clothes would send her into a state of advanced frenzy. This was very hard on Hansl, but unlike Robert he was not easily deterred and always ready to meet trouble half-way and take the consequences.

Two memories come to mind. On one occasion, when Robert, uncharacteristically, tore himself away from his mother and running after us fell – the damage was slight, merely a bruised knee – Auntie Rosa made a real drama of it. She yelled at him and shook him until he was breathless and wheezing while tears were streaming down his face and he was whimpering away in his usual style. Then she checked to make sure that the poor mite had not broken any bones – what a vindication of her maternal concern it would have been if he had! – and, finally reassured, pressed him to her enormous bosom calling him her sweet noodle and bestowing other terms of endearment on him. Hansl and I thought poor Robert's mishap extremely funny and laughed fit to burst, until Aunt Ida, who had regarded the entire scene with an air of total disdain, ordered us to be quiet.

The second incident occurred only a few days later in the yard. I was on top of my usual haunt, the dung heap, enjoying one of my favourite roles, when Hansl appeared, all clean, shiny and uncomfortable in his white suit. 'What are you doing?' he wanted to know. 'I am the King of the Wolves,' I replied in my most grandiloquent manner, flourishing my sword. 'Can I be King of the Wolves too?' he inquired. 'You cannot be Chief King of the Wolves,' I replied, but to comfort him (as tears were beginning to glisten in his eyes) quickly added, 'But you can be Second King of the Wolves if you like.' Then I declaimed, 'Come over here Sir Second King of the Wolves, come to the Castle of the Wolves.' However, to reach me, Hansl had to get across the 'moat', a ditch filled to the edge with black liquid manure which surrounded the heap on all sides. For him, a 'townie' with rather short legs, this was no easy matter. However, being a brave little boy and eager to join me, whom in those days he still admired greatly, he simply ran at the ditch, jumped and landed up to his neck in the stinking effluent. I, of course, thought that this was unbelievably funny, but Aunt Ida was madder than hell and really made Hansl pay for it. I cannot remember how I fared, but Aunt Sali being Aunt Sali I probably got away with it.

I have no idea what became of Robert, but Hansl emigrated to Israel, married and had, I believe, three children. A sanitary engineer, he travels from kibbutz to kibbutz, and being very musical he always carries with him a gramophone and a selection of records, which he plays at the end of the day. This has made him a popular visitor especially in the more remote settlements. After my grandparents' death – they died within six months of each other – and my return to Vienna I used to see a lot of Hansl, whose family also lived in Vienna, and we became great friends. But when I met him again in London after the war, we did not find it at all easy to recapture the easy relationship of those days which then seemed a million years away, our lives having diverged too much for any comfortable accommodation.

Nowadays I find it difficult to understand why I thought my cousins' mishaps so funny – perhaps because 'normality' no longer means as much to me as it used to. Besides, what we think of as funny may be simply a kind of half-way house between pain and not feeling anything at all. Loving her Robert as she did, Auntie Rosa obviously shared in his misery (this surely must be the idea underlying the term 'compassion') although her suffering was of a different kind. This might explain her hysterically violent reaction. A total stranger who was not at all involved would probably have remained indifferent, as I myself have often been when I have witnessed some minor accident which has not affected me directly. As for Hansl's famous leap into the ditch, that eventually became part of our family's tradition, and in time even Aunt Ida came to think of it as funny – further proof it seems to me that humour is simply a reaction to mild irritation.

If that, in fact, is so, it must surely apply to humour at all levels, from simple jokes about banana-skins, mothers-in-law and ethnic or racial inferiority to the most sophisticated satirical literature. In my opinion, for what it is worth, all types of humour are based squarely on the notion that anyone to whom ridiculous things happen is bound to be stupid – and, in consequence, different from the narrator and his public, who it is understood are not stupid. However, such a person is also perceived as constituting a menace, precisely because he is different. *Dead Souls*, for instance, deals with many types of base corruption and stupidity disfiguring Russian society in Gogol's day, which he, a man who loved his country passionately, must have resented bitterly. Merely recounting his observations might or might not have been enough to make us respond, but by distortion, exaggeration, understatement and excessive repetition of those events which he holds up to ridicule, the writer focuses our irritation and increases it, thus, incidentally, making certain of our laughter.

... Today, in my intermediate class, we were practising questions and answers. Time and again I could think only of questions such as 'Is the fat lady wearing a yellow straw hat?' and 'What do fat ladies eat for breakfast?'. Eventually Mrs. Snyder, who is truly elephantine, wiggled a bulky finger at me saying, with perfect poise and unclouded good humour, 'Plump or possibly stout, but never fat.' All the students were roaring with laughter, at my expense of course. Sometimes I simply cannot resist the temptation to say outrageous things, and people laugh, but I am quite aware of having overstepped the mark. Is it perhaps simple curiosity about how far it is possible to walk the tightrope between making people laugh and giving offence?

... What, I wonder, has become of that Finnish course Dr. P. threatened to saddle me with? He hasn't mentioned it again, nor has anybody else. Perhaps he simply invented it in order to make me think that he was offering me a rosy future and not merely a dead-end job. On the other hand (and he is certainly devious enough to do so) he may have wanted to tell me – obliquely, without actually spelling it out, which would have been counter-productive and quite possibly a waste of a good interview – that he was not taken in by my story about having been to university (I have again forgotten where) and knowing all those languages. Be that as it may, the prospect of having to run a Finnish course still worries me on occasion, and I wish I could be certain that that project is dead or never existed at all. Still, if the worst came to the worst, this wouldn't be the first time that I taught a language which I didn't know at all.

… Have been trying to screw up courage to ask Catty to the cinema.

On his way home from TTTW, M, for the past hour Head of the German and various other departments but not the French one, most of them being as yet without teachers or students, decided to celebrate by taking lunch at 'The Masticating Bull', that well known up-market restaurant near Marble Arch. He ordered meatballs in tomato sauce and boiled potatoes followed by American apple pie and coffee. The meatballs proved to be dry and uninspiring, the potatoes bland, and as for the apple pie and the coffee, the less said the better. Not surprisingly however, this frugal meal was by no means cheap. Still, mindful of what had brought him there in the first place, he chose to tip the waiter – a bespectacled, elderly gentleman all in regulation black and white with a stern, condescending manner – most royally and not merely, as was his custom, generously, to which end he had to rummage through his pockets, extracting a penny here and a few halfpence there. However, the waiter refused his gift, demolishing him neatly with a crisp 'You need the money more than I do, Sir!'

For some reason the waiter reminded M of Dr. Schwalbenkopf, a senior colleague at Nuremberg without whose advice he might never have become a simultaneous interpreter at all. For when M, together with many other candidates, sat for his test – extracts from past court proceedings were read to him, which he had to interpret 'simultaneously', namely, speaking his translation into a microphone while listening to the examiner through earphones – it was found that although his rendering was fair, his voice was far too high-pitched, far too squeaky, to be acceptable. Besides, under pressure his Viennese background tended to affect his choice of idiom and grammar to an extent obviously regarded by his listeners as both hilarious and mildly revolting. This might well have disqualified M for good, had Dr. Schwalbenkopf, a member of the examiners' panel, not called him over and suggested that he approach a Herr Wranke, a former actor and friend of his, who, in return for reasonable remuneration, might be prepared to give him elocution lessons.

M followed his advice, and during the following three months he and Herr Wranke did much sterling work together. Herr Wranke taught him how to project his voice ('My dear Maskenbusch, you really must speak as clearly as a bell, so that you can be understood even at the most remote point of the gallery'), enunciate clearly (M, a latter-day Demosthenes, with corks between clenched teeth), and breathe correctly, an essential skill apparently much neglected in M's development so far. He also offered M some valuable insights into the art of acting as practised by some of the great luminaries of the German stage. 'The important thing, my dear Maskenbusch,' he explained, 'is to stress and modulate, stress and modulate at all times. When you say "love" you must also clutch at your heart like this, and when you say "hate", you must clench your fist and shake it threateningly like this.' He accompanied these gestures with suitably dramatic contortions of his face and entire body. Had he not known better, M might well have been alarmed, for Herr Wranke was a big man and M, by comparison, somewhat puny.

In due course, when M presented himself for another interpreting test he passed with flying colours and was offered a position as a member of one of the teams, not merely because his microphone technique had improved but primarily because he had made good use of the intervening months, during which he employed Frau Breitenfach, one of the ladies of the cleaning department, to read to him hour by hour from *The Art of Cross-Examination* and other suitable texts while he whispered his interpretations.

M spent two good years at Nuremberg, well insulated from the post-war ravages surrounding him on all sides. Indeed, the widespread destruction, the air of all-pervasive corruption as well as the manifest desire of the Germans he met to forget about the past, to shake off the shackles of poverty and failure and to make a fresh start, produced an effect both romantic and curiously optimistic. Corruption, in particular, was widespread. Scrip dollars, for instance, US Army notes, which in theory were not available to Germans and could legitimately be exchanged only at American Express offices, were collected from black-market operators, many of them 'displaced persons' (i.e., people from the liberated territories and without domiciliary rights in the region) living in remote camps, and from prostitutes – indeed, the very stench of prostitution still adhered to many a crumpled and filthy note. In due course they were passed on in multiples of 1000 to co-operative members, both military and civilian, of the occupying power and, after conversion into legitimate money, smuggled abroad. This, of course, was *streng verboten* but hardly anyone cared.

However, when, after much arm-twisting, poor old Professor Hampel, a British subject by naturalisation and employed as a lowly reviewer in the translation section, finally allowed himself to be seduced by the offer of 25 dollars for exchanging illegally collected scrip at the American Express, he was promptly caught, taken to court and, as a warning to others, sentenced to a term in prison. A more adroit colleague of Professor Hampel, on the other hand, who used to convey large amounts of 'laundered' money to Switzerland, was by the end of his stint in Nuremberg able to purchase a factory and has since become a millionaire and supporter of worthy causes. Whereas, prior to the reform of the German currency, Marks were practically useless, virtually anything at all could be obtained in return for cigarettes, soap, chocolate-bars and nylon stockings. The latter, in particular, smoothed the way to many a *Fräulein*'s heart.

M was popular with his colleagues and reasonably successful at his work, which, though by no means as difficult as people thought, was frequently very boring. Concentrating, as they did, on the immediate conversion of words into words, albeit in another language, the interpreters had as a rule no clear idea of what was actually going on in court, and as the prosecutors piled horror upon horror while, on the other hand, the defence counsels kept arguing that their clients had merely obeyed orders from their superiors or been totally ignorant of what was happening in their areas of jurisdiction or had tried to prevent yet greater evils by sticking to their 'jobs', to mention but a few of their more common assertions, the proceedings became so repetitive and predictable as to lose any dramatic impact. Boredom, incidentally, was by no means confined only to the interpreters. One of the judges, for instance, made a point of holding a pencil in his hand, which would drop to the floor whenever he was about to fall asleep, thus recalling him to his duty.

Under conditions such as these any genuine human response was bound to sound odd and even ridiculous. A witness from the extreme north of Norway, asked in cross-examination whether he could remember any atrocities committed in his area, replied, once he had understood the question, that seeing how long his part of the country had been occupied it was difficult to pinpoint any particular incident. When the counsel for the defence insisted, all he could recall was that the arrival of the Germans had caused the engagement between his cousin and his cousin's fiancée to be broken, in spite of the fact that they had been promised to each other for many years. His cousin had later committed suicide but he did not know what had happened to the girl. This reply caused much unwarranted hilarity – unwarranted, for surely it is always easier to identify a particular atrocity of a kind generally accepted as such than it is to define a more personal and, in its continuing effects, equally atrocious state of human misery and degradation.

Burdened with an excess of spare time and unable to find a teacher of Japanese, a language he would dearly have liked to master, M embarked on Russian lessons with Trude Hansing, who had been born and bred in Russia, where her father, an 'ethnic' German, had until the outbreak of the war been manager of a sawmill. Trude, a woman in her late thirties and endowed with a very passionate nature, used to call M her 'eagle'. In Russian this did not sound as silly as in English and was in fact what she used to call her former lover, a real Cossack, who was more frequently drunk than sober and, in the time-honoured tradition of his homeland, used to prove his love for her by beating her regularly with a whip, a feature of their relationship which Trude liked to describe to M in vivid detail. M, while not above enjoying a fairly torrid relationship with Trude, who kept assuring him that she could not bear children and was therefore 'perfectly safe', was not inclined to follow seriously in his predecessor's footsteps. He was, however, extremely appreciative of Trude's cooking, in particular the way in which she used to prepare mushrooms.

Yet, paradoxically, it was mushrooms that triggered the break in M's friendship with Trude. The difficulty arose when on one occasion, after she had cooked for him a particularly succulent dish of mushrooms in a thick white sauce, M made the mistake of telling her how highly he thought of her culinary skills in general, how much good food meant to him and how greatly he had enjoyed her latest offering in particular. She took this to mean that in future only mushrooms prepared in this special manner and nothing else would do for her adorable 'eagle'. However, after a week or so, M had had quite enough of this particular delicacy to which she kept treating him with monotonous regularity and told her, perhaps not as tactfully, not as gently as she had a right to expect, that he was utterly sick of her disgusting mushrooms and hoped never to see another one as long as he lived.

Faced with her student's unexpected and, of course, unmerited brutality, Trude burst into copious tears of bitter recrimination – the very type of tears M had never been able to cope with – and generally gave him a rotten time. However, at that time M was already getting tired of her dog-like devotion and the way in which she, an unreasonably jealous woman, attempted to keep him away from other, frequently more desirable, female company and seemed to regard him as somehow belonging to her. Once again, M fought for his freedom, inflicting much pain in the process, for he simply lacked the courage to make a clean break such as the situation clearly required.

During his stay in Nuremberg M also devoted much time to the local branch of the German-American Youth Club, a grand place in which to feel really important, arguing with more or less idealistic and some entirely pragmatic youngsters about matters of political morality, art or even less serious topics such as whether girls should or should not use lipstick. Intent upon opening windows to the world and restoring the treasures of German culture, he headed a small circle, in which they discussed – over cups of coffee, crackers with slices of processed Kraft cheese and other toothsome goodies which he contributed – Goethe's *Faust, The Merchant of Venice* (with special emphasis on the relationship between Antonio and Shylock), Schopenhauer's analysis of honour, and a few paragraphs from Immanuel Kant.

Not surprisingly, quite a few relationships – such as M's friendship with Anni – originated at the club, some of them fleeting or purely physical but others quite permanent, eventually culminating in marriage. M came to rely in ever-increasing measure on Anni, who combined a freedom-loving and poetic spirit with great generosity and kindness. As his dependence on her increased, he even went so far as to ask her to lend him the money which he required to pay for her Christmas present – money which she could ill afford. M never repaid that debt, but many years later they would still recall this episode with some wondering pleasure.

It took M a very long time to become aware of the fact that he had committed himself to Anni as to no other, a revelation which he, a veritable Don Juan, who loved the chase but was frequently too fastidious to pick up his quarry once he had brought it down, would use as a kind of shield to protect himself against potentially complex relationships. Also, having for a long time suspected that his personality was in some important ways inadequate – he thought of himself as utterly lacking in human warmth and unable to form meaningful and lasting relationships, deficiencies which he blamed on the untimely death of his mother – Anni's seemingly unquestioning friendship and patent sincerity as well as her physical presence had become essential to him, his only hope, as it were, of being released from clammy frogdom and through the kiss of a pure and compassionately loving maiden becoming the handsome, ravishing prince he in his innermost heart knew himself to be.

Anni was a very private, even secretive person racked by contradictory instincts and emotions, but when it came to the point her judgment was sound and her loyalty, once bestowed, total. Whenever they were apart they would exchange long, romantic letters. This correspondence meant a lot to M, as indeed it did to his friends, to whom he would read her letters, without the slightest misgiving that this might not be entirely proper. This became quite a ritual among them and an occasion for much indulgent banter – something of which they never appeared to tire.

M also counted among his friends such talented, interesting people as the physicist Munkel, later one of the leading lights of NASA, Dr. Meyer, who explained holistic medicine to him, and the poet Fischer, who in spite of a hare-lip was a handsome, almost ethereal fellow. When sober, he would often recite his latest poems, among them such splendid gems as *Landscape in my face* and *I spit for the freedom of my soul*, but when he was drunk, which was more frequently the case, he would go on and on about the virtues of living alone – he had been married three times and divorced three times – or tell funny stories about Karli, his little son, whom he saw only occasionally (not, in fact, as often as he would have liked), when he himself could spare the time and Karli's mother did not have other plans for her offspring. According to one such story, albeit of doubtful authenticity, Karli asked him to lie on his back, which Fischer, a truly indulgent parent, hastened to do. Once he had assumed the required posture, Karli spat straight between his eyes. But Fischer, keenly aware of his obligations as an educator, spat right back. Karli, an intelligent boy, apparently drew the right conclusions from this reaction, which, as his father explained, contributed greatly to their friendship, while teaching Karli a most valuable and practical moral principle.

When M arrived at No. 12 Westlake Crescent he immediately made for the kitchen, where he found Silversmith busily polishing his black shoes. Silversmith, currently in the process of preparing for a posh party in the evening, attached great importance to looking his best on such occasions and 'not letting the side down'. Told about M's experience at 'The Masticating Bull', he pointed out that the waiter's unexpected reaction had in his considered opinion (and he knew what he was talking about) been due not so much to any kindly impulse as to the wholly understandable desire not to waste a perfectly good table on someone like M when it might be taken by high-tipping business tycoons or tourists, and to discourage him from ever coming again. M, while accepting the logic of this argument, continued to agonise about the waiter's identity.

CHAPTER NINE

M STOOD FACING a brand-new class of beginners, all of them eager to master the German language. As always in these classes, most of the students were housewives or secretaries, and only two were men – one haggard, jolly and middle-aged with a loose, coffin-shaped jaw, and the other reticent and in his early twenties, with dark glasses hiding his eyes. In the front row sat a pleasant girl, not as young perhaps as M might have wished, but glowing with good health and extremely welcoming. M warmed to her immediately. Looking at all those upturned faces so hopeful and expectant, M, not by nature a cynic, experienced a flush of goodwill, for at this stage he too was awash with hope and agreeable anticipation.

He started the lesson by introducing himself and explaining that his memory being unbelievably bad he was not likely to remember anybody's name, not for weeks and weeks, so would they please bear with him. This raised a giggle or two, whereupon M, sensing that the class was now with him, turned to the blackboard and, after rearranging its coating of chalk with the aid of a yellow duster, wrote on it:

'*Ich heisse Maskenbusch. Wie heissen Sie?*'

Having explained the meaning of these sentences, M made the class speak them in chorus and then passed from student to student asking their names in German, according to the pattern set out on the blackboard. This was a task at which almost all of them acquitted themselves most creditably, the only exception being the student with the coffin-shaped jaw, who had major problems due mainly to the fact that he had studied the language on previous occasions and was therefore irretrievably confused. The young man with the dark glasses, on the other hand, launched into a lengthy statement, in conscientiously structured German, to the effect that his name was Spencer Willoughby and that he was studying German with a view to reading the poetry of Wagner in the original. Suspecting that Mr. Willoughby might well create quite a few problems, not least by being excessively critical, M decided then and there to encourage his early transfer to pastures new, especially since his German was far too advanced for any beginners' class.

M knew from personal experience that deviant black sheep not in step with the flock had to be dealt with firmly and without prevarication. This he had learned, not so long ago, when he, a black sheep himself, had been employed as a teacher/gardener at a small, private school in Hampshire, an establishment for the care and education of some thirty boys and girls of all ages dumped there by absentee parents and guardians or by local councils because they were 'difficult'. The school, which was strong on psychology – everybody was forever understanding and explaining everybody else – but positively feeble on the scholastic front, was run by a Mrs. Appler, a formidable lady of craggy countenance, who, even at the height of summer, was forever shivering with cold. She was assisted, not all that ably, by her husband, a brandy-loving country gentleman of advanced years, who in spite of his paunchy, apoplectic appearance still fancied himself as a bit of a ladies' man. He had a particular *penchant* for pretty young girls, including one or two at the school whom he used to ogle and follow about like any romantic, love-sick youngster, providing thereby an ever-fertile source of merriment much appreciated by one and all. As for the headmistress herself, neither the children nor the members of the staff liked or trusted her – something which she knew very well but never managed to accept or alter. She used to insist, for instance, on everyone addressing her as Mabel, which was indeed her Christian name. However, when the children voting in General Assembly resolved unanimously to call her Mrs. Appler instead, she threatened to withdraw all their privileges, particularly those commonly associated with the Arcadian tradition and nowadays, alas, described more crudely as 'permissive'. It stands to reason that the *status quo* was quickly re-established – at any rate when talking to her direct.

Many, often difficult, accommodations were needed to cope with this situation – pretence, hypocrisy and lies of every hue marking every relationship. So when, in the course of a particularly treacly staff-meeting – they were discussing an article in the *New Statesman*, according to which schools such as this were the laboratories of British education – M, not by any means the most tactful of persons, took it upon himself to point out that no institution – and certainly not this one – was entitled to call itself a laboratory of any sort unless it was run by scientists who knew what they were doing, had at their disposal appropriate equipment and were in a position to conduct serious scientific research, he immediately became *persona* definitely *non grata*. There followed an acrimonious argument, punctuated, on his part at any rate, by several powerful, even earthy, observations, whereupon Mabel, who in any case had good reason to detest him – after all it was he who had initiated the barbaric game in which hordes of children (nasty, unruly brats) kept dragging away her mauve shawl without as much as a 'by your leave' – declared that he had a problem. Next day M was called to the Office, where Mabel told him curtly that quite obviously he did not, after all, appreciate the aims of the school and its value to society. Then she handed him his letter of notice, which read as follows:

To whom it may concern:

Mr. Morus Mushenbush has been a teacher/gardener in the employment of this school from March to May, during which period he performed various duties. We wish him well in whatever other occupation he may choose to follow.

Mabel Appler,
Headmistress

M never ceased to enjoy this letter and to admire the neat way in which his amputation had been effected.

The lesson continued without incident, with M explaining how to pronounce German words. Doris, the pleasant girl in the front row, kept saying '*Herr Lehrer*' whenever she reasonably could, embellishing this courtesy with a warm smile, which M interpreted as intimate and full of delicious promise. The fact that apart from Mr. Willoughby and Doris the students found it difficult to pronounce the '*ch*' in '*ich*', gave M a welcome opportunity to explain about this sound, its rendering in various dialects and sundry other points about which he knew little but which were more or less germane to the subject, thus making it plain that he, M, was no ordinary teacher, not simply a purveyor of information, but a man of profound learning, a potential professor at London University.

At the end of the lesson the students declared themselves to be highly satisfied, except Mr. Willoughby, who had been hoping for news of the subjunctive in indirect speech – a point about which he questioned M at some length after the others had left for their various destinations. M, in turn, suggested to him that he would be well advised to join a more advanced class, seeing that his German was as good or even better than that of any university graduate (as far as M could tell, this particular piece of flattery went down quite all right), but since M could not offer any suitable alternative and Mr. Willoughby had already paid for the term, nothing practical was after all achieved by this somewhat tentative recommendation.

Catty, at the House of Pasta, was picking away without much appetite at her salad. M, opposite Catty (at last!), would undoubtedly have enjoyed his *spaghetti al burro* more if Catty's presence had not made him tremble so with suppressed desire. Their conversation, such as it was, proceeded in fits and starts, with Catty venturing this or that observation and M racking his brain for scintillating things to say, albeit without any signal success. To complicate matters further, his sense of achievement at having progressed to the point where he had actually invited her to have lunch with him and she had, as it seemed to him, accepted eagerly so that they were now sharing a table, away from the office and to the exclusion of all others, was spoiled by a distinct if inexplicable sense of shame at being seen in her company at all, as if somehow he had settled for second best and had become a kind of Esau selling his birthright for a mess of porridge. So, torn between his desire and the deeper wish to escape while he could, he listened as Catty told him about her ambitious mother (it was she who had insisted on Catty taking up typing), her father (ever such a nice man but he didn't have much to say for himself) and her little brother (quite a genius – everybody said so). Then Catty embarked on her favourite subject – the foibles and odd behaviour of various members of the staff.

'I can't stand that Mr. Daker,' she now commented, 'Can you? There is something weird about him, the way he looks at you, you know … and he is always after more money, I wonder why.'

'Well, to tell you the truth, I am not all that keen on him either. Frankly speaking, he bores me stiff.'

'The other day when I was walking with Angela, my best friend ever since we were in school together (we were looking round the shops, you know, they had such a nice black dress at Dickins & Jones, a bit pricey though, but you would have loved it), I saw him in Charing Cross Road with a young bloke, ever so chummy they were, so I said to him I said "Hello, Mr. Daker," but he acted as if he had never seen me before in his born days. I wonder why?'

'Perhaps he really didn't see you.'

'Didn't want to see me, more likely, the old queer.' was Catty's worldly-wise if uncharitable reply. 'Mind you,' she continued, quite animated by now, 'he's not as bad as that Dr. McGill.'

'I have never met him,' commented M, 'but I understand he is keen on pretty girls.' M couldn't help himself. The conversation, which was approaching deliciously delicate but also dangerous matters, was carrying him along, and there was nothing he could or would do about it.

'You can say that again,' Catty agreed, blissfully unaware of M's dilemma. 'You have no idea what he gets up to with some of those girls in his classes. He's even had the cheek to try it on with me, the mucky devil. As if I would.' Catty, lowering her eyes, blushed furiously.

'What did he want you to do then? You can tell me. After all, we are friends.' There it was, that awful and yet so delightful next step down the ladder. M would have given anything if he could only have recalled that word, for 'friends' meant commitment, a commitment he did not really want, not to this vulgar girl who was not even particularly pretty. But a word once spoken could not be recalled and there was nothing he could do about it. Like the professor in *The Blue Angel* he was powerless to resist and at the same time glorying in his abandon.

Some of M's turmoil seemed to have infected Catty, for she did not answer, merely keeping her eyes, now sultry and close to tears, on the few unpalatable leaves of salad still languishing on her plate. Her blush had disintegrated into inflamed blotches on her forehead and neck which were set off by the natural paleness of her skin in general. Now she was somehow reminiscent of a rat, hunched up and unlovable. The corners of her mouth were turned down, making her look both discontented and hungry. ('Hungry for what?' M wondered.)

'You don't really want to be with me,' Catty said, getting up abruptly, 'I'll pay for my own lunch.' And off she went. M, left behind, was in despair over his clumsiness. The pendulum of his emotions had swung again the other way.

Miss Pratt was not one to take her responsibilities lightly. She had offered to take M in hand to help him with his spoken French, and this is precisely what she did. Under her firm, if somewhat pedantic, guidance he really did make progress, though not indeed to the point where he could have been safely entrusted with even a beginners' class – at least in the opinion of Monsieur ('call me Antoine, if you please') Chanteclerc, the recently appointed head of the French department. Monsieur Chanteclerc – in his native France an only moderately successful song-and-dance man – had joined TTTW at roughly the same time as M but had already become Dr. Pendlebloom's right-hand man and confidential adviser, a meteoric rise which surprised no-one, seeing that in many ways he was the exact opposite of the Principal, complementing him to a T. He was a mobile little fellow with expressive simian features and an ever-ready Gallic wit, who was universally popular and could make any party go with a swing.

Dr. Pendlebloom, on the other hand, did not like many people (nor did many people like him) and was totally devoid of anything even remotely resembling a sense of humour; his effect on a party was simply devastating. Antoine was a dab hand when it came to mending a fuse, painting a poster or replacing a broken window, whereas the only tool which Dr. Pendlebloom could use without danger of accident was his elegant fountain pen, and his hands trembled so badly that even lifting a cup of coffee from the table presented him with major problems. Women, particularly the young and pretty ones, melted to Antoine's indubitable charm, which he could turn on and off like an electric lamp, and the list of his conquests, both real and imagined, was endless. As for his employer, women in any role other than that of handmaiden were definitely beyond serious consideration. They did, however, have certain qualities in common as well. Both were outstanding organisers quite capable of coming up with utterly brilliant solutions before giving even a moment's thought to the problem in hand.

Naturally, the consequences of their organising activities were not always as felicitous as they might have wished. For instance, when after a spate of scurrilous messages on various TTTW blackboards, some of them throwing doubt on the Principal's paternity (and worse), Monsieur Chanteclerc decided, with Dr. Pendlebloom's wholehearted approval, personally to unmask the evil-doer and thus put an end to the outrage by spending a night at the school, accompanied and abetted by his trusty Frascatti, a poodle of admittedly frisky temperament, the outcome was not as hoped for and expected. For on the following morning poor Antoine was found by some students fast asleep and snoring away in a state of advanced inebriation beneath a blackboard bearing yet another offensive message, while Frascatti, perhaps from a desire to assimilate knowledge as copiously and quickly as possible, was sitting nearby surrounded by items of literature at various stages of dismemberment, assiduously chewing a Spanish dictionary which one of the students had forgotten to put away the previous day. It is only fair to add that his output for the night was by no means limited to the foregoing activity but had taken other forms as well, with results that can only be described as inappropriate to a place of learning. In spite of such minor mishaps, everyone was agreed that the head of the French department was indeed a paragon. He did, they would hasten to add, have certain minor faults (as indeed who had not?), none of them particularly grave from the point of view of TTTW but all of them quite charming. If he gave a promise, for instance, it was quite certain that he would never keep it, and like some highly imaginative children he was quite unable to distinguish fact from fiction.

However, those who have risen high are, like Humpty-Dumpty, always prone to the danger of a great fall. Following a serious disagreement on a point of moral duty, Dr. Pendlebloom, who in any case had been growing more and more suspicious of Monsieur Chanteclerc as his dependence on the latter increased and who had been looking for just such an opportunity, rid himself, boldly and at a single stroke, of this embarrassing and potentially dangerous incubus. Whereas moral duty, moral superiority and, conversely, the moral inadequacies of others were never far away from Dr. Pendlebloom's or Antoine's thoughts, their ideas in this respect frequently differed. Dr. Pendlebloom, for instance, considered it a moral duty to write and actually despatch a frank letter of warning – every word in it, of course, gospel truth and the result of much soul-searching and deep consideration – to the intended new employer of any member of his staff who, wishing to leave TTTW, had had the temerity to request a letter of reference. Antoine, on the other hand, was more inclined to see his moral duty in captivating and pleasuring any female person – of whatever age, complexion or spiritual background – whom he believed to be in need of his ministrations.

Antoine, out of a job but only briefly at a loss as to what to do next, first opened a ballet school and then, when this failed, set up as a business efficiency consultant. However, following three separate bankruptcies on the part of clients and two of his own company he turned to the manufacture of shirts from synthetic materials. Years later, M, still a respected and well-thought-of member of TTTW, met Antoine again in Edgware Road, where the latter told him that he was now the proud owner of a factory nearby and insisted on showing M the premises. M obliged, not without some admiration and even a touch of envy, in spite of the fact that the 'factory' proved to be simply a number of workshops dispersed within a rather ramshackle, once purely residential house, but now a veritable hive of economically productive activity. Before he left, his former colleague, very much a Captain of Industry, presented him with two semi-transparent green nylon shirts, and they exchanged addresses and promised to keep in touch, but in the event never did.

Miss Pratt – Emilia, was her given name, but in spite of many invitations M could never get used to addressing her thus – did not by any means confine herself to improving her *cher professeur*'s French but did her best to improve him in other ways as well. Herself a talented maker of ceramic figurines and other ware and a lover of fine art, she introduced him to various museums and art galleries, took him to the theatre and to operatic performances – the latter very much under protest, for M never managed to grasp the, to him, perverse partnership between music and words known as 'opera' – and even repeatedly tried to get him to go with her to a concert. In this, however, she failed dismally, for having been told by Professor Bergenau at the Klappenhorn Gymnasium that he was a *Musikschwein*, he had made up his mind once and for all that, apart from a few musical items which he did enjoy, music was for him simply too emotional, with nothing to get his intellectual teeth into. This he claimed to regret deeply, for surely so many brilliant people both past and present could not all be wrong.

By 'enjoyable' music M meant mainly uplifting or sentimental songs which he had known a long time and could hum proficiently (with numerous improvised variations) in the bathroom, and also *Eine kleine Nachtmusik*, as well as certain catchy tunes from Austro-Hungarian operettas mainly by Lehár and Kálmán, for according to him some operettas were definitely all right whereas all operas, with the exception of *Carmen* and, perversely, Wagner's *Ring* cycle, were boring. To make his point, M even devised – although he never actually wrote – a short story in which the devil attends a concert given by a world-famous violinist at the largest and most prestigious concert hall in the world and causes ripples of laughter to bubble up here and there in the auditorium. As intended by the evil one, this laughter rises in a crescendo and eventually culminates in a veritable storm of derision, the inevitable result being that, after fruitless entreaties in turn by the management, the violinist himself – with tears in his eyes as he begs his public to give him another chance, however undeserving his performance – and finally the violinist's own mother, the concert hall is burnt to the ground, thousands of music-lovers perish in the fire or are trampled to death in the ensuing panic, and the famous, now alas disgraced, violinist throws himself and his priceless violin into the all-consuming flames, to the everlasting perdition of his immortal soul.

Miss Pratt firmly believed that M had a 'divine spark', and like any faithful believer she found evidence of this wherever she looked. She admired his various literary efforts – mainly unreadable and certainly unperformable plays, short stories dimly reminiscent of Dostoevsky, Gogol and Kafka and 'nonsense poems' which M fondly believed to be in no way inferior to those of Christian Morgenstern, one of his literary heroes – and when he was fool enough to show her some of his watercolours, basically doodles in paint produced on Saturday evenings while listening to the 8-o'clock play on the radio, she immediately concluded that it was her moral duty – like Dr. Pendlebloom she too was very keen on this concept – to develop his, as she saw it, strong, if primitive, talent. Armed with sable brushes, cartridge paper and selected paints in tubes – a far cry this from the humble paintbox and a pad of lowly drawing paper from Woolworth's which he had used so far – M tried his hand at washes (but how on earth could genius express itself in a routine wash?), sundry brushstrokes, the mixing of colours and 'composition' – activities which bored him no end and with the results of which he was not at all satisfied. Miss Pratt nevertheless applauded M's efforts uninhibitedly, making him wonder whether 'art' – a concept which was never far from her thoughts – was not simply what self-styled experts chose to regard as such. However, when on one occasion she went so far as to declare that the effect of a blob of dismal brown paint which had dripped from his brush was 'marvellous' and 'pure Sutherland' (whoever that was), that proved to be the last straw. M, in a fit of revulsion, decided then and there never to paint another stroke, and neither the progress of time nor Miss Pratt with her endless arguments and tearful entreaties were ever able to change his mind.

If Miss Pratt had been merely trying to flatter him, he would not have minded her virtually uncritical approval so much – in fact he might even have developed a sense of some superiority of his own – but her tendency to go 'overboard' in ascribing to him all manner of 'talents' which he knew himself not to possess was, on occasion, more than he could bear. Sometimes, indeed, he felt that for Miss Pratt he was simply an object on which to lavish her Pygmalion-like tendencies – an as yet only partly finished but most promising creation. It is hardly surprising that M was not exactly keen on playing this dubious role, which did nothing for his in any case shaky self-esteem.

CHAPTER TEN

THE JAPANESE used to give the prisoners in M's camp a small weekly ration of cigarettes, enough to keep the smokers smoking but by no means enough for their needs. This, inevitably, led to splits in the camp community, with most of the non-smokers in a position to buy food, clothing, soap and sundry services, while, to satisfy their craving, the smokers would, for a cigarette or two, sell whatever they could and would have sold their souls as well, had there been any takers. The 'haves' – capable traders, respected bullies and prisoners good at 'organising' such as some of those loading and unloading railway wagons at Michigawa station or working at the local soy-bean factory – were doing all right and, however unpromising their antecedents, tended to acquire middle-class and even upper-class attitudes. In the fullness of time they came to believe in the sanctity of private property and the need for tidiness and personal cleanliness. Those who could afford them would buy such little luxuries – mainly food 'organised' at work and smuggled into the camp – as happened to come their way, and the most successful lorded it over cliques of devoted and sycophantic henchmen, whom, in return for their company or services, they befriended and with whom they shared the spoils of their enterprise.

The 'have-nots', on the other hand, tended to decline into poverty and often ill-health, and came to be thought of as scroungers or even beggars. With certain notable exceptions – Dr. Cullan, for instance, who, in spite of increasingly brutal and persistent discouragement by the Japanese, did what he could to obtain medical supplies for the camp, only to disappear in the end to God knows where – the officers too became demoralised. This was mainly because, for reasons of status, they were not allowed to join in the work but were instead compelled to lead working-parties or otherwise act as intermediaries between the prisoners and the Japanese. They were therefore always in the limelight of attention and expected to set a 'good example' to the lower ranks, which, for them, made 'organising' extremely difficult and hazardous. Besides, they did not, of course, find it easy to come to terms with the fact that such possessions as they had brought with them into the camp tended to wind up in the hands of former Borstal boys and worse. Incidentally, in that particular camp, prisoners caught by the guards in the act of 'organising' or in possession of 'organised' goods were only likely to be slapped about and shouted at a lot, slapping as a form of punishment for minor misdemeanours being common in the Japanese army and by no means confined to the prisoners, so that it was well worth their while to accept the unavoidable risk of discovery – another circumstance which contributed to this social turnabout.

After the war M came to realise that, considering what so many other prisoners had had to endure, he and the others in his camp had been inordinately lucky. This was due to a variety of reasons, such as the fact that the camp was situated in the heart of Japan, where the brutalising effects of war were less pronounced than, for instance, in Burma or the Philippines. Besides, the Japanese climate with its clearly marked seasons, hot summers and cold winters resembled that of Central Europe, and the conditions, both at work and in the camp, happened to be such that most of M's fellow prisoners remained reasonably fit and able to cope with their work, which from their captors' point of view was undoubtedly an important practical consideration. Indeed, rumour had it that the camp was a kind of showplace, which seemed to be borne out by the fact that from time to time it was subject to inspection – on one occasion even by representatives of the Red Cross. If it was true that M's camp had a 'public relations' function, very harsh treatment of the prisoners would obviously have been counter-productive.

M was also fortunate in that most of his fellow prisoners were British soldiers and seamen, an easy-going lot, imbued with the same spirit of innate decency and cheerful adaptability as he had found during those nightly bombing raids on London, when he, together with so many others, used to seek shelter on the platform of an underground station. Once he had been fully accepted into their intimate, tightly-knit community – which took him the best part of two years – he felt perfectly at home and at ease among them. There were, of course, many divisions, and no-one would deny that there was a tendency for cliques to form and reform in ever new patterns as does the foam on the crests of waves, but personal friendships too flourished and there was much agreement across all the divides. Besides, based as it was on natural preference for their own kind rather than any sense of exclusivity, the cliquishness of the inmates tended to make life in the camp more colourful than it might otherwise have been, without giving rise to destructive discords.

While still on the *Bergano*, M had been in the early stages of becoming a smoker, but once in the camp he gave up the habit, which, as he was only slightly addicted, he did not find particularly difficult. Convinced that some personal gesture was called for in view of the social and moral ravages resulting from the cigarette trade and hoping for the approval of his fellows, he announced that he would not be selling his cigarettes but would give them away, one at a time, to anyone in need of a smoke. He stuck to this decision firmly, without, however, achieving much popularity as a result. Many thought him a bit odd though harmless, and he was often referred to as that 'creeping Jesus', a rather hurtful nickname, which he did his best to ignore. Indeed, he might well have joined the ranks of the 'no-hopers' but for some redeeming qualities such as a moderate 'organising' ability – he generally managed to get hold of at least some sweet potatoes, tangerines, sugar or other produce which happened to be 'on offer' and insufficiently guarded – and the fact that he alone could, thanks to a schoolboy knowledge of geography (a subject forced upon him at the Klappenhorn) and a chessplayer's understanding of strategy, read and interpret maps from Japanese newspapers written in Katakana syllable script. Inasmuch as this enabled him to explain and 'predict' the progress of the war in Europe, he became a much appreciated source of information and came to be regarded as something of an oracle. People also liked to talk with him when they felt in need of 'serious' conversation, and on one occasion he was even entrusted with devising and directing the annual summer show, a variety event much looked forward to and enjoyed by both prisoners and Japanese and usually presented by the British and American officers in the camp.

The following incident occurred in the second year of M's captivity. He happened to be on a wagon shovelling coal with Sergeant Griffith, while discussing such perennial questions as good and evil, the meaning of death and whether the end, however noble, could ever justify the means. Sergeant Griffith had just challenged M to prove that he was indeed, as he claimed, capable of rising above the imperatives defined by his personality and circumstances by doing something entirely against his grain, when who should appear but Petty Officer Bramwell asking M for a 'fag'.

P.O. Bramwell, one of M's 'regulars', was known to be a spineless, treacherous creature and a scrounger to boot. With his airs and graces and la-di-da accent, which contrasted oddly with his threadbare uniform and altogether dishevelled appearance, he was despised by one and all, and although nothing of the kind could be proved he was widely suspected of having, time and again, betrayed fellow prisoners to the Japanese in return for a bowl of rice or a few cigarettes. Until that day M had never refused P.O. Bramwell a 'fag' whenever the latter asked him for one, but on this particular occasion M, responding to Sergeant Griffith's challenge and, in any case, no longer certain that his 'moral strategy', however well-intentioned, served any real purpose, felt compelled to bet him a packet of cigarettes that he would not be able to stop smoking for two whole weeks. Egged on perhaps by M's barely concealed contempt, P.O. Bramwell accepted the bet, thus agreeing to a contest which was to become, under the confined conditions of the camp, something of a *cause célèbre*. Many were hoping that M would be knocked, once and for all, from his high moral perch, whereas others were particularly eager to see P.O. Bramwell thoroughly, even crushingly, humiliated. There was much speculation as to the probable outcome, and many a side-bet was placed, although in all likelihood hardly anyone really cared which of the two protagonists would carry the day.

He had confidently expected P.O. Bramwell to be caught within a short time, but as day followed day it became increasingly obvious that this might not be the case. All of a sudden the boot was on the other foot. Now it was P.O. Bramwell who looked ever more confident, whereas M, who never once doubted that his adversary's means were foul rather than fair, was faced with the, from his point of view, shameful possibility that the latter might 'get away with it'. He was convinced that he himself was on the point of becoming the laughing-stock of the camp, that the other prisoners were looking at him with malevolent delight at his humiliation or, which was even worse, with pity.

Still, it seemed to M, a latter-day Raskolnikov, that there was one way in which he could stop P.O. Bramwell, and, driven by the irresistible need to find out once and for all whether he was man or mouse – capable of determining the course of events by the power of his will, or a mere follower blown this way and that by the whims of others – he took it. In the event, however, his efforts turned out to be pathetic and degrading, eventually forcing him to the mournful conclusion that he was, after all, no 'superman' and that, moreover, his lofty moral stance had never amounted to more than a pitiful sham.

For instead of accepting defeat like a man and paying up, M chose to turn for assistance to 'Frosty' Icing and 'Dusty' Miller, two infamous camp bullies who gloried in a reputation so fearsome that no one had ever dared to put it to the test, which suited them fine. Their plan, for the execution of which M promised them twice as many cigarettes as his bet would have cost him, could not have been more simple, and there was not the slightest reason to doubt that it would succeed in every particular.

The hour of decision came the very next day after this dastardly plot had been hatched, which from M's point of view was not a minute too soon. Since it was the lunch-break, there were prisoners everywhere, relaxing in the scorching sunshine on large, fragrant, freshly unloaded tree-trunks. Some were fast asleep, others were deep in conversation, and yet others were enjoying their *korean*, a kind of pinkish-mauve millet, which was their staple diet. Their *hanchos*, Japanese workers in charge of the various teams, were devouring genuine rice-balls and fish, wholly unaware of the impending drama.

Far from enjoying the sleep of the righteous, M, who for this occasion had spent a miserable night going over the various events which had brought him to this particular pass, was still hoping against hope that what he knew was bound to happen wouldn't. But suddenly there was no more room for hope, for P.O. Bramwell, who, for this occasion, had spruced up his uniform and now looked positively shiny and festive, was coming from one side of the yard to collect his prize, while from the other side came Frosty and Dusty, ready to swear that they had seen him smoking that very morning, in the 'bog' at the end of the yard. As soon as he saw them, P.O. Bramwell knew the score, and so did everybody else. He turned white as the proverbial sheet, but did not attempt to argue. M, on the other hand, blushing furiously and with the blood pounding in his temples, felt thoroughly miserable, just as he used to feel at the Klappenhorn when a professor, having caught him in one misdemeanour or another – M was always in trouble – would make a point of shaming him before the entire class. He knew that he was lower than a snake's belly, an outsize bastard, a Maskenbusch unmasked.

And yet he also experienced some triumphant pride at having been able to descend to depths such as these. But when it occurred to him that he had done similar things before – at the Klappenhorn, for instance, when he had nearly brought about the unwarranted dismissal of his Mathematics professor, who had never done him any harm – and that he had, in fact, not been acting 'against the grain' at all, every vestige of elation vanished and all he was left with was a profound sense of self-disgust. However, unlike his predecessor in literature, the hero of Dostoevsky's *Crime and Punishment*, who had been redeemed through suffering and the love of a 'worthless' creature – the prostitute Sonya – M's 'crime' had a rather different outcome, for, strangely enough, this mean, unsavoury episode seemed to have gained him considerable popularity. Only one or two people with whom he had so far been on friendly terms took exception and avoided him whenever they decently could, as did P.O. Bramwell, who never asked him for another cigarette or, for that matter, anything else. Still, M continued to give away his cigarettes, mainly because this course of action seemed easiest, and there was never any shortage of applicants.

'Come in, come in, my dear fellow,' boomed Dr. Sombrero-Domingo welcoming M to his home in Brixton.

'Let me introduce you to Mrs. Doctor,' he continued, as his wife, thick-set and stubby and somehow reminiscent of a short, brown Christmas candle, appeared behind him, giggling in helpless delight.

'Hee-hee, isn't he a scream!', she gurgled. 'Come in, hurry up, the schnitzels are waiting if Puffy hasn't had them already, hee, hee-hee. That stupid dog is always after my schnitzels.'

'But Bertha,' exclaimed her husband with mock reproval, 'don't be so boisterous. You will be making a bad impression on our young but honoured guest.' Now turning to M 'Still you will find she is an exceptional cook, a cook and a half, you might say, haw, haw, haw, forgive my little joke.'

'Don't listen to him. Rudi loves joking, I often say to him: "What a joker you are, Rudi," but he only jokes away like nobody's business.'

M had at last insinuated himself past his hosts, who were manifestly pleased to see him, into their house, a Victorian terrace house both excessively narrow and exceedingly high, with a flight of well-worn brick steps leading up to the front door. The hall too seemed to be inordinately tall and narrow, an impression heightened by the dark, stained wallpaper, the muddy-brown, peeling woodwork and the feeble light shed by the unprotected bulb dangling forlornly from the ceiling. Wherever one looked there were vast amounts of clutter covering and filling every available space: piles of old books grey with dust, bundles of newspapers with titles long forgotten, and a rolled-up, severely stained mattress.

A large, black cat with a white nose and white paws lay stretched out on top of the mattress in an attitude of perfect repose, weighing up the scene. 'Who's a naughty puss then?', Bertha intoned. 'She'll be wanting her fishy, Mummy can always tell! Come on now, fishy upstairs, up you go.' Naughty puss did not deign to respond to this invitation in any manner whatsoever. She was a wise cat and knew from bitter experience that this might well be a trick to displace her from her comfortable perch. Bertha, by implication admitting that in the past she had indeed on certain occasions stooped to such practices but having, on this occasion, a clear conscience, felt that a more persuasive approach was needed. 'Fishy really upstairs this time,' she affirmed accordingly, 'Cross my heart, it's true this time.' And to show that she really meant it, proceeded to cross her heart. Naughty puss, considering that there was, after all, nothing much to lose and deciding that for the sake of amicable domestic relations she had better give Bertha another chance, got up, stretched, and jumped onto the rickety staircase. Having arranged her tail in an elegant curve, she now led the way to the upstairs kitchen, followed closely by Bertha, M and the master of the house, in that order.

In the kitchen there were yet more animals – lots of them. The Sombrero-Domingos did not have any children, but their animals – some of them very intelligent and with great personalities – ensured that they were never short of emotional experience and intellectual stimulation. One of them was a floppy-eared spaniel which, when so inclined, answered to the name of Puffy. Having somehow missed out on the schnitzels he was currently engaged in a violent disagreement with a big, apparently most argumentative rubber bone. In a large gilded cage a most colourful but predominantly green member of the parrot family sat rakishly brooding, while in a glass tank lit from behind a number of exotic fish were having a fine time blowing bubbles. Looking, at Bertha's proud invitation, out of the window into the 'back garden', a tiny area devoid of greenery but rich in well-churned mud, M could not but notice 'Ducky', a white hen so named (hee-hee-hee; haw, haw) because of the prodigious size of her eggs, and, as if this were not enough, the S-Ds also kept a pair of hamsters and a tortoise – an animal so lethargic that without a most thorough examination it would have been quite impossible to tell whether it was still alive.

There were a number of Chinese prints sprinkled about the walls of the kitchen. Asked about them, M's hosts, both talking at once and vying for his attention, explained that back home in Berlin Bertha had been a student of classical Chinese and that, having originally met at the university but lost sight of each other during the war, they had again in Madrid, where Bertha was employed as a nanny and Rudi was earning a frugal living as a humble clerk in a solicitor's office. Several years later they had decided to join their lives in holy matrimony. Eventually, motivated by dreams of dignified and serene intellectual endeavour at the British Museum and other similarly hallowed places, they had moved to London. They liked what they found, in spite of the fact that they had never become properly rooted in their new environment and were far from successful in the more practical spheres of life. Fortunately, however, Dr. Sombrero-Domingo had inherited some money from a wealthy relative in Brisbane, Australia, which he had used to buy their present home.

The schnitzels served with potatoes mashed in milk and with cucumber salad (the way mother used to make it, hee-hee) were an unmitigated triumph, as, indeed, was the pale Liebfraumilch they were drinking, and the evening passed very pleasantly indeed. Dr. S-D had a wonderful time reminiscing about this and that, Bertha had an equally wonderful time making him thoroughly mad, and M too enjoyed himself hugely, explaining, expounding and elucidating, while his hosts were happily bickering away, in turn exhorting one another to pay attention, to listen to what young M was saying, not to be so naïve etc. But when Bertha told them about her fat white rabbit – a creature gentle in the extreme and positively saintly, that wouldn't hurt a fly – M really took wing.

A fly having been mentioned – thus, in a manner of speaking, making its appearance on the conversational menu – M, now in a schnitzel-happy state of expansiveness, launched into a recital of his favourite thoughts on flies. Always eager to paint as complete and balanced a picture as possible, he mentioned an elderly gentleman of his acquaintance who managed to achieve a genuine friendship with a fly – the latter used to visit him regularly every morning and settle on the right-hand top corner of his newspaper, where he would feed it with spots of jam and similarly delightful morsels – and quoted Gogol's vivid description of flies on a hot summer's day deporting themselves like perfect gentlemen in black smoking-jackets at a party, fastidiously rubbing their front paws together and then taking off again, circulating, as it were, in a manner appropriate to such an important social occasion. And he described how Aunt Ida – Uncle Georg's wife and Hansi's vitriolic mother (Hansi, it will be remembered, was the cousin who jumped into sewage while wearing his white sailor suit) – used to catch any passing fly on the wing, chameleon-like but not, of course, with her tongue (an organ which was, however, every bit as deadly as that of the above-mentioned reptile).

From flies and their quirky ways M managed to pass effortlessly to his favourite adventures with wasps, at which point Rudi, naturally eager to match him on every point, interjected that his Uncle Eberhard, on such occasions every inch a hunter, used to enjoy stalking any careless wasp with his deadly pocket-knife at the ready and would, once the moment was ripe, neatly split his quarry in half, to his young nephew's great disgust but even greater relief. He also pointed out that he himself had never been able to distinguish between bees and wasps – a fact he obviously regarded as both noteworthy and somehow significant. M reciprocated by telling his hosts how, in those happy, long-gone days on a training farm for Czech refugees, it had been one of his tasks to go to the meadow every morning at the crack of dawn in order to catch four wily horses and get them ready for the day's work. The horses were laughing at him, of course, but who could blame them.

Encouraged by the interest and general approval of the S-Ds, M now launched himself, with great verve and gusto (inspired partly by the Liebfraumilch), into the subject of mosquitoes. Having during his seafaring days spent much time in exceedingly hot and humid regions, his experience in this respect was also considerable. 'When we were in Galveston, Texas,' he explained, 'mosquitoes as large as the top of my thumb' (he wiggled his thumb to illustrate) 'used to be so densely packed upon the white-tiled walls of our galley that many could not find any room at all on those, as it would seem, highly desirable surfaces. However, fiendishly intelligent as they were, they – the mosquitoes that is, not the surfaces – managed to solve this problem as follows: one group would be resting on the walls – possibly asleep, although I cannot be certain of this as I did not have a magnifying glass through which to observe their eyes – a second group would be sitting on the shoulders of the first lot, ready perhaps to change places with them once they had had their turn, while those pertaining to a third group were out hunting and gorging themselves on the blood of such unfortunates as myself. I cannot, at this point in time, tell which I found more distasteful – the swarms of whining and stinging beasties or the Texan immigration officials, with their ridiculous hats covering, for good and valid reasons no doubt, the best part of their faces and with their outsize boots on the table, who, on some flimsy pretext or other, refused me permission to go ashore in order to stretch my legs, see the sights and perhaps "take in a movie". The captain of the *Bergano* having bluntly refused to curtail my freedom by preventing me from going ashore, they even went so far as to engage a beer-swilling tramp, to whom they entrusted the grave responsibility of ensuring my continuing and uninterrupted presence on board. This, incidentally, made me so mad that I bought five dollars worth of Wrigley's Spearmint gum and chewed my way through the lot in only three days.'

M, having exhausted this particular item, passed, naturally enough and after only a brief mention of cockroach-racing on the good old *Bergano* (a popular, competitive sport in which cockroaches were made to swim across a bucket of water), to his really favourite creepy-crawly topic, that is to say bed-bugs, where again he had every reason to regard himself as rather an expert.

He started by recalling some of the principal facts about these unlovable creatures – the way they smelled of almonds or, more precisely, cyanic acid, particularly when squashed, the colonies in which they lived under wallpaper, in mattresses and in the joints of old furniture, and how some of them would roam the ceiling at night and, with the reckless abandon of kamikaze pilots, drop on to people sleeping below, preferably into their open mouths, while others – the massed infantry, so to speak – would attack in great and wholly irresistible pincer movements from the sides. He dealt briefly yet fully with the feel, appearance and duration of their bites, comparing them learnedly with those of fleas, lice and other insects, and concluded this section of his monologue by giving various examples from his personal experience.

All his bed-bug stories were rewarded with huge applause, but his most successful and, in a way, most instructive tale related to an incident which had occurred when, but a fledgling refugee, he was passing through the Jewish ghetto of Cracow. He had been fortunate to find accommodation in a tiny flat in Josefova where, at a price he could just about afford, he was offered the opportunity of sharing a bed with only one other person in similar straits. 'When I went to bed – not, let me assure you, without considerable misgivings but reminding myself that beggars cannot, after all, be choosers – my bed-mate had not yet arrived,' M explained, 'but several others were already asleep on mattresses strewn about the floor of that airless room. The landlady, a balding old woman with a thin, bitter mouth and a veritable grappling-hook of a nose, locked the door behind me. God knows why. Perhaps she wanted to make certain that no-one would get out and notify the Polish police about the inadequate amenities and standards of hygiene at her establishment, or she may simply have been afraid of being attacked by one or several of us in her bed, murdered and – perish the thought – robbed of her possessions or whatever. Be that as it may, the enforced proximity of several men, some of whom had had a lot to drink or eaten stimulating food such as sauerkraut or beans, could not fail to have unpleasant consequences, but in those days we had other things to worry about.

As for me, I went to bed immediately and, being worn out with fatigue, fell fast asleep as soon as my head had sunk into the none-too-salubrious pillow. However, having woken up suddenly in the middle of the night, I witnessed the following scene: a man about forty years of age – a class-conscious member of the German proletariat to judge by his light-blue dungarees and general demeanour – was kneeling on the bed – my bed, that is – with a lit torch in one hand and a needle with a long black thread in the other. At first I thought that he was merely mending some patch of the enormous feather-bed which engulfed me on all sides, although I could not for the life of me understand why. However, as I was turning away in order to return to my habitual sleeping position – I always sleep in the foetal position, on the right-hand side with my knees slightly drawn up – I heard him mutter in what sounded to me, used as I was to the mellower speech of the South, like Prussian or some such revolting dialect: "Skin disease, indeed! I'll show the old bitch once and for all who has a skin disease!" By now, as you may imagine, I was wide awake and, moreover, aware of intense itching sensations of a kind by no means unfamiliar, seeing that in my Viennese days bed-bugs were, to coin a phrase, the ever present, inescapable companions of my nights. But to return to my story. When I looked more closely, I saw that my bed-fellow-to-be was in fact spearing bed-bugs with his needle and sliding them down the thread as if to make some kind of outlandish necklace. This latter-day Nimrod, clearly a bugger (in the strictly literal sense of course) of great skill and distinction, was going about his grizzly business in a most efficient manner, directing his deadly beam hither and thither and spreading terror wherever it fell. When he noticed that I was watching him, he explained in a whisper that he now had the evidence that would settle his dispute *mit der alten Hexe* irrefutably and force her, once and for all, to do something about this pigsty in which he had already spent three truly miserable weeks and might well have to stay another three weeks, for nothing was happening and there was nowhere to go. It would appear that in the event his *démarche* to the landlady did not do him much good, for I never saw him again. Still, this episode taught me the valuable lesson that it is not always wise to insist on one's point of view, even if – especially if – one has incontrovertible proof to show that one is absolutely right.'

Finally, in order to round off what had already been a most satisfactory evening, M decided to play his trump card and read his latest poem, which, for the record, is given here in full.

UNCLE SNORUS

Snorus's proboscis like a periscope
Scans the monotonous expanses of his bed –
Wide-awake, perceptive and intent –
Firmly anchored in his pillowed head.

Snorus – sleeping – gently rocks the ceiling
With his penetrating, vibrant snores,
Flakes the paintwork, loosens all the mortar,
Rattles all the windows and the doors.

Yet his snoring is melodious and true,
And it has a grace we all admire –
To its sound we tune our instruments
In the evening, strumming round the fire.

Having read out the English version of this contemplative piece, his hosts repeatedly interrupting to give vent to their obvious enjoyment, M read also the German version entitled *ONKEL SCHNORUS*.

'I bet there never was such a person as this *Onkel Schnorus*, hee-hee-hee,' ventured Bertha and was immediately pounced upon by her husband, who explained in a tone of great and kindly superiority, 'Of course not, Bertha, can't you tell that this is a creative work of literary genius? A periscope in bed, haw, haw – who ever heard of such a thing?'

'Can't say I have. And I've never heard of anyone breaking up a house with snoring either, hee-hee.'

M, who felt that any explanation might take too long, let it go at that. In any case, it was by now quite late and, afraid of missing the last bus to Bayswater, he took his leave. After numerous protestations and mutual compliments he was eventually on his way.

In fact, M could have told his hosts that his poem had been composed in memory of Uncle Georg, the carpenter, who had always been kind to him but particularly so during M's last days in Vienna, when he allowed him, his by then destitute father and his stepmother (M never managed to think of her as 'mother') to stay at the small flat behind his workshop, which even without them was already severely over-crowded. Uncle Georg happened to own a small pillow with the embroidered text *A Rua will i hobn* (Viennese for 'Let's have some peace'), on which he spent many a happy hour of siesta allowing the world and its hysteria to pass him by. On such occasions he would snore away gently, as befitted his character and disposition, greatly adding to the good cheer of all who happened to be present. It goes without saying that if the flat had not been in a state of advanced dilapidation (Uncle Georg was a poor man who could not afford even urgent repairs, and it was highly inadvisable – especially for a Jew in those troubled times – to approach the landlord about such matters) it would never have occurred to M that a snore could have caused such structural and surface damage as described in his poem.

CHAPTER ELEVEN

WHEN I think of my grandparents' house it is always the kitchen which comes to mind. At the time I never became really familiar with any of the other rooms in the house, for anything of the slightest importance took place within that welcoming and friendly room. The kitchen was the place where we had our meals and where I had my bed, where visitors were received and where, from the ripe old age of five years onward, I used to do my homework. Homework was, no doubt, a necessary evil, but apart from sums, which I enjoyed (particularly if, at the same time, I could give my poor Aunt Sali a bad time, catching her out in this or that mistake), I found it excruciatingly boring, a real waste of my valuable time, when I would have much preferred to be out and about doing interesting things.

In the kitchen, with its large cast-iron range on which the food was cooked, there was a massive table, which my grandmother would scrub daily with untiring devotion until it was perfectly spotless and fit for any king, and at which, by the friendly light of the brass paraffin lamp, she and Aunt Sali would sit in the evenings mending clothes and chatting about the events of the day. I also remember distinctly those blistered olive-green walls, from which I – unlike other children, who would merely bite their nails and pick their noses – used to remove loose flakes of paint and eat them. In the kitchen it was warm and cosy, except, of course, during the night, when I was alone, with every noise magnified and every shadow sinister. Then the gaunt window with its crossed centre beams would fix me with its blind, malevolent stare, a stare from which there was no escape – however firmly I would hide my head in the depths of my pillow, closing my eyes tightly and forcing myself to think of agreeable things – for after a time I simply had to come up and take a peep, when there it would be again, that horrid grey rectangle with its hideous stare. Only when I was older did I manage to break that spell, through direct communication with the Almighty, with whom I eventually managed to strike up quite a satisfactory relationship.

We even had our baths in the kitchen, in a wooden trough used at other times for washing the laundry, while large pots of water were steaming away on the well-stoked range. We all used the same water, one after the other, but I can no longer remember whether I was the first to get in, when the water was still hot and clear, or the last, when it had become lukewarm and bluish-grey. What I do, however, remember is my sense of earnest wonder as I lay watching the others from the feather-soft profundity of my bed. It was from that safe haven that I watched my Viennese cousin Olli, my very first love, who was a year or two older than I, while she was being given a bath. Poor Olli! She was pale and kind and lovely but never really well, and she died when she was only twelve years of age. After our return to Vienna I often used to visit her and, sitting by her bedside – she was then already very ill indeed – read to her stories as well as bits from Goethe's long epic in verse about the cunning fox Reineke, the sonorous hexameters and rhythmic regularity of which I found both satisfying and exciting. I hope that Olli too got some enjoyment from my recital.

One day we had an invasion of ants and all of a sudden the safety of our kitchen was shattered. (Whatever its night-time terrors, in daytime that kitchen had always seemed to me to be an eminently safe place.) There were ants everywhere – on the window-sill and under the window, on the table and about the range. I could not bear even to look at them, for, away from their natural environment – the ant heap at the back of the garden – they seemed unspeakably menacing and downright evil. It was as if the kitchen, for me at that time the very centre of the universe, had sprung a leak through which the devil and all his cohorts, the wicked queens and wolves and all the man-eating giants could and would now enter, to do their ghastly worst, so help us God.

We all fear chaos such as these ants symbolised for me. The following story, which I wrote after a bout of severe depression, has nothing to do with ants or any other insects whatsoever.

SCREW

In spite of his advanced state of mental deterioration, Rasmusson was aware of the fact that the rooms of the apartment had grown even higher and now resembled a huddle of upright green bottles linked by a series of mysteriously beckoning doors. Some of the doors had not been opened for years whereas others could no longer be opened at all. Rasmusson stopped in front of the mirror specially made to reflect his image in an infinity of frequently surprising ways, but he did not really see it at all, nor did he pay any attention to Gordon, the robot, and his flashing messages. His eyes, bright with suppressed excitement, were directed towards the door of the broom-cupboard, through which Welling, his brilliant friend, had passed so long ago, never to emerge again.

Once upon a time this had been quite an ordinary apartment with reasonably low ceilings and large, pleasant windows, with greenish light filtering through the leafy trees outside. That was in the early days when Rasmusson and Welling, finding that they were soul-mates in every way, had first joined forces, foreswearing all other company. As a result and indeed for many, many years, the apartment remained untainted by the presence of dogs, cats, birds or any other creature, however splendid its fur, tail or plumage.

Rasmusson and Welling were in many respects exact opposites. Rasmusson was tall, thin and a man of many talents, all of which he had long devoted to the pitiless pursuit of Truth. Having delved deeply into the stores of accumulated wisdom, earnestly digested the quality weeklies for years and years, and after many 'insights', with Truth like a flirtatious young thing forever beckoning and forever retreating, he had finally arrived at the conviction that the elusive damsel was to be found only in the pages of the popular press, maturing in proportion to the time elapsed since publication. He accordingly entered into an arrangement with Mr. Krokodilsky, that well-known international purveyor of pulp, to supply him with Clarions and Heralds and Stars in all available languages, even and especially if they were no longer in the least topical. Rasmusson put them into assorted shoeboxes, of which he had managed to acquire a goodly stock, and stored them carefully, so that Truth might blossom undisturbed to reveal herself in due course. Having failed to trap Truth – the cunning creature descending into unheard-of depths – Rasmusson became extremely taciturn, since – as he might have (but did not, in fact) put it – 'What is the point in speaking if you do not have the faintest idea what you are talking about?'

As for Welling, he could best be described as a short, fat man of engineering and science. He had at his command such splendid powers of combination, such marvellous techniques by which to find solutions that the scope of his inventive genius was bounded only by the existence of problems which managed utterly to avoid his probing attention. And he did not accept as valid the widespread view that certain problems are by their very nature insoluble. 'A problem,' he used to say, 'which cannot be solved' (read: 'which I cannot solve') 'is sick and will soon be quite dead. All that remains is to dispose of it in an appropriately hygienic manner.'

There was nothing Welling craved more than a really good chin-wag – a craving Rasmusson was not at all able to satisfy. This, in fact, was the very circumstance which lay at the root of the conception and development of Gordon, the mechanical man. The idea of a *ménage à trois* with a versatile automaton as a third partner first came to Welling one evening in winter when he and Rasmusson were locked in one of those interminable games of neo-chess which, being poly-dimensional, can be played only at an infinitely slow rate, with the position frequently still unresolved when one or even both partners have quite forgotten what they are about or, at the more advanced levels, gone to their just reward. While Rasmusson meditated on how, or indeed whether, to continue, Welling considered how pleasant it would be to have someone – preferably a controlled substitute person that could be switched on and off at will – to whom to communicate the superior intricacy of his own moves and where Rasmusson had gone wrong, and who, in turn, would be able to reciprocate by making both intelligent and edifying comments. Such a partner, it seemed to him, might also be able to enliven their frugal meals by responding verbally and visually to the brilliancies of his, Welling's, infinitely fertile mind, a veritable cornucopia of a mind, thus giving rise to much stimulating conversation. Last but not least, he should, of course, be capable of mastering certain simple tasks such as preparing their meals or stacking and occasionally watering Rasmusson's shoeboxes.

There were the considerations to which Gordon owed his origination, not perhaps in the most auspicious manner imaginable, from a humble Meccano set left to Welling in the will of a cousin thrice-removed.

Making excellent use of this set and such other materials as were to hand, Welling assembled and duplicated, tested and optimised until Gordon began to take shape, and in next to no time there came the memorable day when Gordon, the versatile automaton, was able to take his place at table, ready to learn, to respond and generally to contribute to the quality of life as lived in the apartment.

Gordon's initial efforts were fairly modest. His main visual display with its rotating lights in vivid red kept flashing messages of good will such as 'Gentlemen, Gordon awaits your commands' and equally affable questions such as 'Gentlemen, do you wish Gordon to clear the table?'. As a matter of fact and putting it mildly, Gordon's attempts at clearing the table and similar domestic chores tended, at that early stage of his development, to be rather feeble. His 'hands', still very far from perfect, left deep claw-marks in the mahogany furniture, and on one never-to-be-forgotten occasion Rasmusson caught him *in flagrante delicto*, chewing up several 'hydroponic truth breeders' (HTB's), as Rasmusson used to designate his information-charged shoe boxes. At the time this resulted in a terrible scene but may well have been beneficial to Gordon's eventually quite astonishing intellectual development.

With the passage of time, as winter turned to spring, spring to summer and so on, Gordon's repertoire of skills increased by leaps and bounds. Once he had been fitted with appropriate acousto-systems, he learned to add voice to vision, but at that stage he also moved about more surely and speedily on his sturdy, well-sprung legs, the feet at the ends of which consisted basically of disused jamjars which Welling had polished and improved to such an extent that they shone and sparkled like crystal, and had, moreover, mastered certain social accomplishments such as puffing at his very own Meerschaum pipe and playing patriotic tunes on the pianola in the corner, all of which added greatly to the relaxed conviviality of their evenings. Particularly striking, however, were his newly developed, ever-expanding conversational skills. Thanks to an incredibly complex system of precisely heated and switchable differential-pressure tubes through which flowed molten candle wax (although, as Welling explained, molten bacon fat or any other viscous fluid would have done equally well), he had become able to respond to any statement such as 'The stove has gone out' in a variety of ways. He might say, for instance, 'I agree with you, the stove has indeed gone out' or enquire 'What, in your opinion, has caused the stove to go out?' In his philosophical mode he now was capable of asking questions such as 'What do you mean by stove?' or of commenting wisely 'Stoves do go out from time to time'. Faced with such sagacity, the two friends could not but marvel at Gordon's most gratifying progress, and Welling especially would take the discussion yet further by adding another apt observation or answering Gordon's question in as concise and illuminating a manner as possible. Ever more sophisticated, increasingly self-induced techniques followed, until in the end Gordon fairly dominated the conversation. At this stage he could ring the changes on any statement, adding or omitting elements 'at will'.

Foreign languages too were now firmly within his grasp, and he would frequently come up with choice morsels of information gleaned from Rasmusson's HTB's as he was watering them. Thanks to Welling, Gordon even developed a somewhat technically oriented sense of humour, of which his famous joke linking 'switchcraft' with 'which craft' is a fine example. When they heard it for the first time, Rasmusson and Welling could barely contain themselves, as the rumble of their laughter reverberated through the apartment, deforming its walls and ceilings. It goes without saying and is, therefore, mentioned solely for the record that Gordon soon became a dab hand at neo-chess, whereupon, still guided by Welling, his originator and mentor, he set about mastering various specialised activities such as mother-craft, chair dancing and particulate hygiene, thus augmenting his general usefulness and acquiring the potential for economic independence. It was, indeed, a proud day when Oxford welcomed him as a student of theology and an even prouder one when he received his doctorate *summa cum laude atque honoris causa*.

How splendid he looked in his red doctor's robes and with his tasselled mortar board, as at the head of his peers – both of them unsteady on their legs with drink and barely tottering – he made his way down the centre aisle of the festively decorated graduation hall, to the ceremonious strains of *Bésame mucho* originally recorded on the giant Wurlitzer but now decelerated in a manner most solemn. It was a swelteringly hot afternoon in mid-summer, but although both the faculty members and the spectators were at various stages of incipient dissolution – hair oil bubbling away gently and mascara dripping from the eyelashes of the fair ones – it seemed, when it was Gordon's turn to receive the signal honour, as if the applause would never end.

Ah, those were the days – halcyon days! Would that they had never ended! But already the shadows were growing longer and fearsome night was on the point of spreading its cloak over our heroes, ready to engulf them for ever and ever more.

As Gordon's mundane and social accomplishments multiplied, Rasmusson and Welling became increasingly dependent upon his ministrations. Rasmusson ceased to be interested in his HTB's, and in a fit of murderous depression set fire to them, thus undoing the work of a lifetime and depriving himself forever of any chance of encountering Truth. To repair his loss as best he could, he ordered from a mail-order company a mirror capable of reflecting his image in an infinity of utterly astounding ways, and for a time he spent endless hours contemplating the reflections of his face in a stupor of wonderment and delighted self-adulation. But this device, ingenious though it undoubtedly was, could not satisfy him for long, and he subsided into a state of progressive lassitude and demoralisation from which he never even began to recover.

As for Welling, he bitterly resented the fact that his creature had in all essential respects become his superior. He wanted to destroy Gordon but could not summon the will-power necessary to commit such an act of total, irreversible vandalism. So he limited himself to minor acts of violence and spite, some of which permanently impaired Gordon's emotogenic circuits, depriving him of all self-confidence and leaving him with a permanent stutter and a severe limp. Far from releasing Welling's compassionate urges, this only served to make him more aggressive, but he now turned his destructive drives against his own person. In the end he constructed a most unusual machine capable of reducing anything and everything to absolutely nothing. Having installed this machine in a broom-cupboard, he eventually stepped inside and turned on the energy. This event more than any other promoted the upward distortion of the apartment, with the various rooms increasingly resembling a huddle of melancholy green bottles.

Initially Rasmusson and Gordon managed well enough. Gordon took care of the domestic chores – that is where his domestological studies proved most useful – and saw to it that Rasmusson took his proper ration of tastily prepared nutritive tablets. Rasmusson, on the other hand, made various attempts at a fresh start, applying, for instance, for the position of chief apron-designer to a mystical brotherhood of American businessmen. He also wrote several letters of considerable distinction to the *Hinkley and Surrounds Property Advertiser* in order to attract the editor's attention to various topics of major interest. In one such letter, for instance, he examined the question of whether the fact that even highly experienced practitioners of 'the noble art' were so frequently observed to collide with their opponents' gloved upper extremities was perhaps due to poor, uncorrected eyesight. This letter in particular might well have given rise to a heated public debate lasting many months if only it had been received at the *Advertiser's* offices. But this, regrettably, had not been the case – the postman, who had misread the address, having delivered it instead to the municipal dump.

With Rasmusson quite unable to undertake such minor repair and servicing operations as even the most versatile automaton cannot do without, Gordon's systems went into a gradual but accelerating decline, and matters became even worse when, in a state of absent-mindedness, Gordon swallowed a bottle of instant water tablets. Following this mishap Gordon's optical sensors became prone to leaking brownish fluid, which laboratory analysis would have shown to consist largely of instant water and various ferrous oxides (rust!).

Gordon's progressive deterioration was, indeed, pitiful and would have brought tears to any but the most callous beholder. Rasmusson, however, whose mental condition was at that time already well past any hope of recovery, did not even notice the sad state to which his faithful companion had been reduced. He still spent long periods of time staring into his mirror but without even realising what he was about, and one day he simply walked through the door through which Welling had passed so long ago, leaving the apartment for ever.

Gordon, now quite alone, quite stiff in his joints and rapidly falling apart, kept repeating plaintive messages from his early days such as 'Gentlemen, Gordon awaits your commands' and 'Gentlemen, do you wish Gordon to clear the table?' This went on for a number of days but eventually, his battery recharger having failed, his energy supply dried up and he came to a dead end.

At this point the apartment reached its greatest height, the rooms looking every bit like gaunt and mysterious dark green bottles. But soon a gradual reversal to the initial state set in, in which the apartment reassumed a peaceful, soothing appearance, with its ceilings again quite low.

Several years after these events, two elderly gentlemen came to the apartment having but recently acquired this most desirable residence. One of them, a tall, bespectacled fellow, was carrying a cardboard box bulging with what appeared to be assorted reading-matter. Without initially putting down the box he awkwardly extracted a tape measure from his left trouser pocket – nearly dislocating his right shoulder in the process – and started measuring a wall, which on this bright and sunny morning looked bare but definitely encouraging. Having satisfied himself that the dimensions were exactly as required, he carefully deposited his box in a corner of the room and then left the apartment, returning again shortly with a watering-can and another box which he stacked neatly on top of its predecessor. In due course other boxes of similar appearance were to follow, slowly covering the wall.

While the bespectacled gentleman, Robertson by name, was busy with his boxes, his friend Lessing, a short, chubby man, was examining, with great attention, the contents of a tea-chest in the middle of the largest room. He appeared to be particularly delighted with a network of copper tubes now in a state of collapse, a number of jam-jars, and a collection of mechano-electrical contraptions, some of them immensely ingenious. Once he had completed his preliminary examination, he dragged the tea-chest to what was to be his very own workroom and laboratory, muttering 'These will do very nicely, very nicely indeed.'

A man of great scientific and technical insight, Lessing could see at a glance that many of these bits and pieces might come in very handy for what he had in mind, namely the construction of a caninoid – a mechano-automatic device in the general shape of a dog and with various judiciously selected functions and characteristics of these lovable creatures. The way he planned it, it would, for instance, be programmed to learn and spontaneously perform various tricks (some of truly acrobatic complexity), prettily raise its foreleg at appropriate moments to signal that it wished to be cuddled, and keep any passing burglar or feline (Lessing had an almost pathological aversion to cats, and the hair on the back of his neck would bristle whenever he saw one) at bay. On the other hand, it would refrain from barking, slobbering and any other indecorous activities such as dogs are prone to. Free from all impediments of a biological kind, it would also be able to render certain operatic arias and play neo-whist, a game of which both Lessing and Robertson were extremely fond. In brief, Roger (that was to be their new companion's name) would be perfect in every way, fully capable of brightening a solitary walk or providing intellectual stimulation on a long winter evening.

A caninoid is indeed what Lessing might eventually have designed and constructed, had he not happened to come across an old cerebroton, which when actuated responded, albeit haltingly, with 'Gentlemen, Gordon awaits your commands'. Greatly intrigued by this interesting find, Lessing prodded and tested, soldered and tuned until he managed to elicit many other utterances as well, for instance a highly original restatement of Emmanuel Kant's concept of the categorical imperative, which made him realise that the contrivance in front of him was far from ordinary in more ways than one. This, of course, changed everything. Setting aside his original project for the time being, he henceforth devoted himself entirely to the task of recreating Gordon, whose powerful personality came increasingly to dominate his every thought. His indefatigable endeavours were rewarded with brilliant success, so that one day he was able to introduce the reconstituted and reconditioned Gordon to Robertson, who – as could be gathered from the fact that he allowed his pipe to drop from between his jaws into one of his boxes, which he happened to be mulching – was immensely impressed. It stands to reason that Gordon in his new guise differed in various repects from his former self (in the absence of technical drawings and proper specifications this was, of course, quite understandable) but in all essentials it was him alright, and in some ways he was even greatly improved.

Time thereafter passed happily enough for the three of them, with one busy with his boxes, the other assiduously tinkering and combining, assembling and making good, while Gordon managed the more mundane aspects of their comfortable, harmonious existence and took care of their cultural needs. And one fine day – on Gordon's rebirthday – Lessing came up with Roger, a caninoid of truly amazing potential, after which their contentment reached a peak never to be surpassed. By this time the rooms of the apartment had again grown much higher and again resembled nothing so much as a huddle of upright green bottles linked by a series of mysteriously beckoning doors. The screw of life in the apartment having undergone another turn, further events followed, for nothing ever stands still, even though everything, of course, remains eternally the same.

Silversmith has failed to win any prize whatsoever in the Exobrill competition. According to him this was clearly a put-up job, for, to judge by their names, virtually all the winners appeared to belong to three or four families, with only a few minor prizes – the odd five shillings or so – going to people with other names. Still, he is not too depressed, for he has got himself a new girlfriend. So far we have not seen her, but he says she is rich and exquisitely lovely. He also insists that she is highly intelligent but God only knows how he has managed to find this out, seeing that her English is rudimentary – she hails from Bavaria or thereabouts – and he, to all intents and purposes, does not know a word of German. I put it to him that for an adequate fee I should be prepared to act as interpreter. I thought my suggestion was really funny, but he clearly did not think so and still refuses to speak to me.

The other day, when I had lunch with Catty at the H.P., she suddenly seemed utterly repulsive to me. I really wished that I had never met her. This, of course, didn't last, and the moment she left I found her again as tantalising as ever. I keep thinking about the things I should like to do with her ...

CHAPTER TWELVE

AT THE House of Pasta, Dr. McGill of the English department, a shortish man with wide shoulders and a lovingly groomed pointed beard speckled with grey, and M were enjoying lunch and arguing (not perhaps the right word, seeing that M hardly managed to get a word in edgeways) about the way in which they earned their living, which Dr. McGill described as being highly peculiar, not to say odd.

'You are a clown, my dear Maskenbusch, of course you are, and so indeed are all of us,' said Dr. McGill, who could never resist the temptation of making a point forcefully. 'You don't, I hope, seriously suggest that your so-called students are genuinely interested in improving their minds – always provided that they have any minds to improve, which I personally doubt. No, no, they simply come to this particular establishment in order to make believe that they are a cut or two above the other intellectual pygmies of their acquaintance – please forgive me for mixing my metaphors – or merely to get away, for a brief hour or two at least, from their dreary husbands or wives or whatever. All they really want is "a bit of a laugh", a little stimulation, which is in fact all they do get, the poor swine.' Dr. McGill took a sip of tea, belched demonstratively and, taking advantage of the occasion, blew his nose with a trumpeting, elephantine sound into a handkerchief well beyond its hygienic best. Having concluded this intermezzo, he continued: 'Now, my lot are, of course, equally moronic, but at least some of them have the excuse that they do at least acquire a smattering of English – although, in the process, frequently raping that poor, long-suffering but oh-so-delightful language – in order to earn a crust or two. Yes, my dear Maskenbusch, in their case the overriding motive tends to be economic ambition rather than any urgent need to escape from their own mediocrity or simple boredom with their nearest and dearest.' He took another sip of tea, and having again blown his nose – a veritable cucumber of a nose but of a reddish rather than greenish appearance – in his 'handkerchief', he used the latter to wipe and even scrape about in his right ear, from which – as from its partner – grew a rich crop of whitish hair. This done, he proceeded: 'Mind you, I cannot for the life of me comprehend why anyone should wish to come to London, when almost any other place that comes to mind has evidently so much more to offer.'

'But surely,' M managed to interject as Dr. McGill gurgled and slurped down the remains of his brew, 'if what you say were entirely true – mind you, I am not saying that you are totally wrong – they could go to a cinema or a club and not waste time on an uneven struggle with declensions and conjugations and similarly unnatural activities. Take, for instance, my Mr. Allbright ...'

'Ah, but that is where their guilt-feelings come in – their quite justified and understandable sense of inferiority – don't you see? It would be no exaggeration to assert that your average adult student is a person who feels atrociously guilty if he is not constantly "improving" himself, however irrelevant such an improvement may be to his particular situation and however far beyond his intellectual reach.' (Dr. McGill was quite happy to change the basis of his argument whenever it suited him.) 'We have here a kind of masochism, to which especially you people on the foreign languages side pander in return for money. Not that any of us are entirely free of blame. After all, it would be quite fair to describe us as intellectual prostitutes selling tinsel and pretending that it is gold. We are, as you will no doubt agree, mere conmen catering for a kind of perverse tourism – that other branch of socially acceptable prostitution.' Having thus contrived to bring in the concept of prostitution, Dr. McGill was positively aglow with satisfaction.

'I do agree, at any rate up to a point,' M cut in, 'But as for my students, they all appear to have perfectly good and valid reasons for studying. Some – the majority in fact – intend to spend their holidays in the Alps, or they may be studying for business reasons ...'

'What utter rubbish,' Dr. McGill interrupted, his hands shaking with ill-suppressed excitement, causing him to knock the by now fortunately empty cup to the floor, where it promptly broke, causing Ben, who had been asleep in his corner, to come scurrying along with his dustpan and brush. 'Do you seriously believe any one of your so-called students can hope to master the intricacies of a business discussion after only a few lessons even with an experienced and gifted teacher such as yourself?' Dr. McGill was prone to paying such purely rhetorical compliments, but in fact he regarded every one of his colleagues at TTTW with barely disguised contempt.

'Of course they couldn't ...'

'I should think not. Nor would they dare to speak in a foreign language after such sketchy preparation, unless, of course, they happened to be suffering from some serious mental or psychological aberration over and above the ones I have already outlined. Then again, just imagine what would happen if one of your students were actually to reach that horrible village in the Alps. We have then three distinct possibilities: he – I really ought to say "she", seeing that almost all your charges are female – but no matter. Where was I? Oh yes, he can cut his losses and revert entirely to his mother tongue, in which case he will find that the locals also speak English of a kind – at any rate quite enough for the usual bullshit tourists seem to expect and love. Or he may obstinately insist on speaking what he mistakenly believes to be the lingo of the region, only to find that he doesn't understand one blessed word of what people say to him, which may be just as well. And then again he may, at immense personal sacrifice, master the language sufficiently to speak it with some fluency, in which case he will bore everybody to death and have his lovely German or French or whatever criticised severely by every local yokel, who resents the competition and hates all foreigners anyway. Whatever he does, one thing is certain: he is going to be cheated, as indeed he deserves to be, so spare me the violins.' M was on the point of challenging this extravagant, highly pessimistic statement, when they were joined by Mr. Galbraith, who told them in great detail about certain domestic difficulties involving an aged aunt with whom he shared a flat and whose unenviable task it was to look after him. Eventually, however, he faded away again, leaving them free to resume their conversation.

His hobby-horse, which had been at the point of exhaustion, having somewhat recovered, Dr. McGill continued to ride it, although in a slightly different direction. 'Tell me, my dear Maskenbusch,' he intoned, 'when did you last visit your tailor?' This question was manifestly absurd, for, apart from the brief period during which he had been the proud if unlikely owner of the aforementioned camel-hair coat which he had inherited from his Uncle Moritz but which, alas, was no longer in his possession, M was not in any sense noted for his sartorial elegance – Dr. McGill did not therefore waste time waiting for an answer but proceeded in only slightly meandering manner to the heart of the matter. 'Culture by the yard. That, my dear friend, is the common ambition today – a kind of pseudo-ideal, in fact – and nobody seems to be aware of the fact that this is an aspiration as pointless as going to one's tailor in order to buy up all the cloth in the shop rather than to select a suitable material and be measured for a suit. For just as a suit which is perfect for me may be quite wrong for you, so culture – I use this term in its widest sense as including even a knowledge of foreign languages – can never be a mere off-the-shelf commodity but must, like a well-tailored suit, fit the wearer exactly.' Having driven home his point with customary force and clarity, Dr. McGill devoted himself to careful excavation of the contents of first his left and then his right nostril.

Dr. McGill, who in spite of great early promise had never quite managed to make the grade in the academic world, suffered from a severe sense of inadequacy aggravated by the fact that both his grandfather and his father had been very successful in their respective domains – the former as the founder and guiding spirit of McGill's Haberdashery in Edinburgh, and the latter as a widely respected man of learning. Incapable of coming to terms with the fact that he was merely second or even third best, just another common-or-garden Ph.D. among thousands, Dr. McGill, once an idealistic young man devoted to the energetic pursuit of various good causes (in addition, of course, to the equally energetic pursuit of pretty young girls, whom he liked to 'chastise', although, of course, very few would allow him to do so), had become a veritable culture-vulture with all the awful characteristics of that ilk such as intolerance, a tendency to envy and self-pity, and pride in his numerous limitations and inadequacies. One of his numerous standard clichés was 'Even when I am wrong, I am still right, relatively speaking', and he used to make much of his inability to hit a nail with a hammer, repair a fuse or wash the dishes – chores which he left to lesser mortals not so richly endowed, such as his long-suffering wife. He affected to despise all intellectuals and used his cynicism as a cover for his considerable mediocrity. Politically he was left of centre, and as a humanitarian – although not a philanthropist, being far too parsimonious – he loved the disadvantaged, provided that the latter belonged to a category approved by the quality press and could be kept at a safe distance, making no demands on him and confining themselves to the anonymity of statistics. As for real people, he did not like them much. This, however, did not prevent him from acquiring a large circle of 'friends', every one of whom was, according to him, outstanding in one way or another – by virtue of intellect, achievement or simply wealth, for which latter attribute he had a very healthy respect. His attitudes to women were, to put it mildly, ambiguous, but he venerated his wife and was a good if somewhat over-indulgent parent, paid his taxes honestly although grudgingly, and was a valued member of his local congregation.

From time to time, seized by a powerful desire to improve his mind, M would gobble up large chunks of this and that – poetry and history of art, psychology and the principles of literary criticism, logic, philosophy, and indeed anything likely in his opinion to make him more acceptable to the select circle of academically qualified and, as it were, legitimate intellectuals, to whom, on many occasions, he felt deeply inferior. But to be acceptable was, from his point of view, not enough, for knowing himself in his innermost heart to be greatly superior to these people, whose frequently pretentious ways and narrow-minded conventionality he despised profoundly, he had set himself the aim to do better, to become a giant in the land of Lilliput. The fateful day, on which as a result of a test taken for fun he would have to admit to himself and to an – as he hoped – incredulous world that his intelligence was not so much that of an Einstein as that of a 'clerk', whatever that might be, had not yet dawned, and he was therefore as yet unshakeably convinced of being a kind of potential 'mastermind'.

Still, he could not but agree with Dr. McGill that 'culture by the yard' was both senseless and vulgar, and the analogy of the tailor's shop certainly appealed to him. After all, he himself had argued time and again that it was absurd to acquire knowledge without any regard for one's real needs. When studying languages, for instance, he always used to classify new words and even rules of grammar according to their importance to him personally, allocating different amounts of learning effort to every group. Not infrequently, however, the very words which he had rejected as being totally useless – words, the meaning of which he did not know or which he was certain never to require – came to stick in his mind for ever and ever, turning eventually, as was bound to be the case, into chunks of imperfectly rotted intellectual compost.

To illustrate this point M had even written a short story, the hero of which, an obsessive fellow named Rosper, whose every waking thought and dream had in the past been taken up with matters such as the Welsh word for 'fish' or the longest word in the Portuguese language, happens to fall in love with a beautiful foreign girl, whom he teaches English and whose own language he alone can understand. To begin with, impressed with his knowledge and since he is her only bridge to the outside world, she admires him and even responds to his feelings for her with some mild affection, but as her English improves – not so much due to her mentor's assistance as thanks to her attractive appearance and generous nature – she becomes increasingly bored with him and his endless prattle. In other words, she, as many another before her, begins to realise that there is not much point in knowing how to say things if one has nothing to say in the first place. When at the end of the story Rosper comes to her laden with yellow flowers as well as a selection of splendid dictionaries in order to offer her his hand in marriage, he finds her in bed with a bald-headed, large-bellied lorry driver, who knows only English – and that not very well – but can clearly offer her much more of what she wants and needs than her poor admirer, who naturally goes away to seek solace in the acquisition of yet another language.

Dr. Pendlebloom was having a really busy day. To begin with, there had been his meeting with Mr. Smallgrove, the company's adviser in matters of accountancy and his close personal friend, who had put before him a most ingenious plan for reducing overall staff costs while actually increasing the number of people employed by TTTW. Then he had seen Mr. Woodlock of Woodlock, Woodlock and Spring, his publicity consultants, with whom he had discussed a new poster advertising the services of his organisation. The poster was to be all in green, Dr. Pendlebloom's favourite colour, with – by way of principal attraction – a photograph of all the TTTW staff at its centre. He had already drafted the wording of this as yet unrealised work of art and given much thought to the grouping of those privileged to appear in the photograph. In order to achieve the desired result, he had drawn up a list of tutorial members and administrative staff, grading them all according to height. His artistic aim was to suggest a large ceremonial bird with its wings outspread, with himself as its head and body. He toyed briefly with the idea of placing several telephone directories on his chair in order to increase his own height when seated but eventually rejected the idea as not sufficiently *comme il faut*, deciding instead to stand on a box wearing mortar-board and gown (by courtesy of that well-known firm of gentlemen's outfitters which specialised in hiring out garments of distinction for memorable occasions), with the others to his right and left, their eyes firmly focused on him while he extended his right arm in a gesture of neo-biblical leadership.

There were still certain points of detail to be resolved but, luckily, solving problems was Dr. Pendlebloom's favourite activity and indisputable forte. Who, for instance, was taller – Mr. Clematis, the emaciated Esperantist and also a most valued member of the TTTW panel (although so far there had never been any actual need for his services), or Glub, the caretaker, a highly gifted man who knew just what to do when it was a matter of exerting pressure (psychological pressure, of course) or accepting the odd minor donation for services rendered? Dr. Pendlebloom having made two notes – 'Gomberg to supply required dimensions of height Clematis and Glub 3 o'clock latest' and 'Instruct Glub to supply sturdy box app. 10" high for P. to stand on' – checked them carefully and placed them in the out-tray.

And now Dr. Pendlebloom, from time to time pensively stroking his handsome, well-groomed moustache or – another aid to concentration and creativity – absent-mindedly looking out of the window into the office on the other side of the courtyard, was making notes on one of his most recent and currently favourite schemes – the diversification of TTTW by adding to it a multilingual escorting service for foreign visitors and others wishing to tour and inspect the prime sights of London or, more ambitiously and only by special arrangement, to gain, within a relatively short period of time and at appropriate rates, a really intimate acquaintance with such delights of London as are not generally accessible to the uninitiated.

Everything would of course be perfectly above board and in impeccably good taste. Dr. Pendlebloom jotted down: 'Impeccable taste essential. Pale green uniforms (?) – to be discussed.' Then he added 'TTTW Escorters', underlining this three times with such emphasis that a drop of ink flew from the nib of his exquisite and highly tasteful Parker, splattering his previously whiter-than-white blotter. This minor mishap dismayed him slightly, but he was too determined, too forceful a man, for its effect to be anything but temporary. He simply rang for his faithful Gomberg, and, once she had replaced the offending blotting paper, continued with his deliberations. He was, understandably, very pleased with what he had achieved so far. 'TTTW Escorters,' he thought, 'has a real ring to it. It sounds much better than TTTW Hostesses – far more refined and to the point.' Then he wrote yet another note: 'Contract to specify wearing of uniform at all times, also when not on duty', underlining the words 'contract', 'uniform' and 'not on duty'.

At this point Dr. Pendlebloom, who would not have achieved his present eminence without a considerable flair for improvisation, had yet another flash of inspiration. For, having given the matter much thought and carefully weighed the pros and cons of retaining Madame Bellringer's services as a teacher of French, he had arrived at the mature conclusion that it was his indubitable duty to make her relinquish this post, particularly as he had received a very formal, even quite unpleasant letter from

Miss Almondgreen of the 'Clean up Soho' campaign. Still – and although, as a matter of principle, he would never go back on a decision once taken – he had not felt entirely comfortable about this particular decision, for he regarded himself as a friend and moral guide to his staff – always just, always in their corner, as it were. Besides, he had been quite unable to discover any real evidence proving that Madame was indeed guilty as charged, and she might well cause a lot of trouble leading to the loss of students (and hence of their fees) and worse. But, all of a sudden, there it was – the perfect solution: he would ask Madame Bellringer to manage the TTTW Escorters – a position for which by all accounts she would be admirably suited. Besides (like any chess master or head of an intelligence organisation, Dr. Pendlebloom always considered all the possible ramifications) even if she refused – and with women you never knew, for in his experience a woman was always likely to cut off her nose to spite her face – she would not have a leg to stand on in the classroom or, for that matter, in a court of law.

Dr. Pendlebloom again pressed the bell on his desk. When Miss Gomberg appeared he instructed her to bring him Madame's file and to send her to his office at 4 o'clock sharp, as he had important matters to discuss with her. Miss Gomberg took the notes relating to the photographic session from the out-tray and left. Finally, Dr. Pendlebloom, rightly feeling that he had done a good morning's work, put on his hat, scarf and black overcoat and went to lunch in a nearby restaurant – a select establishment much frequented by members of the business community.

CHAPTER THIRTEEN

SHORTLY after his grandfather's funeral, M, then about eight years of age, was taken back to Vienna by his father, who had only recently married a very much younger, very passionate and extremely attractive woman. After so many years of living alone, Papa had hoped to create a real family – slippers waiting for him in front of the stove when he came home in the evening, home cooking and every personal comfort, not to mention the fact that his son would surely benefit from parental advice, guidance and loving care such as he and M's new Mama would now be able to provide – but in the event things did not, after all, work out that well. Under the lengthening shadows of Adolf Hitler's Reich, Papa's health and fortunes rapidly waned, and Mama, who had been so eager to escape the narrow life of provincial Bielsko in order to partake of the social and other delights of Vienna, soon discovered that, although they were there for some, they were certainly not there for her and that she had simply found her way from the frying pan of boredom into the fire of drudgery. Saddled as she was with an ageing husband, who even when he was at home – from Friday evening until Monday morning – was mostly ill and of little if any use to her and with an annoying little boy, her life was not as she had hoped it would be. Besides, she increasingly resented her stepson, particularly once she had been obliged to admit to herself that she would never be able to bear a child of her own – a failure for which, obscurely, she appeared to hold him responsible. M, an introspective, highly-strung boy, thus became ever more afraid of that half crazy woman who was his stepmother, until fear dominated every facet of his at the time not very happy existence.

Rummaging among his papers half a century later, M happened to come across a faded photograph of his father and stepmother taken shortly after their wedding. His father's rigid pose concealed almost every quality which had distinguished him, only the merest trace of vague hopefulness and the neat way in which his tie was knotted giving some slight indication of the kind of man he had been. On the other hand, it seemed to him that Mama, wearing her well-remembered jaunty hat and elegant suit, was again staring with cold, pitiless eyes at the cringing boy – himself as he once was – before her, still, even beyond the grave, quite capable of arousing in him fantasies of terror and fascination.

Yet, initially, life *en famille* in Vienna was not all that bad, for the Maskenbusches were still able to afford a reasonably comfortable flat near the Karlskirche, undeniably one of the more elegant parts of Vienna, ate good food – whatever her faults, M's stepmother was a marvellous cook whose poppy-seed cake was simply mouthwatering – and were able to keep a maid. Liesl, in fact, stayed with them for a long time, even though her wages were increasingly in arrears until eventually they ceased to be paid altogether.

Liesl treated little Morus as a friend and shared all her best secrets with him. She told him about her family, a subject of great interest to him, for he himself would have dearly loved to be part of such a friendly clan. When Mama was out shopping, Liesl would allow him to stay with her while she did the ironing or other household tasks, and she did her best to answer his many questions and to respond sagely to what he had to tell her. One story in particular used to fascinate him. Indeed he never grew tired of hearing how on the 5th of December, the eve of St. Nicholas's Day, her grandfather would dress up as that good and saintly man, all in red and white, put on a massive white beard and a bishop's mitre, firmly grasp a shepherd's crook in his powerful, gnarled hand and, accompanied by Herr Franz, the hairdresser, who for this occasion only had put on the guise of an all-black devil, would set off to visit the children in the neighbourhood in order to enquire whether they had been good little kiddies throughout the year, meriting such rewards as he himself carried in his bag. However, if they had been thoroughly bad and in need of correction, there was Herr Krampus Franz, who for this purpose would carry a sack in which to take away naughty children, chains with which to bind them and a bundle of birch twigs with which to beat them. The answer, after some purely formal hesitation which greatly added to the tension of the moment, being in general benign – namely, that they had, on the whole, been good children but promised faithfully to be even better next year – he would give them various goodies, in particular little devils made entirely of prunes on toothpick skeletons and with sugary red tongues.

M's memories of those early years were, on the whole, confused and altogether unreliable, but certain experiences and events did remain with him, such as reading the legends of ancient Greece at the Belvedere Gardens and making the rounds of the many local consulates in order to ask them for postage stamps from letters and other items of correspondence received. His favourite port of call was the Turkish consulate with its flag sporting a white crescent and star on a sombre red background, where the porter inspected him through a tiny circular window above the massive oak-wood door but never admitted him, rather as St. Peter might have considered and then rejected a sinner knocking at the gates of heaven. Then there were mystery plays on the steps of the Karlskirche and visits with his parents to the Café Schwarzenberg on Sunday afternoons. On New Year's Eve, when Vienna was alight with gaiety and the spirit of celebration – they would give *Die Fledermaus* at the Opera, which was also broadcast on the radio, while on New Year's morning, when as often as not the sun was shining brilliantly, the snow underfoot was crisp and clean, and the bells in all the churches were ringing gaily, welcoming the as yet untarnished newcomer – M and Mama would go to Julius Meinl's coffee emporium, a place fragrant with the scent of coffee and spices from far-off lands, in order to collect their free calendar. This, it must be understood, was not an ordinary calendar but one printed in deep, glowing colours on solid, even massive, cardboard of the very finest quality, on which that chocolate-coloured boy with the tasselled red hat kept carrying a cup of steaming hot coffee through a Rousseauesque jungle.

The various holidays – Chanukka and Christmas, Easter and Passover, Purim and Carneval – became jumbled up in M's mind, and he could have sworn that every Christmas Eve he was given one present and one present only – a book, pleasant to hold and with beautiful, satisfying colour illustrations – which, alas, he had to give back again at the end of the festivities, only to receive it again, neatly repacked and with seasonal good wishes, the following year. Be that as it may, M was certainly a most avid reader, with his nose forever in this book or that, such as *Robinson Crusoe* or *Münchhausen*, whose inspired and inspiring lies he admired greatly, Grimms' *Fairy Tales, Die Schildbürger,* stories of simple villagers who used to do silly things such as carry sunlight in barrels into their windowless church in order to light it up, or *Till Eulenspiegel*, an ancient work recounting the adventures of a famous migrant jester who used to make fools of everybody. Karl May's noble savages, Sherlock Holmes and the Greek Gods and heroes – all of these and many others vied for his attention with roughly equal chances, and he would have loved to be one of the *Höhlenkinder* – cave children at the dawn of history, to whom everything was new and who, with marvellous intelligence and vigour, solved every problem that came their way.

In the Belvedere Gardens he would wander among the fountains admiring the statues or sit on the stairs leading to the Temple of Theseus, chewing a pencil as he racked his brain trying to write the story of his life. And even if the results of his labours were not exactly overwhelming, it was hardly surprising that he too, surrounded as he was by so much classical elegance and man-made beauty, felt called upon to join in the general chorus of creative endeavour.

On Christmas morning at No. 12 Westlake Crescent Mrs. Bingley was in the process of preparing for the annual tenants' get-together. In this monumental task she was assisted most ably by her husband, Mr. Bingley, and by her Australian niece, a young woman answering to the name of Audrey and currently on a visit to the old country with her two little girls, Pamela und June, nine and eleven years of age respectively, who had been firmly sat down in a corner with a picture book to keep them out of mischief.

Mrs. Bingley was arranging the 'spread' – various *petit-fours*, sausage rolls, assorted nuts and tiny pretzels, to mention but a few of the delicacies on offer.

Audrey, whose artistic flair was proverbial among the Bingleys of two continents and who had already decorated the Christmas tree, was performing miracles with twigs of pine and sprigs of holly and mistletoe, while Mr. Bingley, his thinning, grey hair neatly brushed and parted, his toothbrush moustache daintily trimmed and generally neat if mousy, was polishing the wine glasses under Mrs. Bingley's ever watchful eye.

'What do you think, Mavis?', asked Mr. Bingley, addressing his better half. 'I should think they are all right now.'

'Well, if you are quite sure, leave them now and give Audrey a hand with the decorations. And when you have finished, get out the crystal and the Crown Derby for when they have gone again.' Having thus programmed her husband, who without her guidance and instructions would not have known what to do, Mrs. Bingley went to have a look at the turkey, a large, once matronly bird, now – as befitted the season – sizzling away peacefully in the oven and giving off a right royal fragrance, much appreciated by one and all.

Her festive lunch well in hand, Mrs. Bingley busied herself at the cocktail cabinet, carefully moving her 'specials' to the rear, where they would be less obtrusive. The door of the cocktail cabinet being open, the inside was illuminated, discreet sea-green light bringing out the mysterious quality of the bottles.

'At home in St. Kilda it would be mainly Foster's,' ventured Audrey. 'That's what they would expect, especially the men.'

'Well, they can have beer if they want it. Arthur's got more than ample from the off-licence.'

'I reckon it's mainly sherry they drink here at parties and such like.' Audrey had a philosophical turn of mind, and the differences between St. Kilda, that very pleasant suburb of Melbourne, where she and her husband, a prosperous builder, had made their home, and the odd places where other people chose to live were to her a source of incessant wonder.

'Sherry is what they mostly take, but some do prefer beer,' said Mrs. Bingley, who had far too much to do to allow herself to be drawn into an argument.

'You can't beat Watney's pale, that you can't,' commented Mr. Bingley, who in the true spirit of Christmas had had one or two already and felt an uncharacteristic urge to add a male point of view to the conversation. Mrs. Bingley, however, far too experienced in the ways of marriage, especially her own, to allow her hubby even this poor vestige of independent opinion, reminded him sharply that there was no time to chat, that their guests would be arriving shortly and would he kindly concentrate on what he was supposed to be doing.

At this point Pamela said something to June which made the latter roll about with shrieks of laughter on the carpet, whereupon they were promptly told off by their mother, who promised to speak to them later – a prospect sufficiently unattractive to reduce their excessively high spirits to a more acceptable state of simmering hilarity, turning them again, however briefly, into 'good little girls' not requiring any special attention. Their great auntie, while fully appreciating that a firm hand might well be needed as far as those two were concerned, gave each of them a glass of pink Tizer to show that there were no hard feelings. Knowing better than to tempt fate again, they thanked her politely.

The first to arrive were Silversmith and M, both in their Sunday best as befitted the occasion. Mrs. Bingley introduced them to her niece, who was most interested to hear that M had been to Melbourne during his seafaring days and had even met a ship's fitter whose home was also in St. Kilda. Silversmith, afraid of being dislodged from the centre of the stage which he regarded as his natural territory, invented, on the spur of the moment and remembering perhaps the popular ballad of *My brother Silvest*, who, it would appear, had forty medals on his chest, big chest, and so on and so forth, a Great Great Uncle Bob, who had gone to Australia when he was still a young man in order to make his fortune, and – at the end of his days a millionaire and the major shareholder of a well-known beer-brewing concern – had died in his sleep at the ripe old age of 100 years exactly. They found him (so Silversmith explained) with his enormously wide chest bedecked with all his medals from the Crimean war, where thanks to his unparalleled bravery and incredible talent for leadership he had risen to the rank of a colonel of infantry. Still clutched in his powerful fist was a telegraphic note of congratulation from Her Majesty Queen Victoria, who knew him personally and valued his friendship and advice.

During this recital, which elicited many an 'ah' and 'oh' from the ladies and gave Mr. Bingley a chance to pour himself another Watney's pale, M found himself on the flowery carpet with the girls, telling them an improvised story about the funny adventures of an elephant named Vindaloo, a certain panther Featherbone and Mildred, a mouse, the climax of the story being a truly wonderful party at which the three of them, but especially Mildred, disgraced themselves utterly, in various side-splittingly funny ways. The girls were delighted and, finding that M was rather a push-over – and that neither their mother nor their great aunt was paying any attention to them – progressed from much giggling and charming disrespect to such enjoyable pursuits as giving him an entirely new hairdo, pulling his nose and climbing all over him. They were having a quite marvellous time until Mrs. Bingley, who was the first to surface again, decided that enough was enough and told them that they were bothering Mr. M, so would they stop it immediately. To everyone's surprise but much to M's regret, since he could not but suspect that the reproof was really meant for him rather than his playful tormentors, they chose on this occasion to do as they were told.

The next to arrive were Mr. and Mrs. Bradley from the top floor, he a scoutmaster and she a florist's assistant. They were a shy couple only rarely seen in daylight but much given to press-ups and other fitness-promoting exercises at night, when various bumping noises became clearly audible in the room below, which happened to be Silversmith's room. Their significance being naturally interpreted in the most conventional way, these noises never failed to give rise to much optimistic speculation and considerable hilarity.

Mrs. Bingley, firmly convinced by now that M ought to be separated from the girls forthwith, took him over to the Bradleys, disingenuously suggesting that they were sure to have many interests in common. M did what he could to make them talk by asking them in his best TTTW manner lots of questions about modern scouting, and also told them about his own experiences as a Young Falcon or some such thing in Vienna and how his membership had come to a speedy and abrupt end when on his very first excursion he managed to stumble over a rock and break his wrist. He held out one of his wrists for their inspection (not necessarily the damaged one, as he could no longer remember which one it was), as if this somehow proved the veracity of his account. Mr. Bradley, not one of the most stimulating conversationalists, tended to confine himself to rudimentary replies, and neither did his wife, a tall and thin person with many protruding teeth, who insisted on holding his hand throughout the proceedings while gazing at him in wrapt admiration, contribute much to this exchange of thoughts. She came alive only when M managed to swing the conversation to floral displays, at which point she took over and could not thereafter be stopped or even side-tracked. It turned out that she considered herself rather an expert on the making of wreaths for funerals and similarly lugubrious events. The Bradleys were also keen on ballroom dancing, another interest which they and M certainly did not have in common.

The last of the guests was Jim, the friendly young policeman who lived on the ground floor. Rumour had it that he was an expert in various oriental martial arts, and as a result he was held in great esteem by both M and Silversmith. M, who was keen to impress the master with his knowledge and prowess where matters of unarmed combat were concerned, and who had by that time enjoyed two sherries already, lay down on the carpet, raising one bent leg while keeping the other straight in order to demonstrate and explain a complicated but potentially deadly judo routine. Jim, for whose benefit this exhibition was mainly intended, made no comment, limiting himself to an enigmatic smile which gave nothing away, but when Silversmith, who had also had more liquid refreshment than was good for him, blotted his so far spotless record by suggesting that in this position M reminded him above all of a dog which had fallen over in the very act of obeying a call of nature, the girls, no longer able to restrain themselves, burst into shrieks of unbridled laughter, while Mr. and Mrs. Bradley looked in dire need of a really secure hiding-hole. Audrey raised and wiggled a threatening finger at her unruly daughters, again warning them of her intention to speak to them later. By this means she actually managed to subdue them for a few seconds but no longer.

In order to prevent the situation from getting even more out of hand, Mrs. Bingley, who was viewing the proceedings with considerable consternation, instructed her husband to put on the record of *The Twelve Days of Christmas*. Mr. Bingley tried – indeed he tried very hard – but Watney's pale, not to mention a succession of other intakes, had incapacitated him severely – a fact which eventually compelled Mrs. Bingley herself to take over. Events had definitely taken a downward turn, but there was nothing she or anyone else could do about it. The *Twelve Days* were followed by various other well-loved carols and eventually, ably accompanied by a woefully wailing Mr. Bingley, a solo rendering of *Good King Wenceslas* by Jim, which gave the latter an opportunity to prove that he was not merely a useful man in a fight and a pretty face but also a most accomplished singer of Christmas carols. Then M sang, in a variety of different keys, *O Tannenbaum*, which proved to be a comic event rather than the heart-warming experience it should have been. Once this phase of the proceedings was over and a modicum of proper decorum had been restored, Mrs. Bingley, determined to put a stop to all this nonsense forthwith, thanked everyone for coming, to which the others responded with 'Not at all' and other most suitable expressions of appreciation. 'Goodness me,' exclaimed Mrs. Bingley, 'Is that the time?' and rushed out into the kitchen, where Audrey was already doing useful things to the succulent, fragrant bird which was to be the crowning glory of the Bingleys' Christmas dinner.

Mrs. Bingley's guests, realising that their welcome was now definitely at an end, got up – albeit with considerable reluctance, for their noses told them that the best was yet to come – and having thanked their hosts for a truly wonderful time, departed.

CHAPTER FOURTEEN

IT STILL felt bitterly cold, although the roads were no longer frozen over and the snow – now in dirty brown and dismal heaps – was in the process of melting, when Lipkin, of whom nothing had been heard or seen for several weeks, presented himself at No. 12, with his arm in a sling and looking generally bedraggled and out of sorts. His tale was both shocking and ludicrous. While walking along Queensway during the recent season of good will towards all men, minding his own business and deep in thought, he had been hit – suddenly and without the slightest provocation – by a flying egg. The latter had landed squarely and with an unpleasant splosh on that part of his overcoat which covered his chest, broken, and having broken, discharged much of its gooey substance downward, over his trouser-legs and, further, onto his shoes. This unexpected, startling occurrence had deprived him, if only for the vital fraction of a second, of the concentration necessary in order to remain upright on the icy road, causing him to slip, fall and upon impact fracture the wrist of his right hand and dislocate his shoulder. Try as he would, he had been quite unable to get up by his own efforts and might well still be trying to do so, had not a couple of kindly elderly folk come to his assistance. The rest was NHS history.

While listening, not without some show of earnest attention, to Lipkin's tale of woe, both M and Silversmith were picking away at the skeletal remains of a tough old bird prepared for them by Mrs. Bingley herself, in order to remove and devour the last remaining morsels of accessible meat – an undertaking in which they were presently joined by Lipkin, whose inability to make use of one of his hands did not appear to hamper his progress in any way.

They balanced this diet with some jam tarts left over from a former meal, had some tea, and then went into the fascinating question of *mens rea*. Silversmith, who prided himself on having a powerful, even brilliant, legal mind, was quick to point out that the facts of the case – an egg, by all accounts fresh and of good quality, coming from nowhere and hitting Lipkin with such regrettable consequences – did not *per se* warrant any assumption of guilty intent. Objects in motion for whatever reason had, after all, to go somewhere, and occurrences such as the one under discussion were, therefore, inevitable. He himself had on one occasion almost been hit by just such an object in flight, a sweaty sock hurled in his general direction by a former landlady – not, of course, anyone in the least like Mrs. Bingley, who would as they must surely agree never stoop so low – but aimed in fact at his room-mate as the presumed owner of the offending sock in question, so *mens rea* did not, on the face of it, come into it. Still, if that wretched object had made contact with his, that is to say Silversmith's, person and if this had been an actionable case, which to the best of his knowledge it would not have been unless actual physical, psychological or other, for instance financial, harm could have been shown to have ensued, the fact that Mrs. X (her name was neither here nor there and he would rather not mention it) had not intended him, Silversmith, to be the target would, of course, not have helped her much in a court of law, for, as everybody knew and as he himself had on many an occasion pointed out, *ex turpi causa non oritur actio*, which might be rendered freely as 'Even the most skilful lawyer cannot make a silk purse from a sow's ear.' M, who, in spite of the merest doubt about the aptness of the *turpi causa* bit, could not but agree wholeheartedly with his friend's brilliant analysis, confined himself to quoting from a story as yet unwritten but very much in the planning stage, where in the course of a marital argument a baby is hurled through a window, hitting or nearly hitting – he had not as yet decided which – the hero, a man of but few talents and accomplishments, who is involved in an epic and eventually tragic conflict with a dog of the neighbourhood.

The burning problem of *mens rea* thus clearly disposed of, they considered the role (if any) of the law in cases such as this and, more generally, whether a highly specific network of prohibitions, decrees, byelaws, directives and full-blown acts of parliament were more or less likely to be ineffective than a few all-embracing laws, seeing that the former might reasonably be defined as a very large number of loopholes held together and bounded by a kind of abstract regulatory string, whereas the latter usually required much interpretation, thus lending themselves wonderfully well to every kind of misinterpretation – not unlike the biblical commandments, which were, after all, better known for being ignored or used as moral sledge-hammers than for being observed as guides to righteous living.

Other aspects of the case also came under scrutiny, such as the estimated size of the egg and the force of its impact, the possible and probable intentions of the thrower (if indeed it was thrown and not merely dropped, for example, by a passing magpie or eagle), and whether or not certain people were more prone to being hit by flying eggs than others, conjuring up and thereby, in a manner of speaking, devising their own particular misfortunes. This brought them (as so often before) to Bishop Berkeley, Descartes's *Cogito, ergo sum* and to Hume's theory of solipsism. And, quite naturally, all this heady talk reminded M of his glorious days at Cambridge, where shortly before the outbreak of the war he had spent two or three happy months as the guest of some students reading Mathematics at St. John's College. Not, as it happened, because at Cambridge he personally had met either with much thought that was highly original or with great intellectual effervescence, but rather because he had always expected this to be the case, wished it to be the case and – dazzled by the sheer medieval grandeur of the place – still could not imagine it not to have been the case after all.

Initially – at any rate while he was partaking of food and drink, Lipkin had been listening in a reasonably attentive manner to the sparkling display of verbal peacockery which had been triggered by his misadventure. But once, as was bound to be the case, he had reached the conclusion that none of it made any sense whatsoever, he produced a pocket chess set from his overcoat (formerly a plain grey garment but now well matured to a more interesting, more variegated colour) and for the rest of his stay devoted himself to finding the solution to some particularly intractable problem. In debate, Lipkin, tongue-tied and chronically in a state of conversational ineptitude, might be no match for Silversmith or, for that matter, M, but no-one could deny that he was very good at chess, much better in fact than either of them – in spite of the fact that, in the absence of proof to the contrary, each considered himself a potential world champion.

While Lipkin was struggling, as yet unsuccessfully, with this approach and that, and Silversmith was sitting there with a fixed grin on his face – a grin half absent-minded and half approving, such as a busy uncle, who really had much better things to do, might exhibit while listening to his nephew reciting some familiar, seemingly endless poem – M worked himself into a fine lather of sentimental recollection as he told them, not by any means for the first time, about his, alas, all-too-brief stay at that fount of wisdom – the University of Cambridge.

It all started with a note on the public notice-board at the premises of the Czech Refugee Trust Fund, where together with many others in the same situation M attended once every week in order to collect his subsistence grant – a note requesting the services of a mathematician with a sound knowledge of German and English, capable of translating a book on the history of mathematics in the 19th century. Having not the slightest doubt about his suitability, M applied forthwith and was duly selected for this task after only the most perfunctory of interviews. However, when it came to the crunch, both his mathematics and his translating ability proved woefully inadequate – a fact soon realised by his hosts, who were, however, sufficiently good-natured and sufficiently well-heeled to continue with their support – more or less regular payments based on collections enabling M to buy food and whatever else he required. They had also arranged for him to live at the 'Blue Gate', a private house inhabited by several people – all men except for a black-haired beauty with long and slender legs, at all points most appealingly formed, who would often wander about in a state of advanced undress and, having washed, in the communal kitchen, various articles of most provocative clothing, would hang them up for drying. Unfortunately, at any rate from M's point of view, she happened to be the live-in girlfriend of a fellow 'Blue Gatonian' and was, accordingly, strictly out-of-bounds, which did not, of course, prevent her from playing havoc with his fevered imagination and immodest cravings.

Once his utter uselessness as a translator had been realised, no work whatsoever was expected of M, who, at the fringes of student life but free from any of its usual burdens, was in a position to make this a truly wonderful summer – his last before the outbreak of the war. He went to what seemed to be innumerable parties, took part in hitch-hiking expeditions and spent much time at the College library delving into this book and that, half convinced that he was a 'real' student and not merely a kind of camp-follower. He made friends and, since most of the people he met regarded themselves as socialists, pretended to be a red-hot firebrand of a Marxist, which – with the civil war in Spain still fresh in everyone's memory – met with considerable approval, although he could not entirely avoid problematic, even highly embarrassing situations. On one occasion, for instance, when at a party he was invited to sing *Vienna is red* or some such song in German, he found himself in some difficulty, for he had never even heard of that song, and improvising a credible alternative while his ears were aglow with understandable distress proved to be almost more than he could manage. His audience, however, let him get away with it, or so at least it appeared, but he was never quite certain whether he had really managed to pull the wool over their eyes or whether they had seen right through him and were simply having a sophisticated good time at his expense.

M in turn learned certain songs, his favourite being *I am the man, the very fat man that waters the workers' beer*, and when, in his best beer-barrel voice, he bellowed 'And what do I care if it makes them ill, if it makes them terribly queer' he sounded as if he really couldn't care less and indeed positively delighted in those poor men's misfortunes. Many years later, long after he had lost all his teeth and become as bald as an egg, he used to sing this song – together with several others popular during the First World War and taught to him by Professor Bergenau at the Klappenhorn – to Timothy, his little grandson, in order to pacify the little lad – a stratagem which hardly ever failed. In actual fact, M never did have much truck with the beer-watering variety of 'very fat man' and should perhaps, for that reason if no other, be forgiven his patent insensitivity.

Songs, of course, were not by any means all he learned during his stay at Cambridge. For instance, he also managed to improve his command of the English language – particularly the spoken variety – to a most gratifying extent. This was due largely to the efforts of his good friend Beaverman, who – in return for an excellently designed if largely fictitious list of German words and phrases not generally to be found in dictionaries – supplied him with a similar English compendium. Alas, when put to the test, Beaverman's list, though indubitably of great practical and theoretical interest, also proved to be less reliable than might have been wished or expected. This was brought home to M with great clarity after a fact-finding expedition to one of the less favoured counties of England, where some of his friends hoped to study the state and customs of the working masses at first hand.

Getting to their destination by the time-honoured method of hitch-hiking had not been a problem, but their return journey proved to be rather more difficult. Indeed, to judge by the way in which such cars as happened to come along – fewer and fewer as the afternoon faded into evening – sped past without so much as a tiny hoot to acknowledge their existence, they had good reason to fear that they might have to trudge every last dreary mile back to Cambridge, which they had left in such high spirits only a few hours previously. As tempers were on the point of becoming frayed, M, not under such pressure as his companions, for unlike them he was not subject to any curfew, tried out – with a view to light relief and in order to cheer them up – one of the more vivid exclamations specially recommended by Beaverman for use among students in a state of advanced misery. The effect was, to put it mildly, stunning. Indeed, the general reaction of his fellows was even less encouraging than on that famous occasion when, having been introduced to a young lady unprepossessing in more ways than one, M, attempting for the sake of politeness to pay her a compliment, had come out with 'You strike me as a highly pregnant young lady'. This *faux pas* was quite understandable, for in the vernacular of his native city 'pregnant' meant 'highly impressive'. However, to make matters still worse, he had recalled, as soon as this word was spoken, the conventional English meaning of 'pregnant' and nearly collapsed laughing.

In due course, as a result perhaps of this and certain other events, as well as of the erosive action of time itself, M's welcome started to wear rather thin. He did not receive as many invitations as before, and the donations so essential to his continued well-being were beginning to show signs of petering out. With nothing but London and the Czech Refugee Trust Fund to look forward to, and feeling increasingly unloved, unnoticed and irrelevant, he decided on a last grand gesture – a *lecsó* party to which all his friends and benefactors would be invited. What he had in mind was a luncheon party at which only one dish would be served, namely, *lecsó*, a simple concoction of eggs, tomatoes and Hungarian paprika, which, apart from semolina pudding, was the only dish he knew how to prepare. In order to add interest to his invitation, he let it be known that *lecsó* was a dish greatly prized not only in Hungary, where it originated, but also in Czechoslovakia, the country whose passport he had the honour of bearing. He also made it plain that in organising and staging this important occasion he would welcome help of any kind that might be on offer. In the event, his affluent friend Wolmer promised to help with the shopping and eventually did all of it and paid for it too, while Wanda, Polish and therefore specially qualified, declared herself ready and willing to do all the cooking, which was just as well seeing that *haute cuisine* was not one of M's stronger points. Most of the guests, expecting to receive no food at all or, at best, pretty spicy food requiring a tough palate and a cast-iron digestion, brought tins of this and that, cakes and bottled beverages of various descriptions. Some of this fare was in fact consumed but most of it wandered into the capacious larder, for later use. The party itself – and in particular the *lecsó*, which Wanda prepared and dished out in great dollops – proved to be a great success and led to quite a number of return invitations. Besides, many felt, albeit mistakenly, that this event must have cost M a pretty penny and – if only for a week or two – again shelled out their shillings and pence, which were also most welcome.

However, nothing lasts for ever, and all good (and, for that matter, bad) things are bound to come to an end sooner or later. Although he did manage to hang on for another two or three weeks, he eventually had no alternative but to return to London and more normal arrangements.

CHAPTER FIFTEEN

I HAVE always thought of the year between our departure from Vienna and my escape to Poland as one of the best years of my life. This was, after all, the year in which I managed – or so it seemed to me – to shake off the chains of childhood and family while gaining a large and, on the whole, highly satisfying measure of independence. Indeed, it is more than likely that if I had remained in Vienna and quite simply continued along the road on which I happened to find myself, I would eventually have wound up as just another *Herr Professor*. I would have had a steady salary to be sure, but never would have been able to afford anything much. Confined within a narrow circle of mainly cultural preoccupations, with little to look back upon and nothing much to look forward to, I would have been convinced that I knew all the answers to everything that mattered without in fact knowing anything of the slightest real importance – in short, I would have been a rather boring, irrelevant man hiding his ineptitude behind a threadbare façade of wisdom and authority, but fooling no-one, least of all my unfortunate students.

It could, of course, be argued that instead of a *Herr Professor* – in a manner of speaking, therefore, a minor pillar of society, but a pillar nonetheless – I am now merely, as Dr. McGill keeps pointing out, a would-be funny-man in the service of a pseudo-educational establishment, not very well paid and with very dubious credentials. But this would be missing the point, for the very variety of my experiences has given me an insight into life – Dr. McGill would say a worm's-eye view – such as *Herr Professor* Maskenbusch could never have hoped to achieve, and it is precisely that insight which makes even the most mundane happenings in my life much more interesting and meaningful to me than they would otherwise be. By contrasting Faust, that wide-ranging and powerful spirit, with his attendant Wagner, as narrow-minded an intellectual nobody as ever there was, Goethe, I think, was trying to make a similar point. And when Pushkin referred to the intelligentsia of his native land as 'rabble', he was simply expressing his contempt for barren, impotent intellectuality, such as might well have been my lot if I had followed the course initially charted for me.

Although some of our *Herren Professoren* were pretentious second-raters, there were others to whom I shall always be grateful. Take for instance Professor Nagel, who tried, alas without much success but none the less valiantly, to teach us the elements of classical Hebrew and who persuaded my father, when the latter was much tempted to have me transferred to a craft college, to leave me at the Klappenhorn after all, thus preventing a sudden, premature break in my academic education, in spite of the fact that at the time my father really could no longer afford my school fees (as a Czechoslovak citizen I was not entitled to full exemption) and there were ample practical reasons for such a move. Then there was Dr. Bergenau, who, accompanying himself on the guitar, taught us songs from World War I and whose lessons were in general so lively and interesting that most of us actually enjoyed learning English. Kindly Dr. Hirsch taught us all about *Gallia est divisa in partes tres* and made us realise that ancient history and ancient languages were very much part of our present and even of our future, and not, as generally assumed, dead and useless. Last but not by any means least, there was Professor Schmitz, who did his best to teach us German. Endowed with a great, if somewhat peculiar, sense of humour, he always came to school on a motorbike, wearing slippers and carrying on his back a tattered rucksack in which he kept his books and, as rumour had it, his sandwiches and beer. There was, of course, no direct evidence for this, but to judge by certain stains that regularly disfigured compositions returned by him to their proud (or not so proud) owners, it seemed very likely. I can still hear him bellowing '*Kritik bitte*' to wake us up and restore our thought-processes, such as they were, when, after a particularly boring discourse by a fellow student (these discourses, a compulsory weekly feature of our curriculum, were, it would seem, intended to turn each and every one of us into a latter-day Cicero), we had sought refuge in a state of stupor or were daydreaming about whatever subject we happened to be interested in at the time – in my own case, girls and especially blonde and lovely Gretl Navratil, who had captured my heart but in the event proved herself to be rather fickle.

No longer able to make a living in Austria and in obvious danger from the new régime, my father – still the holder of a valid Czechoslovak passport, although he had quite lost contact with the country which he had left so many years ago in his quest for 'the good life' and could no longer speak its language – needed hardly any encouragement to leave Vienna in order to seek refuge for himself and his family in Moravská Ostrava, which by train was only an hour or so from Klimkovice, the village where he was born and where I spent a large chunk of my early childhood.

Moravská Ostrava, with its busy streets, well-appointed shops and numerous cafés, seemed to me, at any rate, far more attractive than Vienna and every bit as interesting. And, of course, also the fact that quite a number of our relatives and friends lived there did much to make us feel at home. Although not by choice, I saw quite a lot of my hen-pecked Uncle Emil, a photographer by profession and a true artist at heart, whom I remember chiefly for his magnificent, ticklish moustache and for the elegantly drawn design with which he embellished my very first pencil-box, and Aunt Gusti, his unbelievably vulgar, horribly loud-mouthed wife, who owned a shop selling cosmetics, little mirrors, turtle-shell combs and other 'fancy goods' in one of the arcades near the railway station. She, like my stepmother, came from Poland and was said to have been a great, haunting beauty in her youth, much desired and pursued by every red-blooded young stallion in the village but eventually carried off – an odd phrase this in the circumstances – by poor, not at all red-blooded Uncle Emil. I sometimes visited their son Eduard, who was pale, kind and a good listener. He played the violin most beautifully, and although, generally speaking, music bores me since I love clarity above all things and am too impatient a person to waste time on what I cannot clearly understand, I did enjoy listening to him. I have been told that he eventually became a *Kapellmeister* in the Russian army, so he must have been quite a genius.

Another person I remember fondly was Mrs. Blumenfeld, whose cooking and hospitality (in my mind the two are inextricably linked) were simply phenomenal. My mouth still waters when I think of her goulash and her plum dumplings topped with fried breadcrumbs and hot molten butter. Her tall, vivacious, dark-haired daughter Helli, who was one or two years older than I, must have inherited some of her mother's generous nature, for it was she who, when I was only a little boy, initiated me into the early wonders of carnal enjoyment. Mrs. Blumenfeld's son, Leo, on the other hand, although forever in and out of prison for fraud, was greatly respected by one and all for his profound understanding of all matters financial and for the soundness of his advice.

In Moravská Ostrava my father, whose financial resources were then – even by his usual modest standards – at a particularly low ebb, but who – ever the optimist – was still firmly convinced that one day soon his luck would change for the better and that such hardships as could not be avoided were bound to be purely temporary, managed to rent an 'apartment' barely large enough for two people but quite definitely not for three, and it was accordingly decided that I should, for the time being and in certain expectation of better days, go to stay at Klimkovice. Fortunately, two old schoolfriends of my father – Dr. Semmler, the district judge, and Herr Hager, the timber merchant – agreed to look after me, at any rate during the summer months, after which other arrangements would, no doubt, have to be made.

Both my grandparents had died long ago – grandmother, they said, of a broken heart only six months after her beloved husband. As for Aunt Sali, she was dying slowly of a wasting illness at a municipal hospital in Moravská Ostrava. (The last time I saw her she was already too weak to talk to me but, brave and selfless to the end, still managed – and this was the saddest thing of all – to smile at me as if to welcome me and put me at my ease.) I could not, therefore, stay at my grandfather's house, in which nobody had lived now for a long time and which – much smaller than I remembered it – stood sadly dispirited and with its doors and shutters securely bolted and barred, a mere shadow of its proud and hospitable former self. I stayed instead at Dr. Semmler's house but took my meals with Herr Hager's multi-headed family and, more importantly, Susi, my dearly beloved of that summer.

Dr. Semmler's house, where I was installed in my host's study, was a stately, elegantly furnished villa with a large rose garden at the rear, situated at the very end of the village. From my window I could see far into the distance – past the pond with its velvet-headed, brown bullrushes and its splendid choirs of frogs, in which as a child I used to wade together with the other children, sharing its cool, muddy water with various domestic animals, to the green and yellow fields beyond, where I used to 'help' with the hay harvest. On a clear day I could see even the edge of the dark forest, which, rumour had it, stretched all the way to Bohemia and was so deep and mysterious and unfathomable that a wanderer inadvertently or misguidedly straying from its sun-drenched outskirts might easily lose his way and never again meet anybody except perhaps Hänsel and Gretl, Little Red Ridinghood and her wolf or, possibly, a witch or two. But in the most unlikely case that he did find his way out of the forest, he would be changed beyond all recognition, and we all knew well enough what that meant.

Dr. Semmler, an inveterate bachelor of porcine appearance but kindly disposition and with a mind as keen as any razor, was hardly ever at home, since in his official capacity he had to travel a lot. However, an elderly and, in the main, invisible housekeeper took care of the place and, incidentally, saw to it that my bedding (I slept on the sofa) was always fresh and well aired, and the study clean and tidy. I cannot remember many places in which I felt so totally content, so entirely at one with my surroundings. To a large extent this was undoubtedly due to the fine mahogany furniture, the dark wood panelling and a general air of restrained luxury, but what attracted me more than anything was the large and select collection of books, ranging as it did from a *History of the Popes* to *Anna Karenina*, from *The Psychology of Murder* (with a wealth of gory illustrations) to *Boccaccio*, and from *Mathematics for the Million* to *A History of Western Philosophy*. A fast and voracious, although not very discriminating reader, I ploughed my way through this work and that, unsystematically and incompletely but with very great enjoyment.

Much of the time I also spent longing for Susi – dark-haired, impish, lovely Susi from Prague – who slept at Herr Hager's house and was, as I had every reason to believe, extremely generous to her cousin Emil, Mr. Hager's eldest son, a boorish fellow, whom for the life of me I could not stand. Me she unfortunately regarded merely as a friend. On one occasion, when she came up to my room in order to see, as she put it, what I was up to, I feverishly tried various gambits, gleaned from some such work as *Seduction in the Middle Ages*, in order to gain her co-operation. I even showed her one of the more aptly illustrated works hoping that it would plead my cause, but, alas, to no avail. She was not at all interested, and since I did not have the slightest inkling what to do about it, she went away. Next day, however, when we were all having lunch in Mr. Hager's kitchen, she told all and sundry, as a kind of marvellous joke – and that indeed was how it was taken – about what I had asked her to do, which I denied hotly. Nobody, of course, believed me for a second, but when, at our next meal, I came up with quotations from one of Dr. Semmler's learned books in order to prove that Susi was the liar and not I, kindly, down-to-earth Mrs. Hager looked distinctly worried, wondering perhaps whether I was quite normal and why I should go to so much trouble merely to prove a point.

This was nearly the end of what had been a grand summer, and it was a pity that it was ending on such a sour note. Not by any means the only one, as it happened, for various events were beginning to point to the impending annexation of the Sudetenland and the end of the Czechoslovak Republic. My former headmaster, for instance, seemed to have forgotten or was trying hard to forget his friendship with our family and made a point of ignoring my very existence whenever our paths crossed (which in a small village such as Klimkovice was bound to be the case frequently), obviously in order to avoid any suspicion of hob-nobbing with Jews. Heini, his son, not such a bad fellow, with whom I used to share a school desk, on the other hand, did talk to me, if only to inform me that whereas some Jews were perhaps not as noxious as it was natural for them to be and might even, if they worked hard and did their best to repair such harm as emanated from their detestable race, enjoy a measure of protection, the vast majority deserved to be burned alive and would in due course be dealt with in a manner not to be forgotten. 'It is all quite logical,' Heini explained, basing himself on such sound tenets of political philosophy as were, for instance, enshrined regularly in the *Stürmer*, 'No good saying a Jew cannot help being a Jew. After all, a rat cannot help being a rat, and even you would kill a rat, now wouldn't you?' All this was, of course, meant kindly and intended to reassure me, but somehow I couldn't quite see it that way.

It was a truly marvellous summer, nevertheless. I visited all my favourite haunts such as the hill with the old chapel and the small cemetery – both of them long out of use but still very popular with all the children, who loved to climb about on the low wall, jump over the graves, and, when they had had enough, sit in the tall grass under the shady linden trees. Long walks along endless roads took me through avenues of apple and cherry trees, where I would eat my fill without anyone caring, and I spent many an hour lying in tall meadow grass watching bees and butterflies as they went about their mysterious summer business, enjoying the glorious sunshine and listening to the birds in the cloudless, blue sky. I talked with the old folk, who marvelled at the way in which Mori – but yesterday, it seemed, a small boy with big eyes, clever too, you could tell – had grown so tall and handsome and commiserated with me about the passing of the Maskenbusches. Most of my former friends, though, had gone, and as for those still around, they had become strangers. Even talking to Milan, formerly my best friend and guiding spirit, had become a strain, and we were both greatly relieved when it was time for him to return to Prague, where he was a student of engineering at the University.

At the end of that summer, I returned to Moravská Ostrava, where my father had rented a sofa for me in the bedroom of a very old lady, who never said a word but used to tie up her jaws before going to bed, in order, perhaps, to prevent them from dropping open and becoming dislocated during the night. Listening to her stertorous breathing whenever I happened to be awake and before drifting off into more pleasant thoughts, I used to wonder whether she would still be alive in the morning, which thankfully she always was.

According to Miss Pratt – I suppose I really ought to call her 'Emily' as she continues to ask me to do so, although 'Praying Mantis' would be more appropriate, but God only knows what she might make of that – clay has the mysterious ability of 'remembering' former states and reverting to them. For instance, she tells me that if she were to bend a corner of a slab of wet clay of absolutely even thickness and consistency and then smooth it down until it was again quite flat, it would, in the course of drying and firing, warp to a shape reminiscent of its earlier deformed state.

I find this really interesting, for if even an object as basic as a slab of clay is governed by its past, how can there possibly be such a thing as 'free' will? To illustrate my point: if it were conscious and capable of reacting in much the same way as a human being or animal, a mountain stream displacing as it flows downhill a large obstacle such as a fallen tree would, no doubt, believe that it had prevailed by dint of superior will-power. If, on the other hand, the tree formed a barrier entirely blocking the flow of water and eventually forcing it to follow a different path, our sentient stream would initially feel frustrated, but once it had circumvented the obstacle, it would feel that it had acted in a very cunning or intelligent manner. However, since its behaviour (as indeed that of the tree) would in fact be determined entirely by the interplay of physical factors such as the mass and velocity of the water and the resistance and shape of the tree, any notion that it was free to act as it pleased, that it was in some mysterious way exempt from the laws of cause and effect, would clearly be illusory.

But – some might argue – a stream is not a person nor even an animal, so there is no point in assuming that it may have feelings, and as for it actually being capable of emotional reactions to external events, that is simply ludicrous. I am not so sure, not by any means. What, after all, could be more wrong than to assume that anything with which we cannot communicate must also be inanimate and, therefore, incapable of feelings, thoughts or other manifestations of conscious life? This, after all, is the very fallacy which is at the root of so much prejudice against strangers, ethnic jokes and the widespread idea that anyone whose mother tongue is not one's own is bound to be stupid, uncultured and uncivilised. It also, for that matter, explains the fact that since time immemorial 'sportsmen' have found it convenient to believe that foxes are so perverse as actually to enjoy being hunted or that fish do not mind having their jaws impaled upon hooks because 'they cannot feel pain'. Surely, if I, Morus Maskenbusch, cannot understand another person because I do not speak his language, this only proves an inadequacy on my part but not necessarily on his, for until we have exchanged ideas I cannot possibly judge his intellectual and cultural attributes.

As I recall, the noise in the engine-room of the *Bergano* used to be quite deafening. Initially, at least, when I was still quite inexperienced as a greaser and before I had learned to differentiate between the various parts of the engine, I could not deduce anything whatsoever from this noise nor could I discover the slightest sense in it. Not so the engineer with whom I shared the watch. He was alive to every change in sound pattern and would draw appropriate conclusions from what he heard. If he said, for instance, 'This pump is knocking again, I think the bearings are worn, I shall have to have a look', you could bet your bottom dollar that the bearings were indeed worn and had to be relined or replaced. After all, the pump was, in its own way, telling the engineer, 'I am highly uncomfortable, there is something wrong with me, see what you can do'. So, who is to say that apparently inanimate objects are not, in fact, alive after all and capable of feelings as well as their own brand of speech and even thought. Nor can it convincingly be argued that what is man-made cannot be alive. After all, any process of 'becoming' is in its essence no more than a transformation, by whatever means, of what already exists, and this, of course, is bound to be true also of human beings.

God only knows to what extent, albeit without the slightest malicious intent, I personally contributed to problems which might have become critical but for my watch-mate, the third engineer. Formerly a heavyweight boxer in the Norwegian navy, he was a very easy-going, good-natured man and quite content to leave me to my own devices while he sat on an empty barrel under one of the ventilation shafts, reading comics or novels (quite a few of which he used to borrow from me) about 'love', preferably of a mildly pornographic kind. It seemed to me that he (lucky fellow!) had nothing whatsoever to do, except, of course, in the event of a problem, of which, mercifully, there were not many. As for me, this suited me fine, for it meant that apart from my routine, which occupied exactly eight minutes of my time every quarter of an hour, I was free to do as I pleased – in fact to sit under another ventilation shaft, the one next to the ship's telegraph, also enjoying a good read.

Like most ships of the Norwegian merchant navy, the *Bergano* had a well-stocked library, of which I managed to take full – according to some even excessive – advantage. However, for me to be able to get around the engine in what amounted to a record time, it was, of course, essential to refine every technique, every movement even, to the point of ultimate efficiency, and I spared no effort to this end. One such refinement consisted in hitting the oil nipples (the inlets of copper tubes conveying oil to bearings and other parts in need of lubrication) with a squirt of oil from my can, rather than inserting the pointed, elongated spout of the can into every nipple, which was the conventional method practised by less accomplished greasers.

I might quite happily have carried on like this for ever and a day, had not on one occasion a squirt of oil impinged upon the egg-bald head of the engineer when he happened to be standing almost directly below me. As he looked up to see what was the matter he received yet another squirt, this time in his upturned face. Quite understandably, he was somewhat dismayed and gave vent to his feelings through a string of very expressive and, in all fairness, not inappropriate phrases, some of which have indeed become indelibly fixed in my memory. I had to admit that my brilliantly efficient method was not, after all, quite 'spot-on' and that the oil only seemed to reach its intended target without in fact doing so. It was, perhaps, fortunate that the greasers on the other watches were less creative, for otherwise the consequences might have been dire, but if the engine was indeed a sentient being, as I strongly suspect it may have been, it must have taken a very dim view of my efforts.

For some time after joining the *Bergano*, I was employed as a greaser on daytime duty, which meant that I had to look after the firemen's mess and take care of the cabins in their section of the quarters. This, however, was by no means all. Once I had finished washing dishes and tidying bunks I was expected to go down into the engine-room, lend a hand wherever required, polish the ship's telegraph – a beautiful device made of the very finest brass – and oil the floor-plates to make them look spick and span. And, as if this were not enough, I was expected to repaint the entire engine-room. To this end I had to crouch for hours in the bulkhead where I happened to be working, chipping away at the rust and scraping at the loose paint, prior to treating the exposed metal with red anti-corrosive paint. And, of course, as any experienced greaser will readily confirm, there are millions of these inclined, watertight compartments covering the walls inside any engine-room worthy of the name.

Since the *Bergano* spent much time in tropical waters, the heat in the bulkheads was, as a rule, oppressive and the air quite foul. Besides, it was only too easy to touch the tangle of hot pipes and suffer really nasty burns, which happened to me several times each day, nor was it any picnic for me to be constantly hunched up while trying to maintain my balance. But worst by far, almost impossible to bear, was the grinding boredom of this particular job. Small wonder, therefore, that my attention shifted away from what I was supposed to be doing, to more creative pursuits such as teaching myself the ancient art of knocking-signals by which inmates of prison cells and other places of confinement are said to communicate with one another. Indeed, I became quite good at it, although, apart from the odd dolphin that happened to be passing, there was absolutely nobody about with whom I could possibly have wished to make contact. Whenever I felt that I needed a change from this indubitably worthwhile exercise (it did, after all, make time pass) I hacked out areas of paint resembling the shapes of Germany, Italy and their occupied territories, to which I then applied streaks of red oxide meant to represent invading allied armies moving deftly and quite inexorably towards the heartlands of the enemy and eventually covering them entirely. This activity too proved useful in its way, for it sharpened my instinct for pincer movements – an instinct to which I owe many a spectacular victory at the chessboard.

In due course, perhaps in appreciation of the fine quality of my work, I was promoted to the proud position of fully-fledged regular greaser – at the time the very pinnacle of my ambition. Free at last to engage in shift work like everybody else, I chose to serve on the dog-watch – 12 to 4 at night and 12 to 4 in the afternoon. As most seamen hate this watch like poison since it virtually cuts out any chance of proper sleep, I did not encounter any competition. As for me, I liked this particular arrangement because on the *Bergano* the dog-watch was more peaceful than the other watches, on which there was always some job or other in progress, mainly because the other engineers were men of restless temperament.

CHAPTER SIXTEEN

ON A rain-sodden afternoon in late October Mr. Galbraith and Mr. Daker were playing chess at the House of Pasta. Inside, the tables were lit discreetly, and it was fairly dark but also warm and cosy – definitely not an afternoon to be hurrying outside. M, who had come over to join them, was watching the two protagonists while sipping a cup of coffee.

As the struggle progressed – slowly, ever so slowly – from one unexciting move to the next, time for M seemed to be standing still (the only evidence of its passage being the ticking of the clock on the wall, almost directly overhead), and even Ben, their genial and voluminous host, had snoozed off over a cup of cappuccino and was snoring away gently in his corner, dreaming perhaps of his beloved Palermo, the town where most of his family lived and to which he hoped to return one day, his financial position permitting. M too felt an overpowering urge to close his eyes, which, having a lesson with Mr. Allbright to go to at five o'clock, he tried to overcome by concentrating on the game in progress. This did not help, nor was there any point in looking out of the window since, owing to the heavy, unremitting rain, nothing much was to be seen except for an occasional umbrella hurrying by outside. Desperate to stay awake, M even forced himself to look at some of the paintings on the walls, but as always these excessively realistic, rather gross representations of Parisian night-life in the Naughty Nineties – a special feature of the establishment – made him feel somewhat queasy. In the end, however, sleep did overtake him after all, and he woke up only when, sounding exactly like a pair of outraged hens, his friends protested vociferously because in changing his position he had lowered his head onto the chessboard, disturbing the pieces and making it impossible for them to carry on with their game. Looking at the clock, M realised that it was by now far too late to return to TTTW for his lesson. He decided, therefore, to stay where he was and, having woken Ben, who was still in the land of Nod, ordered a dish of *spaghetti al burro*.

On and off, M had been involved with chess for almost as long as he could remember. As a rule, he derived much pleasure from playing this game, but there were times when he felt that he was being taken over by a demonic force and that his mind was no longer his own. He recalled, in particular, one long, hot summer in the country, when his father and Uncle Georg – both of them on holiday – had spent many long hours hunched over the board, neither of them able to bring the game to its proper conclusion. Assuming (and who could blame them?) that he was still far too young for such mental exertions, they did not, of course, bother to explain the rules to little Morus, who stood at his father's side watching intently. But one day he simply understood, and it didn't take him long to appreciate some of the finer points which seemed constantly to elude his elders and betters. So he challenged first Papa and then his uncle, winning both games, to everybody's delight – particularly his father's; he was a generous man and exceedingly proud of his son's every achievement. In later years it was one of M's favourite myths that he – a prodigy if ever there was – had been able to play a fair game of chess ever since the very early age of three and a half, whereas the illustrious Capablanca had already reached the ripe old age of four when he started, also by watching his father.

M did not play again for several years, but rediscovered the game when he was about twelve years of age. During the summer vacation he would play chess in the *Türkenschanzpark* with other children whose parents, like his own, could not afford to send them away from Vienna to a holiday camp, as well as with old men and others with time on their hands and nothing better to do. He also had three regular partners – Stengel, Birkenfels and Josef Brunner. With Stengel he played many a game during poor Professor Nagel's Divinity and Hebrew lessons, with the chessboard concealed under the desk, and he also frequently played chess with Birkenfels, whose father was a wealthy banker and who had a room of his own.

But M's main and most regular partner was undoubtedly his friend Josef Brunner, with whom he played literally hundreds of games at great speed – often as many as thirty in an evening – for they seemed to share a passion for statistics and were interested, above all, in watching the numbers of wins, draws and losses accrue at a satisfyingly high rate. To this end they would break off their games by agreement as soon as one or the other felt that a decisive advantage had been gained or that the game had become 'boring'. Their chess bible in those days was Dufresne's famous, if indigestible, textbook, from which they gleaned openings, unusual combinations and hints on how to play the endgame. On one occasion they even went so far as to learn by heart a game played nearly a hundred years previously and renowned among chess aficionados throughout the world for its 'immortal' elegance and originality. They 'played' this game on a bench in the park, attracting great admiration from the spectators, until somebody recognised it for what it was and rudely called their bluff.

The café where young Morus, his father and his stepmother generally spent their Sunday afternoons – at any rate, as long as they could afford to do so – was yet another centre of chess activity. In those easy-going days nobody was expected to spend a fortune if he chose to dally for a few hours at a pleasantly appointed, even mildly luxurious coffee-house, where the air was warm and fragrant with the smell of coffee and cigars and there was much to delight and entertain the visiting patron. Indeed, a cup of coffee and a piece of delicious *Torte* would entitle one to stay as long as one pleased, and the prices, at least in the relatively modest establishments, were not high.

While Papa read the Sunday papers – large and weighty journals on sturdy wooden frames – or played a game of billiards with one of his cronies and Mama studied the fashion magazines or *Die Fliegenden Blätter*, M would move about among the chess tables kibitzing until, if he was lucky, he managed to get in a game of his own. M always felt that no other institution in the world was as civilised as the Viennese café where one could play chess, and if, during his later years, there was one thing that he missed more than any other, it was coffee-houses such as he had known in his youth.

At seventeen years of age M reached a crossroads of the kind dealt with in innumerable works of classical literature, where he had to choose between love and honour.

A few months after his arrival in England, M went to live at a hostel for Czech refugees near Reading, where he met Rosie, a beautiful dark-haired Hungarian, several years his senior and at the time 'in service' at a place about two miles distant. M fell in love with Rosie at first sight, but she did not reciprocate his feelings, for she in turn was passionately in love with young Dr. Emmerich, an expert on physical education. His heart, however, belonged entirely and without reserve to Frau Dr. Gruber, a lady of considerable charm and culture but old enough to be his mother, who was by no means insensitive to what her devoted admirer had to offer. How Herr Dr. Gruber, a morose, thick-set and silent man of advanced years and bald as an egg, felt about this situation is not known. In any case, he spent all his time writing a major work on something or other, which, it seemed, engaged his attention to the exclusion of every other matter, including, apparently, the way his wife – God only knows why she ever bothered to marry him – felt about their relationship. Day after day he sat in his corner, talking to no-one, never taking part in any of the communal activities and, mysteriously exempt from the hostel chores, covering reams of lined notepaper with his neat, even pedantic, writing. He never deleted or added anything and never stopped to think or to check what he had written. To M he seemed like a latter-day Moses taking dictation from the Almighty Himself.

As for Rosie, she used to visit the hostel every evening after work, on her bicycle. She would participate in such entertainments as were available, make sheep's eyes at Dr. Emmerich, who ignored her, and eventually depart. That was the point at which M was at last able to prove his devotion by pushing her bicycle for her, whatever the weather, although the way he recollected these walks, they always took place at full moon and under a starlit sky. As a rule, they would walk along in perfect silence, her thoughts being presumably with the man she loved or possibly on other matters, while M, whose heart was full to overflowing with the sweet, sweet torment of unrequited passion, could not utter a single word.

On one occasion, however, their somewhat barren relationship seemed to enter a different and, from M's point of view, more promising phase. Several of them, including the main protagonists in this emotional tangle as well as Mr. and Mrs. Prosser – she far advanced in pregnancy and expected to give birth in the very near future – were on a visit to another hostel, where M, substituting for a 'friend' who had suddenly developed a severe attack of 'cold feet', was to give a talk on 'The Jewish Problem'. Seeing that he had had no time to prepare himself, M simply reverted to his standard speech advocating, in a somewhat uncompromising manner, militant Zionism. This speech had been a great success in Slovakia, where, during the winter prior to his escape to Poland, M, in addition to earning a living as a teacher of English, had visited various towns, promoting illegal immigration to Palestine among the local Jewish population. But his present audience, composed as it was entirely of card-carrying Communists, was not at all impressed. Indeed, the reception accorded to M's speech was positively frosty, for the residents were all 'politically aware', whereas the visitors had no idea what he was talking about.

When M, still resplendent in his navy-blue suit with the shiny brass buttons and the odd, wrap-around waistcoat – a charity outfit bestowed upon him by the Jewish Community but still in excellent condition – eventually sat down (a chair had been provided for him on the rostrum), the chairman did his best to elicit applause, but, apart from M's party, who in their enthusiasm went rather over the top, no-one applauded. Instead, various members of the audience came on to the rostrum, attacking M for his 'fascist' views. This induced Dr. Emmerich, not the most circumspect of men, to respond in spirited, explicit Czech, which, in spite of the fact that this hostel too was operated by the Czech Refugee Trust Fund, hardly anyone of those present appeared to understand. M, of course, had spoken in German, which they definitely did understand. Be that as it may, Dr. Emmerich's intervention certainly contributed to the liveliness of the occasion. There seemed to be every likelihood of a fight breaking out (which could well have proved disastrous considering Mrs. Prosser's advanced pregnancy) when one of the speakers, a man with cadaverous features and a wooden leg, addressed the meeting in particularly fiery terms.

Desperate straits, they say, require desperate measures. M had always been very good at curving his fingers backward so as to form an arc, a skill which in the current emergency came to stand him – and, of course, the others – in good stead. Having achieved an almost circular arc with his forefinger, he held it against the side of his nose, which had a most disconcerting effect on the current 'firebrand', who, after some finger-jabbing in M's direction, eventually dried up entirely. This gave M the opportunity to state, in as conciliatory a manner as he could muster, that having heard so many good and convincing arguments this evening, he would be doing his hosts a grave injustice if he were to respond immediately, off the cuff so to speak and without proper, careful consideration. He promised, without the least intention of actually doing so, that he would come again in order to debate these weighty matters as they deserved to be debated and in order to deepen his understanding where it proved to be deficient.

A major concession such as this – it was seen as an important conversion, Saulus turning into Paulus on the road to Damascus – could not but have a most felicitous outcome, and the prevailing mood did in fact change almost instantly from intense hostility to great hospitality. Whereas, only a few minutes ago, violence had seemed to be unavoidable, the air was now thick with congratulatory statements freely proposed and gladly accepted, and everybody was happy. The guests were ushered into a large room with trestle tables along the walls virtually bending under the weight of home-made cakes, sandwiches, fruit, pots of tea, bottles of pink Tizer and of wine, also made on the premises. All this was quite excellent, and good talk flowed freely as they munched and guzzled, burbled and sipped their way through all the food and drink. After this feast the tables were taken away and there was much enthusiastic dancing to such well-loved tunes as *If you were the only girl/boy in the world* and *La Paloma* played on the hostel gramophone. Both Dr. Emmerich and Rosie, having had rather more than was good for them of the home-made beverage – a more potent liquid than they had been led to expect – disgraced themselves slightly but not to any serious extent and not with each other – he by challenging all and sundry to a one-legged race, a challenge nobody accepted, which was just as well, since in his present state he would have found it difficult to maintain himself in an erect position even if he had had four feet or more, and she by dancing a most unusual version of the can-can and in the process showing rather more of her private garments than befitted a member of the class-conscious proletariat.

When M, who would have liked to join in the dancing but was too inhibited to do so, mentioned to one of his hosts that he was a keen chessplayer, hinting that his eyes were on the championship of the world, he was taken in triumph to meet an old gentleman from Pilsen, the best player in the hostel and formerly, M was told, one of the most formidable chessplayers in Czechoslovakia. A chessboard and pieces were found, and presently they were locked in relentless, if somewhat one-sided combat, while all around them other jollifications were in progress.

Having lost the first game without any apparent effort on the part of his opponent, M also managed to lose the second. They were halfway through the third when Rosie, who was upset because Dr. Emmerich, more or less himself once again, was unashamedly paying court to Frau Dr. Gruber and had repeatedly and none too tactfully rejected her own well-meant advances, decided to leave forthwith. Not wishing to go alone, she invited M to go with her. Never had she looked more enticing to him, never more seductive, with her face slightly flushed and her tousled hair shining. In her dark eyes M read a promise such as he had never read there before.

He was aching to go with her, but how could he possibly, things being as they were? It was unthinkable for him to resign at the very stage of the game when his defeat was indeed beginning to take shape but was, in his judgement, not yet inevitable, whereas to leave on any other pretext would not only have been most rude to his partner but downright dishonourable. So what else could he do but decline, with a breaking heart and inwardly cursing his bad luck, the invitation he would have loved to accept? Rosie, rejected again, and this time by that little creep M of all people – how could she ever have allowed herself to sink so low? – gave him a look of withering contempt, shrugged her beautiful shoulders – oh, what would he not have given to hold her in his arms – and, not deigning to say another word, left without him. M, in his emotional turmoil entirely unable to concentrate, managed to continue with his game only for another few minutes before it was all over, but this time he hardly noticed and certainly did not care.

Among the very few things M kept to remind him of his childhood and his family was a photograph showing his Uncle Max playing chess in what must have been an important match. All rigid and formal, Uncle Max was wearing a large, black hat, as indeed in all the photographs taken in his later years, although M had seen one photograph showing Uncle Max as a young man and without a hat. However, what impressed him particularly was the fact that the two players were sitting at a separate, prominently placed table, with their names clearly indicated in large, spidery Gothic script, and not, as were all the others, anonymously at long, continuous rows of tables such as could be seen in the background. Although (in spite of repeated defeats at the hands of relatively undistinguished opponents) M saw himself as a future grandmaster at the very least, he always took pride in his uncle's achievement and occasionally wondered whether he had inherited his own 'genius' from the latter. He also cherished the well-used chess set which Uncle Max had given him, his favourite nephew, on some long-forgotten occasion, imagining with some pride that many of the leading masters of his uncle's generation had used it to play games of great interest and distinction.

CHAPTER SEVENTEEN

NEITHER M nor Silversmith ever discovered how it had come about that Lipkin and Rosabelle had suddenly become inseparable. They were, of course, fully aware of the fact (and in the circumstances this was hardly surprising) that Lipkin was 'sweet' on Rosabelle, but on her part no such attachment to Lipkin had been observed. And yet, there they were, as true and genuine a couple as ever there was, going everywhere together and sharing many things. Their personalities too seemed to have changed. Lipkin had become even more taciturn than previously and now walked about with a kind of permanent, beatific, irritatingly indulgent smirk, whereas Rosabelle, who in the past had hardly ever deigned to say anything at all, firmly convinced that no-one could possibly wish to hear what she thought, had become positively garrulous, incessantly venting her frequently tiresome opinions on each and every subject that happened to come her way. Her innate bossiness too became increasingly apparent, with Lipkin its natural, perfectly willing target. She had never been pretty, but now her looks – at any rate, in everyone's eyes but Lipkin's – deteriorated further, as the slight fluff on her upper lip became darker and more pronounced, showing distinct signs of turning into a real, full-blown moustache.

Be that as it may, they were clearly happy with one another. Indeed, their happiness was not in the least impaired by the fact that, apart from having each other, they had every reason for being downright miserable, for Rosabelle was still in a lowly position at a local solicitor's office, copying this and that and making the tea, while Lipkin, largely because of his insuperable romanticism, particularly about the working classes, and his excessively high standards of personal conduct, continued to be virtually unemployable. Still, in her current ultra-communicative state, Rosabelle was able to make ever greater use of such terminology and jargon as she happened to pick up at her place of employment, so that at times she sounded amazingly like a qualified practitioner of the law and a most scholarly authority on legal matters, in spite of the fact that she really had no idea what she was talking about. In the fullness of time she even managed to convince herself that she had indeed been a student of the law but had been compelled by circumstances over which she had no control to abandon her studies.

As for Lipkin, he suffered his latest *débâcle* after only a brief spell of employment (two weeks, actually) at a building site in Paddington, where they were constructing a new school. Work on that site, to which he had been sent by the Labour Exchange, was already far advanced, and he had spent most of his time on precarious planks high above ground, supplying the bricklayers with bricks, while trying to draw comfort – for he was not a naturally fearless person – from the fact that on one side, at least, he was close to a solid wall. To begin with, the foreman seemed to be well satisfied, and on one occasion even remarked to the Clerk of Works or some such illustrious person 'fellow works like an 'orse', which pleased Lipkin (who happened to overhear him) quite a lot and was only fair, seeing that he always did his best and was by no means a 'lead-swinger'. However, as is generally known, pride – or whatever humbler emotion Lipkin may have experienced – comes before a fall. Lipkin, instructed to sweep the future gym hall, observed that the carpenter and his two mates were trying to install an enormous window-frame, part of which had split lengthwise and should quite clearly have been replaced. As he swept within a few feet of the carpenter, he actually heard him say: 'Once it's in and painted, who's to know?', to which one of his assistants responded with 'Lots of bloody kids. God knows why we spent all that money on them!'

This was altogether too much for Lipkin, a true believer in the importance of education, not to mention such old-fashioned virtues as pride in craftsmanship and the dignity of honest labour. So he went over and tried to reason with them, to make them see the error of their ways. Hardly able to believe that a lowly creature such as Lipkin could have the nerve not merely to speak to them – skilled men in their own country and, therefore, the finest in the world – without being asked, but actually to be telling them off, they remained speechless for a moment or two. But when the carpenter had recovered sufficiently to respond, he first enquired as to whom Lipkin thought he was talking to and then advised him, in strong and convincing language, to mind his own bloody business and get on with his job, or else. The others too added appropriate comments, leaving Lipkin in no doubt whatsoever about their thoughts and sentiments.

Of course, the carpenter, a spiteful man and no lover of the 'chosen people', would not leave it at that. He mentioned to the foreman, who happened to be his brother-in-law, that that foreign bloke was a right little troublemaker and a bloody Red to boot, which did poor Lipkin no good at all, inasmuch as he was shifted forthwith to a foundation-digging job outside. With the rain pouring down and the ground thoroughly waterlogged, Lipkin, far from fit and already suffering from a most unpleasant nasal cold, found it very hard to insert the spade into the squelchy clay and even harder to get it out again. He also discovered how difficult, under such conditions, it can be to raise a boot heavy with clinging mud in order to bring it down on the spade, and his back was aching atrociously. As a result, his progress was exceedingly slow, and by the end of the day he was almost relieved when the foreman told him that he was wasting his and everybody else's time, and here were his cards.

M and Silversmith were by no means surprised to hear of Lipkin's misfortune, if losing a job such as that could, in fact, be regarded as a misfortune. Both of them told him what they thought, M more sympathetically than Silversmith, but it was the latter who surely hit the nail on the head when he pointed out that the average working man, far from being proud of his class and what he was doing for a living, had his eyes firmly fixed on the main chance and would do anything to join the property-owning middle and upper classes, and, God willing, to progress to the House of Lords. As for honour and idealism, such airy-fairy notions were strictly for the birds and the likes of Lipkin, whose naïve faith in the basic decency of human beings, when all the best evidence pointed the other way, would get him into serious trouble yet.

In matters of manual labour, M's record was hardly more impressive than Lipkin's, but his problems were, in general, due less to a romantic attitude of mind (M, basically friendly and well-meaning, was not so much an idealist as a pragmatist and middle-of-the-roader) than to an extraordinary ineptitude and, frequently, a quite unbeliev-able – one might fairly say inspired – lack of intelligence whenever practical skills and solutions were expected of him. How else could one explain that famous occasion when, as a trainee farm labourer in Somerset, he thought he was looking at Clara, the black and white Jersey cow, when in fact he was facing Augustus, the bull. The latter, admittedly, was also black and white but quite a bit older – Clara was only recently past the first flush of youth – and unmistakably less sweet-natured than Augustus, quite apart from various other distinctive differences by which M might have known better. Then again, what was one to make of M's misguided efforts to clean the slides on a horizontal milling machine in Manila with, of all unsuitable tools, a file? By this single regrettable act he managed within a second or two to divest that unfortunate object of every last vestige of potential usefulness and to convert it from a proud, if at that period in its history somewhat dilapidated, metal-cutting device – the largest, they said, in the entire Philippines – into (putting it mildly) an engineer's nightmare.

After many months in a burnt-out factory with a roof long since present only in outline and a floor buried in lush vegetation, this poor machine, another victim of the war, was pitted and covered with rust, its spindles bent and twisted and its parts, which in happier times had, no doubt, performed their various tasks harmoniously and lightly, stuck and motionless as if in perpetual *rigor mortis*.

This unfortunate incident occurred while M – only recently released from a prison camp in Northern Japan and by then thoroughly 'fed up' with waiting for the various official actions without which he could not hope to return to England and what he, perhaps mistakenly, regarded as 'civilisation' – was working as an 'apprentice' for an engineer from Munich, a kindly man of few words and with a most melancholy manner. Indeed, M's employer had much to be melancholy about, for his wife had left him but recently, and his partner, a tall, choleric man with glasses, who ran the garage next door, was forever shouting at him and threatening him with various physical excesses. Still, things might have been worse. Once the slides of the hapless machine had been painted in a most workmanlike shade of grey with touches of cheerful red here and there, M's intervention, such as it was, did not prevent a most profitable sale to the down-town Chinese for further disposal.

M was reasonably happy in his job, although not at all happy with his general situation. He would 'mend' the corrugated tin roof of the shack housing the workshop whenever this appeared to be advisable in order to prevent the rain from pouring in through a multitude of tiny and not so tiny holes, or collect, together with some of the other workers and with the aid of a truck and a few simple tools – planks, ropes, rollers and a crowbar or two – such pieces of derelict machinery as were, in his employer's opinion, capable of being restored to a saleable condition. M was familiar with work of this nature from his days in Japan, and it made him feel powerful and virtuous. But when there was nothing else for him to do, his employer would ask him to cut out stars, rings and other shapes from pieces of cast iron, which, once finished, were promptly thrown away. In the process of acquiring this skill M broke many a good hacksaw, until one day he found that he had at long last mastered the technique and could now saw anything and everything with consummate ease. Henceforth he was always a dab hand at sawing and felt that his relationship with any saw was very intimate and very special. There were indeed occasions when he could have sworn that a saw was actually smiling at him in a friendly and at the same time conspiratorial manner as if to say: 'You and I will show these dumb bastards what's what!' Once his employer realised that M had become so adept a manipulator of saws, he made him drill holes into disused cast-iron frames – drills without number met their end in the course of this effort – but M never managed to master this particular skill, nor did he ever develop a worthwhile relationship with any drill, however congenial.

Meanwhile, in Manila, M was slowly clawing his way back from a state of official non-existence to one in which he was again deemed fit to undergo the various forms of administrative processing on which his return to 'civilisation' – in his eyes, friends and relatives to be impressed, real pea-soup smog which you could taste in the mouth, savings to an amount of £50 deposited with a leading bank, and such other attractions as London had to offer – depended. He had been a non-person ever since someone, presumably a fellow-repatriatee, had, in the humid, sweltering heat of an over-crowded, dusty camp in sun-drenched Okinawa, relieved him of his shirt and, incidentally, Czechoslovak passport number something or other – his pride and joy and the only documentary link with his past prior to internment in Japan. At the time, M understandably regarded this incident as a severe blow, for it left him, as it were, rudderless and disorientated on an alien sea, but even then he felt some sympathy for the 'liberator' of his shirt, to whom neither M's passport nor, indeed, his shirt could have been of any conceivable value or interest. In any case, everyone in the camp had been inundated by the American Red Cross with what seemed excessive amounts of perfectly new G.I. garments of the very highest quality, such as shirts, trousers, boots and even heavy greatcoats, more suitable for an arctic winter than for the tropical conditions of Okinawa. Most of these articles appeared to find their way into the outsize waste-baskets, providently situated at numerous prominent locations throughout the camp.

Naturally M turned to the officer in charge in order to obtain benevolent advice and assistance, and the latter, having learned of his plight, did in fact suggest that he might be able to arrange for his immediate return to Japan, an offer M simply refused to take seriously.

It did not take the officer, a very busy man, long to lose interest entirely (this had been an on-going process ever since M approached him) and since M had also been unable to come up with any constructive suggestion, their ways parted for good, without the slightest regret on either side. So while American planes daily ferried former inmates of Japanese camps away to, no doubt, more desirable destinations and other ex-PoW's were brought in, only to leave again after just a few days in the camp, M found himself forgotten and ignored. His prospects at that stage were distinctly unpromising, and by the time he – mostly prone on his bunk, sizzling away in the oven-like heat and vastly depressed – realised that the people whom he had known in former and, as it then seemed, better days had been whisked away, panic set in such as he had rarely experienced before. He pictured himself as left behind forever in that inhospitable place, a kind of intellectual Gulliver among the Lilliputians, a toothsome stranger among cannibals, all baring loathsome fangs and making ready to turn him into an unspeakably disgusting stew. Restless then and motivated by an irresistible desire to 'enjoy', as long as possible, any links, however tenuous, with his life in Japan, which he now remembered as a wonderful time, utterly enjoyable and infinitely satisfying, M took to frequenting the departure area on the airfield. There he watched in considerable, exquisite torment as one lot after another of the camp's inmates, all of them strangers eventually, boarded their planes and flew off to who-knew-what joy and happiness, leaving him behind, lonely, miserable and rejected.

One day, however, M noticed that although, on every occasion, the names of all those allocated to a flight were read out, whereupon each person called would confirm his presence, they were not in fact counted as they boarded their planes. This gave him the idea that by simply joining a group he too might be able to get away without being discovered, at any rate until the aeroplane had reached its destination, by which time – a bit of wishful thinking this – they might not bother to return him to where he came from. The worst thing likely to happen, he persuaded himself, was a spell in prison, but that could not possibly last long, for he was, after all, a war hero and not a criminal. He visualised in his mind how the Norwegian Consul or possibly even the British Consul, the most eminent persons he could think of just then, would visit him in prison, shake him by his emaciated but still powerful right hand and thank him for his fine efforts on behalf of his (and now also M's) country and lead him, metaphorically speaking, of course, out into the radiant sunlight. Besides, nothing could have been worse than his current predicament – a kind of living death.

M, who was very good at self-persuasion and equally good at acting upon his fantasies, did not, in a manner of speaking, allow the grass to grow under his feet. The very same day he packed his bag and went off to the airfield, where he waited until yet another party boarded a plane. Not saying a word to anyone, he joined them and presently found himself inside a large grey American bomber. Seeing that there weren't any seats left and having in any case no desire to share a narrow bench for God knows how many hours with a tightly packed lot of G.I.s – that is what at that stage most of them were – he crept into the baggage space, which was far more comfortable and where, at some ease for the first time since his arrival in Okinawa, he was able to enjoy a cheerful chat with some other G.I.s – members of the crew, as it transpired – who were mildly interested in hearing what it had been like to be a PoW in Japan. In due course M, for whom this had been a long and eventful day, fell asleep and woke up only after the plane had landed in Manila and it was time to disembark.

A military brass band was there to welcome them – and, more especially, him – as one by one, in the gathering dusk, they left the plane. Impelled by instinct and the naïve but laudable conviction that 'honesty was the best policy' and confession good for the soul, M decided to make, forthwith and without prevarication, a clean breast of his peccadillo. To this end he addressed himself to the large, round-faced sergeant apparently in charge of what was going on, in order to acquaint him with his special circumstances and problems. The latter, quite obviously, couldn't care less and simply directed him to a truck, which conveyed M and some others to a disused, partly derelict but still very impressive former monastery in the Spanish style – M's first repatriation camp.

CHAPTER EIGHTEEN

AS A CHILD, and especially during his years in Vienna, M had spent much time and effort in evading or at least minimising – often with most undesirable and even dire results – the consequences of his conduct with lies, subterfuge and much secretiveness. This was due in part to some difficulty in distinguishing between fact and fiction – a widespread human failing, to be sure, which has throughout history been a most potent source of trouble, ranging from irritation and frustration at one end of the scale, to murder, mayhem and tribal beastliness at the other – but also to the assiduous training bestowed upon him by his stepmother and, of course, such techniques for getting by as he had mastered at the good old Klappenhorn. At that fine establishment of learning, survival for such as him – those not particularly gifted with their fists, without rich and powerful fathers or not otherwise endowed with special merits and virtues – frequently depended on their skill in executing a kind of tip-toeing egg-dance about and among the pitfalls of simple, unadorned truth. But M had eventually arrived at the indubitably wise conclusion that his purposes would be served far better if, instead, he were to follow (within reason, of course) the advice of President T.G. Masaryk, revered throughout Czechoslovakia as the founder of the Republic, by becoming 'frank' and 'truthful'. While not depriving him of the facility of uttering a real whopper when the occasion demanded it, and leaving aside such harmless 'white' lies as were meant to please others rather than benefit himself, this new approach was, generally, so successful that in the fullness of time it ceased to be a purely optional alternative but caused M to develop a marked preference for 'putting his cards on the table', whatever his predicament. As a result, he came to be widely thought of as harmless and amusingly simple – a view which contributed greatly to his general popularity.

He himself tended to regard his 'straightforwardness' as a mere strategem, a ploy designed to yield certain benefits (which indeed it did) and he was prone to say so, thus giving rise to much merriment and many a knowing wink. In some cases, however, it may well have protected him from great evil or even saved his life. For instance, after the *Bergano* had been captured by a German raider – a converted banana boat, by all accounts, but to M's knowledge this was never established for certain – thin and lanky as he then was and wearing his tattered, oil-stained working clothes (naturally enough, seeing that he had just emerged from the engine room), he stepped forward in order to announce, in his crispest, most uncompromising German, that he was a Jew. After a seemingly interminable pause – time itself seemed to have come to a stop – the commander of the prize crew did the honourable thing and simply instructed M to carry on.

Whenever he described this event and the way he had handled what might have become a very unpleasant situation, M would feel really proud, not because he thought of his conduct as particularly brave – in his eyes, courage due to a lack of natural fear had never been much of a virtue – but because he had assessed the situation so correctly. At that time, so he would argue, every German worth his salt – and he could tell well enough that the commander and his crew were decent fellows – regarded himself as a latter-day Siegfried, namely a man wholly dedicated to everything that was fine, upright and heroic, in short, 'quintessentially' German. By 'taking the bull by the horns' and frankly stating that he was a Jew, apparently at great risk to himself, M had in fact entered this fantasy, not as a 'subhuman' cast in the role of victim but as an equal protagonist – an enemy perhaps, but an enemy worthy of respect. And, besides, all his shipmates knew all about him and were bound, after a few beers or so, to give him away, so there would have been absolutely no point in concealing this fact.

None of this, of course, had been in M's mind at the time. He had simply acted in the manner most natural to him, namely by instinct. Neither heroism nor devious calculation, such as a chessplayer who had won his game thanks to a particularly 'brilliant' combination might reasonably feel proud of, had anything to do with it.

With its large rooms and thick, whitewashed walls, its many arches and low ceilings as well as its pleasant grounds, San Pedro was definitely a most agreeable spot in which to await further developments, quite apart from the fact that quite a few of the people there were civilians, also in transit to the USA and other countries. Once M had passed through the heady stage of intense self-congratulation and more or less found his bearings, he wasted no time but fell in love forthwith, deeply and tantalisingly – once again it was another who was preferred – with honey-skinned Gloria, daughter of a lady from Hong Kong who was currently *en route* to Seattle, where, so rumour had it, she hoped to find gainful employment for both herself and her sweet charge.

M did not really care. Often he would lie in a state of profound, searing frustration upon his hot, dishevelled bed, chewing – quite literally – at the grey bolster, on which at other times he would rest his head, and yearning for 'his' Gloria, until it was time to go to lunch or dinner or whatever, when he might hope to see her again. Yet his hopeless devotion was not wholly in vain, not quite unrewarded, for it brought him an entirely unexpected insight of a philosophical kind. He observed, once the worst was over – the appalling roughness of his unrequited longings having given way at last to a more contemplative, merely melancholy, state of mind – that his pangs of love were always most intense before meals, whereas after meals he would feel far more relaxed and even drowsy. This caused him to conclude, in a veritable rush of penetrative perception, that his desire for Gloria on the one hand and his fondness of food on the other might well be related in some way and possibly even a single, identical urge in two different guises. Ever suspicious of his insights, however obviously profound and startlingly convincing, he tested this particular revelation by obtaining a supply of munchables, on which he would gorge himself whenever his longing for Gloria threatened to get out of hand. This and a considerable excess of leisure caused his weight to increase dramatically, and people were forever telling him how well he looked. In fact, he felt rather sluggish and was inclined to sleep more than in his previous leaner state, but what of it? At least his sanity remained unimpaired.

Other highlights of M's stay at San Pedro were his long and, for him at any rate, highly satisfactory perambulations in the company of Father Manocampos, a Jesuit priest who tried to persuade him of the wisdom of joining the one and only true faith, as so many of M's more enlightened co-religionists had done in the past, the benefits of such a step, both spiritual and material, being, as he claimed, undeniable. As for M's avowed agnosticism, he brushed it aside as nothing but immature fence-sitting and a barren fear of commitment. Basing himself squarely on experience accumulated over many centuries, he explained that if, to begin with, M were merely to go through the motions of religious observance, he would, in due course, gather a rich and most wonderful harvest of faith. M, who, it will be remembered, enjoyed a very special relationship with God already, although by no means convinced of His existence, regarded these discussions as mere intellectual knock-about fun, such as, for instance, he and Josef Brunner used to enjoy so much on their long criss-cross walks through Vienna. He refused to take them at all seriously, which eventually wore down the trained, dedicated patience of Father Manocampos, causing him to withdraw entirely from their relationship. Before doing so, the good Father did, however, hint (as was, no doubt, his charitable duty) at the dire, indeed persistent, consequences which might well ensue if M continued to walk in the footsteps of his – M's, that is – master, the all-devouring, ever rapacious devil. At this point in their disputation, Father Manocampos expectorated with much venom upon the parched and, no doubt, grateful ground. But M, who in any event always saw himself as a kind of composite of Faust and Mephisto – with, for good measure, a dash of Margaret – felt that he had nothing much to fear from that quarter.

From San Pedro he was, in due course, transferred to a much larger camp. However, with the number of repatriatees continuing to dwindle relentlessly, until, apart from himself there were only two left, the camp – despite the fact that there were still about twenty members of the administrative staff in attendance – became a nightmarish place of cobwebby tents, where, grimy with dust and blind, the very lightbulbs seemed to be decaying. Once again and quite understandably in the grip of a deep depression, M did his best to cope with his predicament in a variety of ways, but might well have failed – and in that case, who knows what might have become of him – had he not enjoyed the firm and unwavering support of good friends such as Dr. Blumental and his wife, both of them old in years but young at heart, and Dr. Geller from Berlin, a man of stern appearance but great kindness and unswerving rectitude. The Blumentals, in particular, made a point of entertaining and feeding M every Monday and Friday, Mrs. Blumental doing her utmost to produce, with the limited means at her disposal, delicacies such as those for which Vienna, Mrs. Blumental's place of origin, is justly renowned throughout the entire civilised world. Her imaginative, if not always entirely successful, attempts frequently gave rise to much hilarity and humorous remarks about banana *strudls*, mango dumplings with breadcrumbs fried in butter, and similarly outlandish concoctions. After dinner, while, sipping their coffee, Dr. Blumental and young Morus swapped stories or brooded over the chess board, Mrs. Blumental would sit at the piano and play medleys of her favourite tunes.

Dr. Blumental, formerly a respected dentist in Stuttgart, had come to Manila when it was still relatively easy to leave Germany, in order to escape racial prejudice and make a new life for himself and his wife. However, unable for one reason or another to practise his profession, he had, instead, become a commercial traveller representing a pharmaceutical company, which provided him with a modest but adequate living. Shortly after the Japanese invasion of the Philippines he was elected president of the local Jewish community and was justly proud of the fact that, in spite of the great scarcity of food, he had managed to shepherd all his charges through the difficult war years, without any of them coming to any serious harm due to malnutrition. Convinced that a much younger man was needed to lead the community into the era of reconstruction, he had, once the war was over, resigned his presidency and, although already in his eighties, resumed his agency work. Frugal as they were, the Blumentals did not find it easy to make ends meet, but this was not in any way reflected in their hospitality.

As for Dr. Geller, M remembered him chiefly as a man of rigid principle, who would stand for no nonsense and as a result was, on occasion, uncomfortable to know. Another of M's elderly friends was a Dr. Moser from Vienna, who ran a surgery frequented mainly by seamen, where, before he took regular employment, M would now and again lend a hand. Dr. Moser seemed to regard it as his duty to enlighten M about the physical and emotional aspects of 'love', a subject in which he was clearly a great expert. To do him justice, however, he would have been the first to admit that his interest was, at that stage of his life, largely academic – a circumstance which he seemed to regard as not entirely unwelcome, since it freed him from such compulsive states as had dominated his younger years and made it unnecessary for him to do anything about such 'opportunities' as still, occasionally, came his way. But when, at his suggestion, M had taken some lightbulbs from one of the vacant tents in the camp, it was Dr. Geller who made him realise that this, far from being a matter to brag about, was in fact an act of theft punishable by law. In a way, M had realised this already, for why else should he have felt so guilty when, passing the camp guard with his loot hidden casually under some perfectly legitimate PX merchandise, he found himself, for a truly dreadful moment, in imminent danger of being caught. But it was also Dr. Geller who stood by M through thick and thin when he got into trouble with the Norwegian Consul – a brutish, bullet-headed man, who never seemed to miss an opportunity to make it abundantly plain what he thought of seamen in general and pretend-seamen such as M in particular. In fact, after M had unwisely written to the Norwegian authorities in Washington in order to complain about the way he was being treated by their representative, Dr. Geller even went so far as to call on the Consul, who was, it appeared, well placed to obstruct M's further progress, entreating him to overlook, in the light of his extreme youth and manifest inexperience, M's lamentable and thoroughly ill-considered conduct. For a man as proud and upright as Dr. Geller, this must indeed have been a very difficult thing to do.

M's dilemma was resolved, eventually, by one Marcus Sebastian Dorens, formerly a member of the Dutch forces fighting in Java and by temperament an adventurer, who had been captured by the Japanese and transferred, at a late stage of the war, to the very camp in which M had spent most of his time as a PoW. Dorens, or van Dorens as he preferred to be known, having listened patiently to M's tale of woe – stolen passport, unsympathetic Norwegian Consul, statements such as 'if a visa were to be granted for you to return to England and you were able to prove that you are indeed Mr. Morus Maskenbusch' etc. etc. – offered to help. He explained that he was currently sharing a flat with a notary public, a very sweet, very pretty and very intelligent lady, who would, within the limits of decency and discretion of course, do anything he asked of her, and that he, Marcus Sebastian van Dorens, would, if M so wished, be very happy indeed to interest her in M's most unfortunate predicament, which he could well appreciate, having been in similar situations himself.

A few days later, M, who found documents of any kind, but in particular official-looking ones, enormously fascinating, held in his hands an affidavit sworn on his behalf by his friend and certified by one Carmen Maria Pedicula, Notary Public, duly sealed and with an imposing number of stamps. Shaking with emotion, he read a highly convoluted statement to the effect that Marcus Sebastian van Dorens, formerly of the East Indies Bank and now of independent means, had, in his capacity as administrative officer of the PoW-camp at such and such a place, had occasion to inspect passport number ..., issued by the Czechoslovak authorities at such and such another place and submitted to him by Morus Maskenbusch, a fellow inmate of said camp and identified as such etc. etc. and was therefore in a position to attest and so on and so forth. Strictly speaking, van Dorens had never seen M's passport nor, for that matter, been the administrative officer at M's camp, but who cared? In all important respects, truth had triumphed, enabling M to escape from the absurd state of being a non-person. It so happened that on the very day on which M re-entered the arena of public existence, a visa had arrived at the British Consulate in Manila, authorising his return to England, which could now be affixed to a proper proof of identity, a matter for considerable satisfaction all round.

The following weeks, while M waited for a suitable ship on which to depart from Manila, passed both incredibly slowly and with unbelievable speed, as is so often the case in emotionally complex situations. But eventually, after all the goodbyes and 'you will write, won't you's', there he stood by the railing of the *Louisiana*, the liner which was to carry him to San Francisco, still waving to his friends on the quayside as the ship edged its way slowly out of the harbour.

M, in front of his favourite German class, was having a wonderful time. He had just been handing back the corrected homework books and was currently enjoying the traffic of comments and questions, the arrival of latecomers, whom he would welcome – not, however, without a certain amount of friendly banter – like so many prodigal sons and daughters, and such quite irrelevant discussions as tended to crop up at this 'social' stage of the proceedings, before the lesson really got under way and greater demands were made on his ingenuity and creative imagination.

In the first year or so of his career with TTTW, before, owing to pressure of work and the emergence of new prospects, his initially keen enthusiasm had given way to what some might describe as a more 'professional' attitude, M used to take considerable pleasure in correcting his students' homework. He had acquired for this purpose a special fountain-pen, which he would lovingly fill with red ink of exactly the right tone and which he wielded with great, even unique, thoroughness. Apart from semolina pudding with raspberry syrup or sugar, cinnamon and hot molten butter – in his childhood years the objective standard of good and evil – few things, if any, in his life had affected the development of his personality as profoundly and extensively as had red ink. Indeed, for him red ink was the ultimate symbol of power, authority and all that was unquestionably and incontrovertibly true. Green ink or red ink with a purple or orangey tint, such as some teachers used, would not do, not do at all, but only ink, the red of which was fresh, bright and middle-of-the-road non-deviant. As for red or blue pencils, such unspeakable devices filled him with utter loathing and contempt.

The results of his efforts *en rouge* were most gratifying both to himself and to his students, for he did not confine himself to merely pointing out mistakes and attributing marks as most teachers do, but would add notes – not always sound but always illuminating and, on occasion, funny – explaining points of idiom and grammar and whatever else appeared to be in need of explanation. To support his notes and make them even more 'palatable', he would add short lists and tables, draw little cartoon-type sketches showing sleeping dogs, a pigtailed girl or two (Gretl, oh Gretl, why did you break my heart, when we could have been so blissfully happy, just you and I?) as well as other popular characters, suggest further work and generally do whatever useful or entertaining thing the inspiration of the moment dictated. Small wonder that his comments were frequently much longer than the original homework and that his students felt, not indeed without justification, that they were really getting their money's worth. When it came to assessing his students' work, his method was even-handed to a fault, for however good or however poor the effort, he would always mark it 'very good minus'.

Challenged about his reasons for such quaint, even odd, uniformity – sometimes by a student, but more often by a colleague who suspected him of being insufficiently serious or was simply envious of M's high course-renewal rates, which in those days were forever being held up by Dr. Pendlebloom as shining examples and targets to emulate – he would neatly evade the question and claim that there were secret features about the way in which he wrote the 'minus' which gave him all the information he could possibly require. Besides – so he claimed – the student concerned could, as a rule, judge for himself how he was doing or, for that matter, ask, in which case he would be given a frank and honest assessment. Not everyone, of course, understood M's mysterious method, motivated as it was by his need – long delayed and barely conscious – to revenge himself on the Klappenhorn establishment, which for seven interminable years had haunted him with any number of infinitely depressing marks. His students too did not always appreciate his humorous intent, as proved, for instance, by that most embarrassing episode when Miss Philippa Phipps, the standard of whose work had been declining sadly over a period of time, burst into tears and, when questioned about the reasons for her distress, accused M of simply not caring, for surely her work should have been graded 'poor' or even 'unsatisfactory'.

The corrected homework books now in front of his students, M summarised their mistakes, which on the present occasion had been due mainly to the perennial problems of gender and case. He drew on the blackboard yet another little girl with pigtails, who was giving a bone to a sleeping dog. Anticipating the sad fate presently in store for it, the poor bone was shedding tears, as well it might, but the dog, its eyes tightly closed, was still quite unaware of the treat which its benefactress was offering. M now wrote the sentence *'Das Mädchen gibt dem Hund einen Knochen'* and went on to explain the difference between direct and indirect objects and its grammatical consequences. 'The bone,' he told the still reasonably attentive class, 'is, alas, directly affected by the girl's action, hence the tears, while the dog is as yet quite unconcerned. In other words, the bone is directly affected but the dog only indirectly. Hence the terms 'direct' and 'indirect' object.

Mr. Willoughby, who in spite of M's suggestion that he might do better in a more advanced class, had continued to attend, made the point that in some German dialects, particularly in the South, there was a distinct tendency for people to confuse the dative and accusative cases, an observation to which M responded by pointing out that in the same region there was a distinct tendency to mix up certain consonants, an observation he was able to illustrate with an amusing anecdote. Doris, as ever keen to please, commented that *now* she understood, and didn't the little girl look sweet. Mr. Fennimore, a butcher by profession, who knew a thing or two about the subject in hand, commented on the interesting fact that the bone was disproportionately large and wondered whether it had once been part of an elephant's skeleton. This encouraged Miss Jones, whom the drawing reminded of her own dear little Scottie, to wonder whether it might not be cruel and even dangerous to give such a large bone to such a small dog, and wasn't it unusual for a bone to cry? Mrs. Snyder, having after several diffident attempts at last managed to draw attention to herself, had not understood any of it and had to be given a private lesson, as it were. After the break, M switched to 'conversation' on a most useful topic, namely, the problems and pitfalls of asking for a hotel room.

After the lesson, which lasted until 9.30 in the evening, some of them went to the House of Pasta for coffee and snacks. As always, they invited M to join them, and although he was by that time very tired and would have dearly loved to go home, he did not see how he could possibly refuse such a kind offer without giving offence. Besides, this was his chance to accompany Doris to her home, a bed-sitter in Lancaster Gate, not far from where M himself lived – an opportunity that could not, of course, be wasted, tired or not.

CHAPTER NINETEEN

DORIS was not by any means the only one of his students whom M regularly accompanied on their way home. There was also Antonia, who lived in a block of flats in Swiss Cottage which M came to know very well from the outside, but as she (whatever his arguments and entreaties) never allowed him to come up to her flat, however briefly, he never got any further. However hard M tried on these occasions to play the role of male enticer and dominator – a role that young men everywhere and in all ages have perceived to be their chief *raison d'être* – Antonia, nymph-like, intelligent and without the slightest trace of the sentimentality which tended to make friendship with Doris such a cloying affair, would have none of it and would quell, effortlessly and even with obvious relish, such not very subtle overtures as M managed to come up with, very well aware of his somewhat frivolous intentions towards her, which did not worry or upset her in the slightest degree,

Antonia, in turn, would play the part of a bee gathering honey from a flower in its wayward path, without regard for whatever else that flower might have to offer. The honey in question, as far as she was concerned, consisted in M's more exotic or at least quaint observations, for she had an enquiring, even voracious, mind, which neither her family (she came from Sussex) nor her other friends, most of them artists like herself (she was an illustrator of children's books but never showed M any of her work) were at all able to satisfy. M on his side did not really mind being kept at arm's length, for experience had taught him that, once you actually possess them, most things are not nearly as enticing as they appear in a well-designed shop window while they are still safely separated from the person casually regarding them from outside. He enjoyed talking to her, drawing much inspiration from her undivided, rapt attention and the way she seemed to appreciate and take in what she heard. Besides, he was proud to be seen in her company, for Antonia was a strikingly beautiful girl who attracted many an admiring glance.

On one of their after-lesson peregrinations to distant Swiss Cottage, M explained to Antonia his theories about language study. '*La plume de ma tante*', he declared, 'never fails to inspire great merriment, and this, no doubt, has been the case ever since French came to be taught in the schools of this country. It is a kind of shorthand suggesting various things such as, for instance, the inherent absurdity of all foreign languages – and, by extension, all foreigners, especially Frenchmen – or the gulf which separates all true English folk (whose heart is in the right place and who are naturally inept at languages) from such freakish bores – such pimples on the honest face of John Bull – as actually revel in the cringing, pedantic pursuit of the languages of others. At the same time it is recognised as self-evident that any foreigner would give his very eye-teeth – whatever they may be – for the treasures of the English tongue. Think only of Shakespeare and all his wonderful works...'

'Why poor old Shakespeare and not Milton or Byron or Shelley or ...' A brave attempt, this, by Antonia to get a word in edgeways – an attempt which M cheerfully ignored. She, however, did not mind this in the least, for she really enjoyed all that purple prose and was in many ways a perfect listener but sometimes felt an obscure, and to M rather irritating, need to demonstrate her presence and identity.

'A very good question, a very good question indeed!' M had as yet no very clear notion why this should be such a good question but was confident that something would occur to him, and so it did. He continued: 'Did I ever tell you what happened to me in St. John's, Newfoundland, which the *Moa*, my very first Norwegian ship, reached after a particularly horrible crossing of the Atlantic?' Antonia, looking interested, shook her head. 'No, I thought not. The Moa, you see, was an old tramp steamer, dirty as hell and slow with it. I was supposed to be the mess-boy, but since I was sea-sick most of the time, I wasn't much use, I suppose, to anyone. Still, I managed to make good use of my time by learning Norwegian, which proved to be very useful on my other ships. But to come back to my story. In St. John's – a fine town, I've been told, but I really wouldn't know, for the day I had shore leave it happened to be hidden in a dense cocoon of fog – I eventually found myself at a very large bookstore, which, of course, pleased me no end. However, I soon discovered that the range of books on offer was distinctly limited. All the shelves right up to the ceiling seemed to be covered with Wild West novelettes and comics, and, unsurprisingly, girlie magazines of the cruder kind also appeared to be in great, even universal, demand. Still, never one to give up easily, I kept on looking and eventually found a complete edition of Shakespeare's Works. This I must have, I thought, and carried my prize in triumph to one of the assistants, who eyed me with some surprise and an unmistakable touch of pity. In reply to his question whether that was really what I required. I assured him that it was and asked for the price, which happened to be one dollar 25 – 25 cents more than I had on me. Not one to bargain, I offered to return with the full amount, but the assistant wouldn't hear of that and virtually forced Shakespeare and all his truly wonderful works on me for a mere dollar.'

'I still sometimes wonder whether he would have been so generous if I had asked for anything less unusual. Still, I used the time before the *Moa* docked again in Southampton or wherever for reading all 37 of Shakespeare's plays, got all those Gloucesters and Kents and Bolingbrokes thoroughly mixed up, and developed a compulsive need to make up verses which were, in my humble opinion, virtually indistinguishable from those of the Bard himself.'

'However, there is your answer. Shakespeare is still symbolic of all that is best in English literature and his name is marvellously useful as a club with which to beat anyone outside the magic circle of Englishness about the head. But when it comes to the point, a good thriller or a love story – and not necessarily a particularly well-written one – will almost always be preferred. Where was I, anyway? Oh yes, I was telling you about *La plume de ma tante* and the indisputable fact that, by and large, the English loathe anyone seriously interested in languages. Not so bad if your linguist is a mere dabbler, forever floundering about hopelessly in the undergrowth of inflections and declensions and what have you. This, after all, proves clearly that he is merely a harmless, possibly even loveable, crank still on the right side of the great divide, whereas if he actually knows what he is talking about then that really is adding insult to injury. After all, being no good at languages is regarded by most people inhabiting this splendid realm as one of the cornerstones of their Englishness and a source of legitimate pride and satisfaction.'

'Now we can,' M continued, 'approach the study of languages in two entirely different ways. We can be matter-of-fact and practical about them, in which case we must tailor what we study closely to our requirements, and in this case too *La plume de ma tante* applies, namely as a kind of criticism of the way in which languages still continue to be taught, as if it were possible somehow to substitute triviality for relevance. You have no idea, Antonia, how I hate all those phoney stories about Hans and Maria swimming in the Rhine, those badly written descriptions of Bonn and Cologne and those joky, pointless conversations which I have to trot out week by week in class. There is, of course, another way as well in which some people approach the study of foreign languages. Greedy for anything knowable, they become (to coin a phrase) collectomaniacs, ever rapacious caterpillars among the leaves of knowledge.'

'What about you then, oh Master, where do you fit in?' asked Antonia, giggling in pleasurable anticipation. 'As for me,' replied M 'and I hope that you will not think me pompous or lacking in modesty (although I expect you will and I cannot really blame you), I have studied languages in both ways. My knowledge of English is, as you know, both profound and extensive' – Antonia, whose critical faculties were always wide awake, giggled again, but M chose to ignore this – 'and this has been the result of long and intensive study, but, on the other hand, I have also studied languages for purely practical reasons or to prove that I, at any rate, can master a language adequately within four to six weeks. Unfortunately I must admit that if I acquire a language too quickly, if, as it were, I do not allow it to settle and mature in my mind, I also tend to forget most of it again in no time at all.'

'But let me explain to you some of my methods for rapid language study and the principles on which they are based. In the first place, it is absolutely essential to be selective, especially as regards vocabulary. I, for instance, am not even remotely interested in football but I have a very good friend who is a keen supporter of Liverpool, I believe. It follows that if we both wished to learn a foreign language quickly, I could safely miss out any word specific to football, but for him such words would be very important. In practice I cope with this problem in the following way: I enter all the new words in the left-hand column of a special notebook, and their equivalents in English or German on the right. Then I assess the importance for me personally of every word listed and mark it accordingly, usually in five categories ranging from absolutely essential to totally unnecessary. The amount of time and effort I allocate to each category depends on its degree of relative importance. However, it seems that some words stick in my memory for ever, simply because I have marked them as totally useless. One such word which I shall surely never forget is the Russian word for 'tree stump' and another one the Spanish word for 'stock', which, I have been told, is a very pretty flower. I hope I'm not boring you?'

Faced with this sudden and unexpected question, Antonia, who in fact had been in some kind of a reverie, assured him that this was by no means the case and suggested politely, though not without a touch of irony, that he continue, knowing full well that she, at any rate, could not possibly stop him. 'It is generally thought,' M now expounded, 'that more work needs to be done in the early stages of language study than at a more advanced level. This, of course, is patently untrue, for the more you know already the more you are prone to forget, and there may come a point where you are actually forgetting more than you learn, in which case you are definitely regressing. It is true that what you learn at the later stages is generally speaking far less important than what you absorb early on. That is why I sometimes work through three or four different elementary courses and don't bother too much about more advanced books. But to get the feel of the language you are studying and to progress quickly from mere pedestrian word-by-word translation and the construction of simple sentences, I would advise you to start reading popular novels or magazines or similar publications as soon as possible after acquiring the mere rudiments, and to read them as quickly as possible. Above all – and this is very important – never look anything up but rely entirely on your subconscious to do the necessary work.'

'The point is this,' said M, ploughing on relentlessly. 'In a novel, for instance, vocabulary, grammar and idiom are, you understand, clearly restricted by the subject, the author's style and similar factors. This means that there is no end to the amount of repetition, but whenever a word or an idiom or a grammatical form is repeated, it is generally in a different context, and so this constitutes yet another clue helping your subconscious to get at the significance of what you are reading. And, of course, you must always bear in mind that dictionaries, however well designed, should be treated only as signposts and never as ultimately authoritative repositories of meaning, for just as butterflies in a meadow are in essence quite different from their counterparts in a collector's box, so are words and idioms altered when they are "pinned down" in a dictionary.' He could have gone on much longer yet but they had by now arrived at the block of flats where Antonia had her home and where, after the usual good-bye skirmishes, she left him.

M found Antonia a very stimulating companion and he liked to be seen with her, although there were times when this proved to be embarrassing or gave rise to ludicrous misunderstandings. On one occasion, for instance, they were having tea (what else?) in a café near Marble Arch, when M noticed a man of swarthy Mediterranean appearance staring at them with undisguised and unwavering interest. He stared right back, hoping thereby to discourage the ill-mannered oaf – for he knew from experience that unless he acted quickly and with determination Antonia might well encourage the fellow and in the process forget him, M, entirely – but when this failed to work he suggested to Antonia that they 'chuck in the towel' and go somewhere else, where they might have their tea in peace. She agreed readily, but as they prepared to leave, the stranger came over and asked in an accent redolent of old Vienna as well as a bouquet of other Central European cities, 'Tell me, my friend, are you by any chance the Morus Maskenbusch who was in Cracow in 1939, when I was there too?' M, not at all delighted – he had, after all, much better things to do – and not having the slightest idea who that perfumed, brilliantined but, above all, indiscreet person might be, replied that he was indeed that Morus Maskenbusch. He also mentioned his surprise that after so many years in which so much had happened (and he himself had changed so much for the better), he could still be recognised, whereupon Mr. Kleinfuss – such was the fellow's name – informed him, bellowing with laughter and to the great amusement of everybody present but especially Antonia, 'My dear Morus, you have not changed as much as you think. Your voice, for instance, has not changed at all. It is still as discordant as in those days and, unfortunately, quite unforgettable.'

Antonia had an elderly friend, name of John, a former publisher of modest but very popular books on a large variety of subjects, from *Coarse Fishing* to *Build Your Own Swimming Pool* and from *Minigolf for Beginners* to *Art for All*. Large, of reddish complexion and in his general appearance reminiscent of an apoplectic carp, he was obsessed with the idea of one day soon marrying poor petite Antonia, and, with this end in mind, considered it essential, one way or another, to get rid of M – in his eyes a dangerous and utterly unscrupulous rival. As for Antonia, she regarded the entire situation as a wonderfully funny joke, and to make it funnier still did her best to stoke the jealousy of her ex-publisher while prodding and teasing M's ever wakeful defensive mechanisms, with, in some cases, rather quaint results. Antonia, impish in the extreme, eventually arranged a meeting, which took place late at night and in the course of which M and his portly rival spent several hours walking in an endless circle about Covent Garden, with John attempting to explain, in terms combining English politeness and respect for 'fair play' with poorly veiled threats, why M should desist – in Antonia's best interest, of course – from any further contact with her. He even suggested (with what he, no doubt, considered as diplomacy at its very best) that M might wish to consider a further change of abode – to sunny Spain, for instance, although what he really appeared to have in mind was the North Pole or, preferably, some other planet altogether. M, for his part, refused to understand and muddied the conversation with various irrelevances and arguably despicable *non sequiturs.* The situation became even more farcical after Antonia took to showing M the long letters – rambling, venomous concoctions in rust-coloured ink applied in spidery handwriting – which she received from John almost every day and in which he drew her attention to the potential perils of her relationship with 'that scurrilous (or untrustworthy or dishonourable etc, etc.) foreign J., whose intentions towards her were clearly ignoble (or totally selfish or in a particularly abhorrent way lustful or …).' M made light of these letters but they reminded him that anti-semitism was not restricted to any particular country, class or time but is always with us and will stop at nothing – something he had been trying hard to forget.

M, who was beginning to feel vaguely threatened by all these neurotically hostile outpourings, was almost relieved when John, coming into the open at last, challenged him to a fight, with bare fists and to the bitter end – whatever that might be. Finding no merit whatsoever in such a contest and – with excellent reason – convinced that he would lose, he answered this challenge, which was transmitted to him by Antonia, by venturing to suggest that John fight Silversmith instead, whose weight he estimated as being closer to John's own, which must have been about eighteen stones.

John's 'challenge' was both the climax and the end of this triangular relationship, for Antonia left London shortly afterwards to take up an appointment in Sardinia, and since neither she nor M were great letter-writers, the contact between them was permanently ended. Antonia's parting gift to M was a rolled-up, neatly tied bundle of all her letters from John in which there were references to her friendship with M, and although she did not say so expressly M gained the impression that this was to be a clean and final break. The gift of the letters suggested to him that not only he but also his adversary was to be excluded from Antonia's future life – a thought which gave him some quiet satisfaction and made parting from Antonia more bearable.

The Sombrero-Domingos and M were enjoying supper at a Greek restaurant in Charlotte Street, not far from Schmidt's German restaurant and delicatessen store. It was warm, cosy and positively soporific – an effect emphasised by the abundance of well-worn, dark-red plush curtains and upholstery, heavily embossed flock-type wallpaper and, above all, the enclosed atmosphere, redolent of homely kitchen smells and cigarette smoke. The candle on their table was melting away in unsightly drops all over the wide-bellied Chianti bottle which served as its holder, looking, as it seemed to M, increasingly grotesque and reminding him of a film he had seen, in which the features of the mad scientist slowly and quite horrifyingly disintegrated as he lay writhing in a foul bath of burbling acid.

'You got a girlfriend?' Bertha, a veritable genius at tactless noseyness, wanted to know, and – as if this were not quite enough – continued, 'I bet you would like her to be here now instead of boring old us, or even better ...'

'But Bertha, don't be so indiscreet,' boomed her husband in a voice loud enough to make every head in the restaurant turn towards them, smirking and intrusive and causing M to blush hotly in confusion, 'Don't you see how you are embarrassing him?'

'Or perhaps you would like an older, more experienced woman who could teach you a thing or two?' Bertha, never one to be quelled easily and certainly not by her consort, insisted on pressing the point. 'Now, you may not believe it, but SD himself was always a great one for the ladies, hee-hee. Did he tell you about the time when he interviewed the naughty girls at the railway station in Berlin, or was it Frankfurt or Munich?'

'Never mind that, Morus doesn't want to hear that. Why must you always bring up these old cheeses, as if you had nothing better to talk about?'

'There they were,' Bertha continued undaunted, 'all those girlies all painted up from top to toe, in black stockings and everything, you know, when SD went up, cool as a cucumber he was, and wanted to know, did they enjoy their work, hee-hee.'

'And what happened?'

'What should have happened? I asked them a perfectly civil, perfectly reasonable question and then we had a most enlightening conversation. I learnt quite a lot, but that is something Bertha would not understand, not in a thousand million years.' Thus spake the male member of this matrimonial double-act.

'He learnt a lot, hee-hee, would you believe it!' Mrs. SD gurgled happily.

'Yes, I used to be quite a lad when I was a student.' Sombrero-Domingo had switched to a more mellow, reminiscent mood. 'Did I ever tell you about the time when I went boating on the Spree and dropped my shoe in the water?'

'That's funny, I also lost a shoe last summer from a rowing boat in Regent's Park...' M was about to delve into the deeper significance of this remarkable coincidence, but SD had not heard a word M was saying and was, in any case, in no mood to listen.

'But what was most funny was that if I hadn't lost that shoe, I might never have made it to Madrid. I might instead have landed in Sweden or Russia ...'

'Sweden where all the swedes come from, hee-hee ...' Bertha had a gift for extracting humour from the most unlikely sources.

'Luckily I was with Rosenbloom, my American friend whom I met at Cambridge. We used to call him Lofty, of course, because he was so small, you see ...' M following his own track.

'Cambridge, eh, fancy that ...'

'Be quiet Bertha, just for once in your life be quiet. Don't always interrupt when others are speaking. Where was I? Oh yes, so there I was with only one shoe, haw haw, but I was really lucky ...'

'So you were at Cambridge? Nice place that, Cambridge. I bet there were some nice girls there, hee-hee.' Bertha, twisting and worrying this choice new morsel of information this way and that, was not about to give up on it.

'That's where I met good old Rosenbloom. He was reading Mathematics ...'

'I certainly had Lady Luck on my side on that occasion, for you see ...'

'Lady Muck more likely,' commented Sombrero-Domingo's 'better half', causing him to roar and bellow like some wounded bull or buffalo, again attracting much attention. But what Bertha and M were meant to see was never revealed, for at this very point in their spirited exchange a waiter, picturesquely got up as a Greek freedom-fighter, brought the food – Shish Kebab for Sombrero-Domingo and rich, satisfying moussaka for Bertha and M. To wash it all down, they had pinkish red wine in a carafe and, after some very sweet, very sticky desserts, they enjoyed some equally sweet Greek coffee.

Never a believer in genteel passivity, Bertha, who after a drink or two tended to sail rather close to the wind, asked the waiter, in tones far from dulcet, where the 'funny outfit', which he was wearing with such manifest pride, could be obtained, as she herself was badly in need of some really way-out gear for a forthcoming party, and whether in his opinion such garments would suit her as well. She also enquired, in a spirit of utmost friendliness of course, whether it was true that all his countrymen were prone to engage in certain unspeakable relationships with sheep and goats, and if so, did the latter enjoy such activities?

Nothing, fortunately, lasts forever. Having left the restaurant and again in the open air – it was a balmy, very pleasant evening – they decided to take a walk in order to clear their lungs and get some much needed exercise. So they ambled down Rathbone Place and into Oxford Street, Sombrero-Domingo – round-eyed and argumentative as ever – swaying gently from side to side, while Bertha, who with her wide-brimmed, brown hat at a most rakish angle and in her brown 'mink' looked very much like some ambulatory mushroom, stopped every few yards to study the shop windows, stare at other people passing by or simply because she was out of breath. As for M, that eager beaver, he kept rushing ahead and then rushing back again in order to impart to his friends such snippets of information, observation and thought as he considered to be of interest. Sombrero-Domingo's zig-zag course led to numerous minor collisions and comments appropriate thereto, without however impairing his obvious enjoyment in the slightest degree.

Down they ambled towards Oxford Circus, passing the Studio and Academy cinemas – at the Academy they were, as so often before, showing *Les Enfants du Paradis* – and then turned to the left into Regent Street, where fine porcelain, fashionable clothing, and gold and silverware were the main attractions. Having reached Piccadilly, they lingered a while as they tried to decide on their further progress. Eventually and after much discussion, they headed for Leicester Square, where they considered which of the films currently on offer there might be worth seeing. Finally, and so as to complete the circuit, they went up along Charing Cross Road, past the bookshops, to Tottenham Court Road Station, the point at which their ways would naturally part. Bertha, who had taken rather more liquid refreshment than was good for her, was by this time badly in need of 'spending a penny'. When she found that the toilets outside the station, towards which she had been steering with so much hope and urgency, were closed, she was keenly disappointed – and who could blame her? 'It's closed, you know,' she exclaimed, giving vent to her understandable frustration, 'I suppose they expect me to do it in my knickers!'

CHAPTER TWENTY

CATTY has agreed to go with me to the pictures at last, on Friday. Still 116 hours to go – and I can hardly bear it. I already half regret having asked her, but there is a touch of danger in the situation, which I simply can't resist, as well as more than a suggestion of sin – the very thing, of course, that makes her so devilishly desirable. I am like a man trying to run in two directions at the same time, knowing that he is bound to regret whatever he does (or, for that matter, doesn't do). Only in my imagination am I totally uninhibited, without the slightest concern for what might happen. I am simply shaking with excitement. But I also understand old Faust who, having seduced his Margaret, complained that pure enjoyment was never within his reach, for whatever he did there was always Mephisto at his side ready to spoil it all.

In the tiny 'front garden' of the house at the corner of Meadows Road and Whitbread Lane there is a large black dog with a particularly nasty disposition. I don't know whether it regards me as a special enemy, but whenever I pass that house, which, unfortunately, I cannot always avoid, the cur growls and barks at me like mad, throws itself against the ramshackle wooden fence (which, it seems to me, is in imminent danger of collapse) and generally behaves in a most hysterical and aggressive manner. This has prompted me to write a story about a solitary, downtrodden man of low mentality – I have called him Agamemnon after that much abused, long-suffering king in the Iliad – and his relationship with a sadistic dog. I have read bits of it to Silversmith, who says that it is 'not bad'. That, of course, is high praise indeed, for as a rule Silversmith is not at all keen on my literary efforts, presumably because he is not only utterly devoid of even the slightest artistic appreciation but in a curious way aware of that fact and dimly resentful of his inadequacy in this respect. At any rate, for better or worse, here it is:

AGAMEMNON AND THE DOG

As a child Agamemnon had been afraid of dogs, but growing to manhood and middle age he also learned to hate them and to distrust them deeply.

Dogs, on the other hand, were well aware of his feelings towards them and responded in a variety of unpleasant and even repulsive ways, ranging from slobbering familiarity – paws upon his shoulders, licking his desperately averted face – to nerve-shattering displays of aggression and, worst of all, slyly menacing disdain, which seemed to suggest that one of these days, once total power was finally theirs, he would be dealt with, summarily and without the slightest mercy.

Agamemnon, a solitary person, did not, as a rule, venture out of doors lest fate confront him with a garrulous neighbour poking and prying, brats squalling or other horrors such as infest the public thoroughfares of our great cities, but once every week he would brave these dangers and flit down to the High Street, where he begged the wherewithal with which to buy such frugal fare as he required to keep body and soul of one piece.

On his way to the shops he had to traverse a housing estate and, in particular, to pass by a certain corner-house, the home of his chief adversary. Whenever Agamemnon approached, this canine, Dozer by name, a black and white, sharp-featured animal of no discernible pedigree but high intelligence, would be standing by the garden gate resting his paws on the wooden rail, apparently quite absorbed in the ever-eventful life of the street. He thus presented as peaceful an appearance as one could possibly desire, but Agamemnon knew better. He had learned from painful experience that this peace was extremely precarious and not to be trusted. Dozer might, for instance, allow him to pass until he was nearly out of reach and on the point of heaving a sigh of profound relief, when he – that is to say Dozer – would hurl himself, with a show of incredible ferocity and with his chest pugnaciously inflated, against the fence, which swaying and creaking under the impact seemed on the point of being shattered.

As Agamemnon – no longer a young man and far from fit – fled, his pulse racing, Dozer would bare his fangs in a gesture of supreme derision. On other occasions, he – Dozer, that was – would suddenly emit a most disconcerting yowl, as if he had been kicked or otherwise maltreated, and this would attract his numerous friends, both canine and human, who scuttled forth looking for a likely culprit. And no-one, of course, fitted that role better than Agamemnon. Yet another trick Dozer had, in a manner of speaking, up his sleeve, consisted in jumping over the gate and confronting the unfortunate Agamemnon with fearsome growls, salivating mouth and the hair of his fur bristling as if he were the very Hound of the Baskervilles in a particularly unfriendly mood. And although Agamemnon knew very well that his tormentor was merely pretending, he did not dare to call Dozer's bluff by taking even one more step forward, so that on those days he never got to the shops at all.

Of course, one can but guess what may have been the reason for all this hostility. It may, for instance, have been due to the fact that Agamemnon was a man of stunted growth, bald-headed and devoid of natural teeth. On balance, however, and looking at the matter from all angles, it seems more than likely that Dozer objected to Agamemnon's social circumstances, both past and present, that is to say to the fact that for the best part of his childhood he had been compelled to make do with a cat-box instead of a bed – with God only knows what undesirable effect on his personal scent

– and now inhabited a dog-kennel, charitably assigned to him by a widow Brownduck in return for various menial services. Previous to his occupancy – so rumour had it – it had been the abode of Trailer, one of Dozer's distant relations and last heard of at the Battersea Home for Inebriate Dogs.

As if to be thus bullied and teased by a mongrel dog were not humiliating enough, Agamemnon had to cope with the Woads, the multi-headed family who shared their home with Dozer. They never missed the slightest opportunity to add their ridicule and aggression to that of Dozer the dog. On one occasion indeed, after he had been pelted with stones by two of the lesser Woads, Agamemnon did, in fact, try (and this was quite against his grain) to take the bull by the horns, as it were, by complaining to the titular chief of the tribe, but his initiative ended in predictable disaster, for before he could even turn towards the gate – and who, after all, knows whether his determination would have been sufficient to see him through this self-imposed ordeal – he was confronted by Dozer, who may well have smelt a rat, and sent packing with nothing whatsoever accomplished.

Small wonder, therefore, that Agamemnon was much given to contriving truly ingenious plots with the sole point of wreaking relentless retribution. He dreamed up a variety of slow and painful means by which to terminate Dozer, his arch-enemy, and, depending on the fantasy he happened to be pursuing at the time, one or all of the detestable Woads. At home, in his kennel, which, incidentally, he shared with an unassuming elderly mouse, he would put on his sheriff's outfit – one of his most treasured and private possessions – and imagine himself challenging the lot of them at high noon, or he considered how he might get hold of the most venomous venom in the world in order to exterminate first Dozer and then the others, root and branch. He saw himself as the invisible man wreaking havoc among them with his sub-machine-gun – rat-tat-tat-tat – in the dead of night and then – by way of a special refinement – setting the whole place on fire, after first barricading the doors and windows tightly so that none could escape, except, of course, the two Woad maidens Mergle and Mandragora, whom he greatly desired and would, in the event, know what to do with.

These were but fanciful projects unlikely to come to fruition, but change being ever with us, it presently came to pass that the screw of Agamemnon's life took yet a further turn, which ultimately proved to be a turn for the worse.

For on one never-to-be-forgotten occasion, when Agamemnon was about to pass the dreaded house, an object flying through the mellow air of that spring afternoon struck him squarely in the face, knocking him clean unconscious. The object in question was in fact none other but the youngest Woad kicked savagely through a first-floor window by Wicklow Woad, his ever-loving Dad, who, in the grip of Demon Alcohol, was always prone to applying stringent parental discipline. His collision with Agamemnon caused young Robbo Woad to start screaming with might and main, which in the general pandemonium might well have escaped notice, had fiendish Dozer not intoned a most mournful call pregnant with deepest gloom and reminiscent of sounds such as long, long ago would curdle the blood of any traveller who, in the dead of night, happened to be crossing the moors on his way to Baskerville. This, as the cunning beast had correctly foreseen, brought out the entire tribe, with Wicklow, who had by now entirely forgotten his original part in the affair, rushing, or rather staggering, again in a manner of speaking, to the defence of his maltreated offspring. The latter, although not yet by any means at the age of reason but – bright little fellow that he was – sensing what was expected of him, intensified his protestations, greatly encouraged and applauded by one and all. Agamemnon was partly dragged and partly carried into the house to await the arrival of THE POLICE.

While being thus transported, he suffered various, albeit minor, fractures but, no matter, once inside he was given a nice cup of tea by Klytemnestra, a motherly woman of ample proportions and gratifyingly hospitable disposition.

When, some time later, the representative of the 'Lore' arrived, he too was treated to a nice cup of tea, as indeed were all the friends, relatives and neighbours who kept wandering in and out of the house throughout these stimulating – nay, festive – proceedings. These culminated in a stern but kindly warning to the effect that Agamemnon was to keep his nose clean in future, for the 'Lore' now had its beady eye on him, and he should never forget it.

Somehow Agamemnon's discomfiture released unforeseeable sources of sympathy in the Woads, who were themselves as often as not objects of the 'Lore's' attention. Indeed they felt that it was all a terrible shame and that the old fellow could not, after all, help being such a cretin. The episode ended in Agamemnon being given yet another cup of tea – the availability of this social beverage being apparently endless – with both Klytemnestra and Wicklow inviting him to drop in and see them 'for a chat and a nice cup of tea' whenever he happened to be in the neighbourhood.

Agamemnon took up the invitation with alacrity and, in fact, came to act upon it with such regularity and frequency that time and again the question was asked (as was indeed bound to be the case) whether he didn't have a home of his own to go to. Social problems could not, of course, be avoided entirely, especially with Wicklow Woad – apart from the public purse the chief provider of the family. Woad senior was, no doubt as a result of his essentially nocturnal trade involving property acquisition, which frequently entailed lengthy absences from his cheerful home, a man of somewhat secretive disposition, endowed with a most violent temper. He was also given to wild fits of jealousy, in the course of which he would accuse Agamemnon of unspeakable acts towards his wife Klytemnestra. Naturally, there was absolutely no truth in these flights of fancy. But Agamemnon's relations with the other Woads were reasonably acceptable. Although they continued to regard him as a 'moron' and a 'creep' and frequently told him so to his face, they were also quite proud of knowing a person such as him, for inasmuch as he had once been apprenticed to a professional night-watchman, he was clearly a man of superior education and culture. Robbo, Wriggler and Sebastian, the three little ones, loved to crawl all over him, extracting such hair as they could still find on his almost barren skull and smearing him with various edible and other messes, while, at twelve and thirteen years of age respectively, Mergle and Mandragora were, quite understandably, given to more sophisticated games far more in line with what Agamemnon himself liked best. Nothing, indeed, could be clearer proof of his novel, if but temporary, popularity than the fact that they even took him along on their outings, mainly to look after the little ones (for Wicklow and Klytemnestra were good parents, who never, absolutely never, neglected their offspring) and, of course, to tote provisions.

Dozer, on the other hand, was by no means prepared to let bygones be bygones, but realising that this was not a good time to pursue his master plan, he simply pretended to be resigned to the new situation. So deceitful was this cur that he would even allow Agamemnon to pass through his gate without manifest displeasure – a subdued snarl or a playful snap at Agamemnon's trouser-leg could hardly be regarded as such – and, cunning beyond belief, would accept such well-chosen peace-offerings as plastic bones which mewed plaintively when chewed and a drinking-bowl in the shape of a cat's truncated skull – gifts which would have melted any but as craven, as stony a heart as that of Dozer. This strategy did in fact convince everyone but Agamemnon, who, thanks to a sensitive nose for danger such as is characteristic of rabbits and other creatures much sought-after by predators, had more than an inkling of Dozer's unbending hostility, but this was exactly what Dozer wanted. Agamemnon had always been prone to vivid dreams abounding in monsters and monstrous events, but now it was Dozer who haunted his nightmares. In one recurrent dream, for instance, Dozer would appear to him in the garb of his long since departed Aunt Sadie, a sharp-featured 'Gothic' woman who had 'looked after him' in his younger years. In his dream Agamemnon relived the terror which this formidable relative used to strike in his heart, although now her implements of torture were fangs and claws, and her raucous voice had turned into an equally raucous bark.

Agamemnon made a last, desperate attempt to appease the formidable Dozer. He had inherited a ring-master's jacket with shiny brass buttons and golden epaulettes from his defunct maternal grand-uncle, and he kept this garment, of which he was justifiably proud, in a special box, together with other prized possessions such as his sheriff's outfit and a sub-machine-gun capable of firing lumps of sugar over short distances and at somewhat odd angles. By now, alas, the jacket had lost quite a lot of its military smartness, for it had become a source of sustenance and comfort to a family of domesticated moths. Rightly considering that neither his sheriff's outfit nor his sub-machine-gun nor, indeed, any of his other treasures were likely to appeal to the wily canine, Agamemnon decided to offer him the red jacket as a token of his goodwill and desire for lasting reconciliation. Dozer, false-hearted as ever, appeared to be pleased with the gift, but far from polishing the buttons or carrying out necessary repairs as might have been expected from any hound of true sentiment and breeding, he, grinning broadly, presented it to Agamemnon when the latter came again next day, by which time it had been dishonoured, disfigured, and torn to shreds. And as if this were not enough, this was the very visit when Wicklow, having arrived at the conclusion that he had seen quite enough of Agamemnon to last him a lifetime, threw him out, quite literally.

No longer able to forego the companionship and interesting goings-on to which he had become accustomed – not to mention Klytemnestra's cups of tea and other ministrations – Agamemnon finally made up his mind to get rid of the satanic hound, whom he blamed for absolutely all the ills which had lately befallen him. Realising full well that great cunning would be needed to achieve his aim, he gave the matter much thought, and after rejecting a variety of plans as insufficiently practical or not totally reliable, he hit upon a deadly one so sophisticated as to make its success inevitable.

As is the case with all truly great initiatives, Agamemnon's solution was simplicity itself. It was based on three main premises: his knowledge of the route the Woads – and Dozer – used unfailingly to follow on their Sunday outings in summer, and the present summer being hot and dry, the time was propitious; Dozer's inability to resist the lure of any upright object appropriately scented; and the principle according to which a heavy object dislodged from a great height is bound to fall and, as a result, cause grave and lasting damage to any dog's head within its path of descent, the extent of the damage depending mainly on its weight – that is to say, the weight of the falling object – and the distance between its points of origin and impact.

Agamemnon went to great lengths in designing and constructing his trap. He found a post regularly frequented by a female chihuahua of the neighbourhood, whose powerful scent was famous and could be relied upon to mask his own, not inconsiderable fragrance, unearthed it (the post, of course) and erected it under a tree along the Woads' Sunday-outing route. Drawing on unsuspected resources of strength and perseverance, he tugged a heavy bronze statue of an avenging angel – yet another of his treasures – to the tree in question and into its branches, balancing it most carefully and precariously. He attached a black thread to the main supporting branch so skilfully that it could not possibly be seen but was sure to act as a trigger when Dozer came to mark his attendance at the post.

On the fateful day, with zero-hour nearly at hand and the sun rising merrily in a clear, blue sky, Agamemnon went to inspect his handiwork. Everything was in perfect order – exactly as he had left it – and in the distance he could already hear the Woads in full hue and cry as they approached the tree of destiny. He recognised Robbo's outraged yell as his father hit him playfully in the stomach with a bottle already much depleted in spite of the early hour, and he discerned the emphatic voices of Mergle and Mandragora in strident sisterly contest. Last but by no means least, there came Dozer straying hither and thither as his inquiring mind impelled him, precisely according to plan.

All that remained now was to make sure that the thread was taut and then to hide. By tugging gently, ever so gently at the thread, Agamemnon was able to demonstrate, beyond even the slightest shadow of a doubt, that its tautness was perfect and entirely as intended.

When the Woads found Agamemnon in the grass with his head split wide open, there was much commiseration and some puzzlement as to how his predicament might have come about. But Wicklow, who had an eye for such things, realised that the *objet d'art* was not to be sneezed at and might well be worth a bob or two. As for Dozer, he used the post exactly as Agamemnon would have wished him to use it. And life went on, regardless.

Agamemnon, now sadly defunct but hardly missed, was interred at a cemetery nearby, with a wooden post to mark his passing. In due course everyone forgot him, except Dozer, who, having developed a liking for the open road, used on occasion to visit his grave, possibly to pay his respects.

Friday, at 6 o'clock sharp and only 15 minutes later than agreed, Catty arrived at the booking office of Tottenham Court Road station, where, in a state of mounting impatience, M had already been waiting for half an hour or longer. Always a neat girl but particularly well turned-out for her encounter with M, she was wearing her navy-blue dress with gold buttons, a new beige coat which looked soft and cuddly, black shoes with stiletto heels and dark-grey stockings – a promise, as it seemed to M, of sweet passion unbridled. Catty also carried a long, slim umbrella with a transparent handle in the shape of a fox's head – a kind of symbolic pointer perhaps to the adventure on which she was hoping to embark this very evening. She had put up her hair, which was the colour of ripe maize, and moved in a faint fragrance of lemony perfume. The overall effect was simply stunning, and M, who looked much as he usually did, could not but feel proud to be walking at her side.

They shook hands, formally as it were, like two protagonists before a sporting contest, and then they were off, on their way to the Camden Odeon, where they hoped to see *Love on the Dole*, a film M had enjoyed repeatedly during his seafaring days but was quite prepared to see again, especially since gentle, dove-like Deborah Kerr, who played the heroine, was one of his favourite, most desired actresses.

Having sufficient time to spare – almost an hour and a half – they stopped off at a small Italian restaurant near Warren Street for an escalope and a cup of tea. M's chivalrous attentions made Catty extremely communicative. As on other occasions, she told him all about herself, her family and the latest TTTW gossip – quite pathetic really in her eagerness to capture and retain M's attention, to be accepted by him as a real person worthy of respect and not merely an object of desire. In this attempt she was, of course, bound to fail, for although M never doubted the genuineness of her friendship, not for a moment, he also felt that her insubstantial prattle blunted her charm, creating a gulf between them and dissolving like acid his romantic feelings towards her. Besides, her voice and her 'genteel' accent seemed to him uncouth, and the way in which she expressed herself clumsy and downright ungrammatical.

Just how common his experience was became clear to him only years later when watching a play on television. In this play, during most of which not a word was spoken, a boy from a 'cultured' background and a 'common' working-class girl met across a wire fence while spending a day at a religious retreat in Ireland where talking was prohibited, and fell passionately in love. Having agreed by sign language to meet later outside the retreat, the boy waited for the girl at a nearby bridge. When he saw her coming, his face lit up, but when she spoke to him, in a raucous voice and vulgar dialect, he was so shocked that he simply turned around and ran away from her as if all the furies from hell were after her. As M watched this play, it again confirmed him, as had various other experiences, in his view that the laws of nature were not by any means restricted to certain specific spheres such as physics, electricity, mechanics or mental phenomena, but were in their application far more and perhaps entirely general. For what, in his opinion, made the play so interesting was the fact that what happened in the story seemed, in all essential respects, to parallel the structure and processes of an electrical capacitor, a device for storing an electric charge well known to specialists in the field, which discharges itself in an abrupt and even violent manner as soon as the two sides of a kind of separating screen, the 'dielectric', are bridged with the aid of a conductive wire.

In spite of his growing dismay as Catty gave him a detailed account of her Auntie Pauline's difficulties with a builder, her granny's state of health, and other matters of, as he thought, supreme indifference, M responded with automatic words of comfort or advice, whichever seemed to him most appropriate – and got away with that. Now she was telling him about Angela, her best friend and a close neighbour. 'Me and Angela, you know,' she explained, 'have been mates for donkey's years, she's really pretty, you know, you'd like her. Wherever she goes,' she continued with a sidelong glance at M, who was trying to look unconcerned, 'men stare at her, quite embarrassing really.' Rising to this bait, M enquired – carefully, of course, mustn't make Catty think that he was really keen – whether it might not be a good idea for the three of them to go out together one evening for a meal or something. He would, he said, like to meet this Angela, who appeared to be playing such an important role in Catty's life. After all, shouldn't good friends such as Catty and he know everything about each other? Catty agreed, non-committally, but with more than a trace of discontent, the corners of her mouth drooping and her upper lip trembling slightly. As always when she felt used or rejected, she lowered her head, became taciturn and seemed on the point of bursting into tears, which compelled M, who cursed himself for having aroused Catty's jealousy after all, to take rapid remedial action by telling her about his unhappy childhood in Vienna, when he was at the mercy of his sadistic stepmother. He hinted at details of this dubious relationship, which both restored his own ardour and made Catty all sympathetic and protective, causing her to take his hand and to squeeze it reassuringly.

At the Camden Odeon they were no longer showing *Love on the Dole* but *The Hunchback of Notre Dame* with Charles Laughton as Quasimodo in the title role. M, who had read and enjoyed the book, was all in favour of seeing this film instead, and since Catty agreed that it might be 'good for a laugh', he bought two tickets and a bag of salted peanuts, and in they went.

They had barely enough time to find their bearings in the dark and to settle down in their seats, when the main film started. Initially M observed the greatest decorum, carefully avoiding any gesture which Catty might possibly have resented, but when Quasimodo chased Esmeralda, that dear, delightful gipsy girl, through the streets of Paris in order to bring her to his master, the evil and lustful archdeacon of Notre Dame, M judged that the time had come for him to put his left arm protectively about Catty's shoulder. When Esmeralda, kind-hearted girl that she was, gave water to poor pilloried Quasimodo, thus kindling a flame in his heart which nothing would ever extinguish, M gave his fair companion a reassuring hug and gently, ever so gently, rested his other hand on her knee. Not quite certain how to respond, she pretended not to notice. When radiantly handsome Captain Phoebus, whom Esmeralda loved with every fibre of her being, descended upon her – presumably in order to consummate their wondrous relationship – M changed the position of his protective arm ever so slowly, ever so cautiously, so as to be able to reach Catty's bosom. After a moment's hesitation, she not only permitted this gesture but even joined in it by pressing his hand against her soft, resilient flesh. The enjoyment of this blissful moment was, however, slightly marred for M by the intrusive recollection that, in literature, flesh in this state of highly desirable resilience had on occasion been referred to as 'pneumatic'.

By the time Esmeralda was more or less safe in the bell-tower of the cathedral and poor Quasimodo had confessed his sad, hopeless love for her, M and Catty had themselves made further, considerable progress in their relationship. Their breath had become urgent and noisy, they were perspiring profusely and their hearts were beating fit to burst. M whispered his most daring desires into Catty's ear, and she did not reject him. Alas, the cocoon of intimacy surrounding them was rudely shattered when a young man sitting in front of M turned towards them and asked with some irritation and in a voice meant to be heard by one and all: 'Why don't you milk her, mate, while you're about it?' This provoked quite a bit of giggling here and there, while – preferring, no doubt, the romance on the screen to the real thing – one or two people shouted 'Quiet!' Catty, deeply mortified by this experience, removed herself from M, which compelled him to return to position one. This stalemate lasted for several minutes, but then M's hand, the one he had used to grasp her to his chest, wandered, as of its own accord, first to her knee and then, encountering no resistance, to the hem of her dress, raising it in barely perceptible stages. His questing hand advanced to the top of her stocking and beyond, but at that point Catty closed her legs tightly, preventing any further progress. 'What do you take me for?', she hissed into M's ear, causing him to draw back. By now the film too was drawing to a close. The King of France had pardoned Esmeralda, and she and her good friend Gringoir were on their way. With the evil archdeacon safely dispatched, they had nothing more to fear, and a happy ending – not, however, as romantic as the ending in the book – was on the cards.

Not quite so happy was the conclusion of M and Catty's evening, in spite of the fact that at certain moments it had seemed so promising. Catty was still very upset, tearful and clinging by turns, afraid that M would now despise her for being 'easy'. She even begged him not to tell his friends or anyone at TTTW about what she had allowed him to do. M for his part felt emotionally exhausted and at the same time deeply worried that he might now be under some permanent obligation towards her and no longer free to do as he liked. By the time they reached Camden Town station, they were both thoroughly depressed, and when M asked Catty as a matter of politeness when she would like to meet him again, she burst into tears, which was highly embarrassing. 'I know you don't care a fig for me, you blokes are all the same,' she cried, and then left, her head bowed and her shoulders sagging, the very picture of gloom and despondency.

CHAPTER TWENTY ONE

M WAS ONLY four or five years of age when his father, who happened to be in Klimkovice on holiday, took him to see his first film, a silent version of *The Count of Monte Cristo*. Of this momentous event M remembered only that he did not enjoy it at all – probably because the atmosphere in the crowded 'hall' (not really a hall but a largish room in the local inn) was very hot and stuffy, and he had to stand throughout the performance, not an easy feat for a youngster as restless as himself, whose generally imperious bodily needs could never be ignored for long. Besides, he could not follow the story and was profoundly bored by the apparently endless ballroom scenes.

In spite of this somewhat unpropitious introduction to the world of the moving pictures, films soon became quite an important item in his entertainment diet, especially Wild West films starring Tom Mix, defender of the good and afflicted and scourge of all evil-doers, who, immaculately dressed in a white suit and wearing an enormous white hat, would perform deeds of almost unbelievable valour (but M and the other spectators believed them to be gospel truth), shooting and riding his way out of the most impossible predicaments. Then there was Rin-Tin-Tin, that noble dog of infinite ingenuity, who – it would be churlish to use impersonal pronouns when referring to such a superior being – naturally attracted no end of vociferous advice, encouragement and approval from the predominantly juvenile audience whenever he appeared on the scene. Extremely popular too were the comic activities of Pat and Patachon, one of whom was very short whereas the other was extremely tall. M never managed to work out which was which, and, although in later years he often used to wonder about that, he did not, at the time, attach the slightest importance to this matter, as long as large, messy cream cakes hurled through the air hit the wrong targets, Pat (or Patachon, as the case might be) kept falling into tubs of water conveniently (or, rather, inconveniently) placed, large meals neatly served and eagerly tucked into proved to be made of rubber, and other jolly japes occurred with adequate frequency.

In Vienna M did not see many films, particularly during his latter years in that city, when his father's financial situation was such as to make such 'extravagant' entertainment virtually inaccessible. He did, however, see a few mountaineering dramas with rugged types such as Luis Trenker picking delicate alpine flowers on steep and forbidding rock-faces for village maidens such as those so finely portrayed by Miss Hansi Knotek. He also attended several films about plain Viennese folk with golden hearts – mainly pert and pretty parlourmaids, buxom and elderly cooks, young lieutenants 'on their uppers' but deeply in love with the pretty parlourmaid on offer, and other types much in vogue in romantic Viennese fiction. These attractive and spirited personages got together, were obliged to part and, thanks to the wise and kindly support of the older generation – perhaps a music teacher with a handlebar moustache and a particularly fine and sophisticated sense of humour who lived in the basement, or an old publisher in the upstairs flat – got together again for a truly happy ending. He found films such as these particularly appealing, for they suggested to him a warmth and an undemanding, ready acceptance such as at that time seemed to be lacking in his life.

M longed to be like everybody else, although – an ardent admirer of 'great' literature – he firmly believed that such bliss was available only to the thoroughly mediocre, and he certainly did not regard himself as one of them. He would point out that, at one period of his life, Leo Tolstoy, being utterly determined to get closer to the 'people', made his own boots and insisted in all seriousness that any Russian folk tune however humble was of greater cultural importance than even the most memorable of Beethoven's symphonies, since infinitely more people knew and enjoyed a simple song than had even heard of Beethoven. And in portraying the simple peasant Platonov in *War and Peace* as a veritable fount of wisdom while making Pierre, his own alter ego, 'go native', Tolstoy gave literary expression to a desire, which, according to M, was characteristic of many men of genius. Goethe's Faust bemoans his solitude – at least before getting involved with Mephisto and the lovely Margaret – and feels that he can be truly human only among the 'happy' throngs of his fellow citizens, while Dostoevsky's Raskolnikov, although greatly superior to them intellectually, has much to learn from the drunkard Marmeladov and his daughter Sonya, who has managed to retain her essential purity and goodness in spite of being obliged to earn her livelihood as a common prostitute. Indeed, so M argued, the idealising attitude to the poor and disadvantaged, which is particularly prominent in the teachings of Christ, may have its roots in a kind of 'culture fatigue' and, again, a desire 'to be like everybody else' – not separated from 'ordinary' people by special advantages, standards or accomplishments. There perhaps lay the appeal of the monastic life with its stringent disciplines, as well as the fascination of political parties and religious cults calling for total suppression of self in the life of the community as a whole.

In the course of a school visit M once saw a film of quite a different kind – a 'cultural' film about Siegfried and the Nibelungs, which dealt with such ancient Germanic themes as heroism and craven cowardice, strength and nobility, loyalty and treachery, undying love and retribution. Based on various Icelandic and other legends, better known from Wagner's *Ring*, it could not fail to entertain and impress its youthful audience. M, himself never remarkable for feats of physical prowess, duly admired Siegfried, as the latter, acting on behalf of Gunther the king, outdid the mighty Brünhild in various sporting contests, and laughed uproariously when Brünhild, having seen through wimpish Gunther's machinations, suspended the latter with well-deserved contempt from a nail on the wall. Spellbound, he loved the scenes in the forest, particularly Siegfried's fight with the fiery dragon. Treacherous Hagen with his sinister black eye-patch, two-horned helmet and powerful sword, which he was forever ponderously stroking and cuddling on his knees as he sat, his legs wide apart, deep in unwholesome thought hatching his dastardly plans, filled M with awe and foreboding. But Siegfried's cruel murder caused him much distress – Siegfried, after all, was such a fine fellow and, it would seem, not in the least anti-Jewish – and when the slain hero's wound started to bleed profusely, thus bearing mute yet eloquent witness to the enormity of Hagen's guilt, he could not bear to watch and felt compelled to close his eyes and ears tightly.

In fairness to M, it should be understood that it was not so much the visual horror of the scene that appalled him as the blatant injustice of the act. Perhaps his detestation of injustice was due to the way in which he reacted to personal experience – his school-years in Vienna were, after all, marred by much that was blatantly unjust – or it may have been due to a longing for messianic peace and tranquillity (lions lying down with lambs, etc.), but be that as it may, it stayed with him throughout his life and was never blunted.

During his first year in England, the British government, fearful perhaps of being accused of excessive and imprudent generosity towards aliens and upsetting thereby the delicate applecart of the employment market, did not permit M or, for that matter, any of his fellow refugees, to engage in paid work of any kind. This suited M fine, for, thanks to a weekly allowance of 25 to 30 shillings from the Czech Refugee Trust Fund, he did not find it difficult to make ends meet, but it did entail the problem of how to fill his time between getting up in the morning and going to bed at night. There was a limit to what could be achieved in this respect by getting up late, elaborately preparing breakfast and now and again some other meal, walking, reading and 'chewing the cud' with like-minded friends. At the time he was, incidentally, very keen on acquiring such skills and knowledge as would give him some advantage in the jungle of human relations, to which end he devoured, apart from works of literature and less elevating but nonetheless enjoyable texts, anything from textbooks on ju-jitsu and ballroom dancing to tomes on philosophy and applied psychology.

But once M had discovered the Trocadero near the Elephant and Castle – at the time his local cinema – his troubles were over. Performances being continuous and front seats relatively cheap – you could get a ticket for as little as fourpence, which was really good value considering that, in addition to two films, the show included highly dramatic, spirit-lifting Pathé News and, at the start of the session, real live entertainment such as organ music, comics or sing-along numbers – he would often go to the first performance of the afternoon and stay until the cinema closed its doors for the day. He did not mind seeing the entire programme three times in succession, although the fact that he was always so near to the screen may well have contributed to his poor eyesight and proneness to pains in the nape of his neck later in life, nor did he mind coming in towards the end of a film and seeing its beginning later.

Much as M enjoyed these afternoons, few films which he saw during this period of his life, and even fewer actors, made any lasting impression on him. Bette Davis and Spencer Tracy, Fred Astaire and Ginger Rogers, The Marx Brothers and Buster Keaton, Humphrey Bogart, George Raft and Edward G. Robinson and many, many others did for him what they could, but in the final analysis he didn't much care what he saw – *Andy Hardy in Love*, *A Day at the Races* or any B-movie being equally acceptable. Most films he enjoyed in much the same way as, thanks to a healthy appetite, he generally enjoyed food, that is to say as means to an end, that end being obliteration of time without boredom, discomfort or undue expense. But just as the memory of Auntie Rosa's plum dumplings topped with fried breadcrumbs and hot, molten butter, of his stepmother's chicken-noodle soup and of his grandmother's *Apfelstrudl* remained with him always, certain films did also, after all, take root in his memory. *The Blue Angel* was such a film (oh, for Marlene Dietrich's legs and the imperious disdain with which she treated that wretched professor!) and so was *Benito Juárez*, in which Paul Muni, arguably the greatest actor of his time, played the famous Mexican President as he slowly but surely crushed luckless Maximilian, whose brother was the Austrian Emperor Franz Josef and who, supported by the French but eventually deserted by them in his hour of need, had come to rule the country.

During his time at sea, M visited cinemas in various parts of the world, where, on occasion, they were showing films which he had already seen previously, sometimes repeatedly. One such film was *Love on the Dole*, and he always claimed that in various ports he had seen *Kind Hearts and Coronets* no fewer than eight times, but since this film was made only long after the war, when M was again firmly settled in England, this could not have been the case.

Even in Japan, M's contact with the cinema was not entirely broken, for on the way to and from Michigawa station, where for about two years he and many of his fellow prisoners loaded and unloaded railway wagons, they passed, riding on trucks or marching through the narrow, crowded streets of that working-class district, a small cinema which, to judge by the gory yellow banners advertising its programmes, the large, crude illustrations and such stills as M managed to catch a glimpse of, specialised in war films, the prime virtue of which did not appear to be objectivity.

But as for *The Lash of the Penitente* and *White Zombies*, he enjoyed those during his stay in San Francisco, where – at last on his way back to England – he spent two extremely stimulating months. There was, of course, much else that impressed him in that fine and hospitable town, and he never held it against the Jewish Community

Organisation that one of its officials, assuming (and who could blame him for that?) that M was an illegal immigrant, shouted at him, as soon as he saw him, to get right back where he came from. The man did, after all, become almost comically apologetic once he had understood that M was only in transit, waiting to join a suitable ship, and did not wish to become a burden on anybody's public purse. In his contrition he even went so far as to give M a handsomely embossed, if somewhat worn, leather purse, to which the latter became very attached indeed, although, being excessively limp, it was never of the slightest use.

After his return to London M made it a habit to visit the cinema at least once every week. No longer interested simply in making time pass, he became more discriminating and more demanding. Many of the films he saw during this period have long since become classics. For instance, to mention but a few, *Ninotchka* with Greta Garbo (what a fuss they made when the great one actually deigned to laugh!), *Meet me in St. Louis* with Judy Garland (who could then have foretold the tragic fate that awaited her?), *Citizen Kane*, Orson Welles' memorable portrayal of a ruthless newspaper tycoon, and *Gaslight*, in which Ingrid Bergman as the hard-done-by wife of Charles Boyer, her rotten husband, manages to turn the tables on him in such a gratifying way. He also saw and enjoyed a number of French and Russian films such as *Les Enfants du Paradis*, *Le Jour se Lève*, the Marius trilogy and *Ivan the Terrible*, whereas his first pornographic film – it took him a long time to find the courage necessary for entering the cinema in which it was being shown – proved to be so boring and filled him with such revulsion that he did not stay to the end but left on a note of intense disapproval. M prided himself on being quite unshockable but this in fact was not the case and his curiosity and enjoyment would normally collapse well before the removal of the seventh veil. Still, from time to time he felt the need to repeat the experience, always hopeful but almost always with the same disappointing result.

M came to prefer the cinema to live theatre. When challenged on this point, he would argue that the cinema was far less restricted in its means of production than the theatre, that at any given time far more films were on offer and coming on stream than plays, and that the director of a film could, by means of close-ups and other techniques, make every spectator see exactly what he wanted him to see, irrespective of where in the cinema the latter was seated (although the two or three front rows, where he usually found himself, were admittedly a bit too close to the screen for comfort). In the theatre, on the other hand, a spectator at the rear of the stalls could not hope to see as much as one sitting in front. And to anyone who insisted that, considering the piecemeal way in which films were made, there was greater artistic merit in acting on a stage than on a film set, he would say that what ultimately mattered was not this or that actor's artistic merit but the impact on the spectators of the production as a whole. After all, nobody cared whether a poem or a piece of music had been composed in a single blinding flash of inspiration or bit by bit and subject to much editing, so why should it be any different when it came to acting?

Following the successful publication of the TTTW poster presently gracing the platforms of every underground station in London and, as everyone assured him, adding greatly to their elegance and interest, Dr. Pendlebloom – never one to let the grass grow under his feet – was now in the process of putting the finishing touches to the new TTTW brochure, a stylistic and commercial masterpiece entirely of his own making. He was absolutely certain and understandably proud of the fact that on this occasion there had been no need for him to consult anyone – not even Miss Gomberg or, for that matter, Mr. Woodlock, his adviser on matters of publicity – and, in any case, he had, in the light of past experience, every reason to doubt that they would have been able to come up with any serious contributions. He it was, and he alone, who had hit upon the felicitous idea of basing his preliminary research on the publications of competing organisations, the occasional merits of which Dr. Pendlebloom, generous and fair-minded to a fault, as everyone kept telling him, was at all times prepared to concede. Such enterprises were, for instance, A.A.A. Activities, a company with little enough to recommend it except for its wise choice of name ensuring a most favourable position in the London Telephone Directory and other alphabetically arranged works of reference, and Lingospread Ltd., that widely renowned establishment, which, in spite of being a relative newcomer on the instructional scene, enjoyed a not inconsiderable reputation for maximum profit at minimum cost and was therefore entitled to some respect. Indeed, Lingospread's sound economic policies had already enabled its owner to acquire a neo-Georgian mansion with some ninety rooms, through which he – wearing knickerbockers, suitably engraved boots and a multi-gallon hat, as befitted his station – would walk daily, perhaps in order to make quite certain that neither they (the rooms that is) nor their number had changed in any way.

The heavy responsibility of procuring the required reference documentation and other background materials had fallen to Miss Gomberg, who, as on so many other previous occasions, was again able to demonstrate that she was not merely a force to be reckoned with but (which was even more important) endowed with major executive ability – in other words, a most fitting helpmate to Dr. Pendlebloom. In the process of carrying out her task she had organised various minions and an ever hopeful band of poor relations and hangers-on (as well as the milkman and other local suppliers) into a fact-gathering team second to none. Not all her initiatives were successful, of course, and, although bound to come in useful at some future stage, not all the publications eventually procured proved to be directly relevant to the project in hand. For instance, thinking, quite naturally, in terms of sartorial rather than tutorial establishments and, by temperament an optimist, ever eager to oblige such a valued customer as Miss Gomberg, the gentleman privileged to carry out minor repairs and alterations to Dr. Pendlebloom's nether garments and other items of apparel had presented her with an impressive collection of catalogues and leaflets from various widely esteemed tailoring organisations. In spite of this little, quite understandable misunderstanding, Miss Gomberg continued to value him as a dab hand when it was a matter of replacing zippers with buttons, for Dr. Pendlebloom was a man profoundly wary of zippers, seeing that in the past they had repeatedly exposed his person to unspeakable embarrassment and worse. She also appreciated his skill when it came to widening the shoulders of jackets and overcoats. After all, Dr. Pendlebloom, who was, in some respects, not unlike the hero of *Antic Hay*, believed firmly in this method of personality enhancement.

Having, in a manner of speaking, separated the wheat from the chaff, discarding the latter and appropriately classifying and marking up the former, Miss Gomberg had inserted such material as was, in her informed opinion, potentially useful into a number of colour-coded cardboard files, placing them, in impeccably neat fashion, on Dr. Pendlebloom's desk – as handsome and tidy a desk as befitted the chief executive of an enterprise as important as TTTW. Dr. Pendlebloom, in turn, had studied these documents – not without some distaste, which compelled him to visit his private bathroom suite repeatedly in order to subject his neatly manicured hands to symbolical purification – and, using them merely as raw materials and stepping-stones, had produced a much superior text of his own, which, glowing with satisfaction and pride, he was now in the process of perusing. This is what he read:

'At the very heart of the United Kingdom, in colourful Soho, where East meets West and South meets North, you will find Tutors To The World Limited, an Institute of Learning second to none in this or any other country of the inhabited globe.' At this point Dr. Pendlebloom hesitated for a moment and then, in his spidery handwriting, added the following elucidatory words after 'North': 'at the cross-roads between the City of London with prestigious St. Paul's Cathedral and the verdant expanses of Hyde Park and Kensington Gardens (the West End's evergreen lungs) on the one hand, and historical Waterloo and the opulent residential districts of Belsize Park, Hampstead and Golders Green on the other'. The text continued as follows: 'Tutors To The World Limited, more generally referred to as TTTW, is an organisation devoted entirely' (he struck out 'entirely' and put in 'substantially') 'to the teaching of languages. Our internationally famous English courses enable adult students from abroad and many others to improve their fluency, their style or, at a more elementary level, their basic knowledge of this important language – the language, as will be generally appreciated, of Shakespeare, Wodehouse, the creator of Bertie Wooster and the inimitable Jeeves (Dr. Pendlebloom knew what he liked), and, in its transatlantic form, Mark Twain – beyond their most sanguine expectations. As for our foreign-language courses, they too are justly renowned, inasmuch as they are major keys to the gates of commerce, understanding and durable friendship between the nations of our world.' Quite overcome at this stage by the exquisite brilliance of his style, Dr. Pendlebloom permitted himself the luxury of applying several strong, expressive exclamation-marks to the margins of his copy, which continued as follows:

'The enviable international reputation of TTTW rests squarely on the twin pillars of sound administration and superior tuition. With TTTW you are in safe, highly experienced hands that guide your every linguistic step on the road to perfection, pointing out every pitfall, offering every insight, describing every facility.'

Leaning back in his armchair and turning his head to the left, Dr. Pendlebloom stared briefly out of the window, through which he could see the rear elevation of an office building accommodating a variety of major and minor enterprises. This helped him to think and was a particular boon during the winter months, when in the late afternoons he could look straight into the offices opposite and below. He was then able to observe all manner of comings and goings and other activities, some of which, he was certain, could and would never have occurred in a properly managed organisation of high moral standards such as his own. Having looked his fill, Dr. P. pressed a button on his desk, a signal for Miss Gomberg to dispatch Catty with the mid-morning coffee and biscuits.

Dr. Pendlebloom again turned his attention to the script before him. 'For how true,' he read, 'even in our advanced day and age, are the words of that famous Chinese sage who said: He who speaks in many tongues embraces the world. And where else but at TTTW would one find such perfect confirmation of this profound utterance?' At this Dr. Pendlebloom smiled a very private smile, for, truth to tell, the Chinese sage was a figment of his own prolific imagination. Still, no-one, not even his most malevolent competitor, could possibly be so churlish as to criticise him for this entirely justifiable publicity ploy, especially as there was virtually no way in which its veracity could ever be tested. Besides, Dr. Pendlebloom, a great believer in the power and, indeed, virtue of positive thinking, was unshakably convinced of the essential truthfulness of his statement – so why quibble about details?

Catty having brought the coffee and placed it before him, Dr. Pendlebloom now devoted himself to the enjoyment of this delightful beverage, which he preferred black and with only one lump of sugar. He also consumed two biscuits and then continued with his perusal:

'Just like any other seat of learning,' he now read, 'TTTW depends on its tutorial staff for the excellence which students throughout the world have rightly come to expect. Our tutors, hand-picked educationalists *par excellence* and of superior academic distinction, are admirably capable of moulding the eager, questing minds of those in their charge – a responsibility which they discharge in a spirit of utmost seriousness and devotion. They assist our students in their ascent towards the commanding heights of linguistic perfection and help them to pass – frequently with brilliant results – the important examinations of our leading academic institutions and professional bodies. (For details of TTTW examination courses and fees, see page ...) These outstanding practitioners of the noble arts of language training are, to a man, dynamic, forward-looking and aware – characteristics particularly appreciated by our numerous students from the USA and the British Commonwealth.'

Dr. Pendlebloom nodded appreciatively, acknowledging, as it were, the marvellous subtlety of his phrasing. Then, having turned the page, he passed a critical eye over a list of 79 alphabetically arranged languages, all of which could, as the brochure had it, be taught to post-graduate and all Institute of Linguist levels. He jotted down 'Gomberg check for possible omission of languages' and then turned to the following stirring announcement:

NEW FROM TTTW!!!

THE UNIQUE TTTW ESCORT AGENCY

A service eagerly awaited and sincerely welcomed by thousands of foreign visitors to the superb capital of the United Kingdom. Charming in their pale-green uniforms, our youthful lady escorters, many of them linguists of rare ability and richly endowed with every other desirable talent, are ever at our clients' command, ready to conduct them about London and to introduce them to the delights and mysteries of this ancient Roman city. If, on your visits to museums, cabarets or famous monuments, or simply while enjoying the sights of London on top of one of our world-famous double-decker buses, you require sophisticated companionship and guidance, you cannot do better than to entrust yourself to one of our delightful escorters. You may be sure that with a TTTW escorter to look after you, your every wish will be taken care of

IMMEDIATELY AND AT MODERATE COST!

There is an old English saying to the effect that experience will always tell, and in the sphere of escorting too TTTW possesses an incomparable wealth of experience. Every step towards our clients' enjoyment and instruction is carefully scheduled and closely supervised by our escort monitors, ladies of mature years and appearance, whose dark-green uniforms contrast prettily with the pale-green outfits of the young ladies in their charge. What better way to enjoy London than in the company of sprightly Marilyn, elegant Louise or gay Marianne?

At this point, Dr. Pendlebloom jotted down 'Special services to be listed under Rates.' Then he turned to the page setting out Rates, Conditions and the TTTW Guarantee, and after due consideration of these important sections instructed Miss Gomberg to arrange a meeting with Mr. Woodlock with a view to discussing the photographs to be included in the brochure. On this occasion he favoured two group photographs – one of all the staff, with himself at the centre and slightly to the front wearing the ceremonial garb of a doctor of philosophy (he jotted down 'Oxford? Cambridge? Other university? To be hired as available') and with the escorters in their pretty pale-green uniforms on the wings, and one of a classroom lesson in progress, with the teacher wearing a black gown and 'mortar board'. He also considered various other possibilities such as a photographic view of the National Gallery, the County Hall or some other suitable edifice, which could perhaps be obtained from an official source at little or no cost, and, alternatively, a head-and-shoulders portrait of himself, but he rejected the latter idea out of hand as he did not wish to be thought at all ostentatious.

Having taken these major steps towards the production of a brochure of superior quality likely to reflect much credit upon his organisation, Dr. Pendlebloom devoted himself to various items of routine business until 12 o'clock sharp, when, once again, it was time for him to lock up his office and go to lunch.

One thing was certain. Whatever Dr. Pendlebloom's exertions and however success-ful their outcome, M, for one, was bound to dislike the new brochure, much as he simply hated the latest TTTW posters, which, far from enhancing the appearance and appeal of the London Underground, did, in his perhaps not entirely unbiased opinion, much to add to its general, although admittedly comfortable, squalour. In this respect he was clearly out of step with the official TTTW view, according to which these posters were both popular and effective. His rejection of Dr. Pendlebloom's brilliant achievement, which some thought due to a perverse desire to find fault, was in fact motivated by his deep-rooted fear of being too easy-going altogether, too ready to be impressed – in short, of compromising his integrity and independence as a person, being less of a man than he had a right to expect of himself.

M, indeed, agreed wholeheartedly with his colleagues Dr. McGill and Mr. Dacre, who, during lengthy sessions at the House of Pasta, would, with much innocent enjoyment, go on and on about the higgledy-piggledy layout of the TTTW poster (a concoction reminiscent of posters advertising wrestling events), its confusion of old-fashioned typefaces and the nauseous shade of green in which it was printed. Their many witty comments on Dr. Pendlebloom's lack of taste, both general and particular, as well as his childlike inability to distinguish fact from fiction likewise proved to be a rich source of good entertainment. Given the total inability of the three conspirators to keep their opinions to themselves, as well as the excellent intelligence service at his disposal, it did not take Dr. Pendlebloom long to find out about their virtually blasphemous disloyalty, and a lesser man than he might well have taken decisive retributive action forthwith. However, having considered the matter from every conceivable angle, as was indeed his wont, Dr. Pendlebloom decided to let that particular sleeping dog lie, at any rate, for the time being.

In general, however, M's attitude to advertising in any shape or form was far less critical and even welcoming, nor did creeping commercialisation, which so many of his friends and acquaintances purported to deplore, worry him in the slightest degree. In fact, he rather enjoyed the combination of facile appeal and, on occasion, downright vulgar assertiveness, which, in his opinion, added much to the vitality and interest of urban life. Vienna, for instance, had offered him a variety of eye-catching devices, ranging from a huge, intermittently illuminated cup of coffee on top of a distant building, with three wavy and parallel lines suggesting steam, to the smiling figure, beautifully worked in every detail as M thought, of a shoemaker, who, in a regular if somewhat jerky sequence, kept raising his hammer, turning his head towards the onlooker, turning back again to his work, and finally bringing down his hammer on the sole of a shoe – M never grew tired of watching this contrivance whenever he happened to pass the shop window in which it performed. He also derived much satisfaction from posters not at all dissimilar to the offending TTTW version and advertising products, services and entertainments of every conceivable kind, which covered the stubby round pillars provided for that very purpose. A special favourite of his was the large green frog which could be seen on every tin of the most popular brand of shoecream and, in an even larger size and three-dimensionally, in the window of every shoe-repair shop.

In London too, advertising, especially poster advertising, formed part of M's daily experience. Inseparably linked in his mind with racist, erotic or simply witty graffiti and, everywhere, in any road, liberal sprinklings of litter, they added much, as he then saw it, to the relaxed mood of the town, making it a particularly happy place in which to live. Not all the posters, of course, appealed to M equally, but he used to look forward keenly to some, such as those suggesting that greater whiteness was somehow synonymous with greater cleanliness and, by extension, a brighter and happier future, not to mention social superiority, those showing large tropical birds with immense yellow beaks and crafty expressions, advertising beer (If you can do, what Toucan do ...), and the display cards in underground trains bearing edifying verses – always of identical structure and contributed by members of the public –

according to which wool was definitely superior to any other type of textile fibre. One such jingle, which haunted M throughout his life and which he used to recite whenever the occasion seemed propitious, went as follows:

> 'Guy Fawkes when caught beneath the House,
> Put all the blame upon his spouse.
> November 5th 'twas bitter cold,
> Which made him desperate and bold,
> But when he asked his spouse to knit
> An undergarment that would fit,
> The wench said 'No', the frost was cruel –
> There is no substitute for wool!'

Many years later, when, in the company of Anni, loyal friend and much loved mother and grandmother, whom he had met during those heady days at Nuremberg shortly after the war but who had by then been his long-suffering wife for fully three decades and more, M, devoid of teeth, short-sighted and nearly bald, but still quite spry, still a chessplayer to be reckoned with, visited Russia, he could not but compare the chandeliery *art-nouveau* splendour of the Moscow Metro with the relaxed squalour of the London Underground. Although by any rational standard the Moscow system was more impressive by far, M considerably preferred the London Tube, since, cheerful and neglected, it at least did not make him feel as if he had stepped into his own mausoleum.

CHAPTER TWENTY TWO

MISS PRATT was showing M around her studio, the birthplace of numerous busts, figurines and other objects mainly in bronze and terracotta. The studio was located above her flat in Belsize Park, that genteel and pleasant area within comfortable walking distance of Hampstead in one direction and Camden Town and Swiss Cottage in the other.

To reach the studio, they had to climb a wrought-iron fire-escape rising in zigzag fashion from the walled-in garden at the rear of the elegant dark-red brick building – a garden dominated by a tall chestnut tree at the centre and with a lovingly cared-for herbaceous border devoted entirely to medicinal plants and a variety of shrubs and bushes along the walls. The studio, a spacious room at the very top of the house, had two slanting walls and an enormous window facing, as Miss Pratt explained, east. This, she said, suited her fine, for she preferred to work in the morning, and from that point of view the room was really quite perfect.

Once inside the studio, Miss Pratt turned on the electric lights, for the afternoon was well advanced and dusk was falling rapidly. Everything was extremely simple and workmanlike. In one corner of the room there was a cube-shaped kiln, and coarse shelves along the walls bore various finished and semi-finished models. On the bare wooden floor and against one of the gable walls there stood an old, rather dilapidated sofa, while apart from a massive working table the only other furniture consisted of two chairs and an old armchair. A staircase led from the centre of the studio down to the flat.

Having given M a moment to look around, Miss Pratt showed him her tools and then pointed to a corner where there were several covered pails, a brush and a pan and a collection of sturdy bags containing various materials. She took the lid from one of the pails containing wet clay and then explained, step by step, how a model is built up about an 'armature', a kind of skeleton consisting of wire and flexible metal tubing, how a plaster mould is taken from the model, and how, finally, a bronze or plaster cast is made. She told M about the extreme importance of keeping the clay reasonably moist at all times and, to illustrate her point, removed the outer wrapping and some damp rags from a model of a child's head which she happened to be working on. She concluded M's conducted tour by showing him some of her creations. He particularly liked two porcelain figurines, a Pierrot and a Pierrette with white faces and long, graceful limbs. Then they descended the inner staircase to Miss Pratt's flat but did not stop there, as they had tickets for a play and time was getting short.

Thanks to Miss Pratt, M had come a long way in matters of 'taste' since, during his last job at sea, while serving as a saloon-boy on the *SS Globetrotter*, he had acquired in Naples certain paintings which he was quite certain could not fail to make his fortune. So as to avoid possibly unaffordable customs charges in England, he placed these precious works of art – genuine signed oil paintings on canvas, showing a Neapolitan street scene with lots of colourful laundry waving in the sun from lines strung between opposite houses, a portrait of a gipsy girl with a most winsome smile and an only slightly asymmetrical chest, and a view, mainly in pink and blue, of the Isle of Capri – under the 'rug' ('rag' might be a more appropriate term) covering the floor in his cabin.

When the *SS Globetrotter* eventually reached its port of destination, M, assisted, no doubt, by the lavish hospitality which the steward had so wisely offered to the gentlemen from Customs and Excise, managed to get away with this piece of deception and, indeed, with five 'gold' watches, four of them intended as gifts for his friends, which he had cunningly concealed in tins of cocoa – he did in fact declare the cocoa – but none of which was endowed with a mechanism such as is necessary for effective operation. These, sadly, were by no means the only fiscally reprehensible acts committed by M on that voyage. At a small port in Tunisia (the main claim to fame of which may well have been a most picturesque and highly efficient brothel in the Moorish style, a place of long queues and rapid turnovers) M, wishing to oblige a friend, also attempted to convey several packets of cigarettes on shore without inconveniencing the authorities. To this end he had stuffed them into the tops of his grey socks – when it came to socks, grey was always his preferred colour – which, since his trousers were relatively tight, made his legs look oddly deformed. God knows what made him think that as feeble a stratagem as this could possibly succeed, for considering that he was, after all, a person of some experience in such matters, he should have known better, but, at any rate, it didn't. The Tunisian customs men marched him back to the ship, where he spent a miserable night wondering whether they would come and get him in the morning in order to lock him up for the rest of his days to rot in some horrid dungeon, in which case he would have only himself to blame. When, next day, the ship departed on the last stage of its voyage to England, he was of course immensely relieved.

However, let us return to the paintings. Visiting his friend Löwenzahn, the one with the dramatically scarred face and radical views on the proper control and handling of women and on how to solve the Palestinian problem once and for all but of late decently married and even an industrialist in a small way, M showed the paintings to Rebecca, Löwenzahn's wife, who had expert knowledge of such things, having but recently completed an evening course in art appreciation. Rebecca, who was just then in the process of applying final touches to a series of powder puffs which she had been commissioned to decorate, burst out laughing and informed M, in none too ladylike terms, what she thought of the paintings. Considerably embarrassed by this episode, Löwenzahn, once he was alone with M, tried to explain that her apparent hostility – and he stressed that her hostility was merely apparent – was due solely to the state of her nerves and not in any sense personal. He did not add, of course, that she resented his friends in general and in particular M, whom she regarded as a 'bad influence'. Still, M bowed to her judgment, but he kept the paintings, as he had become quite attached to them.

One way or another, he had a truly marvellous time in Naples. Leaning against a railing of the *SS Globetrotter*, he often used to enjoy the splendid view over the bay and the manifold activities of that busy port. While on shore leave, he visited the National Museum with its fine collections of Greek and Roman art, roamed about in parks and even went as far afield as Pompeii, where he wandered about among the ruins, hobnobbing with the spirit of history. He considered the goods on offer in the windows of elegant and exotic shops, admired craftsmen carving delicate cameos and joined the crowds gaping at street entertainers. Most of all, however, he enjoyed sitting in the sunshine at a coffee-house table, sipping the froth from a cappuccino or eating ice-cream, watching the passers-by and observing, with some amusement, the street vendors hawking their wares. Some of these were really very attractive, beautiful in design and colour, and luxurious in feel and appearance.

Apart from paintings and watches, M bought quite a few choice items from these traders, including a fine grey 'popeline' shirt, which fitted him perfectly and made him look very smart indeed until he decided to wash it, for in the laundry pail most of it dissolved to a kind of grey sludge yielding up only the cuffs, the collar and the buttons for possible further use. He also bought a scarf of the very finest silk and with an exquisite design of glowing reds and greens, but that too came to grief eventually, when Silversmith, having borrowed it in order to impress a new girlfriend on a special occasion, lent it to her as a protection against the rain and the colours proved to be insufficiently permanent. That he had not bothered to ask M's permission was, according to him, neither here nor there, and, after some discussion and searching analysis, M too was persuaded that he definitely had a point.

Without a shadow of a doubt, however, M's finest purchase was an intricately carved wooden box, an object of rare and exquisite beauty. The day – and what a glorious day it proved to be – on which M became the proud owner of that splendid box came to be indelibly imprinted upon his memory, and in his later years – especially those – there was many an enjoyable occasion when he would regale an audience with a colourful recital of the events following this purchase.

I was sitting at a table in one of my favourite cafés – the one in the glass-roofed arcade – enjoying an iced coffee and minding my own business, when I was approached by a sallow-faced fellow, who offered to sell me, at what he described as a truly unbeatable price, a very fine hand-carved box, made, so he said, from 'the cedar of the Lebanon', padded on the inside and lined with attractive pink material – according to him, finest silk recovered at incredible risk from the most private chambers of the Empress of China and imported after many daring adventures all the way from that far country. Although I had no idea how I could ever hope to hold on to such an exquisite object, seeing that it did not in any way fit in with me or my personal circumstances, no persuasion was in fact necessary to make me buy it, and it did not even occur to me to haggle about its price, although this must have been expected.

Left alone with my latest acquisition – I had successfully resisted all other offers of merchandise – I finished my coffee as quickly as I could, paid the waiter, and set off towards the main road, clutching my treasure to my chest. However, I had not gone far, when I nearly collided with my shipmate and good friend Scottie, whose proudest boast it was that after sixteen years at sea he was still a mess-boy and that in regard to 'mess-boying' his experience was therefore second to none. Scottie, who, when we met, was already somewhat unsteady on his feet, since he had only recently sampled and then emptied a bottle of *Lacrimae Christi* and God knows what else, sniffed at the box, held it up to the light and admired it roundly, whereupon he suggested that a celebratory drink might be in order. Having stipulated one or two cautionary provisos, I saw no good and sufficient reason to refuse. When, after a few drinks at licensed premises nearby, Scottie insisted on travelling somewhere in style, I, myself now afloat on a sky-blue sea of euphoria, again saw no good reason to disagree. So we – I with my precious box and Scottie with a bottle of genuine Italian whisky – hailed a taxi, but since neither of us had the slightest idea of our intended destination, the driver, a man of philosophical temperament, simply drove one way and then another before, having extracted from us what seemed to me an astronomical fare, he eventually dumped us in some dreary, featureless area – an area, where as the Germans have it, 'the cats and foxes say "good night" to one another.'

Since both of us were now quite peckish, we went – or more precisely, stumbled – into a place purporting to be a restaurant, where we, very much the only customers, ordered two large portions of steak and fried egg. One portion would, as it turned out, have been quite sufficient, for as soon as the owner – at least I presume it was the owner – brought the food, Scottie, falling forward, landed with his face squarely on his plate, splattering, as he did so, spaghetti, peas, egg and steak in all directions, causing, in short, a mess quite unbecoming to an experienced mess-boy such as him. As for me, I did my best to remain affable and good-humoured. However, when I was handed the bill, by comparison with which even the taxi-driver's fare seemed quite modest, I decided to switch to a display of cold fury. Squaring my shoulders – not the easiest of tasks, for I was not particularly broad-shouldered – lurching about and looking, as I earnestly hoped, very inebriated, very dangerous indeed, I threatened to 'break up the joint' and every bone in mine host's body if he did not immediately reduce our bill to more acceptable proportions. All this, of course, was pure play-acting, for truth to tell, I have always been rather too circumspect a person to resort to real violence. Still, my mock rage appeared to do the trick. Having snatched such money as I proffered from my outstretched hand and muttering what sounded to me like an unholy mixture of unsavoury curses and abject apologies, mine host did what he could to speed our departure. Seeing that Scottie was still quite unable to walk by himself, I hoisted him over my shoulder – compared to some of the loads I had carried in Japan, he was amazingly light – picked up my box, and, seeing that Scottie had already seized his bottle of whisky, left.

Out in the open again, I found that we had a problem, for I had no idea where we might be, and it was getting dark. So I deposited Scottie on the pavement with his back against a wall and looked about for somebody to direct us towards the docks and the *SS Globetrotter*. Far from assisting us in our plight, such passers-by as could not avoid us entirely hurried away, as if they suspected us of carrying some dreaded disease. Eventually, however, a down-at-heel, seedy fellow, who had, for some time already, been watching us from a distance, came up and offered, in quite reasonable English, to assist us. Naturally enough, I was only too eager to accept and intimated that although we were fully aware that he was simply obeying the promptings of his kind heart, we would not, of course, dream of exploiting this fact but would be happy to remunerate him for his trouble. He, in turn, responded by assuring us that his gratitude to us as the noble and generous liberators of his poor country would never permit him to consider any remuneration but the one in store for him in heaven, whither his dear mama, a saint if ever there was and a true martyr to her poor, suffering feet, had but recently preceded him, and he even offered, no doubt as a token of his good faith, to help me carry part of my load such as, for instance, the box, which in our present predicament had indeed become rather a burden. Judging that our new friend looked like a decent enough chap, I accepted without further ado, and having handed him the box – it would have been churlish to refuse – I again picked up Scottie, who was still firmly attached to his bottle, and off we went.

Walking beside me in the deepening darkness of rapidly approaching night, Umberto, our new friend, conducted us through a veritable maze of shabby, nondescript streets of tall, decaying buildings, such as are commonly found in the poorer districts of every large port. On and on we went, through street after endless street, never meeting anyone, all conversation eventually dead. Umberto, no longer at my side, had dropped back a few steps. The streets being virtually unlit except for the pale bright light of the moon, here and there a faint light from some distant window – what intimate or dastardly acts, I wondered, might be going on behind those windows? – and now and again a street lamp shedding its desolate glow, it was impossible to tell where we might be, but, luckily, Umberto was with us, so there was really no need to worry. Time having ceased to exist, I returned to my daydream. It took me a moment to realise that Scottie's moans and mutterings had taken on a new note of urgency. Listening carefully, I could just make out something like 'Bastard, that bloody bastard!' Looking around, I now saw Umberto running away, hell for leather, with my precious box. Having dumped Scottie on the ground (what a relief!), I raced after him – not, however, without keeping a prudent distance – and, as he zigzagged hither and thither, soon lost him entirely. As for the box, I knew that it was gone for good and that nothing on earth would ever restore it to me. To make matters worse, I found that in running after Umberto I had managed to lose my way and now had no idea where I had left Scottie. Panic setting in, I ran this way and that, but without success. However, just when I was on the point of giving up my search, I suddenly heard voices – one of them I recognised at once – turned a corner, and there they were: Scottie still sitting on the ground, still with the whisky bottle in his grasp, but now, it would seem, attempting to render some homely 'tune', which, for the life of me, I could not identify, and three *signorine* around him, chattering away in Italian and generally having a good time. The scene was in some curious way reminiscent of the Judgment of Paris, although the three were, after all, no goddesses and Scottie was certainly no Paris.

Realising that this might be our one and only chance to get back to the ship, I explained to our unexpected but most welcome new companions our difficulty as well as I could, and humbly entreated their help. They were, indeed, quite prepared to take us to the docks, which, it transpired, were only a stone's throw away and to them quite familiar. They even offered – and this was very nice of them – to help us find the good ship *SS Globetrotter* but suggested as an alternative that we spend what was left of the night in their company, in which case they would be willing to offer us an appropriate discount. By way of response I did my best to convey to them that charming though such an interlude would undoubtedly have been, I could not possibly accept their kindness, since both Scottie and I were supposed to be on duty by six o'clock in the morning and I, for one, needed my sleep. Luckily, it was no longer necessary for me to carry Scottie, who had regained some slight control over his legs, although half supporting him and half dragging him seemed at times to be even more strenuous.

At last we reached the gangway of the *SS Globetrotter*, and never was a sight more welcome. With a deep, sweeping bow I thanked our guides profusely, adding, for good measure, *Las signorinas son unas grandes damas.* However poor, this attempt at speaking to them in something resembling their own language obviously pleased them quite a lot, and I, with a warm glow about my heart and a touch of regret, felt that at that point there was nothing they would not gladly have done for us, even without any remuneration. Indeed, so moved was I, that it occurred to me to take the bottle away from Scottie and give it to them, but suspecting that this might well meet with quite ferocious resistance on his part, I simply doffed an imaginary plumed hat to them with another fine flourish while uttering further words of gratitude, which, incidentally, were meant quite sincerely.

Having dragged Scottie up the gangway, I helped him to his cabin, where we found Keesh – the spelling is not necessarily authentic – fast asleep on Scottie's bunk. Keesh, Scottie's white kitten, was, so it was rumoured, a reincarnation of Mary Anne, his long-lost love, whose photograph, in which she could be admired prettily displayed in the altogether as she sat sunning herself upon a rock, he always carried in his wallet and would frequently show to me, particularly after a few drinks, with bitter tears of regret at what might have been. Once I had dislodged Keesh from the bunk and settled Scottie in her place – none of this was easy, for Keesh did not take kindly to what she was, after all, bound to regard as unwarranted impudence and Scottie kept insisting on having a drink with me, which I most certainly did not want – I tottered over to my own cabin, undressed and immediately fell asleep.

I liked Scottie a lot – as, indeed, did everyone else on the ship except the steward, who hated both of us – for Scottie was kind and intelligent and had a great sense of humour. After I had left the ship, we exchanged several letters, but, in due course, our correspondence dried up, as was to be expected. I still think often of the good times we had together.

CHAPTER TWENTY THREE

TO LISTEN to some people, nothing in the world is as important as good taste. Judged by this standard, a man who is a compulsive liar or regularly beats his wife and children may still be quite all right, whereas even a saint or a genius will be 'beyond the pale' if he says, does or likes the wrong things. Those whose taste is good, 'belong', but bad taste will certainly exclude anyone from the hallowed circle of those with similar likes and dislikes. In this sense, good taste is a special prerogative to be guarded jealously, its function being to protect the group against outsiders and intruders, in much the same way as do the mysterious rituals and identifying signs of secret societies. In Miss Pratt's world, for instance, anyone who prefers artificial flowers – because they are less trouble and last longer than natural ones – or never manages to choose the right wallpaper, or uses the wrong words, demonstrates bad taste, but so does any person who is ostentatiously erudite, whose house is deemed to be too large or whose wife wears a mink coat to do her shopping. Clearly, such standards are certain to keep an awful number of 'undesirable' people at bay.

Matters of taste are most likely to preoccupy those who see themselves as belonging to the cultured and intellectual strata of society, but they concern other groups just as much and in much the same way. Insisting on fresh milk at a beerdrinkers' jamboree or flirting with the bride at a friend's wedding would certainly give rise to hostile reactions, even though it might never occur to any of the people present to think of the matter in terms of taste.

However, good and bad taste can also be considered from a different angle, closer to its original meaning. Children can have a wonderful time gorging themselves, without any thought for the possible consequences, with sweets of every kind. They love garish colours and they simply adore anything 'sentimental'. Their capacity for enjoyment is enormous. Older people, on the other hand, whose palates are – both literally and metaphorically – jaded and whose stomachs weak, are far less able to enjoy, fully and without reservations, such 'goodies' of life as are available to them. They are slaves to their state of health, tradition and acquired standards. Besides, their prospects are of necessity much poorer than those of the very young, all of which adds up to a formidable set of major disadvantages. But still they manage to feel superior, for, after all, children and adolescents depend on them while, generally speaking, they themselves are much higher up the ladder of cultural, social and economic success. In other words, the notion of good taste is one of the devices by which people maintain a spurious sense of superiority in the face of progressive decline.

Ever since we went to see the *Hunchback of Notre Dame*, things between Catty and myself have been going from bad to worse. I don't mind her incessant and boring chatter, but when she looks at me with those tearful eyes, reproachful and entreating at the same time, there is only one thing I want, and that is to get away from her as quickly as possible. I think she expects me to take her out again and become her 'official' boyfriend, for her to show me off to her awful family and her equally awful friends, but that is more than I could bear! Yet I find her as exciting as ever and love thinking about her and what we might do together. I am sure she would do anything I asked of her, but then she would really have me in her claws. Why, I wonder, is life so complicated? Roll on, old age, when hopefully all these problems will have vanished for good.

It was raining again – had, indeed, been raining almost continuously for three whole days – and it was bitterly cold. This was real 'pneumonia weather' and not a good time to be out in the streets. But in the House of Pasta it was warm and cosy, and the TTTW people were really lucky to have found such a haven.

Messrs. Daker and Galbraith were playing chess, with M and Giuseppe, Ben's ten-year-old nephew, a precocious, infuriatingly gifted child, looking on. Giuseppe, who lived with his uncle and served as his general assistant before and after school, had been a keen observer of their games for quite some time. A shy boy, he had initially limited himself to watching the chessplayers from a safe distance, but had lately progressed to stopping – when he had nothing better to do and especially, although not only, when his uncle was asleep – at their table in order to assess and predict their moves.

The players, on the other hand, did not mind him watching – in fact, they quite enjoyed his attention and would even address to him some wise words of guarded encouragement – as long as he did not 'blot his copybook' by going too far. But on that particular day of all days, he finally forgot himself and, failing, after a disastrous decision by Mr. Daker, to resist the temptation of 'putting his oar in', pointed out that the latter could have mated his opponent, a move which the latter had overlooked entirely. This serious infringement of the spectator's first commandment – 'Thou shalt not utter a sound, however hopeless the players' – greatly annoyed the two protagonists. Galbraith limited himself to a sulky snort, but Mr. Daker, who regarded the boy's interference as a piece of unmitigated impertinence – he himself had been brought up properly to be seen but not heard and to speak only when spoken to – asked Giuseppe icily to mind his own business and not to concern himself with things he was too young to understand.

Ben – who had been hovering nearby, dusting some bottles – aware that an outrage had been committed and switching from prideful admiration of his sister's first-born to red-hot, immoderate fury at the youngster's temerity and lack of tact, grabbed him by the throat and, imploring all the saints to bear witness to the way his patience was being sorely tried, propelled the miscreant towards the kitchen, where he read the riot act to him, in a stream of impassioned bilingual invective. However, once Ben had simmered down, which did not take long, M, who felt that poor Giuseppe was being treated too harshly, suggested that the boy should perhaps be taught chess properly and even offered to give him a lesson then and there, hoping that this might be more interesting than the somewhat lifeless duel in progress. However, since the only chess set available was being used, nothing could be done immediately. As for Mr. Daker and Galbraith, they clearly disapproved of M's initiative, which they seemed to regard as dangerously egalitarian and not at all wise.

When M looked at the clock above the bar, he was horrified to find that he was, once again, on the point of missing his lesson with poor Mr. Allbright, his last lesson that day. As he got up to leave, Ben, whose pride in his nephew was again fully restored – indeed, he was now giving serious thought to the possibility of getting Giuseppe, in his mind's eye suddenly a future world champion, a small chess set of his own – rushed ahead in order to open the door for M, which he did with an air combining obsequious gratitude with patronising affability. From M's, and ultimately Mr. Allbright's, point of view, this was not at all desirable, for he also blocked the door with his enormous chest and prevented M from escaping into the darkness beyond until he had been cross-examined thoroughly and repeatedly about Giuseppe's practical chances of becoming an outstanding player, as well as his prospects if he succeeded. Having pointed out that he was quite a poor man, he even offered to pay M a moderate fee for his efforts, which the latter, wallowing in a sense of his own virtue, naturally refused. His refusal gave rise to some conflict, for Ben was too proud a man to accept something for nothing. Eventually they managed to compromise on free tea or coffee while lessons were in progress, which was, indeed, a happy solution. Ben also told him at great length about his poor sister Lucia, who lived in Palermo and had been a widow for the past three years. Thanks to the All Merciful, he informed M, who listened impatiently but with feigned interest, she had seven healthy children, ranging from Roberto, a lovely little lad only two years old but already very smart and a real handful, to Giuseppe, whom he, Ben, was teaching the trade. 'A very smart boy, this Giuseppe,' he said, 'he will go far,' adding 'I was hoping he will be stepping into my boots one day, but maybe he will not.'

Finally free to go, M realised that Mr. Allbright's lesson was nearly over and there was by now hardly any point in exposing himself to the rain, which was still pouring down in buckets. So he telephoned the office, claiming that he had been knocked down by a motor-cycle and, although he had got away with only a few bruises, was now at the Middlesex Hospital for a check-up. Mr. Allbright, when he was told of M's unfortunate accident, sent him good wishes for a speedy recovery. Having done his duty and notified the office, M returned to his seat and continued to watch his two colleagues, who had started a new game.

In due course, once Ben had obtained a chess set, M gave Giuseppe some lessons. The latter had already picked up the basic moves and tactics, which enabled M to concentrate on what he considered the principles of strategy and positional play. In their practice games the boy played quickly, aggressively but without precision, while picking his nose, methodically and with dogged determination. At the end of a game, he would extend an incredibly limp and sweaty hand which M shook with extreme reluctance. Since Giuseppe kept suffering from colds, particularly during the more inclement months, and his nose was frequently inflamed and dripping away sadly, M, who was terrified of being infected, eventually came to curse his weakness in promising to teach the lad. He would have dearly liked to extricate himself from that situation, in which he found himself entirely through his own fault, but could not see how, short of staying away from the House of Pasta entirely. This, clearly, would have been too high a price to pay.

His release came when Giuseppe, who had been given a brand-new bicycle, lost his interest in chess, at least for the time being, thereby compelling Ben to consider whether his nephew might not, after all, be better off if he became one of the world's foremost racing cyclists rather than a chess master.

On his way to the kitchen at No. 12 Westlake Crescent, M met Mrs. Bingley, who was wearing her mauve turban to protect her hair and had, as was her custom, a cigarette dangling from the corner of her mouth. She was in the process of brushing down the staircase, this being her day for giving the house a thorough going-over from top to bottom. Mr. Bingley could be heard using the vacuum cleaner on the ground floor. Mrs. B, never averse to improving her mind by engaging in a spot of conversation with her lodgers, stopped what she was doing and, after proper enquiries about his health etc., acquainted M with the fact that Audrey and the girls were now safely back in St. Kilda, from where she had, this very morning, received a letter, in which they expressed the wish to be remembered to one and all. Since the excellent Christmas party, at which they all had had such a glorious time, M, who liked children and got on well with them although he tended to tire rapidly of their excessively demanding ways, had hardly seen anything at all of the girls – their horrible mother had made sure of that – but was sorry to hear that they had gone.

'You must be missing their company,' he now ventured, injecting an appropriate note of sympathetic concern into his observation.

'That's as may be,' was Mrs. B's philosophical reply. 'It's always nice to have visitors, especially family, but all good things have to come to an end some time. Besides, they had a good innings.'

'I do see what you mean,' agreed M non-committally.

'And then there's the girls' education. Not to mention Bill, who wanted them back the sooner the better.'

Although it was most unusual for Mrs. B. to discuss her family with outsiders, she did occasionally depart from this rule when talking to M, definitely her favourite lodger. She continued:

'Besides, the girls were badly in need of their father's hand, I dare say, as they were getting a little above themselves. Proper little madams, these two.'

Not wishing to be thought intrusive, M decided to change the subject, embarking upon a discourse on his latest 'invention'. He was always 'inventing' things, not, as a rule, with any practical purpose in mind, but in order to astonish and entertain his hopefully delighted audience.

'Incidentally, Mrs. Bingley, I don't think I have told you about my latest and, in my modest opinion, commercially and from the point of view of animal or, more precisely, arachnid conservation, greatest invention.'

'And what is it this time?' reacted Mrs. B, slightly suspicious in case M was trying to make fun of her. Besides, this was not the first 'invention' M had come up with, not by any means.

'Large, hairy spiders in bathtubs,' explained M. 'Have you ever considered large spiders in bathtubs and the problems they pose?'

'Spiders? There are no spiders in my bathroom.'

'Of course not.' (With Mrs. Bingley you couldn't be too careful.) 'But for some people they really are a problem, you know. Just think of some very old, very frail lady who wants to take a bath, or simply of someone who is afraid of spiders, and there is that big, evil-looking monster staring him in the face, not shifting an inch and, in fact, unable to vacate the tub, because its walls – the walls of the bath that is – are too steep and too smooth.'

'I know what I would do. Pick it up and get rid of it.'

'But that's just it. There must be millions of people – myself included – who could no more pick up a spider than eat the rear legs of a frog. What about them?'

Mrs. B. shuddered, remembering a trip to Calais.

'That is why my invention is so important,' M continued, not with the slightest intention of persuading his landlady but purely for comic effect. 'My new 'Spider-Trap and Disposal Unit' – SDU for short – will enable people who in the past would have found it impossible to take a bath or who regard it as unlucky to hurt or kill a spider to remove the repulsive horror safely and without causing it any harm whatsoever. This, I am quite sure, will be appreciated by any person who loves spiders or simply believes in the sanctity of animal life in general. You might even say that the SDU will make a major contribution to the quality of our lives and should be available on the National Health.'

'How does it work then, your spider's wotsit?' Mrs. B, having entered into the spirit of M's revelation and wishing to humour him, enquired.

'Very simply indeed, as indeed do all major inventions. This, after all is a device which anyone should be able to afford. In its simplest form a short tube of cardboard – let us say about four inches in length – will do.' (M did not go into details about the most obvious source of such a tube.) 'You simply block one end of the tube with paper and then place the open end carefully over the spider, which, obeying its instinct to save itself, will climb up into the tube and stay there. The tube can now be taken to the nearest window and shaken out. It is then ready for further use on any number of other spiders that one wishes to remove, and it goes without saying that the application of the SDU is by no means limited to bathtubs. In other words, you could also use it to remove spiders from ceilings or curtains – in which case, however, a longer model may be preferable in order to increase the user's reach. It stands to reason that the SDU would be especially useful if a spider happened to be sitting – and I do not, of course, wish to be indelicate – on one's bed.'

'Now, now, watch your language,' interjected Mrs. Bingley, who – always zealous where the spotless respectability of her house was concerned – made a point of keeping her lodgers on a short leash, and did not, in any case, hold with potentially smutty talk about beds.

'Scientifically controlled experiments will, of course, have to be carried out in order to determine what other creatures my method might usefully be applied to. I suspect, for instance, that it would be a great help in dealing with stag-beetles, cockroaches and, on a miniature level, ants. On the other hand, it seems, at least in its present form, less likely to be of use with small, fast-moving animals such as mice, or flying animals such as moths, wasps, or small stray birds.'

'Mice and birds, indeed! Whatever next? Really Mr. M, you mustn't let that imagination of yours get out of hand.'

'Commercially appropriate designs and international marketing will be essential, of course.' (M chose to ignore Mrs. B's discouraging interjection.) 'There is no end to the possibilities. A company – or, considering the vast scope of the project – a consortium of companies may have to be formed, in order, for instance, to produce SDUs in the required ranges and from the most suitable materials – not necessarily cardboard – and to sell them both in this country and abroad. The capital involved is likely to be enormous, and the shares of SDU Industries – that is the name I shall be proposing to the Board of the new enterprise – will no doubt be traded on the Stock Exchange. I hope that you too and Mr. Bingley, whose acumen in matters of high finance I greatly respect, will decide to invest in this great venture of the future.'

'Well, we shall have to see about that, shan't we?' At the mention of money, Mrs. B. immediately turned very cautious, for money was no laughing matter and, besides, she could not, for the life of her, imagine any of her 'boys', however pleasant and however punctual when it came to paying their weekly rent, ever becoming even mildly prosperous, not to mention seriously rich. 'At any rate,' she continued, 'it's time I carried on. Mustn't stand here jawing the rest of the morning.' Shaking her beturbaned head in what M chose to take for pure, delighted wonderment, she added: 'Spider traps, indeed! Whatever will you think of next? Still, Mr. Bingley will be very amused when I tell him.' Whereupon she continued 'cleaning' the stairs.

No-one in his right mind and certainly none of her lodgers could have denied that Mrs. B. was a very jewel of a landlady. She was, after all, not unduly sensitive to cheerful banter, never failed to take a positive, intelligent interest in her 'boys' and their doings, and, provided that the rent was paid promptly and the proprieties were observed, she did not seem to mind if one or other of her lesser rules were infringed. Besides, she was genuinely helpful, and although she ruled her household with a firm, unwavering hand, was never oppressive. She even permitted parties, tolerating, within reason, such general upheaval as they entailed – it being understood, however, that she and her husband would also be invited.

Yet, when talking to Mrs. B, it was never wise to cross certain boundaries – 'take liberties', as she would have put it – for she was quick to react, and even the slightest hint of rebellion, disrespect or discontent was prone to end in a summary sentence of seven days' notice. This very nearly happened to M on one occasion, after he had read to her the following 'poem', which is given here in full in order to show how unaccountably easy it was to fall foul of dear Mrs. Bingley.

> Cutting all the corners,
> Bucket, mop and broom –
> The trouble with this place is,
> I haven't any room.
>
> The engine on the table
> Is ready to depart –
> A dozen whistles blowing,
> It's time to make a start.
>
> The pressure gauge is gauging,
> Watch the pistons churn –
> A butterfly aflutter
> As the flywheels turn.

Double-ended levers,
Scintillating switch,
Valuable valve gear
Discovered in a ditch.

Long-nosed indicators,
Multi-headed screws,
Greaseproof lubricators
And a pair of shoes.

The trouble with this room is
I haven't any space –
I'll have to build a station
Or get some other place.

Mrs. B. did not go into the literary merits of this work of art, nor did she concern herself with its technical content or the personality of the lamenter, but wished to know merely whether she was to understand that M was unhappy with his accommodation, finding it too small, in which case he might be well advised to look for more suitable lodgings ... etc, etc. On that occasion it took all M's not inconsiderable powers of appeasement to prevent the catastrophe he had so carelessly conjured up. Only when he explained that, far from finding his room too small or in any other way whatsoever unsatisfactory – he could never hope to be so happy again in any other room – did she appear to relax ever so slightly. But what really caused her to relent was his assurance that he had composed this admittedly worthless poem expressly for her and Mr. B. as a token of his appreciation and gratitude, and meant, if she approved, to write it out in his finest calligraphic script, for her to mount over the kitchen sink or in such another place as she and Mr. B. deemed suitable.

Silversmith, in the kitchen, was far from happy, and it showed. When, trying to cheer him up, M mentioned that the fair Audrey and *les girls* were back in sunny St. Kilda, sending love and kisses to all and sundry including Silversmith no doubt, he merely growled something or other about this being highly unlikely and, in any case, who cared? And when his friend endeavoured to acquaint him with the details of his latest money-spinning invention, he, most untypically, responded by going to his own room in order, as he put it, to be spared all that boring nonsense. Silversmith, in fact, was suffering from a seriously broken heart and had, moreover, been severely humiliated. For Silversmith – in his humble way as devoted a pursuer of feminine beauty as that notorious voluptuary and corruptor of Seville but not averse either to the higher things in life such as yachts, chauffeur-driven cars, large, elegant houses and very healthy bank accounts – had until last night been deeply and tenderly involved with Nancy, a most appealing but, alas, excessively level-headed brunette, whose father was somebody or other somewhere or somewhere else and whom Silversmith had been hoping to make his very own, as soon as at all possible. Unfortunately however, as fate would have it, all his fine plans, subtly laid though they were, had come to grief when after a visit to the Old Vic – a visit in which he had invested a great deal seeing that the stakes were so high – a shower of rain caught Nancy and him on their way to the underground station at Waterloo, leaving him no alternative but to offer her, for the protection of her lovely, beautifully groomed hair, M's multi-coloured headscarf, which he had borrowed on the off-chance that it might come in handy.

Silversmith swore and ever afterwards maintained that the sole reason why he had not informed M of his wish to take with him, on this one occasion only of course, that precious piece of cloth, which, pinned to the wall at the side of M's bed, reminded the latter daily – and, indeed, nightly – of his wonderful time in Naples, was due entirely to his sure, unwavering conviction that M would fully appreciate his crucial need and would – true friend that he was – be certain to insist on his – Silversmith's that is – putting the article in question to such good use as he could find for it. In the event, Silversmith's appraisal of the situation proved to be seriously flawed, for M was, after all, not nearly as sympathetic as might, perhaps, have been expected. In fact, he came as close to being 'hopping mad' as he was capable of being, for the crumpled, discoloured rag which his honest friend returned to him had little, if anything, in common with that cherished souvenir which had given him so much pleasure in the past. Eventually, of course, M had to admit that no harm would have been done if the headscarf had lived up to its promise and not turned out to be a piece of elaborate fakery, which had virtually tricked (and in that respect M could surely not escape a certain amount of responsibility) poor Silversmith into a potentially fatal course of action.

Once he had bowed to the justice of Silversmith's case, M simmered down again. He could even see the humour of the situation, a splendid example of *sic transit gloria mundi* for both of them, it appeared, although in rather different ways. For Nancy, whose lovely face and, which was yet more serious, special hairdo (not to mention her elegant beige coat with the mink collar) had been so cruelly inundated, rivulets of this and that hue having flown this way and that way all over her, had been rather less prepared to see the joke and let bygones be bygones. Indeed, the taxi ride to Golders Green, where she lived, had, from Silversmith's point of view, not been worth the money it cost him – had, in fact, not been worth anything at all, for she would not exchange a single word with him, freezing him all the way with her outraged disdain. And, to cap it all, a letter had arrived this very morning, in which

Nancy informed him – in a manner so utterly horrid, Silversmith could hardly believe his eyes – that, as he could clearly not afford the pleasure of her company, there was, in her considered opinion, no point at all in continuing their association. Daddy had thought so all along, and so did Mummy and Nigel (dear Nigel!), whom she hoped to marry in the not too distant future.

She was not one to bear a grudge – in fact, if she had one particular fault, it was that she was too easy-going by far, far too ready to forgive and forget – but, be that as it may, she did not expect to hear from him ever again. She concluded by advising him as a friend to restrict himself in future to girls more of his own class and background, whatever that might be – perhaps a typist or a cook. No doubt he might find happiness that way. As for herself, she could not and would not deny her disappointment, etc., etc.

'Mind you,' commented Silversmith a little later, when he had recovered his usual cheerful optimism. 'That bitch really was a bit on the expensive side. One way or another she cost me a fortune, you know. Not that I was getting anything in return, so I'm probably better off. After all, when it comes to women, the real secret of success is to know when to cut your losses. Besides, when I consider all those posh bores she was always introducing me to at her so-called parties, not to mention "dear Daddy" and "dear Mummy" and, of course, "dear Nigel", that fat slob, it makes me quite sick ... Or take that show at the Prince of Wales, where they had that comic with a badly-fitting sort of rubber wig, which was meant to make him look bald but was a bit too large for him. The funny thing was that I had seen him before, with exactly the same act, at some local fleapit – also, as it happened, from the third row but for a mere fourpence. Not that he was worth watching at any time. Still,' he added somewhat inconsequentially, 'nothing ventured, nothing gained.'

Having thus unburdened himself, Silversmith was feeling a lot better. Indeed, he was feeling well enough now to enquire about M's latest invention. M was only too ready to oblige.

CHAPTER TWENTY FOUR

I REMEMBER MY grandmother as a tall woman with silvery-white hair and a radiant smile. She always wore a starched, spotlessly clean apron in which she went about her various tasks, in particular the preparation of our meals. She didn't say much but her very presence was such as to make her the dominant spirit of the house, the tranquil and steadfast centre of all its activities. She had been married, happily by all accounts, to my grandfather – a veritable patriarch with a long and flowing grey beard – for thirty odd years, two previous wives having died leaving numerous offspring, to whose number she had added another two, my Aunt Ida and Papa, who was the youngest. When, after a long train journey with Papa, which I remember chiefly for the endless succession of telegraph poles flitting past in the wrong direction, I first came to that friendly house which was to be my home for the next five years, my grandmother was, I believe, in her late fifties but nearly thirty years younger than grandfather, whom she and Aunt Sali worshipped with unquestioning devotion, ministering indefatigably to his every whim. As for him, he hardly ever left his room, where he supposedly spent all his time praying, studying the Bible and generally keeping his Maker on his toes.

My grandfather was far too remote and my grandmother too reserved to make any great impact on my imagination or feelings. But my relationship with Aunt Sali was quite a different matter. It was she who took care of my bodily and spiritual needs, she to whom I turned with my anxieties and delights, she who spent much time with me playing games or reading to me, and she who helped me with my homework once that became necessary. Above all, it was she who introduced me to semolina pudding as a true indicator of good and evil, right and wrong. Her method was simple. If I had done well at school, been kind or helpful, or was in need of comfort and encouragement as, for instance, after a visit to the dentist (God how I feared that dentist, a brute of a man, who – I remember this distinctly – actually knelt on my chest in order to gain access to my poor, outraged mouth), she would prepare for me, as only she ever could, a semolina pudding, smooth but of firm consistency, serving it piping hot and with a large dollop of yellow butter melting away on top and with simply lots of raspberry syrup or cinnamon and sugar, whichever I happened to prefer at the time. If, on the other hand, I was fractious or rude or rebellious, she would threaten me with the temporary or even permanent loss of my beloved semolina pudding – a possibility sufficiently serious for me to mend my ways instantly. Of course, she never did act on these threats. That would have been quite out of character for her, for she was a person of boundless kindness, especially towards me, indubitably her favourite nephew. In short, she enveloped me in her love, and as long as she looked after me I felt utterly secure.

Incidentally, semolina pudding was not only the main standard by which I learned to make appropriate moral judgements. Much later, during my engine-greasing days at sea, when I was (to the extent at least to which anyone ever is) my own master and in matters concerning food free to make my own choices (within the limits of availability, of course), it also taught me the merits of moderation. For when, on the *Bergano*, I had made a habit of swapping all my eggs, meat and cheese for this, my favourite delicacy, drenching it with raspberry syrup and devouring large helpings of it in a state of delirious self-indulgence, it caused me both a nasty toothache and an unpleasant, disgusting facial skin disease, which – resisting all pills, ointments and lotions prescribed for me by doctors in a multitude of ports – departed only once I had returned to a more conventional diet.

It would not be true to say that I have never tasted a better sweet than semolina pudding. Plum dumplings topped with breadcrumbs fried in butter, for instance, were something else again. And I find poppy-seed noodles such as they serve at Ye Olde Budapest in Dean Street mouth-wateringly irresistible. But unlike semolina pudding none of these or any other delicacies ever managed to acquire great moral significance in my eyes. The other day I told Sombrero-Domingo about this, and he responded by telling me that as a child he had never been forced to eat spinach or finish his soup. I think he was trying to impress upon me that his childhood had been much happier and far less inhibited than mine, and that anyone such as myself whose moral values were based upon a stodgy pudding was bound to become a hopeless pessimist and develop a nasty puritan streak. I didn't bother to argue the point, for poor SD hasn't been very happy lately. He says he is feeling his age.

When I asked my father why Aunt Sali had never married, he explained that on account of her delicate health this would not have been such a good idea. I, of course, did not really understand what he was driving at. However, be that as it may, once all her brothers and sisters had left home she regarded it as her God-given duty to look after her ageing parents – a duty to which she did in fact devote the best part of her life. When I lived in Klimkovice she was far from well, always suffering from this pain or that, and, indeed, she survived my grandparents, both of whom died in quick succession, by only a few years.

I am quite sure it wouldn't take much for Catty to fall in with my wishes, but this I might well come to regret, so I had better not try. Still, Christmas is not all that far away, and who knows what may happen at the office party!

M's monday class was showing distinct signs of terminal strain, for as ever more of the old students left, frequently after a period of irregular attendance, a kind of flat spin resulted, in spite of the fact that certain stalwarts who had been members of the class from the very beginning – for instance, stout Mrs. Snyder, jolly, confused Mr. Fennimore and, of course, Doris – continued to attend regularly. M, however, had a shrewd suspicion that what motivated them was not so much the wondrous quality of his teaching nor, indeed, any burning desire to learn his language, but rather personal loyalty, perhaps even pity, for him, their unfortunate teacher, as they watched him trying, not very convincingly, to look cheerful and unconcerned through it all, and the fact that, for the time being at any rate, they could not think of anything better to do on a Monday evening. Nor was there much hope that matters would improve, for some of the students were by now far too advanced, tending to hog every conversation and generally muscle in on whatever happened to be going on, whereas others were making no progress at all and appeared to be forgetting even such little German as they had once known. And all the time the office was sending along new students without the slightest regard for their suitability, inspired, no doubt, by the notion that it was sinful to turn away good money.

Small wonder, therefore, that M sometimes felt he was losing his grip. The failure of his class came in his mind to be inextricably linked with a sense of personal failure and an equally potent feeling of guilt. However often he told himself that he had no reason whatsoever to feel guilty – after all, classes, like any person, had a limited lifespan, and this particular class had already lasted longer than most – he was really convinced that the impending demise of his Monday evening class was the result of his own inadequacy as a teacher and a human being.

In moments of black depression he could not in fact but agree with Dr. McGill, who never failed to point out to him that teachers at establishments such as TTTW were mere clowns, a species of pretentious frauds, with little, if any, impact on their students. And it was M's distinct impression that even as a clown he wasn't doing too well. Surely Mr. Desmond, one of his more capable students, hit the nail squarely on the head when he pointed out that whatever, in or out of class, the topic under discussion – whether it was life after death or the properties of shoe cream – they always wound up with the same ideas and the same well rehearsed arguments. Surely, Mr. Desmond – and, no doubt, he was not the only one – was by now fed up to the back teeth with M's not-all-that-stimulating paradoxes and would-be profundities, although, being well brought up and English, he didn't, of course, say so in so many words. Needless to say, observations such as this did nothing to lighten M's spirit or to make the decline of his class any less painful.

He was, of course, by no means the only teacher stumbling along in this manner – indeed, what else could be expected given the way in which TTTW was organised – and not all was doom and gloom, not by any means. His re-enrolment rates continued to be relatively good – only recently had Dr. Pendlebloom complimented him on how well he was doing, hinting with more than one 'You and I, Dr.

Maskenbusch' and similarly pleasing expressions that he and M were somehow set apart from the common herd and far above it. The common herd had its uses, of course, but could never manage without the leadership of persons such as themselves. Indeed, M had good reason to conclude that what his employer was talking about was promotion and a more permanent, far more central role for M, to be discussed in the very near future. More promising yet, Miss Gomberg had taken to smirking at him whenever they met at the office or elsewhere, proof perhaps that she had at long last come to terms with his existence.

M's Monday class was the last class of the day, and it had become customary for some of the 'old guard' to take M after their lesson to the House of Pasta and to buy him a cup of coffee. They would chat endlessly about their holidays, the outrageously rising prices of this and that, or other topics of similar interest. As for studious and obnoxious Mr. Willoughby, he always made very good use of this opportunity to extract yet further linguistic information from poor old M, who, dog-tired as he was by then, would gladly have done without this 'treat'.

But as if this were not enough, M also felt obliged to take Doris home to her bed-sitter in Lancaster Gate. Doris was very nice of course, very kind and friendly, but outside the classroom they didn't have all that much in common, nor did M find her exactly irresistible. Indeed, he found her a bit too plump for his taste and not really desirable. Parting company (at last!) in front of her house, she would look at him expectantly, and once or twice he had actually been on the point of kissing her, but remembering other, similar occasions and what they had led to, he had managed to resist this particular temptation.

That failure and guilt were so closely linked in M's mind was almost certainly due to the fact that his mother – an angelic person, by all accounts – had died only a few days after he was born and that he had neither brothers nor sisters. After all, a small child cannot tell whether such misery as may come its way is due simply to circumstances or events entirely beyond its control, or the result of its not being up to standard, that is to say, punishment. Since the concept of unhappiness other than by way of retribution is bound to be incomprehensible to it, any child with more than its fair share of unhappiness is bound to develop an exaggerated sense of inadequacy and, in consequence, guilt. A lonely child who feels neglected or starved of natural affection – and this certainly applied to M during long periods of his very early life – will tend to respond by becoming ever more inward-looking, a state in which it wastes much energy trying to come to terms with its feelings (generally without success since they are in any case irrational), thus leaving it drained, confused and quite unable to take any action, however futile.

How different, by comparison, are the reactions of a person such as Silversmith or Sombrero-Domingo, whose childhood had been a happy one and who as a child was at all times and regardless of his behaviour in general and in particular assured of his parents' affection, never lonely and always at the centre of things. A person such as this is far less likely to search for faults and errors in himself, and if things go wrong he often becomes aggressive and blames everybody and everything under the sun rather than himself. Such a person was, for instance, M's schoolfriend Birkenfels, who – it will be remembered – used to throw the pieces at M whenever he lost a game of chess, which really illustrates the point to perfection.

It would be misleading, of course, to suggest that M was incapable of facing up to adversity whatever his predicament. On the contrary, he proved on occasion to be most determined and a veritable man of action, always provided that his conscience was clear and his path, as he saw it, straight. This was certainly the case when, only a few months before the end of the war, the following series of events led to his transfer from a camp on the outskirts of Tokyo to one in the North of Japan, where he was employed alternately in mining iron ore and feeding 'pot-roasters', smallish steel furnaces with a voracious appetite for both ore and coke.

It all started with M – still at the PoW camp where he had by then spent nearly three long years – on sick-leave and not, therefore, obliged to go to work at the goods yard of the local railway station. After a day or two of being left entirely to his own devices (a welcome break this in his daily routine before boredom and lethargy set in), he was declared sufficiently fit to join a group of fellow 'sufferers' delegated to plant potatoes in a nearby field, an area on which until quite recently had stood a colony of small, flimsily constructed houses – the modest homes of local workers and their families – which had been totally destroyed in the course of numerous incendiary raids. After every such attack small detachments of prisoners had been sent out from the camp – as if by a miracle, but more probably because its whereabouts were known to the American pilots, it had remained unscathed – in order to clear away the debris and restore the ground to its original arable and highly fertile state.

M felt no special hostility towards the Japanese in charge of the camp and certainly none towards the population in general. Indeed, he was much impressed by the absence of aggression or any apparent resentment with which these poor and dignified people would meet the prisoners while an air-raid was in progress, as, separated only by a few soldiers, they and the prisoners all stood there in the open, staring into the flames of burning houses or at the turbulent, fiery sky, a deep glow as from a myriad infernal furnaces. As for the way in which he and his fellows were treated by the Japanese in charge of the camp, M was convinced that under the circumstances (and it must be borne in mind that at the time he had no idea what was going on in Burma or the Philippines or any of the other territories in which prisoners were being held) they could not be expected to behave very differently from the way they were doing. After all, he argued, prisoners are not exactly welcome and honoured guests and cannot, therefore, expect to be treated in any especially favourable way. But although he understood their point of view and, on occasion, sympathised with it, he never lost sight of the fact that they were the enemy and that it was quite in order and even commendable to inflict damage on them, however extensive or ridiculously slight. How else, after all, but as totally ridiculous could one describe the deliberate destruction by M (albeit in a manner virtually undetectable) of a consignment of crockery on its way through Michigawa station? Yet, on that occasion too, he was acting in the same passionless spirit as when, after the *Bergano* had been captured, he plotted (or at any rate thought that he was plotting when in fact he was merely day-dreaming) how she might be retaken from the German prize crew, although he rather admired those of its members whom he came to know personally and even, to some extent, identified with them. Certainly, the fact that he shared their language and cultural background created a bond between them which could not readily be denied. When he dreamt up his 'heroic' plans, he could not, of course, have foreseen that one of them – throwing live shells into the engine room in order to immobilise the ship while she was close to land so that everybody would have to take to the lifeboats, the idea being that they would soon be picked up by the Australian navy – was to miscarry so badly and with such disastrous consequences, since it had not occurred to him or anyone else that it was critical to prime the shells. In the event, when some of the Norwegians decided to act on this plan the shells simply tumbled down to the lower levels of the engine room, causing no significant damage whatsoever. This attempt was made long after M had been removed from the *Bergano*, and he heard about it only after the war in Manila, when he happened to meet Petersen, one of his former shipmates, who had been directly involved and had, as a result, spent two wretched years in solitary confinement in a Japanese punishment camp. Petersen, smiling all over his broad face, as if the entire affair had been some huge joke and not the tragedy it in fact turned out to be, told him that at the time in question the *Bergano* was on her way to the Philippines, under another German captain with ideas very different from those of the gentlemanly commander who had taken her to Tokyo. Although M had not participated in this unsuccessful action and could not in any case have influenced its outcome – after all, he too had not the slightest notion of what to do with a shell in order to make it explode – he always felt that its results were his fault and his alone, since it had been his idea which set the entire process in motion.

However, since he was squeamish about violence in any shape or form and not very brave, his acts of defiance, such as they were, generally had more in common with futile schoolboy pranks than with such acts of valour and daring as perhaps deserve to be universally admired.

So back to the planting of potatoes: marching along in single file and two by two, each pair of prisoners was connected by a pole from which swung a heavy wooden tub brimful of stinking, yellow human excrement, writhing with fat white maggots. Walking slowly and carefully in order to avoid being splashed, they were carrying this succulent load, the only type of manure available at the time, to the field where, with the aid of a kind of wooden ladle, they were to distribute it in the black, fertile furrows. M, at the head of the column, came to a sudden halt (nearly causing a multiple collision with who knows what dire consequences) as the camp commander, Lieutenant Takahashi, crossed their path. The Lieutenant, as neat and fastidious an officer as ever there was, waved them on, but the men of the potato-planting detail would have none of that. Taking full advantage of the situation, they saluted him at great length and with great obsequiousness, strictly according to the rules, compelling him to respond in the appropriate manner, although on this occasion at any rate he would clearly have preferred a less formal and certainly less protracted encounter.

Once in the field, they decided first of all to make a fire and to warm themselves. Looking, a few minutes later, into the friendly blaze, it occurred to M that there was really no point in planting the potatoes entrusted to them by the medical sergeant, seeing that the end of the war was manifestly at hand and that they were most unlikely to benefit from their labour in any way. When he put it to the others that they might as well plant stones and eat the potatoes while the going was good, they agreed heartily. They skewered the potatoes on to wires (which would make it easy both to get rid of them if a Japanese were to approach and to find them again once the danger had receded) and put them into the fire until they were thoroughly cooked. Then they shared them out and had themselves a feast.

They really thought that they had got away with it and, no doubt, should have, but in the evening, shortly after their return to camp and before supper, all members of the potato-planting detail – about ten prisoners altogether – were instructed to go to the office. In the mistaken belief that they were to be rewarded with cigarettes, one of their more enterprising fellows joined them, in spite of the fact that he had been hard at work all day unloading chromium ore at Michigawa station.

To judge from the way in which he yelled at them and kept hitting them with his stick while exhorting them to admit their terrible crimes against the Japanese people, who had been good to them and treated them well, not as the scum of the earth they in fact were, nothing was further from the mind of the medical sergeant – it was he who had ordered the planting of potatoes and, as it appeared, had worked out what had really happened – than to reward by any means whatsoever the unfortunate creatures now lined up dismally in front of him. He screamed that the most guilty men must confess or be indicated to him immediately, for although all of them were guilty and would receive their just deserts, never you fear, there were some so steeped in depravity as to require very special attention. To begin with, this harangue did not cut much ice, but when he threatened that all the prisoners in the camp would have to stand all night in the freezing yard, M, who had been through just such an experience before – in summer, when it was reasonably warm and not all that unpleasant to be out in the open – stepped forward, followed closely by Canada, a young lad who frequently followed his lead. As ever, M's motives were not all that simple. He wished, for instance, to prove himself a 'real man' quite prepared to 'be counted' and to 'take responsibility', whatever that might mean, seeing that he was unshakably convinced that nothing untoward could ever happen to him, and, being intensely curious, could in any case never resist a 'challenge'. He certainly was aware of the likely consequences if his fellow prisoners were made to suffer because of him and would rather face anything than their fury, but almost equally persuasive was his frequently aching back, which made standing in the yard seem the most agonising fate imaginable. This, of course, was quite some time before the arches of his feet had sunk so low as to require permanent supports and had become his chief source of physical misery.

Contrary to what might have been expected, the medical sergeant, fundamentally as decent a chap as one might wish to meet, took M's revelation in a calm and even relaxed manner, perhaps because he was relieved that he had not been made to 'lose face' or because, unlike many of his comrades, he did not, in spite of his apparent anger, cherish any kind of confrontation. Besides, he may well have thought that this was a fine opportunity to deal, at least in part, with a far weightier matter, namely how to ensure a reasonable standard of cleanliness throughout the camp in time for the forthcoming inspection by some general or colonel or other big-wig, of which he had been notified only a few days previously and which already constituted one of the burning issues of the day, eagerly discussed by both prisoners and staff.

In fact, the medical sergeant's problem was by no means an easy one, for much of the clothing worn by the prisoners – mostly British Army apparel captured at Hong Kong or Singapore – was very far from clean and most unlikely to pass muster. But what else could have been expected, seeing that hardly anybody had any soap and that after a hard day's graft only obsessively clean people, of whom there were some but by no means many, could contemplate an activity so lacking in appeal as the washing of their clothes? There was, however, not the slightest truth in the malicious rumour that if at full moon a shirt or a pair of trousers were to be hung at either end of one of the washing-lines spanning the yard, it might with luck be seen moving slowly towards the other end, carried along in solemn procession by veritable armies of resolute lice. Still, no one could deny that there were lice in the camp, and, looked at closely, many a vest or shirt was oddly reminiscent of a grassy hillside in autumn with sheep grazing in the distance.

Such perhaps were the thoughts which the medical sergeant was pondering as he sat on his chair and considered what kind of punishment he should inflict on the two wretches standing at some kind of attention on the other side of his desk. He certainly took his time but eventually pronounced sentence to the effect that they were to wash, every day and for an unspecified period, thirty articles of clothing each, after returning from work at the railway station. Since he was not an unreasonable man and, on this occasion, concerned mainly with finding a practical way of dealing with the irksome matter in prospect, he also provided each of them with a bar of soap and sent them on their way.

The procedure, they were told, was to be as follows: M and his partner in crime were, after their nightly return to camp, to collect altogether sixty shirts, jackets, pairs of trousers or major items of underwear, record them in writing and submit both the dirty clothing and the list for his approval. Following this initial stage, they could return to their room in order to enjoy their supper. After supper they were to wash the clothing in the bath-house, where there was quite a large, white-tiled sunken bath in the floor. Next day, when the now clean washing was dry, they were to show it, again together with their list, to the sergeant, who would pass or reject their efforts, as the case might be. Having returned the clothes to their no doubt grateful owners, they would collect other garments in need of laundering etc, etc *ad infinitum*.

To say that M was profoundly dismayed at this prospect would indeed be putting it mildly. How, he asked himself, was he, who even under normal circumstances had not the slightest leanings in that direction, or, for that matter, poor Canada – who hardly ever spoke but smiled a lot and was loyal and generous to a fault, and for whose plight M felt responsible – to manage this monstrous assignment after loading and unloading trucks all day at Michigawa station? How could he have been so stupid as to risk so much for such a poor return as a few charred potatoes, when, after all this time in the camp, he might have known that the medical sergeant was far too much of a busybody to assume, without further ado, that his instructions had been carried out well and truly? These and many other questions passed through his mind as he contemplated the predicament in which they found themselves, but at that stage he couldn't see any way in which to avoid the unhappy fate in store for them. As for young Canada, formerly a deck-hand on a British cargo vessel, he faced the future with far greater equanimity, possibly because he was confident that his good friend M would, as so often before, be sure to come up with some perfectly satisfactory solution – so why worry?

Back in their 'room' – small and very cramped, with four bunks on either side in two tiers and only a narrow aisle in between, but home nevertheless – M and Canada found that the story of their avowal had preceded them, putting them, however briefly, at the centre of their particular stage. Every detail of their ordeal was gone into, as was the wisdom or foolishness of what they had done, and there was no lack of good advice and critical comment. Basking in all this fuss and 'glory', M was delighted and not a little surprised to find once again, as on several occasions since he had tricked Petty Officer Bramwell how many friends he now seemed to have, whereas Canada, who really was quite blameless in the matter, clearly regarded all this attention as highly embarrassing.

Inspired by so much solidarity and encouraged by so many offers of help, the following plan emerged: the dirty garments would be collected and presented to the medical sergeant together with a list, entirely as requested. However, as soon as he had inspected these articles and checked the list, they would be returned to their owners immediately, unwashed, of course, for them to deal with as they saw fit. While M and Canada were at the office, clean articles would be collected in the exact proportions laid down in the list and thrown into the bath. Soap would be added to the water to make it look turbid, and more water would be spilt on the floor, enough to convince any passing guard or soldier or, for that matter, the medical sergeant himself, that the two culprits were hard at work. Of course, the light in the bath-house would be left on all night. Taking advantage of the fact that there were always some prisoners – mainly old men – who could not sleep and spent the nights prowling about the camp, M let it be known that anyone alerting him and Canada that a Japanese was approaching the bath-house would receive, subject to proper and trustworthy evidence, of course, five cigarettes – a high price but certainly worth it. In fact the situation never arose, but if it had, they would simply have jumped from their bunks – they were already fully dressed, with their sleeves turned up – dipped their arms into a conveniently placed bucket of water, and rushed to the bath-house pretending that they had been away for only a minute or two. Early in the morning, well before dawn, M and Canada would rinse the clean washing and hang it up to dry. In the evening the dry clothes would be shown to the medical sergeant and in due course returned to their owners, whereupon the entire cycle could recommence.

This charade went on for a week or two, during which even fewer clothes were washed than before, largely because for much of the evening the bath-house had become virtually inaccessible. As for the medical sergeant, he eventually realised that his ingenious plan was not working and that the prisoners were simply making a fool of him, but he never managed to work out just how they were doing it. At any rate, he stopped the punishment but included both M and Canada in a list of 'undesirables' to be sent to a newly established camp up north, and it was there M found himself at the very end of the war.

CHAPTER TWENTY FIVE

THE KITCHEN at No. 12 was full of acrid smoke, with a kind of whitish haze lending an air of unreality to the scene. Silversmith, at the sink, was in the process of scraping some black deposit from the one and only saucepan, while Lipkin, whose face was grotesquely battered and in part swollen and discoloured, was gnawing away cheerfully at a lump of charcoal or something very much like it. They had opened the window – to get rid of the smoke, obviously – and, the year being already far advanced, it was bitterly cold.

'What on earth is going on?' M, who had just arrived, wanted to know, once he had more or less recovered from a fit of coughing.

'Nothing that need concern you,' replied Silversmith, adding with a touch of desperation 'My God, I'm hungry. I could eat a horse.'

'That dumpling was not bad, I wouldn't mind having another,' said Lipkin, revealing thereby what he believed the mysterious food object which he had devoured with so much enthusiastic approval to have been.

As a result of relentless questioning by M (who was particularly well equipped to carry out this investigation inasmuch as during the last days of his stay in Japan he himself had had grave problems cooking a dumpling of quite similar characteristics, which, as distinct from the dumpling in the present case, had turned into a watery mess of no discernible taste) it eventually transpired that Silversmith, having decided to cook a steamed dumpling for his lunch, had, with the aid of a large red-and-white chequered handkerchief, suspended the dough – a rich concoction of choice and very nourishing ingredients such as (in addition to two eggs, milk and some flour) bacon, apples and lumps of cheese, to mention but a few – in the saucepan. After filling the latter one third with water (good thinking this!), he had jammed on the lid to hold the handkerchief and its precious burden in position, finally lighting the gas flame under the saucepan in order to initiate the process of cooking. Then, as was his custom, he had gone to the public library to study the morning papers and thus work up a reasonable appetite, leaving Lipkin, who happened to be visiting, behind to keep an eye on the proceedings. The latter, in turn, had immersed himself in a chess problem, waking up to the developing crisis only when it was already well advanced.

Subsequent analysis suggested that, apart from Lipkin's stewardship of the dumpling, two things had gone seriously and irretrievably wrong: the steam generated as the water boiled had, to judge by such evidence as was still available, lifted the lid from the saucepan thus causing both the 'dumpling' and the handkerchief in which it rested to sink to the bottom. And, of course, once the water had boiled away, there was nothing to prevent what Silversmith, at any rate, understandably regarded as a major culinary tragedy. Luckily, Mr. and Mrs. Bingley had been away on yet another house-viewing expedition, and Lipkin had coped well enough with this difficult situation. Indeed, the entire event amounted to no more than a minor storm in a teacup, for nothing really disastrous had happened and there had, thanks to Lipkin's ever lively appetite, been very little waste.

Once the debris had been cleared away and everything restored more or less to normal, Lipkin told his friends about the injuries to his face – injuries sustained not in fair contest at the gymnasium he sometimes attended in order to practise his boxing skills, but in a fight at his most recent place of work, a 'factory' specialising in the production of costume jewellery ('plastic ornaments' according to Lipkin) for ladies. It all started with the secretary (who, among other things, prided herself on her close, indeed intimate, relationship with the owner) fining Lipkin a penny for being one minute late for work. Lipkin, understandably, had let her know what he thought of her in rather emphatic terms, causing a certain Bill from the brooch department, who had never liked Lipkin – in fact, as he was never loth to point out, he 'simply hated the little foreign bastard's guts' – to seize the opportunity and leap to her defence. In the ensuing struggle, Lipkin, of course, had been at a clear disadvantage for, honestly believing himself to be a trained pugilist, he had felt compelled to fight with, as the saying goes, his hands tied behind his back. In any case, a brawl with Bill went very much against his grain, seeing that in his eyes Bill was a fellow worker and potential comrade at arms. Bill on the other hand, although formerly a regimental boxer, had no such misgivings – hence the result. Lipkin concluded his story with a painstaking description of the job from which he had just been fired. 'It was very interesting,' he told them, 'and there was a great feeling of solidarity among us. Only one thing I did not understand: plastic ornaments – why should anyone want to own a plastic ornament?'

M and Miss Pratt had been to see a new production of *The Key*, Bacharach's latest play about a man with a clockwork heart and his untimely end. Now they were sitting at the 'Frying Pan' in Belsize Park waiting for their toasted 'specials' and discussing that evening's entertainment.

'A very interesting effort, I thought, but wasn't it a pity that it was so poorly attended?' said Miss Pratt of the claw-like hands, who on that occasion was wearing a black tailored suit and an enormous black hat.

'But isn't that always the case when you get a really worthwhile play rather than the pitiful rubbish they normally show in the West End?' When talking to Miss Pratt about 'cultural' events and anything else that 'really mattered', M, like a well-trained circus horse, knew precisely what was expected of him, and his opinions on such occasions tended to be impeccably correct, at any rate in the early stages of their discussions. In return for his right-mindedness, he was, as a rule, allowed to get away with rather exaggerated language. For M all this was, of course, merely a kind of game, as he would have been the first to admit, but as for Miss Pratt she was deeply serious and it never occurred to her that what filled her with such intellectual satisfaction were simply echoes of her own voice.

'I wouldn't disagree with that – after all, that is exactly how it is – but considering some of the better reviews and, in particular, Angela Stroud's piece in the Arcadian, I certainly would have expected a much better attendance.' In matters relating to the theatre, Angela Stroud was Miss Pratt's ultimate authority.

'What the theatre-going public enjoys and what the reviewers praise are, you must admit, two entirely different kettles of fish. I, for my part, would not dream of paying the slightest attention to what the reviewers say, no more than do most people. After all, some reviews are so loosely related to what they purport to describe that I have often wondered whether they should not perhaps be regarded as an entirely independent genre of literature and whether they would not be equally valid – or invalid – if the play or book in question didn't exist at all.' The real M was not to be denied any longer. 'The same argument applies really to any form of art. The Sunday papers, for instance, are full of reviews of this or that musical event, in spite of the fact that most readers cannot have been present and are probably unacquainted with the works in question. Clearly it follows that reviews have something to offer which is independent of their subject, and it is equally obvious that a person who enjoys reading such a review might well have been bored to death by the actual piece of music. Take Thomas Mann's *Dr. Faustus* with its pages and pages of music theory, which to me are entirely incomprehensible but which, nevertheless, I would not wish to skip inasmuch as my very lack of comprehension adds an air of mystery, which in turn increases my enjoyment. In any case,' he concluded, reverting to the play and Angela Stroud's contribution, 'phrases like "symbolic masterpiece" and "colourful extravaganza reminiscent of Gogol's Overcoat" can be a bit daunting.'

'Still, we enjoyed it, didn't we, and that, as far as I am concerned, is the main thing,' intervened Miss Pratt to calm M down, for here at last came the waitress with their 'specials' – soggy toast bearing greasy bacon, a fried egg each turning on them its blind, indifferent stare, and tomatoes, with the whole unappetising dish buried in wilting, brown-edged lettuce leaves and smothered in mayonnaise.

'Not exactly what we had in mind,' said Miss Pratt probing gingerly at the swill now in front of her, 'Still …'

'Oh I don't know, I have eaten worse.' M, who had, indeed, eaten much worse, set about his 'special' with a will, making short shrift of it. As for Miss Pratt, who in any case suffered from a chronic lack of appetite, she merely picked away listlessly at her portion, looking every bit like an elderly black vulture suffering from a bout of indigestion.

206

'A highly claustrophobic play, I thought. It reminded me a lot of Kafka's story about the man who waking up one morning finds that he has turned into a beetle.'

'No question about it, none whatsoever,' responded M. 'This, you will agree, is basically a satire with two main themes – the utter pointlessness and emptiness of life once personal survival has become the only reason for living, and, on the other hand, the unutterable futility of science when its sole purpose is achievement without real benefit to anybody, in this case the prolongation of life without regard to its quality. What, after all, is the point of Newt's existence, seeing that his only interest in life is to keep his clockwork heart in good working condition?'

'At least he has that interest, unlike some people I could mention,' interposed Miss Pratt, pushing the dispirited remains of her 'special' away in disgust. 'But didn't you think that the way in which the various objects appear to have lives of their own came across very clearly? As Angela Stroud put it ...'

'No doubt about it! The clock, the chair and the rat's tooth but above all the key itself certainly have lives of their own rather more interesting than that of Newt himself. Surely all that is part and parcel of the irony pervading all aspects of the play. Take, for instance, the final scene in which Newt panics and tries this and that because he cannot find his key, with two keys turning up eventually, neither of which can be used because Newt has damaged the lock. I particularly enjoyed that splendid conclusion, where the mechanism continues working perfectly for nearly a quarter of an hour after Newt has actually died, and Professor Trauermann ...'

'Wasn't he great fun, with his thick German accent and all those assistants following him about?' giggled Miss Pratt.

'He was indeed, but what really got me was the Professor's virtually obscene delight, because 'his' mechanism had been such a success, with never a thought for poor old Newt. The message comes over loud and clear: As far as Professor Trauermann is concerned, Newt's sole function in life was to be a guinea-pig serving the greater glory and advancement of science and, of course, Trauermann's own glory and advancement. In a way, this suggests that science, in particular applied science, can be really irrelevant and even absurd if it lacks what I would call a moral dimension.'

'I thought Moira Shingle as the landlady quite outstanding. This, surely, was comic acting at its very best. In my opinion, Angela Stroud was absolutely right ...'

'With her extraordinarily silly prattle she (it was understood that he meant Moira Shingle, not Angela Stroud), of course, symbolises yet another aspect of Newt's futility,' said M, sipping at the black 'coffee' and scalding his tongue in the process.

'I quite agree. But wasn't the set absolutely marvellous? All that stuffy Victorian furniture and that ghastly clock – wasn't it simply divine?'

Their discussion continued in this happy vein for quite some time yet, but eventually they decided that it was time to go, and Miss Pratt having settled the bill that is what they did. It had been a most enjoyable evening for both of them.

'Dr. Pendlebloom will see you now.' Miss Gomberg once again smirking broadly presented M with this horn of plenty, hoping, no doubt, against hope that he would prove worthy of it.

By way of preparation for this important meeting M had just finished sucking two *Snoozoferons*, sedative lozenges highly recommended in numerous advertisements. By this means he hoped to achieve the detached steadiness of purpose essential, in his opinion, to the matter at hand. On other occasions he had emerged from meetings with Dr. Pendlebloom as the indubitable loser, his impetuosity and, in a manner of speaking, sense of lacking appropriate substance having let him down at crucial stages. (In his masterly and profound work *Dead Souls* the Russian writer Gogol suggests that the qualities of spirit and character required for worldly success are almost inextricably linked with physical bulk, whereas a thin, lanky appearance and a poor posture point to unreliability, shiftlessness, a naïve attitude to life indicating a poor value-structure and, to coin a phrase, plain pauperism. A similar lesson can be learned from the works of Charles Dickens, whose truly solid citizens tend to be solid also in their physical attributes. To comprehend fully why M felt compelled to resort to a drug and thereby, as it were, alienate himself from his real self, it must be borne in mind that at that particular time of his life he was indeed tall, thin and lanky and, being short-sighted, had a tendency to look at the ground in front of him rather than straight and manfully ahead, which of course did his posture no good whatsoever.) Having arrived at the door of Dr. Pendlebloom's inner sanctum, he knocked cautiously and was presently, after only the briefest of pauses, invited to enter.

'Come in, come in, my dear Dr. Maskenbusch.' Dr. Pendlebloom, courteous and affable as always, ushered M towards the man-eating armchair. 'Make yourself quite comfortable, and please tell me what I can do for you,' glancing semi-surreptitiously at his watch to indicate that his time was in fact limited.

'Thank you very much for ...'

'What a terrible pity that our meetings at the office are of necessity always so short, but you know how it is. At the office time is always at a premium – a million things to do, particularly now, with our Escort Agency well and truly launched and already a considerable success. Others may think that they can afford to fritter away valuable time but you and I, toilers in the vineyard of TTTW, know that to waste time is to waste the future.' Realising that this felicitous phrase might come in handy under other, perhaps weightier circumstances, Dr. Pendlebloom made a note of it.

After numerous similar encounters only too familiar with his managing director's impressive range of tactics (which he enjoyed and even admired for the skilful way in which they were executed, while no longer taking them as seriously as might have been expected from one whom Dr. Pendlebloom had repeatedly described as a pillar of his organisation), M confined himself to looking interested while waiting for the *Snoozoferons* to work.

'One of these days we must have lunch together at my club,' continued Dr. Pendlebloom, who in his present expansive mood actually meant what he said, but was in fact most unlikely to follow up this near-invitation, since, quite apart from the cost-factor, a lunch with M, even at a less prestigious venue, could only lead to needless embarrassment while, quite possibly, raising unwarranted expectations. M, who liked to feel relaxed while taking his meals, sincerely hoped that, as in the case of previous similar invitations, nothing would ever come of it. Dr. Pendlebloom, incidentally, knew all about embarrassing situations arising from ill-conceived invitations. After all, he himself had, in his younger years, repeatedly triggered such events, for instance on one unfortunate occasion shortly after the inauguration of TTTW, when he had been the luncheon guest of two hopeful advertising executives who could ill afford to be too finicky in their choice and pursuit of prospective clients. What happened at that luncheon could be fairly described as a classic case of social misunderstanding, for while his hosts were waiting for him to start eating, he, not to be outdone in matters of politeness, had waited for them to make a start, and all the time the food, so succulent and delicious-looking when it was served, had been getting colder and colder and less appetising in appearance. Although for many years he had been able to exclude the memory of this experience from his conscious mind, it had returned lately on a number of occasions whenever he was pondering on the significance and direction of his life.

'They make quite a fair fillet steak with onions, which I can highly recommend. As for me, I like my steak medium rare but you may prefer it rare or even well done. Still, here I am going on about steak when you have far more important matters to discuss. So, once again, what can I do for you?'

'May I, to begin with ...?'

'But, of course, my dear fellow. The second door on the right, you know your way.'

'Very considerate of you, Dr. Pendlebloom, but that is not what I had in mind, not this time. I should simply like to congratulate you on the launch of your new venture and to wish you every success with it.'

'How very clumsy of me and how extremely kind of you! I hope you will believe me that no offence was intended. However, it has not escaped my attention – I may as well call a spade a spade and come straight to the point – that you apparently need to relieve yourself rather more frequently than one would expect from a person of your relatively young years. I know from personal experience and as one whose family has suffered much from ailments in that region that there are problems which have to be tackled head-on and with determination. Believe me, a much older man...'

'Not at all ...'

'Yes, indeed, much older, however much I might wish that this were not the case. But here I go again, wasting your valuable time.'

There was a knock at the door. Catty came in, carrying a tray with two cups of coffee and some biscuits.

'Sugar, Mr. M?'

'Yes, please, two lumps.'

'Milk?'

'A little.'

Once Catty had gone again, Dr. Pendlebloom, now clearly impatient and every inch the managing director rather than a benevolent older friend eager to guide and advise, decided to get on with it. 'Now to the business at hand,' he said. 'What was your purpose in requesting this interview?'

This, at last, was the crunch-point. Everything now depended on the *Snoozoferons*. Having cleared his throat, M began: 'You will, no doubt, be aware that I have been with TTTW now for a considerable time ...'

'And I trust that you are entirely happy with us and will stay with us for many a year to come, that, in fact, you will be one of those to whom I shall be handing over the reins of management when the time comes for me to retire, which is bound to be soon, indeed very soon.' The latter was said imploringly, almost tearfully. There followed the usual exchange of expressions of dismay and affirmation. 'We think of you as one of the mainstays of the organisation, one of the very bedrocks of TTTW. Not a fly-by-night like so many, here today and gone tomorrow ...'

'I am certainly happy at TTTW and regard it as a great honour to be a member of this particular team but ...'

'I know exactly what you are going to say and believe me, my dear Maskenbusch, we are seeing entirely eye to eye. Yes, the time has indeed come for you to be promoted, and it accordingly gives me great, indeed very great pleasure to offer you the important position of head of the German and Rare Languages department. Please let me finish. I fully realise that you are at present our only regular German expert and have so far not been able to make full use of your, if I may say so, quite exceptional linguistic range and accomplishments. However, plans are in hand, which, for reasons you no doubt fully appreciate, I am not yet at liberty to disclose but which will in due course astound you by their range and magnitude. Eventually I foresee – and I hope you share my vision – a major centre for German studies and rare languages arising, a veritable phoenix (where the mythical bird came in was not entirely clear, but in full flow Dr. Pendlebloom was no respecter of pedantic points), with hundreds of students and dozens of lecturers all working busily under your direction and sole authority. As soon as our meeting is over, I shall instruct Miss Gomberg to draw up an appropriate agreement ...'

'Thank you very much indeed. I shall certainly do my utmost to merit your good opinion of me. But will the new agreement entail also a commensurate rise in salary? (The *Snoozoferons* were beginning to work.) You see, I am finding it a little difficult to make ends meet, and, besides, I should like to enrol for an extramural course in mathematics or a language or two at London University. I have, however, not yet made up my mind which it is to be.' M felt that this was as good a point as any at which to raise this particular hare.

'Please forgive me for interrupting you at this point. Does a linguistic expert of such ability and experience as you – not to mention your important new status – really need a degree? Might it not in fact prove counter-productive? May I, your senior by many a year, advise you to search your heart carefully before you answer this question, for what, after all, is the value of a degree if you are out of a job? TTTW, you will agree, is primarily about total commitment, and, in the light of your remark, I am now bound to ask you: Are you prepared to make such a commitment, yes or no? For if you are not, we may have to think again, very carefully.' Dr. Pendlebloom stopped in order to contemplate the impact of his words, fully expecting that M's resolve, if such it was, would now begin to crumble.

'But a degree has always been what I wanted more than anything else, for as long as I can remember. At four years of age already ...' M, patiently polite, was beginning to show his teeth.

'I understand your aspirations perfectly and should not, on any account, wish to stand in your way.'

'That is extremely kind of you, I am really most grateful.' M, now fully at ease, was beginning to feel agreeably indifferent to his employer's blandishments and other devices, a fact which did not escape the latter's attention. A manipulative man, he did not like what he perceived and it upset him considerably.

'We must be practical in this.' Dr. Pendlebloom's hands were beginning to tremble quite noticeably, preventing him from drinking his coffee, while a worried frown appeared on his face. 'As for your plan to enrol at London University, I am prepared to await developments and see how it all works out. But as for the matter of an increase in your salary, the situation is far more complex. As you doubtlessly appreciate, TTTW London currently employs about 150 tutors and other staff, some of whom have very high professional and academic qualifications whereas others are blessed with large families. Indeed, there are some to whom both these descriptions apply. Now if, as I would very much like to do, I were to offer you an immediate increase (scribbling rapidly on the block of paper before him and underlining the result of his calculation in emphatic red) of, let us say, 40 per cent of your present salary or £200 per annum – and please do believe me, my dear Dr. Maskenbusch, that I would gladly offer you more – what am I to say to all the others when they come knocking at my door asking for a similar rise?'

'I take your point, Dr. Pendlebloom, indeed I do,' said M, doing no such thing but continuing to feel pleasantly detached, much as on that rather different occasion in Japan when he had woken up in the middle of the night firmly convinced that he had died and had therefore no longer the slightest reason to fear the event of dying, as distinct from all the other poor mutts snoring away all about him, who still had their futures to worry about. 'But what am I to do? Without a satisfactory rise in salary...'

'Please consider if you will. 150 times £200 (another rapid calculation on the block of paper) would amount to £30,000 per annum. Please correct me if I am wrong. In the present economic climate, for which I in common with many other members of the business community blame the intolerable profligacy of the present government, this would, of course, be quite impossible.'

'Surely not everybody ...'

'There is, of course, one possibility – one way out of our present predicament. TTTW might be able to offer you an additional £50 per annum to recompense you for your new responsibilities. This would make you one of the highest paid practitioners in our profession – I say 'our' advisedly, for like you, my dear Maskenbusch, I am proud of belonging to what I consider the most noble and perhaps the most ancient of all the professions – while avoiding the necessity of paying inflated salaries and rates to people whose contribution is in no way comparable to yours. May I take it that such a solution would be agreeable to you?'

'£100 would be more in line with what I had in mind and actually require in order to make ends meet.'

'All right, I do not wish to haggle,' conceded Dr. Pendlebloom looking anxiously at his watch, which told him that it was high time to go to lunch. 'Let us split the difference. £75, that is my best offer, take it or leave it.'

Hardly able to believe that he had actually got the better of his wily opponent, agreed smartly and the appropriate parting formalities having been completed, M left on a high note of triumph and, after using Dr. Pendlebloom's toilet on the way out, general relief.

CHAPTER TWENTY SIX

SOMBRERO-DOMINGO, far from well of late, had been complaining a lot of shortness of breath, pains in his chest when walking, and general exhaustion. Following a severe heart attack on his homeward journey from TTTW he was now in a hospital bed, recovering slowly but still by no means out of the woods.

In his mind, the way in which he had – by good luck really but, as he insisted, mainly by a series of razor-sharp, spot-on decisions – escaped almost certain death had become a heroic exploit, perhaps the most heroic exploit he had ever been involved in. When M came to visit him he was obviously very tired indeed, but such was his desire to communicate his experience that virtually nothing, not even the look of mock disapproval the ward sister gave him as she passed by on her round, could have prevented him from telling his friend all about it.

'You have no idea how lucky I was,' he panted. 'If the door had closed before I managed to get out of the train, yours truly might no longer ...' this with a rueful grin '... be here to tell the tale.'

'We none of us live for ever,' commented M, who, since he had not the least idea of how he might be expected to react to a statement as manifestly realistic as this, decided to be matter-of-fact. Besides, he was busy picking away at the bunch of grapes he had brought by way of propitiatory gift and which, quite clearly, would have been wasted on poor, bed-ridden Sombrero-Domingo. This pursuit therefore engaged a considerable part of his concentration. 'So tell me, my friend,' he continued, 'What actually happened?'

'What happened? What do you mean, what happened? On my way to Tottenham Court Road I all of a sudden got this terrible pain in my chest. I am not afraid of a little pain, you know – not even my worst enemy could call me *wehleidig* – but this was getting beyond a joke. So I went to the chemist and asked for something to stop it. I had, of course no idea what was wrong.' Sombrero-Domingo, looking utterly worn and exhausted, asked M to hand him the glass of water from the overloaded bedside table. He took a sip but did not like it. 'This water is warm,' he complained, 'but the doctor says I must drink a lot.'

'Shall I get you some fresh water?'

'Would you? Would you do this for poor old S-D?'

M took the jug and went looking for water. He meandered hither and thither trying to find a suitable tap but without success until he happened to bump into a nurse, who, clearly not in the least surprised at M's incompetence (what, after all, could one expect from a mere visitor, who in any case had no business wandering all over the place, getting into people's way and, more especially, hers?), she took the jug away from him and told him that she would bring Dr. Sombrero some water as soon as possible. He would just have to be patient and wait his turn like everybody else. She was rushed off her feet and had, after all, only one pair of hands.

Once again at Sombrero-Domingo's bedside, M roughly outlined what had happened. After some merely perfunctory grumbling, S-D continued with his tale. 'Aspirins or codeins, that was all the *schmock* said he could give me, so I took the codeins because they are stronger. He also told me to see a doctor, as soon as possible. Easier said than done, the way I was feeling already. Pains in the chest I have had before but never such pains. But the doctor here – between you and me he looks worse than I – tells me not to worry, there is nothing much wrong with me and I shall yet live to be a hundred. For a man of my age, he says, I'm really quite fit.' (It was obvious that even in his present sorry state the doctor's testimony to his fitness still filled him with considerable satisfaction.) In any case, fit or not fit, I thought the pain would go again as it had done before, many a time, once I was in the train sitting down.' He stopped for a moment, gazing at M with his large, brown, almond-shaped eyes both sadly and with an air of total trust. Looking like this he seemed oddly reminiscent of Puffi, his schnitzel-loving spaniel. M could not but feel that it was somehow up to him to solve all his friend's problems – to restore him to youth, health and vigour – and the awareness of his absolute impotence filled him with guilt and profound despondency.

'At any rate,' S-D continued, 'old fool that I am, I carried on regardless but the pain was getting worse all the time.'

'So what happened?' M had nearly finished all the grapes.

'Happened? What do you mean, happened? By the time I was in the carriage sitting down – for once when I don't need it I don't have to wait for hours – it got so bad I thought I must die. So I said to myself "S-D, my friend, you must not be quite right up there (he pointed vaguely in the direction of his large, mottled head), sitting in this carriage when you really ought to be in hospital," and I got out just as the doors were closing and dragged myself up the stairs. God knows how. Still, I was lucky – you have no idea how – for there was a taxi which took me straight to this hospital. A decent chap, the driver, he didn't even want any money, but I gave him what I had in my pocket.'

'Who says guardian angels are simply figments of the imagination? You really were dead lucky.'

'Don't use that word in this place, even as a joke,' protested S-D, who like many agnostics was profoundly superstitious, 'And do me a favour, don't even speak to me about luck. What sort of luck is it to land in a place like this, if you please? Still, I am better now – the worst is over, touch wood.' Sombrero-Domingo extended a skeletal, brown-speckled hand to touch the table but couldn't reach it. His hand dropped, dangling limply at his side.

'Never mind,' said M somewhat disingenuously, trying to cheer him up. 'Anyone can see that you are getting much better. You will be up again and back at TTTW before you know it.' He did not really expect to get away with this but Sombrero-Domingo was eager to clutch at any straw.

'Do you really think so, scout's honour? I certainly feel a lot better.' However, just then a very pretty nurse carrying a tray passed by without S-D showing the slightest interest in her. Nothing could have proved more convincingly how desperately ill he still was. 'During the first few days, in intensive care, I had to have oxygen, you know,' he continued feebly but again with a definite touch of pride, 'not to mention the green tube in the back of my hand.'

'What is the food like?' M enquired, eager to change the subject.

'What can I say? Some people like it – good luck to them, I say – but as for me, I simply can't get it down. It all goes back to the kitchen. I have lost a lot of weight, you know – simply pounds and pounds – which is good, of course, in my condition and pleases the doctor, but I can't even finish my boiled egg in the morning. Even the eggs taste terrible, but there are some who can't get enough. Take Bill, for instance – the man with the glasses in the bed opposite – you would not credit what that man can eat.' M turned around to look at Bill, which seemed to be the right thing to do in the circumstances, and as Bill for his part happened to be looking in his direction they smiled at each other and waved cheerily.

Sombrero-Domingo, who had been looking with an air of ever increasing impatience towards the entrance of the ward for quite some time, was on the point of becoming petulant. 'She is late again, Bertha.' he complained, 'That woman is always late. Last week, on two days running she actually managed to arrive just when they were ringing the bell at the end of visiting-time.'

'Perhaps she got stuck in the traffic,' suggested M, helpfully. 'What do you mean, stuck in the traffic? If she didn't leave everything to the last minute, she wouldn't get stuck anywhere. The trouble is, Bertha has not the slightest idea of time – never had – and, besides, she enjoys nothing more than to make me wait.'

'And what are the other patients like?' M felt that another change of direction was called for. 'Do you have any contact with them?'

'They are not too bad, not too bad. We get on all right, on the whole. Bill over there is a bit bossy but he means well. He brings me tea in the morning and comes over to chat. I only wish he wouldn't keep coughing half the night, but there is something the matter with his lungs. That is why they brought him here in the first place. And then there's George, the fat fellow in the bed next to him. I call him my son, which is very funny when you think that he will never see seventy again, and he calls me father! Mind you, his wife comes twice every day and she really hates me.'

'Can you blame her?'

Sombrero-Domingo, choosing to ignore this attempt at light banter (or perhaps he had not even heard it), turned to the subject uppermost in his mind. 'Only yesterday we had a real tragedy here. Very sad it was and very upsetting. I am still very upset, let me tell you.'

'Why, what happened?'

'In the morning they brought in a patient – Wolfson I think was his name – and they put him in the bed over there.' Sombrero-Domingo did his best to indicate which bed it was. 'At about eleven he came over on a little visit and told me all about how he had sold his business – cuddly toys, he told me – and was going to take it real easy, living from his savings. His heart had been giving him trouble lately and he had had a slight coronary – that's why they brought him in the first place – but the doctor had told him that there was no reason why he shouldn't live another twenty years doing everything he wanted to do – even playing tennis – as long as he watched his weight and didn't overdo things. He also showed me some photographs of his family and especially his three-year-old grandson, a nice little chappy with fat cheeks and big eyes, clearly the apple of the old man's eye. In the afternoon his wife and his daughter – the mother of his grandson, you know – came to see him. They stayed quite a long time and had even brought the grandson along. Before they went again, they came over to me – both of them very agreeable people, I must say.' Sombrero-Domingo paused as if to contemplate his story so far and allow it to sink in.

'But in the evening,' he eventually continued, 'Wolfson wanted to be taken to the toilet, so the nurse made him sit on that squeaking wheelchair over there and pushed him along – he was waving to all of us as he went past, a great sense of humour he had, that man – and then nothing happened for a long time, nothing at all. Then they were rushing about all over the place, nurses and doctors everywhere, and the visitors were being kept out although the visiting-time had started already long ago. Nobody, of course, told us anything – they never do, you know. But one has an instinct about this sort of thing, and I with my journalistic nose simply knew that there was something terribly wrong. And then, all of a sudden, we heard a woman shrieking. It sounded quite awful, like from a wild beast in the jungle it was. That is when we all knew that the poor fellow was gone for good. Later on the charge nurse came and told us that he – Mr. Wolfson that is, or rather was – had had a cerebral haemorrhage – bleeding in his brain, you know – and was gone for good. Well, that's life and that's how it goes.' Sombrero-Domingo, visibly moved, took off his glasses and started to polish them.

At this point in his story Bertha arrived, all breathless, giggly and apologetic. 'I'm not late, am I?' she enquired. 'The traffic was terrible, you know, it was really terrible, and then I met Beryl from the Poly, and she never stops yapping, you know what she's like.' Turning to M 'Hello M, nice of you to come. Mind you, S-D is looking much better now, you should have seen him a week ago. I had such a shock, you know, I can't tell you. I really thought he was going to snuff it this time, hee-hee.'

'Must you always paint the devil on the wall, Bertha?' His annoyance seemed to be giving S-D new strength.

'Why not, if it is a good painting?', contributed M, making Bertha choke and splutter in pure delight.

'Bertha, please come and tickle me now. I want to laugh. M is so funny.'

Having recovered from her bout of the giggles, Bertha chose to ignore this, unpacking instead a variety of goodies and then embarking on a lengthy account of what Beryl had said to her and what she had said to Beryl. She had not nearly finished when the bell rang, marking the end of visiting-time.

'Goodness me,' she spluttered, 'Is it that late already? Their clock must be fast, I bet.'

But it wasn't, and a few minutes later it was definitely time to go. Sombrero-Domingo, looking again very old and thin and parchment-transparent, waved feebly after them as they made their way slowly down the endless aisle.

'I really do miss that man,' said Bertha suddenly, 'and can't wait to have him home again, you know, whatever he'll be like. I wouldn't care even if he was deaf and dumb and couldn't move an inch.'

M, rather touched by so much devotion, reassured her, and for a brief spell they walked on in silence.

Near the exit they passed by a curious contraption, a kind of elongated box which looked as if it were made of lead. Bertha explained that it was used to move newly deceased patients to the mortuary. 'Yes, that's exactly what they do, you know, isn't it awful? I wouldn't like to lie in one of those, would you?'

M said he most definitely would not, but if that was what it was used for he could see the point of all that lead, whereupon they went their separate ways, he – late as always – hurrying to a lesson with long-suffering Mr. Allbright and she home to feed the animals.

When M put it to Dr. Pendlebloom that he was determined to study for a degree and would not shun any sacrifice to achieve this aim (there being tacit agreement between them that for M to forego his prospects with TTTW would be nothing less than the supreme sacrifice) he was in fact talking on impulse – off the top of his head one might say. However, from this dubious seed had sprung a very real desire – quite distinct, he felt, from the self-indulgent daydreams of what he now thought of as his younger years – to acquire some academic distinction such as a B.A. or a B.Sc. which might one day lead him to such glories as M.A., Ph.D. or even a D.Lit. Having discovered himself to be a man of action, a man to be reckoned with, as the magnificent rise in salary which he had so cunningly wrought from his reluctant employer proved beyond a shadow of a doubt, he decided to take the requisite steps forthwith, without any prevarication.

Realising, however, that for London University to accept him as a student he would first have to pass the relatively minor but none the less unavoidable hurdle of matriculation, M decided to enrol, in the first place, with a reputable tutorial establishment able and willing to prepare him for that examination without requiring him to attend its courses in person. He accordingly wrote off for the brochure of Dr. Johnson's Correspondence College, an institute of learning which, to judge by the advertisement, combined first-rate tuition by highly qualified and experienced academics – every one of them a teacher of distinction (where had he come across this phrase before?) – with a solid tradition, the cause and result of virtually innumerable successes (testimonials from highly satisfied students proved the point), and a modern approach closely tailored to each student's individual needs. Besides, the range of subjects on offer was said to be very wide indeed – a distinct advantage from M's point of view, seeing that he had not yet quite made up his mind which subjects to select.

The choice was indeed a hard one. It had always been M's ambition to become one of the world's foremost mathematicians and be acclaimed as such, another Newton perhaps or a Leibniz. At the good old Klappenhorn in Vienna they did, after all and surely not without good cause, call him Einstein – at least on those rare occasions when they did not actually hate him or, having some ulterior motive, wanted to butter him up – and, besides, in his eyes Mathematics was easily the most prestigious as well as the most romantic of subjects, the very highest pinnacle to which the human spirit was capable of ascending. Magic it was, purest magic, particularly when things worked out. M positively gloried in every correct solution of even the most routine problem, regarding it as proof positive that he was indeed a mathematician of rare genius, as yet perhaps a trifle short on actual knowledge and technique but clearly with a great future to look forward to. Always, apparently, on the point of squaring the circle or achieving some other notable triumph of the intellect, Faust M and Wagner Stengel knew very well what they were about, as they beavered away in that tiny, airless room in old Mr. Stengel's hardware shop, where the warm, cosy light of the paraffin lamp was mysteriously reflected in the eyes of Dora, the Stengels' large black cat.

However, M was well aware of the fact that if he were to choose Mathematics, he could hope to get to the very top and attain the coveted transformation to graduate status only by unstinting commitment and much hard work on his part, presupposing qualities of character and personality which, as distinct from sheer genius, he could, after all, not be certain to possess. And although he had not as yet set out on this particular journey, he knew only too well and from ample personal experience what it was like to be staring at a problem without the slightest idea how to set about it or how it felt when, after racing with eager anticipation towards a 'solution', one eventually wound up again at the very beginning, nothing whatsoever achieved. After much detailed self-analysis and cogent reasoning, he eventually arrived at the wise conclusion that if, after all, he was perhaps not cut out for consistent hard work, it might perhaps be better for him to approach his goal by a less arduous road.

Such was his conundrum. The simple answer, which a more down-to-earth person might well have opted for, would have been to take a degree in German, but M, a purist in such matters, disdainfully rejected this choice as one that would give him an unfair advantage and was therefore utterly unworthy of him. Indeed, when he mentioned his aspirations to, among others, Mr. Daker, such a course was precisely what the latter suggested, pointing out that at the end of that particular road nobody would care in the slightest measure what, if anything, had been the subject of M's initial degree. 'I would care,' was M's somewhat prim reply, 'and I would never be able to look myself in the face again.'

Once his free brochure from Dr. Johnson's Correspondence College arrived – all 128 pages of it – he finally made up his mind and enrolled for three subjects – Elements of Psychology, Foundations of Electrical Engineering and French Stage I – a combination particularly judicious in as much as it left all sorts of options open.

Elements of Psychology in particular offered much promise, for it had always been one of M's chief aspirations to achieve and dominate by insight and persuasion. Besides, there was always a chance of odd glimpses into the more private spheres of human personality and experience (for 'human', of course, read 'female'), and he, by no means very pure when it came to this his main interest and preoccupation, felt that that might be both instructive and highly enjoyable. The acquisition of knowledge and enjoyment of 'life' being always uppermost in his mind, M tended to see himself as a latterday Dr. Faust such as Goethe presented him in Part I of his immortal masterpiece, that is to say as an indefatigable seeker after knowledge most lofty and most profound, as well as akin to Mephisto, the spirit of doubt and negation. As for his interest in poor Margaret, innocence obscenely abused but triumphantly redeemed at the end of Part II, that tended to fluctuate between the sublime and less lofty sentiments and attitudes, depending on whether Faust or the arch-cynic Mephisto happened to be in the ascendant. At that stage in his life, M, incidentally, had not yet matured to the deeper insight that there was also a fair streak of Margaret in his make-up.

As for French Stage I, M picked this subject largely by way of light relief, hoping to astound his tutors at JCC (such was the acronym for Dr. Johnson's Correspondence College) by the rapidity of his progress and the uncommon breadth of his knowledge. However, he also believed that in attempting to master a foreign language he must do his utmost to lay sound and impervious foundations, reinforcing them again and again, for if the foundations were weak they would only be able to support some poor, ramshackle structure totally inadequate for any useful purpose whatsoever, and not the mighty edifice of all-embracing linguistic prowess that was his ultimate goal.

Now as for Electrical Engineering – virgin territory indeed – that was the kind of challenge M felt almost honour-bound to accept. It was precisely the fact that M was entirely uninterested in this highly recommended subject and had, in the light of past experience, no reason to assume that he would even be able to understand its very principles, which lent it such a curiously irresistible appeal, for he liked, even expected himself, to do the unexpected from time to time, and what could be more unexpected than for him to take a course in Electrical Engineering, of all things. Incidentally, M's truly remarkable inability to cope with matters electrical – even changing a fuse was well beyond him – may have been due to the fact that as a child in Klimkovice he was frequently tempted and induced to put his hand into a glass vessel filled with water, through which flowed an electric current, in order to extract therefrom a coin, the equivalent of several succulent sweets. His friend Milan too used to take part in these attempts, but the experience must have affected him differently, for he eventually chose to study aircraft engineering at the university in Prague, a subject in which a sound understanding of electricity must have been essential. During the war poor idealistic Milan took up arms against the occupiers of his country and lost his life in a famous uprising.

Following instructions, M had provided himself with several no doubt excellent textbooks and was now ready and willing to attack the first set of lessons which JCC, having safely cashed his cheque, had forwarded to him. The various instructions, presentation notes, study notes and assignments – all of them in suitably sober and scholarly print – were relatively simple, but M was more than somewhat dismayed at the exceedingly large chunks of study required of him at even this early stage. He was, for instance, instructed to study and master chapters 1, 2, 7 and 9 in *Electrical Engineering Science* as well as pages 15-37 and 49-74 in *Principles of Electricity.* However he was also sent various notes, for instance to the effect that on page 97 of EES the 'h' had been omitted from 'heating elements' and that on page 33 of PE 'osculation' should be read as 'oscillation'. It is only fair to mention these notes lest anyone arrive at the misguided opinion that JCC's own contribution was perhaps inordinately small. Perish also the thought that the excessively heavy demands made on students at this and other stages of the course were intended to discourage them from going through with it, seeing that the full fee had already been paid and, no part of the fee being refundable, such sections of the course as were abandoned by the students could be regarded as clear profit for the college. Whatever the rights and wrongs of JCC's policy, M, his enthusiasm in no way impaired, set about his self-inflicted task with a will and completed these first assignments with great gusto and in record time.

Since their visit to the cinema M's 'relationship' with Catty had passed through a number of phases, from dull misery on her part and an almost total inability to talk to her on his (an inability about which he felt particularly guilty, for she was, after all, a nice girl who deserved better) to veritable orgies of self-revelation in the course of which they told each other things far more intimate than ever before when there was still a possibility of their really coming together.

It was during this latter stage that M learned from Catty, when by chance they met near Tottenham Court Road Station, that she had but recently acquired a 'real boyfriend'. An older man he was, of great experience and ever so clever, she told him with just a hint of reproach, the merest suggestion of 'you could have had me, body and soul, I was there for your taking but you failed to take me'. Catty and her paramour would meet regularly on certain afternoons, go to a show or a restaurant and would finally wind up at a hotel in Bloomsbury, but Robert had to be ever so careful, for if his wife were to find out there was no telling what that woman might do, nor could she herself afford to take any chances seeing that she was still living at home with her parents and brother.

'He is ever so good to me,' Catty explained, 'giving me things and he can be really nice, but he is also very strict with me, teaching me lots of things.' M could imagine and did, but continued to probe, which was both delectable and tantalisingly painful, for he was racked by a feeling very close to jealousy and a sense of regret for what might have been.

So far, it transpired, Catty and her avuncular boyfriend had not yet spent a whole night together but, she affirmed, he was planning a weekend with her at the seaside, had in fact already booked a hotel room for them, and she was really looking forward to it, she really was.

'Would you have liked to spend a weekend with me?' M enquired, but they both knew very well that his question was purely academic and quite devoid of any practical significance.

'It would have been lovely,' Catty replied, 'I would really have loved it, but knowing you, you wouldn't have gone, would you?'

'I would have adored being with you in a nice hotel at the seaside,' answered M, choosing to ignore the implied disdain, 'just you and me, walking and talking and you know what ...'

'What would you have wanted to do with me in the room, you know, when we were alone?', asked Catty, entering at last into the spirit of this their favourite game. M, giving his torrid imagination free rein, now expounded his fantasies, painting a cosy, rosy picture of premarital bliss. Having booked into that hotel they would go straight up to the bedroom, lock the door and then ... M now went into great detail, presenting her with a choice cocktail of the possible and the impossible but all of it quite delightful, while she, romantic to the end and, no doubt, for old times' sake, squeezed his hand fervently with her own clammy one. Then it was her turn to question him earnestly, searching him out, and together they spoke the ever potent words over and over again, they could not get enough of them.

However, they were not in a hotel room by the sea but walking along Oxford Street towards Marble Arch, and it was a cold, drizzly afternoon late in November. Dusk was descending about them gradually deepening into night, and the pattern of lights all around and above them was becoming increasingly dense. When they reached Bond Street Catty had to leave; she was late already.

'I enjoyed our talk,' Catty said, 'I truly did. But I have to go, I really must, or there'll be such a row!'

M considered for a moment whether to accompany her, go with her all or part of the way just in case the carriage was empty, but before he managed to make up his mind she was off, M looking after her wistfully, his eyes fixed firmly on those slim, well-turned ankles and high stiletto heels. He was deeply depressed.

CHAPTER TWENTY SEVEN

MY YEARS at the Klappenhorn in Vienna may fairly be said to have been marred by fear, boredom and other types of misery. Being younger by far than any of the others in my form and unable to cope with pain, I was hopeless at gym and quite useless at games. This, in the eyes of my classmates, was unforgivable, even more unforgivable than my being a Jew or the fact that I was, by comparison with most of them, a pauper. Although, generally speaking, I was a mediocre student just good enough to get by in most subjects – on one occasion I nearly had to repeat an entire year because of my inability to take geography seriously and to buckle down to some serious work – I was pretty good at certain others, notably Latin and Mathematics, in which I enjoyed a reputation for being a bit of a wizard. As a result I had a number of fair-weather friends, who were quite ready to treat me as their equal or better when they thought that I might be of use to them, but would brutally disown me once my usefulness had come to an end.

As for my teachers, most of them seemed to me uncouth or stupid or both, although some such as Professor Bergenau, who taught us English, and Professor Schmitz, from whom we learned German, were really quite decent. The teacher I hated most was Dr. Pollak, a silly little man with a whining, high-pitched voice, who was supposed to teach us history and geography. To this day I still resent this wretched man with his 'When Maria Theresia ascended the throne, continue Maskenbusch' and 'Maskenbusch, name the towns on the left bank of the Isar', the idea being that I should reel off large chunks of undigested and indigestible information, preferably verbatim as it appeared in the textbooks. I still see myself walking up to that awful map, at least one of my socks drooping (in anticipation, no doubt, of my impending failure) and the rest of the class howling with laughter at my despondent, degrading state and inevitable humiliation, in order to point out some ghastly locality or other, which I was certain not to be able to do. I am convinced that my almost total lack of any sense of direction, my – on occasion – most inconvenient inability to tell where exactly I am, is very largely due to Dr. Pollak's 'instruction' and perhaps its only lasting result. And I still fail to understand why it was so important to know precisely how high in metres (but not in centimetres or millimetres) was some obscure mountain in South America, which, in all probability, I would never see and most certainly never ascend. Assuming, I used to speculate, that a rock exactly one metre in height were, by an explosion or other means, dislodged from the top of a certain mountain in the Andes, would this necessitate the withdrawal and reissue of all the school atlases in the world or would it suffice to print and distribute erratum sheets? Would it be necessary to mount an expedition and restore the blemished mountain-top by placing upon it another rock, the height of which was identical with that of the rock displaced initially? Incidentally, the perfect solution of this problem occurred to me quite recently: A mountain-top extension kit comprising a retaining device and an extensible rod would do the trick, seeing that what appears to matter is not the mass, volume or shape of the mountain, not what grows on it or lives on it, but solely its height.

Bullying was rife at the Klappenhorn, and I especially got my fair share of that, but our top people such as Geiger, who was simply outstanding at almost everything (even at Mathematics his results were better than mine), had a rich father and may, for all I know, have been a very decent chap, simply ignored the likes of me, for which I in my abject state was duly grateful. As for some of the others who were not so easy to live with, I used to go to great lengths to avoid them, dodging in and out of corridors and up and down staircases, varying my homeward route daily. In general, such tactics of avoidance were quite adequate to keep me out of trouble. However, with Lebenswurm, whose background was working class and who should have known better but was really stupid, nothing seemed to work, his one object in life apparently being to persecute me wherever and whenever he could. Apart from the usual types of physical bullying, he specialised in taunting me about my more obvious failings and weaknesses. The situation eventually became so intolerable that one day after Woodwork (this was another subject at which I was absolutely hopeless, having neither patience nor the slightest manual ability) I attacked Lebenswurm with an inkwell, pouring ink all over him and reducing him to a blubbering jelly. This incident, which happened towards the end of my third year at the Klappenhorn, gained me the dubious reputation of being quite mad and potentially dangerous. On the other hand, it freed me from the unwelcome attentions of Lebenswurm, who in any case left the school by the end of the term, his father, I believe, having accepted employment in another part of the country, and brought me, at least for some time, a little grudging respect such as one might accord to a rabid dog.

Although, for reasons of financial insufficiency, our family frequently had to change accommodation, we continued to live in the same area. On my daily way to school I used to pass several shops of great interest, in particular one where, in addition to notebooks, pencils and compasses, rulers and similar scholastic aids, they offered second-hand textbooks in varying condition ranging from as good as new (for those lucky enough to be able to afford them) to totally dilapidated. The windows of that shop held a curious fascination for me, making me forget time and school and everything, and, as I stood there in a kind of mysterious trance, reading all the titles of the books and thinking God knows what or perhaps nothing at all, I would fail to notice how the stream of students on their way to school was gradually thinning down to a mere trickle and eventually ceased entirely. By the time I managed to tear myself away and, by then thoroughly panic-stricken, run the last fifty metres or so to the

Klappenhorn, I didn't have a chance. The tall, massive oak door now forbiddingly closed would creak open with manifest, grim reluctance, the corridors, olive-green and heavy with stale odours, seemed to sneer at me contemptuously, and a storm of scornful laughter rising to a crescendo would meet me as I entered the classroom.

Come to think of it, things were not as bad as all that. I did, after all, have two steady friends: Brunner, with whom I played innumerable games of high-speed chess and took long walks, on which we would practise, in as noisy and generally demonstrative a fashion as possible, 'English conversation', not so much with a view to improving our fluency as in order to astonish the passers-by with our erudition; and Stengel, black-haired and with his round head, arched back and softly-softly approach to all matters as cat-like a person as ever there was. With Stengel, in particular, I spent many very agreeable hours trying to break down certain mysteries of geometry (at least for us they were mysteries) and purporting to translate *The Tempest*, another activity from which we derived immense 'scholarly' gratification, largely due to the fact that we were so woefully ill-equipped for it, seeing that we were then in our very first year of Klappenhorn English.

I have, at long last, had my very first bunch of corrected assignments back from the College. Unfortunately I have by now virtually forgotten what they were all about, and as for Electrical Engineering I cannot even remember how I arrived at the solutions for which I have been awarded an 'A'. The French tutor has, in two different sentences, seen fit to change the gender of 'auto' from feminine to masculine. I have checked this point, and he is definitely wrong. I am racking my brain how to point this out to him without making him lose too much face. Perhaps I shall write that Larousse uses only the feminine form, as indeed does Harrap's, although in this respect modern usage may well be uncertain. That should really impress him!

Silversmith is beginning to worry about his finals, it seems. He has become very jumpy and avoids company. I do believe he has given up girls (for the first time in my experience) and may, in fact, be frequenting prostitutes again.

M, who, together with his parents, had left Vienna in the nick of time, spent a very enjoyable year in Czechoslovakia, this being the very first year in which he, released at last from the stringent constraints of both home life and school, was able to try his wings and sip his fill from the chalice of personal freedom. But in an initially radiant sky there soon appeared dark clouds heavy with menace, gathering swiftly until eventually the storm broke and friendly, hospitable Czechoslovakia, but recently a haven of peace and safety, was overrun and annexed by its greediest and most powerful neighbour. In order to ensure their acquiescence, other neighbouring states were allowed and even encouraged to tear away and take over bits of this region and that, a bonanza of which they – veritable curs devouring titbits from their master's table – took full, treacherous advantage.

At the time, M, like a person under the influence of some potent hallucinogenic drug, did not fully comprehend the gravity of these developments but was nonetheless firmly in the grip of the general mood of anxiety which had come to pervade and dominate all life throughout the Jewish community. Where previously there had been a great diversity of concerns and interests, people were now entirely preoccupied by the single, overriding question of how to save themselves from the events which, to judge from what had happened in other territories newly annexed by the Reich, were about to unfold.

For Jews too poor, too old or too infirm to leave the country the future looked bleak indeed, and in the event few of them managed to survive the war years. This group included, for instance, M's father as well as his favourite cousin, who, although reasonably well off and only in his thirties, suffered from a nervous disability which made it impossible for him even to cross a busy road, let alone travel abroad. Anton lived with his aged mother, Auntie Sibilla, in an elegant ground-floor flat in a quiet part of Moravská Ostrava and used to give English lessons to a few private students who would visit him in his home. He introduced M to such classic works of English literature as the plays of Bernard Shaw and *The Pickwick Papers*, and they spent much time playing table tennis. M also accompanied Anton on his daily walks around the block. People with wealthy relatives or friends in England, America and other countries were in many cases able to obtain the necessary affidavits of support, guaranteeing that they would not become financial burdens to the state, and were therefore able to emigrate quite legally. Those who were less well connected but able to afford it could hire a guide to smuggle them out of the country. For the guides – local people with an intimate knowledge of the border regions – this was an extremely lucrative though hazardous business. Incidentally, it was not all that difficult to obtain the services of a guide, for they were widely quoted in whispers on a kind of black market. And, of course, anyone rich enough could bribe his way to at least temporary safety.

As for M, who had neither money nor, as far as he knew, any well-wisher likely to send him an affidavit (but was unshakably convinced of his romantic 'destiny'), it was his good friend and fellow Zionist Gerlinsky, whose father happened to own an inn near the recently revised border with Poland, who eventually helped him on his way. Gerlinsky, a veritable wizard at billiards – there was no end to the variety of impossible trick shots which he was able to play – and immensely strong, could, of course, be presumed to know the region in which his home was situated like 'the back of his hand'. So when he, perhaps in a mood of excessive optimism, intimated to M that he could help him to escape, as indeed he had helped lots and lots of others, and would be glad to do so, the latter, never one to let a great occasion pass him by, asked Gerlinsky to take him across to Poland there and then. Fascinated by a sense of impending adventure, M felt no desire to say goodbye to anyone, not even his father, nor did he see any point in going home in order to collect some luggage. In the face of such masterful decisiveness, what else could Gerlinsky do but act out his commitment – a commitment which upon sober reflection he might well have regretted and even denied as foolishly rash?

It was a beautiful morning in spring and the air was crisp and clear. The fields, meadows and forests through which the two friends walked were bathed in sunlight but, mercifully, it was not too hot. As it was a public holiday, there were quite a few people about, many of them also on the way to the revised border, which was still something of a nine-day wonder. Time and again M, whose trust in Gerlinsky's leadership seemed to know no bounds, enquired whether they were already in Poland, only to have his unrealistic hopes dashed. But at long last there it was. Wooden posts marked the border between two facing tongues of forest, with huts for the border guards on either side. There were German soldiers on one side, and Polish soldiers on the other. Slightly further back, again on both sides, there were groups of spectators gawping in silence at the soldiers, some of whom clearly felt uncomfortable to be stared at as if they were animals in a zoo.

This finally was the point at which the bubble burst. Gerlinsky, his large ears – which seemed to project from his head nearly at right angles – red with embarrassment, admitted that he had never taken anyone across any border and did not feel that he could help any further. He also suggested that they go back home in order to consider more realistically how M could be helped to leave the country. However, M had already progressed too far in this particular dream to let sweet reason prevail. So he merely scribbled a brief message for his father on an old postcard and gave this and the key to the flat in which he had occupied a sofa during the past two months to Gerlinsky, told him to take care, and set out in the direction of the forest, apparently unobserved. Driven by a sense of destiny and unafraid, he penetrated deeper and deeper into the forest but might well have lost his way if, by a stroke of good luck, he had not come across a group of gipsies camping near a cluster of tall trees. M, who spoke to them in the local Czech dialect, would never know whether or not they believed his story that he was an apprentice house painter trying to get back to his family in what was now a village in Poland. Be that as it may, they showed him where to cross over, warning him to keep away from the road until nightfall. M, who was grateful to them, gave them whatever money he found in his purse – barely enough to buy a meal – and went on his way. Hearing a shot not far away, he stopped briefly, wondering whether he was being pursued, but when nothing else happened decided that the shot had probably been fired by some hunter and continued as he had been told. After a few minutes he came to a post similar to those he had seen at the border and having gone past it knew that he was in Poland at last.

Rosabelle had finally made up her mind to follow her friend Chloe's advice and leave London for good. Chloe, currently employed as an assistant cook at a small hotel in Hastings, where she was lonely but otherwise content, had written that what sounded like a most interesting position (ever so friendly, full of interesting people, well-paid and with all mod. cons.) was vacant at a private establishment for elderly ladies, not more than five minutes from her own place of work. Rosabelle, thoroughly disenchanted with life in London and hoping to put some distance between herself and Lipkin in order, as she explained to him, to give both of them a chance to work out how they really felt about each other and whether their relationship was strong enough to justify tying the ultimate, insoluble knot between them, had applied and in due course been invited to come for an interview.

In the course of their meeting, the owner, an extremely plausible lady of truly elephantine proportions, confirmed that all of them – she, her staff (a tall girl, Susan, one of whose regular tasks appeared to consist in keeping her employer supplied with cups of strong, black tea, a deaf old handy-man, George by name, and a former nurse with red, badly swollen eyes and an equally red, bulbous nose, whose hunched-up shoulders were at all times covered with an enormous brown shawl) and, of course, her charges (ever such nice, genteel ladies) were indeed one happy family and would be pleased for her to join them. Rosabelle's by no means onerous duties would consist in certain domestic functions such as a little cooking, their requirements in this respect being extremely modest, occasional light cleaning, and, which was most important, keeping the administration on course. In her spare time she would also be welcome to take care of the vegetable garden, where everything was grown 'organically', that is to say without using spades, forks or any other soil-violating implements nor, for that matter, any 'unnatural' artificial fertilisers. From time to time she might be called upon to lend a hand with one of the ladies, an activity she was certain to find most rewarding. When Rosabelle pointed out that she had no nursing experience whatsoever and that her culinary skills were at best mediocre, her interviewer immediately reassured her, explaining that specialists and experts were the very last thing wanted at a genteel establishment such as hers, where everybody helped everybody else and intelligent exploration, even experimentation, was the rule.

In due course Rosabelle was taken on a guided tour of the house and garden and introduced to a few of the 'ladies'. This convinced her that at 'Roselands' she would be really appreciated, which was, of course, very important to her. She did, however, have fleeting misgivings when she was told that, funds being temporarily low, pocket money was all she could hope for, although there was every prospect of the situation improving in the very near future, in which case a proper, substantial wage would certainly be offered to her. Besides, she might find even her pocket money difficult to spend since all her needs would be generously provided for.

At any rate, Rosabelle had been persuaded to give it a try. So here she was at Victoria Station with M, Silversmith and Lipkin as her seeing-off escort. M had bought her a bag of assorted nuts as a going-away present, while Lipkin, who had insisted on carrying her blue rucksack, was twisting a somewhat unappetising handkerchief between his long, bony fingers – a sure sign this that he was most unhappy. Still, Rosabelle had promised faithfully not to forget him and to answer his letters if she could find the time, and, after all, Hastings was not all that far away. Silversmith, practical as ever, asked her whether she would, now and again, be prepared to do some typing for him and intimated that he would not mind spending a short holiday at her new residence, preferably in spring or summer when the weather was good. Rosabelle's response was minimal but Silversmith interpreted it as enthusiastic assent. 'That's settled then,' he declared. 'Just let me know when and I'll be right there.'

Intrigued by the notion of 'organic' gardening, M and Silversmith considered at great length whether artificial fertilisers were in any sense less natural than compost or animal manure and whether anything could possibly exist within nature that was not also entirely natural. According to Silversmith, the distinction between 'artificial' and 'natural' was simply one of practical linguistic usage, a kind of signposting as it were, but M felt that that was altogether too simplistic. 'After all,' he argued, 'we tend to assume that anything man-made, for instance Rosabelle's rucksack, is fundamentally different from anything in the evolution of which man has not had a hand. Nobody thinks of a bird's nest, however skilfully made bearing in mind the limitations to which birds are subject, as artificial, but a house for people to live in is a different matter entirely. Yet it is difficult to see where we could draw a definite line. A cave inhabited by people would be a kind of house, yet no one would claim that it was in any way artificial unless major alterations of a structural or decorative nature had been carried out in it. The question is, what, in this context, is major?' And without bothering to wait for an answer, he continued, 'This, of course, would not matter in the least if it were not for the fact that we tend to base our value-judgments on these concepts, in spite of the fact that a clear, factual distinction between them is not possible. I am trying to say that it is qualitatively quite immaterial how Rosabelle's blue rucksack has come about, that is to say whether it has been manufactured in a factory or grown in a garden.'

Before Silversmith was able to point out that, to the best of his or, for that matter, anyone's knowledge, rucksacks of whatever colour do not grow in gardens, the train came into the station and Rosabelle got on. Lipkin insisted on helping her with her rucksack, making sure that it was safely deposited in the luggage rack, his reward being a comradely handshake. Feverishly searching his pockets for something to give to her, he eventually found a battered roll of mints, which he pressed into her hot, perspiring hand. By the time Lipkin got out of the carriage, the train was beginning to move out of the station. So he had to jump off and, landing awkwardly, managed to sprain his ankle. With Rosabelle gone, all three of them were, in various degrees, depressed. To cheer themselves up Silversmith and M decided to go to a pub, while Lipkin, limping painfully, followed behind.

CHAPTER TWENTY EIGHT

SITTING despondently in an empty classroom, M was wondering if this spelt the end of his Monday class. It would not be the first time a class had died on him, not by any means, but, adaptable though he was, this was one experience he simply could not get used to. Besides, the Monday class had been his very first and in its time most successful class, and he felt that its cessation would be a kind of death, almost a personal bereavement.

It had, in fact, been on the cards for quite some time that this class was on its way out. For a long time now the number of students had been hovering near the danger-mark where it was barely economic to keep the class going, there had been excessively wide variations in the levels of knowledge and aptitude of the students – whereas some like Mr. Willoughby were very advanced indeed, others could not, with the best will in the world, be described as anything but absolute beginners and likely to remain so – and the attendance figures had been so erratic that even a semblance of systematic teaching had been out of the question. Every lesson was tainted now by an air of general gloom and lack of direction, so that after only one or two visits new students dropped out, never to be seen again, and even they of the 'old guard', who had, so far, stood by him through thick and thin, were clearly getting restless, clearly hoping for something to happen that would release them to pastures new. 'Teachers in proper schools don't know how lucky they are', thought M wistfully. 'Their classes, at least, cannot descend to such hopeless states of terminal confusion as at TTTW or simply cease to exist.'

Classrooms – at the best of times dusty, dirty, inhospitable places – are particularly desolate when they are not in use, and the one in which M now found himself was in no way an exception. Automatically, as he had done so many times before, he shuffled over to the blackboard, stared at it aimlessly, and returned again to his seat. As nearly always when he discovered himself doing something without proper concentration, the Japanese term for 'absent-minded', which he had picked up somewhere or other and could no longer exclude from his mind, flashed into his consciousness. The silence was oppressive and somehow nightmarish, as if in anticipation of some horrible event. Wondering whether there was any point in waiting any longer, M looked at the large clock on the wall and saw that the lesson should have started ten minutes ago. He decided to wait another five minutes just in case someone, anyone, were still to come. Mr. Fennimore, perhaps, or Mrs. Snyder or Doris – surely she would not let him down, not Doris. Even Mr. Willoughby would do, insufferable bore though he was.

In some ways this situation was of a kind with which M had been familiar as long as he could remember. In the innermost recesses of his mind he had always been quite certain that he would never be able to come up to standard and avoid personal disaster, and so deep was this conviction and the anxiety which it entailed as to afflict him with a fine set of nightmares which haunted him throughout his life and in which he saw himself, for instance, in some bare, ghostly classroom or office, useless, forgotten and virtually invisible, while all around him people, many of them former friends and colleagues but now utterly unaware of him, were busily engaged in a multitude of meaningful activities.

'*Guter Abend, Herr Lehrer,*' and there, thank goodness, was Mr. Fennimore. There was not the slightest probability of Mr. Fennimore ever mastering even the rudiments of German grammar, but, no matter, he was more than welcome. 'Where is everybody?' he enquired cheerily, 'Don't tell me I'm the first! I had trouble parking, that's why I'm even later than usual.'

'*Guten Abend, Herr Fennimore,*' responded M, 'Am I glad to see you – *Bin ich froh, dass Sie hier sind.*' He went to the front of the class in order to write this sentence on the blackboard.

Mr. Fennimore, having removed his hat and coat, sat down in his favourite place in the front row. 'You have no idea what the traffic – *Verkehr* ('furcair' was what he actually said) – is like at this time. Take my advice, Herr Mask, never travel anywhere during the rush-hour. I wonder what's keeping the others?' A diffident knock on the door seemed to provide the answer, and in came Doris and, trailing behind her and out of breath, Mrs. Snyder.

'I'm ever so sorry I'm late,' panted Doris, 'but I had to work late at the office.'

'So am I.' Mrs. Snyder was equally apologetic. 'My feet are simply killing me. How do you say "My feet are killing me" in German?'

Bouncing back from his depression, M told her several ways in which this could be done, drawing attention to various pertinent points of grammar, idiomatic differences between English and German, and so on and so forth. And to give his three students further value for money, in spite of the fact that he knew and they knew that they had reached the end of their common road he did his best to engage them in some German conversation. However, none of them felt in the mood for work, and after a few minutes they decided to go instead to the House of Pasta, where Ben welcomed them in his usual exuberant fashion. They discussed the sorry state of the class and what might be done to revive it. They all tried desperately to sound optimistic, but when Doris told them that Mr. Willoughby was apparently not intending to continue and might in fact not be able to come again, this brave attempt fizzled out. Mrs. Snyder said that, on account of her rheumatism, she was finding it increasingly difficult to undertake the long journey to TTTW and, in any case, felt that real progress was perhaps beyond her. Perhaps she was simply not intelligent enough, what did *der Herr Lehrer* think? As for Mr. Fennimore, he announced that he might be going north for several months to open a new shop in Manchester. Reacting to this last blow almost with a sense of relief, M brushed it all aside with a jaunty '*C'est la vie!*'

The following Monday, Doris was the only one who came. After about half an hour, they decided to go and, as so often before, M accompanied Doris on her way home. This time she invited him to come up to her room for a cup of tea, and he accepted. The room – small, neat and at the same time extremely feminine – seemed to match her personality in every way. The table in front of the large, curtained window – Doris mentioned with obvious satisfaction that as the window faced west, she got a lot of afternoon sunshine – was covered with an embroidered linen cloth, in the centre of which stood a pot of red geraniums. Next to the door there was a large 'utility' wardrobe, and on the chest-of-drawers opposite Doris's bed were two ancient, somewhat battered teddy-bears. A framed print of Constable's *Hay Wain* graced one of the Regency-papered walls, and a shaggy red rug lay on the greyish-brown hair-cord carpet. As for the narrow bed in the corner, that was positively buried in lots and lots of cushions and cuddly animals. Doris explained that collecting cuddly animals was one of her hobbies – apart from studying German actually her only hobby, although until a few years ago she had also been very keen on ballroom dancing and had even won several prizes – but that the teddies were her favourites and had been so ever since she was a child.

On that occasion M stayed with Doris, and they spent the night together. Doris, when it came to making love undoubtedly more experienced and more relaxed than M, took the initiative, and, thanks to her tact and sensitivity, he for once really enjoyed what he was doing and what was being done to him. When he left in the morning, he had every intention of returning again soon but in the event never did. As for the Monday class, that was officially dissolved only two days later.

The morning after the liquidation of his Monday class M received a note informing him of the sudden and untimely death of his friend and colleague Sombrero-Domingo. The note also advised him of the time and place of the funeral – Sombrero-Domingo was to be cremated – and suggested that instead of sending flowers a donation to the local hospital would be welcome.

In spite of being deeply shocked by this distressing news, M's first instinct was to forget all about it, to distance himself from this sad event as if it were no concern of his. Unable as he was to give vent to his emotions and, as a result, afraid of surrendering to such natural feelings of sadness and bereavement as he experienced, M had frequently taken this line in the past – in particular when after his return from Japan he had learned of the death of his father – but never without a deep sense of shame and betrayal, which, even many years later, would still be with him. So as to justify his behaviour in his own eyes and those of others, he would put forward various 'philosophical' arguments, mainly to the effect that the concept of the immortality of the soul was simply due to man's inability to come to terms with his own finality – the end, as he saw it, of a road leading inevitably from infinite potential, at least on the human scale, to absolute zero – and with the fact that, in the absence of an immortal soul, there could be no common bond between the living and the dead. However, he himself was not entirely convinced of this reasoning, there being more than a spark of hope within his mind that he might, after all, be utterly wrong. That M regarded it as a 'waste of time' to engage in any kind of mourning or 'last rites' was perhaps forgivable. Less forgivable, however, was his readiness to cut himself off – at a stroke, more or less – from the deceased's other friends or family, who might have been grateful for his support at such a difficult time. Nor would it be true to say that M's lack of solidarity was entirely due to his personal fears – sheer laziness also played a part in this. Cemeteries were often inaccessible, unattractive places, which M avoided whenever he could. And he could never understand why anyone in his right mind should actually choose to attend funerals or visit a cemetery as if it were indeed a park or a 'garden of rest'.

Lately, however, M had become aware of the fact that his attitude to death and its paraphernalia was due not so much to firmly held, consistent views and strength of character as to various defects in his own personality, as well as a certain irresponsibility, and it was this awareness that prompted him to telephone, albeit with great reluctance, Bertha in order to offer her his sympathy (for what it was worth) and to find out more about the circumstances of her husband's death.

M's call was answered not by Bertha but by an elderly lady, her sister-in-law, who explained in muted tones befitting the occasion that it was she who was taking care of the arrangements since Bertha herself was far too distraught to cope. She told M that her dear brother – God rest his soul – had, after a most remarkable recovery from his recent heart attack and only four days ago, been run over by a car while, according to a neighbour who had witnessed this sad event, pursuing a letter which he had been reading when a gust of wind carried it from his hand on to a busy road. He had died on the way to hospital without regaining consciousness. She did, however, remember that on the regrettably all too few occasions when she and her poor brother had got together in recent months he had repeatedly mentioned M by name, and she hoped to see him at the funeral. M, who had not even known that his friend had a sister, assured her that he would certainly be there.

On the day of the funeral – a cold and bleak but mercifully dry day – M, who normally stayed in bed until all hours, sometimes even until well into the afternoon, got up early, and, having taken great care to achieve a reasonably well groomed and sombre appearance in keeping with the sad occasion ahead of him, set out on his journey to far-away Brixton several hours before the time scheduled for the cremation, which was two o'clock in the afternoon, in order to make quite certain that he would not be late. This proved to be a wise precaution, for in the event he not only spent an inordinate amount of time waiting for his food at a local café but did indeed experience all kinds of difficulties in actually finding the appointed place.

Still, M was in good time – in fact, one of the very first to arrive. Since he did not know any of the other mourners already present, he went to look at a display of floral tributes from other funerals, reading, in desultory manner, the names and messages of condolence on the various cards. Then he strolled among the nearby graves, studying the inscriptions on the headstones and speculating on the messages they bore. In the meantime, more people had arrived, among them two tutors from TTTW, whom he knew vaguely. Glad at this stage of any contact that might help him to feel less isolated, he went over to talk to them, whereupon they exchanged the usual observations about how sad it all was and who would have thought it, how sudden and quite unexpected was Sombrero-Domingo's demise, and how greatly he would be missed. It did not take long for this 'conversation' to flag and, not finding anything else to say to one another, they drifted apart again.

The funeral cortège was late, and people were beginning to get restless. In life, Sombrero-Domingo had never managed to be anywhere on time, and it seemed that this tradition was going to be continued. The cleric in charge of the proceedings, worried no doubt about fitting in this ceremony before the next one was due, and hiding his manifest impatience behind a façade of mild resignation, had come out repeatedly, and M had, on at least two separate occasions, observed him glancing surreptitiously at his watch. At long last, however, the hearse and the attendant cars appeared, slowly and in solemn procession meandering up the drive towards the wide open doors of the chapel, from which could now be heard music by Vivaldi. Supported by her sister-in-law and followed by the congregation, Bertha, grey-faced and shaky, slowly entered the chapel and was guided to her seat in the front row. As always on public occasions, M chose to remain inconspicuous at the rear. While the congregation were finding seats, the coffin had been borne in and was now on the dais at the front of the chapel.

After a short, excessively expeditious service and a brief eulogy on the deceased, remarkable mainly for the way in which the officiant kept stumbling over the numerous unfamiliar names of persons and places with which he had been supplied, there came the macabre moment when the coffin started to move slowly, again to the strains of Vivaldi's music, through the doors at the back of the dais and towards its ultimate destination. M joined the queue of friends and relatives proffering their condolences to Bertha, who stood there, dazed and forlorn (the really bad time would come once she was alone in her house with only the animals to keep her company), going through the motions expected of her. Then it was all over. As the next funeral congregation gathered and their ceremony got under way, those who had come to take their final leave from Sombrero-Domingo went their separate ways. As for M, it took him over two hours to get home to No. 12. In a way he was glad to have 'done the right thing' but he also felt relieved that the funeral was now a matter of the past. However, Sombrero-Domingo's personality had been too vivid for his image ever to fade from M's mind, even after many years when he himself had become an old man. He did lose touch with Bertha, who – so he heard – eventually sold her house and returned to her home town in Germany.

The sequence of recent events, from Rosabelle's departure to Sombrero-Domingo's death and funeral, left M with a distinct feeling of increasing isolation or, as he put it to Silversmith, the impression of rapidly disappearing up his own intestinal duct. This state of mind is clearly reflected in the following story written by him, with great travail, a week or two later. Its literary antecedents as well as the true identity of 'Pomfrit' are, of course, quite obvious and do not require any comment. However, less apparent – and, at the time of writing, not perceived even by M himself, although eventually, many years later, pointed out by him time and again *ad nauseam* may be the fact that 'Pomfrit' is a generic rather than a personal name, inasmuch as every other operative in the Department is called 'Pomfrit' whereas his neighbours on either side bear the designation 'Frankie Chipolata'. This, it will be understood, was an essential feature of the binomial system of administration, the system managing with perfect smoothness (at least until the improbable occurred and some spectacular breakdown took place) not only Pomfrit's but all the departments, the number of which was virtually unlimited. That 'Pomfrit' and 'Frankie Chipolata' were generic designations did not, by any means, mean that they did not have personalities and lives of their own (Pomfrit, for instance, was known more particularly by the number 2673977ABD), but from the Department's point of view these were, of course, totally irrelevant.

THE OFFICE

Pomfrit was early.

Today, as on any other day, he had arrived at the Department exactly 25 minutes and 30 seconds before zero-time, and had, as on the way to his office he passed through a multitude of virtually endless corridors, managed to navigate a path through the crowd of cleaners, who with their buckets and mops, their pans and brushes, were hurriedly scurrying to their cubby-holes and lockers, whence to continue to their various abodes in the City. None of them paid the slightest attention to Pomfrit, nor did he waste as much as a single glance on any of them.

In spite of the uncertain light from the illuminator overhead (the supervisor of the cleaning team was responsible for extinguishing this device), he spent the time still available to him (until the door of his office would, seemingly as if by magic but in fact as a result of highly sophisticated technological wizardry, open to admit him) in reading, re-reading and then once again reading the various notices – a veritable feast provided for his edification and instruction – in that section of the corridor which to him was home from home, or, more precisely, his real home, inasmuch as it communicated directly with his very own office. Many of the notices, relating as they did to events long past, evoked – very much as do the inscriptions in such venerable locations sacred to history as rural chapels and churchyards – the transitoriness of all things, whereas others, of a prohibitory nature and phrased in fascinating legalistic language, engaged all his powers of formal reasoning while at the same time giving him a sense of belonging, for was he not one of the many to whom these notices were addressed?

His favourite notice, however, the one which he always left to the very last, was to be found on the door immediately preceding that of his own office. Very many years ago, when he joined the Department, this notice had already been there, part of it mysteriously disfigured. Indeed, all that could be read on it now were the words '... strictly forbidden on pain of ...... The Director'. It was clearly very satisfying to speculate what act it might be that was so dire as to necessitate such a strict prohibition, and what – doubtlessly dreadful – retribution might follow in the wake of heedless disobedience; but what really made this notice so particularly fascinating, made it so worthwhile for Pomfrit to forego, earlier than strictly necessary, the comforts of his humble though convenient dwelling and, every day and in every weather, to hurry to the office in a state of tremulous impatience was, of course, the fact that the document purported to emanate from no less a personage than the Director himself. All the other notices in his part of the corridor appeared to have been issued by Clerks of the 23rd Degree or Deputy Assistant Processors or other officials of elevated rank, but this instruction alone came from the most illustrious centre about which all things revolved. Whenever Pomfrit regarded this notice or pondered upon it (and when did he not?), he experienced a deep sense of gratitude and – yes, it must be admitted – virtually unbounded, ultimately very understandable, pride. After all, not everyone was in the fortunate position of being the recipient, however unworthy, of such an undoubtedly important order. It gave meaning and perfect dignity to his existence. In short, it made him a happy man.

Zero-hour, the time when the Department resumed its manifold activities for another day, was marked by a high-pitched whistle. As soon as he heard this to him by no means unwelcome signal, Pomfrit went to the door of his office, where he inserted a coded access-control card into a slot provided for just this particular purpose. This simple action set the oxygeniser inside the office in whirring motion and, in addition, caused a compartment in the wall to open, from which Pomfrit now extracted two items – a head-lamp and his personal heating harness. Whereas the former would give him, without the slightest waste and in a manner conducive to total concentration, all the light he could possibly require in the execution of his duties, the latter, a particularly ingenious device, served, by pleasantly heating certain strategic areas of his body, to ensure that the blood in his arteries and veins would course right merrily throughout the day, thus keeping him alert and in admirable physical and mental trim. Having put on these items, Pomfrit withdrew his access-control card, which caused the door of the wall compartment to close again and the door to his office to open. Pomfrit entered and sat down at his desk. His weight on the chair triggered the door-closing mechanism and actuated a trap in the ceiling, from which fell a document landing precisely in the middle of his desk.

His daily routine had begun. Pomfrit's office was long and narrow, with walls so tall that their height could only be guessed at. It did, however, possess certain distinguishing and, it is pleasant to report, distinguishable features setting it apart from other offices and giving it a note of class. The wall facing Pomfrit's chair, for instance, was adorned with a frame, which may well have contained a picture – possibly the likeness of some illustrious administrator or the jubilee photograph of the Clerks of the 23rd Degree – but this was a point Pomfrit was never able to resolve, since the beam from his head-lamp did not reach that far. By moving his desk to the wall, putting his chair on it and then balancing tip-toe on the latter, he was indeed able to touch the frame – a facility of which, in his less busy hours, he took full and stimulating advantage, both intellectually and physically.

The usual position of Pomfrit's desk was close to the door and in line with the longitudinal axis of the office. Another, larger desk, such as a supervisor might have used, was situated on an elevated rostrum at the other end, and, standing, as it did, at an angle of 90 degrees to said longitudinal axis, divided the room into two unequal sections. It goes without saying that, in the course of his day and whenever his none-too-arduous workload permitted, Pomfrit would often find himself near the rostrum, wondering, but knowing his place he never went any further and certainly never disturbed the ancient cobwebs connecting the desk with the walls on either side and quite possibly also with the ceiling above.

This office, so agreeably devoid of undesirable distractions and yet so profoundly stimulating, was Pomfrit's favourite place. There he was wholly content, and he showed his appreciation of what was being done for him and his gratitude to a wise and munificent administration by his untiring devotion in carrying out such duties as were routinely entrusted to him. These were of two distinct types. Whenever a document landed on his desk – some of them thick and heavy, and all of them destined for the disintegrator – he had to search it for soup, tea and any other stains as might disfigure its pages, and, having done so with meticulous care, register any such blemish in a secret log-book provided for that very purpose. It will be noted with some relief that Pomfrit – who was in fact the only person ever to lay eyes on this unique record before, in the fullness of time, it too fell victim to the voracious machine in the basement – would lock it away carefully whenever he had to leave the room for any reason whatsoever. But that was not all, not by any means! It was also his task to search for such objects as might inadvertently or through negligence have been left between the pages of the document currently in front of him. Over the years he had found numerous such items, but none more remarkable than a fried egg of tough consistency, on which someone – obviously a person of considerable artistic flair and superior education – had carved a woolly animal's head and the mysterious legend *ADMINISTRATIO GRATIA ADMINISTRATIONIS*, which can, of course, be rendered loosely as 'What an incredible waste of time!'. This was perhaps the only occasion in Pomfrit's long and honourable career that he actually coveted what he had found. He would have dearly loved to be the proud possessor of such an unusual artefact and felt sorely tempted to take it home in order to display it above his humble bedstead. However, as might have been expected from one so eminently worthy of trust as himself, he resisted and overcame this temptation most manfully, and, having made the proper entries and completed the proper forms, forwarded the treasure to the canteen administration – in his educated opinion the proper authority to deal with this matter.

On this particular morning, Pomfrit, while sitting at his desk, gradually became aware of some subtle change in his surroundings. Having brought his penetrating mind to bear on the situation, he soon managed to pinpoint the nature of the change in question. Whereas hitherto every step he took, every movement he made, used to cause dense clouds of dust to arise, which on occasion made him cough or sneeze but at other times gave him much pleasure as he watched the enchanting gyrations of the dust particles in his beam of light, this did not prove to be the case today. He stamped his feet tentatively but not even the tiniest cloudlet of dust could be discerned. The conclusion was inescapable. His office, or at any rate that part of it which was readily accessible, had been thoroughly dusted or, more precisely, dedusted – possibly even electro-cleaned. And since there was bound to be a very good, a very important reason for such an event, unique in Pomfrit's experience, he now endeavoured, by logical analysis, to resolve the mystery. His thought-processes took roughly the following course: he had always done his duty without fear or favour, incorruptibly, loyally (no trouble-maker he!) and strictly according to the rules. If he was indeed right in this assessment, the removal of his office dust was more likely to be a measure of reward than of rebuke. On the other hand, as he realised full well, there had, apart from the notable case of the fried egg, been but few, if any, occasions when temptation had come his way, and the qualities he had so proudly cited in his own favour might not, after all, be seen by those in authority as particularly meritorious. And what about his indubitable curiosity, his tendency to allow his thoughts to wander, and, of course, his temerity in speculating on the various notices in the corridor and, more especially, the one emanating from his Eminence, the Director? Furthermore, since there was, after all, nothing intrinsically unpleasant about the presence of dust, which could, in fact, be quite entertaining, its sudden disappearance could well be a kind of warning, an intimation of further and more severe deprivations to come (unless, of course, it was simply required elsewhere, in which case the dedustation of his office might not have any significance for him personally).

In other words, it was virtually impossible to deduce anything definite from the occurrence under consideration. Still, such is the frailty of the human spirit that it generally prefers hope, however irrational, to the absence thereof, however well-founded. Alas for the innocence of poor Pomfrit! By brushing aside, at any rate for the time being, such reasonable misgivings as had crossed his mind, he had, in his innermost being, unleashed the very floodgates of boundless ambition, giddy, immoderate speculation and, worst of all, rampant discontent. 'What next?' he wondered. Had the time come, at last and none too soon, for him to be promoted? Would he – oh happy thought! – be joining the Clerks of the 23rd or even of the 22nd Degree? Would he soon be meeting an Administrator or encounter the Head of the Department face to face? 'My dear Pomfrit,' the latter would say to him, 'Thank you, thank you, thank you ever so much! How on earth would the Department manage without you? And to show our deep appreciation of your invaluable services, we have promoted you to a Clerkship of the Very First Degree, which means that you will be near His Radiant Magnificence, the Director, at all times. He will depend on your marvellous advice in all matters, and perhaps one day ...' Thus roughly ran Pomfrit's imaginings, and the office in which he had spent so many deeply satisfying, indeed happy, hours suddenly seemed to him more like a dungeon than the one and only true and glorious pod of his soul, which it had formerly been.

Whereas hitherto he had hardly ever bothered to stop for 'lunch', seeing that he always had far too much to do and, anyway, had not the slightest desire to mingle with the others, things were quite different today, and for once he could hardly wait to get out of his office and make for the canteen, where he intended to treat himself to the finest and most expensive item on the menu. At the canteen he immediately headed for Frankie Chipolata, the incumbent of a nearby office, whom he knew vaguely and would normally have avoided at all costs. Like one demented and by then entirely incapable of exercising the slightest self-restraint, Pomfrit forthwith acquainted his colleague, a latter-day Cicero, as it were, much given to voicing his opinion on any subject brought to his attention, with his aspirations and what he hoped to be his prospects. And Frankie Chipolata did not disappoint him. Embellishing his delivery with splendid rhetorical flourishes, he intimated that the time had surely come for Pomfrit to make a definite stand, to show that he could not be pushed around, to insist on his inalienable rights. Changing direction, he pointed out that this might, of course, backfire. Pomfrit might, at the end of the day, come to rue his temerity, find himself in the outer darkness, hoho! The question was simply: was he a man or a mouse? In a situation such as this, he, Chipolata, would know what to do. But then, it was not up to him, he was not concerned except as a friend. Still, some people had all the luck, but, after all, in some organisations (he could but would rather not name) ability was neither here nor there. Quite on the contrary, it only aroused envy and even demonic malice ...

While this harangue was in progress, Pomfrit was doing his best to cope with an 'Enormo Ham Surprise', a kind of wafer sandwich with a filling of 'mystery ham', which, however, resisted his every effort at dismemberment and mastication. However much he tore at it and worried it with his usually so efficient stainless-steel 'choppers', it would not come apart. This, perhaps, was not all that surprising, seeing that, in a manner of speaking, it was in its present predicament by mistake only, having until recently done sterling service as part of a pinkish undergarment, the function of which was to protect the charms of the porcine canteen manageress. Pomfrit, eventually, dealt with the matter in a most decisive way by swallowing his 'ham' – on the face of it what he had paid for – in one determined gulp and swilling it down with 'Gastrolube', an oily liquid very suitable for this purpose.

Frankie Chipolata too had certain problems. It turned out that his own 'Super Browning Double Wafer', providently acquired by him this very morning from one of the many unlicensed (but, so it was rumoured, officially tolerated, and even encouraged) stalls, did not contain health-giving, satisfying nut-browning as should have been the case but dark, thick masonry glue, which firmly adhering to his upper and lower dentures and causing them to churn about in his mouth in ballet-like unison eventually robbed him, at any rate for the time being, of the power of speech, entirely preventing him thereby from uttering any further fireworks of wit and intellect.

On his way back to the office, Pomfrit again found himself in front of the famous notice, but this time in an entirely novel frame of mind. He had, to all intents and purposes, shed his chrysalis and turned into a venturesome butterfly ready for a life of giddy frolics and abandon. And whereas formerly contemplation and consideration of the notice had been all that he desired, he now felt a quite irresistible urge to enter and explore the room beyond.

Curiously enough, this door was not, as might have been expected, locked but opened easily (albeit with a creaking sound, which would surely have sufficed to warn him if he had been in a more normal frame of mind) to his initially tentative but then impatient pressure. Indeed, so great was his impatience that he virtually fell into the room in a manner that can only be described as most unseemly. Once inside, he quickly closed the door behind him and would now have set about his quest of discovery had he but been able to see. His head-lamp, however, was safely in its compartment, where he had deposited it before going to the canteen, and the ambient darkness was wholly impenetrable. What was he to do? All of a sudden in a deep panic (no trace now of the buoyant, fearless Pomfrit of but a few seconds ago), he lost his bearings and could not find the way back to the door, but even if he had, he would not have dared to use it, for it was terrifyingly likely that it might not be possible to open the door from inside, and then again that he might be caught in the act and 'brought to justice' (as Frankie Chipolata and everybody else would, no doubt, describe his fate). If the former proved to be the case and the door could not be opened again, a horrible although (as he now realised) richly-deserved end awaited him, and if he were discovered and put before the Judges he was sure to be found guilty of dire conduct unbecoming to an operative in a position of trust, from whose office the dust had but recently been removed and who was accordingly under a most special, indeed sacred, obligation to behave in an altogether exemplary fashion. His humiliation would be utter, and his punishment awesome.

As, quaking with fear, he groped about in the unrelieved darkness, it occurred to him that there was something oddly familiar about his surroundings. What exactly, he could not immediately discern. But gradually it dawned on him that the room in which he found himself was indeed his own office, although apparently the wrong end thereof. Exploration revealed a large, transversely placed desk, and he distinctly perceived the fragrance of a toe of garlic, part of his festive fare last Founder's Day, which he had mislaid and never been able to recover. His first instinctive impulse was to rush past the desk and to make for the safety of his own domain, but a moment's reflection sufficed to convince him of the potential perils of such an attempt. There were, as he knew well from previous observation, thick, multilayered cobwebs linking the desk with the walls on either side – he had no reason to assume that they were gone – and if indeed they were still in place, they might well have been coded, for instance by means of strategically suspended insect remains, in order to discourage and, if necessary, trap the excessively inquisitive or, more precisely, himself. It would seem that he, Pomfrit, was the fly for whom this elaborate screen had been constructed and that there was no escape.

Only one hope remained. If the narrow opening between the drawer units of the desk were to prove unobstructed, he might yet get through. Trembling with desperate anxiety he went down on his knees trying to locate the opening and, if possible, squeeze through to the other side. In his eagerness, he arched his back somewhat like a cat, his bony behind projecting in the opposite direction.

This then was his position as the door behind him opened and the Boot walked in......

CHAPTER TWENTY NINE

IT TOOK M several days to finish this story, for he enjoyed nothing so much as editing what he had written and, in particular, adding to it. Having but recently read that it had taken eight hand-written drafts to complete *War and Peace*, he had formed the opinion that with certain authors such as Tolstoy or himself fine writing depended on a process of unceasing amendation, of infinitely patient filing, polishing and other forms of enhancement, and was never simply the result of a single flash of blinding inspiration. However, once his 'masterpiece' was completed to his satisfaction (and he was, indeed, beginning to be slightly bored with the very effort of creativity), he felt a deep need for an appreciative audience. So as to assuage this need, he wandered into the kitchen, where he found Silversmith trying to mend his socks, a chore which since Rosabelle's departure he had as yet not been able to delegate to anyone else. Silversmith, in a manner of speaking doubly captive since he in turn wished to impart to M some momentous news about his very latest and in practical terms most promising conquest, one of the Sparkle-Browns, no less, fitted the bill perfectly.

Galbraith, secretary and eager beaver of the Pantheon Chess Club, had at last succeeded in persuading M to attend one of its Wednesday evening sessions as a visitor. Meeting in an upstairs room of the 'Crown and Bull', this club appeared to be surprisingly popular, perhaps because of what it had to offer to those in need of special stimulation or suffering from habitual dryness of the throat. When they arrived, M and his companion found most tables already occupied with games in progress, while quite a few people were standing around talking club politics or simply watching. One table in particular was entirely surrounded by 'kibitzers', attracted, as Galbraith explained, not so much by the wondrous quality of the game in progress as by the undeniable charms of the club's only lady member. Aware of his impotence in this matter, Galbraith tolerated these outlandish goings-on but certainly did not approve of them.

The room – wine-red plush and gold, with a large, faded chandelier, upholstered chairs and benches and Victorian prints in dark wooden frames on the walls – was overheated, and the air was thick with smoke and the exudations of various alcoholic beverages. Galbraith, having caught sight of the chairman, with whom he claimed to have some important club business to discuss, wandered off, leaving M to his own devices. However, M's solitary status did not last long. Presently, a large, grey-suited gentleman with a manic glint in his bespectacled eyes and a beaming smile enhanced by reflections of the chandelier's cosy light from several gold teeth, bore down upon him, shook, or rather crushed, his hand in a most welcoming manner – to judge by the length of time that seemed to pass before he again released this unoffending member, he was in fact a bit of a sadist – and introduced himself as John Eaglebird, a humble *aficionado* of the game of kings.

'You are new here, I believe,' he intoned. 'I, on the other hand, have been playing at this dubious venue for many more years than I care to remember.'

'Why …' responded M, attempting to put a question, but Mr. Eaglebird cut him short immediately.

'Why indeed. You will, no doubt, wish to know why I describe this venue as dubious. Believe me, my dear sir, I have chosen this word with the utmost care, although you may, of course, not agree with me. However, let me give you a bit of a guided tour, let me be, as it were, your Virgil. You may, for instance, not have realised that this venerable pub is in fact one of London's main centres for boys who would be girls and for girls who would be boys. Still, as far as the members of the club are concerned, this is, of course, of no interest whatsoever, although, to coin a phrase, some of them are without the slightest doubt "on the wrong game". But please do not misunderstand me. I am not trying to discourage you from joining our happy family. Far from it. We have a truly marvellous spirit here, yes indeed, and I am absolutely certain that you will fit in splendidly. Besides, you could hardly hope to find a more colourful bunch of chess-playing individuals anywhere in the country, no indeed. Take, for instance, Mr. Lobrowski over there. He is forever on the lookout, not so much for a chess partner – although he is quite a good player, he would be the first to admit that he doesn't really like the game – but rather for someone prepared and able to lend him a pound or two. And would you believe it? His supply of willing "bankers" never seems to dry up. As for *La Paloma*, the dove-like creature with the large bosom over there – she is the darling of all the over-sixties, who, too old and decrepit for the real thing, simply queue up to get a sniff of her undoubtedly expensive perfume and play with her, *faute de mieux*, at chess. Even Simon Borowski, our current champion, who never misses a chance to point out that on one occasion he nearly managed a draw against Vladimir Borsht in a simul, keeps trying to teach her the moves, predictably without much success, for in whatever other arenas her talents may lie, chess is certainly not one of them.'

Another attempt by M to prove that he too had the power of speech ended in failure, as Mr. Eaglebird continued relentlessly: 'But, of course, as is bound to be the case at any club, we too have one or two members who are not merely colourful but most definitely peculiar. Dr. Magirus, for example, the fellow with the black beard, is a case in point. He is, bar none, the most cantankerous player I have ever come across. Even Smithburton – and he certainly can't afford to be choosy – no longer speaks to him, ever since Magirus accused him of cheating when they were picking colours for a "friendly". Mind you, I myself wouldn't put it past him, for Smithburton is one of those who'll try anything if there is the slightest hope of getting away with it. But actually to challenge him – I ask you! And how about old man Meyerbach, the bald-headed, toothless chap in the corner, whose main ambition in life you might think is to cover his nose with his lower lip. Still, although he has never said so himself, I have reason to believe that he is a close relative of Siegmund Meyerbach, Mr. Milking-machine himself and one of the pillars of our age.'

Just then a young man with sallow features and thick, horn-rimmed spectacles came over to ask M whether he would like a game. However, before M had the slightest chance to say aye or nay, Mr. Eaglebird, not a man prepared to put up readily with interference by a member of, as he saw it, definitely lower rank, intervened to point out that this was a private conversation and that in any case Mr. Bush was his partner, so would he kindly leave. His distinctive, angular proboscis was red with annoyance as the youth, greatly to M's consternation, beat a hasty retreat. 'Some of these young whipper-snappers have no manners at all,' grumbled Mr. Eaglebird, 'but you must not let them take advantage. Where was I? Yes, I remember – Meyerbach. Now, he would never do anything that could possibly be described as dishonest, but he never plays a match without first carefully and ostentatiously removing his ill-fitting dentures, wiping them with his handkerchief and placing them in a plastic bag which, throughout the contest, he leaves in full view of the other player. Some regard this practice as both unhygienic and rather disgusting and there have been complaints about it, but he justifies it by claiming that this externalisation of his biting tools contributes greatly to the incisiveness of his thought while at the same time relaxing him physically. According to one story, which I personally do not believe but many do, he, on one occasion, quite forgot to put his teeth into the bag, balancing them precariously on the chess clock instead. They say that his opponent, a very highly rated player, was violently sick as a result and had to rush off to the Gents. It appears that he was too upset to continue with the match, preferring to lose it by default. But credit where credit is due! Old man Meyerbach is still a valuable member of our fourth team, and even if it were true that some of his former victories – and we may as well face it, the operative word is former – have indeed owed considerably more to his adversaries' squeamishness than the quality of his own play, who cares? Most of our members, however, are perfectly decent folk who pay their subscriptions more or less on time and even attend occasionally. Only one thing is wrong with them – they can't play chess. But what, after all, is chess, why do some of us love it, why do we rather play chess than go to the theatre or engage in erotic pursuits?'

John Eaglebird, who, for his part, clearly preferred talking to playing chess, did not waste time by waiting for M to make yet another attempt at answering, but went on regardless. 'Chess, my dear young friend, is about many things. It is about power and aggression, it is a symbolic exercise in Napoleonic strategy and Machiavellian tactics, it is treacherous, cynical and brutal. It is all that, but it is also sensitive, capable of infinite variation and rare beauty – in short it is the perfect medium for expressing both love and hate.'

Exhausted, perhaps, by this rhetorical *tour de force*, Mr. Eaglebird suddenly and abruptly appeared to lose interest in M, at last, no doubt, seeing him for what he really was – utterly unimportant. 'Ah,' he said, 'there is Mr. Saburewski, our venerable treasurer. I must have a quick word with him. I hope you don't mind.' And off he rushed in the general direction of a ponderous gentleman wearing, in spite of the intense heat in the room, a long, black overcoat and a large, wide-brimmed hat. He did not, however, manage to reach Mr. Saburewski, for on his way he happened to notice that someone was occupying his favourite chair, a temerity which upset him greatly. There followed a heated discussion, involving in ever widening circles many of the other members until the place was in uproar and people at various stages of inebriety were coming up from the public bar in order to take part in what they appeared to regard as an entertainment specially arranged for their benefit. By the time the dust had settled, Mr. Saburewski, who in common with many other members had no great desire to converse with Mr. Eaglebird and to whom the drinking fraternity was in any case anathema, had disappeared.

M, who did not really expect chessplayers to be normal or even quite sane, joined the Pantheon Chess Club at the following meeting.

'Come in, come in, my dear fellows, and meet Rosburga,' twittered Silversmith in a portentous, even pompous, manner suggesting both restrained triumph and major achievement, as he ushered M and Lipkin, who had come to congratulate him on two momentous events – his newly acquired B.Sc. and his engagement to Rosburga Brown, one of the Sparkle-Browns, that well known clan of brewery tycoons – into his room. Having met Rosburga at one of those posh parties to which he was so partial and found that she, superbly nubile in every important way, was not at all averse to his advances, it had not taken him long to decide that an opportunity such as this must not on any account be wasted. What of it that her height was rather above average, that she was not by any means as young or appetising as he might have wished, and that her prominent nose, curved as it was in the manner of a circular arc, suggested both a parrot's beak and, by its virtually incessant twitching, a constant perception of repulsive odours. And although her voice was embarrassingly sonorous, she clearly had a great deal to offer, and even her two impressive degrees from Oxford, no less, did not put him off. As for Rosburga, most of her friends and contemporaries were already in the happy state of being able to flaunt husbands, babies and similar appurtenances, which made her feel unwanted and 'on the shelf'. Besides, she knew herself to be 'ready for love', and in this regard especially Silversmith seemed to fit her requirements better than most. Richly endowed with the practical intelligence and fine organising flair that were characteristic of her family, she was convinced that given appropriate guidance (and who, after all, could apply such guidance better than she?) Silversmith would be most amenable to being moulded into a husband second to none. She did, of course, realise that he was a person of acquisitive, even rapacious, personality, but this merely served to 'turn her on' and made her want to do unspeakable things with him.

'Meet my fiancée,' invited Silversmith imprinting a noisy, proprietorial kiss on Rosburga's bony cheek, while she, smiling broadly and every inch the lady of the manor, bore down on M and Lipkin, her hand extended in a gesture of positively regal welcome.

'Do come in,' she boomed, 'and make yourself comfortable if not quite at home. Silvy has told me a lot about you, so I thought it about time to inspect you for myself and see who exactly it was that was to blame for his evil ways.' If this 'humorous' reception was meant to make everybody feel relaxed – and this, Rosburga being Rosburga, is doubtful – it certainly did not achieve its purpose, as M, who, hopeful as ever, had expected to be bowled over by her wit and beauty but was, all of a sudden, thoroughly depressed, muttered something about good wishes and being very pleased indeed, while Lipkin, too terrified to respond in any way, merely cowered behind M's back. On the other hand, it did not take Rosburga, as shrewd a judge of potential as ever there was, a minute to decide that new friends would have to be found for her intended, as soon as possible. Lipkin in particular seemed to her very alien and quite unsuitable, and it did, in fact, occur to her to mention him to Daddy, just in case one of his pals at the Home Office happened to be interested in him. However, oozing charm, as it seemed, from every pore, she, for the time being, carried on with the conversation almost entirely by herself, ignoring M's purely *pro forma* interjections and Lipkin's abject silence, while firmly frustrating Silversmith's every attempt to get a grip on, as it were, the steering-wheel of conversation.

A little later, Mrs. Bingley, who had also been invited to meet Silversmith's 'woman of destiny', came in. It did not take her long to decide that Rosburga was exactly what young Silversmith needed, and she did not hesitate to make this quite clear. 'In my opinion,' she said, 'Mr. Silversmith – and I would be saying the same about you, Mr. M – needs very firm handling, and I am quite certain your young lady will do very well in that department. Mr. Bingley and I have been married for more years than I care to remember, and he has always followed my advice without being any the worse for it.' This was indeed dramatic stuff. Mrs. Bingley commenting on her marriage when talking to her lodgers was a truly unheard-of, cataclysmic event, showing perhaps how greatly Silversmith had risen in her esteem by his association with Rosburga. 'Be that as it may,' she continued, 'we both wish you all the very best for your future together. I am sure Mr. Bingley will be as pleased as I am to know that at least one of you boys is on the right road, particularly now that we have decided to sell this house and move to a bungalow in Bournemouth, where we have quite a few friends and acquaintances.' This, as it were, 'official' statement of intent did not make any great impact on Silversmith, who in mind and spirit had in any case already put his life at No. 12 behind him, but it came as quite a shock to M, in spite of the fact that he had already heard rumours about the impending sale of the house and the imminent departure of the Bingleys. M had been happy at No. 12, and, as far as he was concerned, the future now looked gloomy and full of ominous question-marks.

Having completed her inspection and made her announcement, Mrs. Bingley, not one to waste precious time uselessly, departed, leaving Rosburga to reoccupy the centre of the stage – her natural domain, as it seemed. As for Silversmith's degree, admittedly not one of his more glorious achievements, no-one mentioned it at all, not even its fortunate possessor, which was perhaps just as well.

Silversmith married Rosburga a few months later. It was an 'elegant' wedding at one of London's socially more acceptable churches, and M was invited, although Lipkin wasn't. The wedding was followed by a grand reception at Cadogan Hall, at which M, thoroughly intimidated by all those grey top-hats that seemed to sway and bob around him on all sides, eventually joined forces with Mrs. Bingley, who was also somewhat out of her depth. They agreed that this was indeed a splendid occasion and that Mr. Silversmith had done really well for himself, and M, never loth to delve into the treasure-chest of his past when this might help to make things move more smoothly (or simply because virtually nothing gave him greater pleasure), availed himself of the opportunity to compare this event with others which he had experienced, particularly during his seafaring days and in Japan. Besides, Mrs. Bingley enjoyed listening to his stories and was greatly relieved not to be left standing about like a lemon, virtually ignored by one and all. However, in due course all good – and bad – things come to an end, and having run the gauntlet of prominent Sparkle-Browns and Silversmiths, who had to be thanked for an absolutely wonderful time and whose hands had to be warmly shaken, M and Mrs. B. were at last free to make their escape – Mrs. B. to a leading store, where they had a sale of furnishing materials, and M to the Academy in Oxford Street, where they were showing an old film with Jean Gabin and Arletty.

After this memorable wedding, M and Silversmith met only on one further occasion and entirely by chance, several years later, outside a theatre in Shaftesbury Avenue. They had a cup of tea together at a coffee-bar. Silversmith, fat, nearly bald and almost indecently prosperous-looking, had become boringly middle-aged, visibly weighed down by the responsibilities of business and family. He told M all about the scope and achievements of his company, according to him a leading supplier to the brewery industry, and showed M photographs of his two little girls in front of a large, impressive country manor – their current home and not a bad little place, as he pointed out with some pride – and one showing him with his 'Roz' in San Francisco, where they had been on a kind of working holiday, at a brewers' convention, at which Silversmith had been one of the speakers.

As for M, he had not changed all that much, in spite of the fact that he too was now married – to Anni, whom he had met at Nuremberg – and had two children, a boy and a girl. He was still employed at TTTW, but with an even more impressive string of titles and at a slightly better salary. M and his family now lived in a small, unassuming house in North London, which he had bought with the aid of a mortgage. He too carried photographs but decided not to show them. Instead he explained, at some length and with numerous embroideries, that he could never have hoped to qualify for a mortgage if the agent representing the Northampton and Derby Mutual had not prevailed upon him to enter on his application form a much higher salary than that to which he was actually entitled. M thought that the agent's attitude in this matter had been rather remarkable and gratifying proof of the confidence which the latter, clearly a man of considerable business acumen and judgement, had in his, M's, probity and prospects, but Silversmith seemed totally uninterested and indeed unable to comprehend the real significance of M's tale. After this, M did not quite know what else to say to his friend, who droned on and on about his various achievements and successes, and accordingly confined himself to making approving noises whenever this seemed indicated, whereas Silversmith viewed M with faint disapproval, dimly envious perhaps because he himself had moved away so much further from the happy, irresponsible past which they had shared. When, recalling old times, M mentioned Lipkin and Rosabelle, with whom he still exchanged an occasional letter, Silversmith first looked puzzled as if he had forgotten them entirely and then brushed them aside with 'They were both Commies, weren't they?'

Caught up in a brief spell of nostalgic sentimentality and too embarrassed to admit the end of their now extinct friendship, M and Silversmith exchanged telephone numbers before they parted, promising faithfully to 'keep in touch'. However, as is generally the case with such promises and resolutions, these too were destined to come to nothing, for the distances between them had grown far too large to be bridged, even if they had genuinely wished to bridge them.

When, neatly rolled up in a cardboard tube, the next lot of assignments arrived from JCC, M was dismayed to discover that the French tutor (whoever he was) had seen fit to respond to his tactfully worded query about the gender of 'auto' not by any rational argument or valid evidence but simply by awarding him a lower mark, namely, a 'B' instead of the 'A' which M regarded as his by rights. M, who had never been able to stand what he regarded as cowardly abuse of authority, of which the despicable tactic used by the French tutor was clearly a prime example, immediately decided to discontinue this and all the other courses, without even deigning to advise the college why it had fallen from grace so irretrievably. Somewhat naïve in matters of this kind, he fondly imagined that his uncompromising, nay pitiless, action would give rise to great dismay and much searching of souls at JCC, that heads would roll, and, in particular, that, bereft of his mantle of false authority, the faceless Frenchman (if that was indeed what he was, and not simply an Englishman or perhaps a Spaniard masquerading as a Frenchman) would be sent into the wilderness, his garments, such as they were, in tatters and with ashes on his guilty head.

Several years later, a friend in the employment of the Department of Inland Revenue told M that in his organisation – and probably in organisations of any kind – even well-written letters of complaint from 'clients' with real vitriolic talent had not the slightest chance of upsetting anybody or changing anybody's mind but were eagerly looked forward to as sources of merriment and welcome breaks in the monotony of daily routine, whereas the total absence of such a letter was merely a non-event of the most absolute kind. By way of evidence he mentioned that fine old working-class ditty 'You can't get me, I'm part of the Union'. Only then did M begin to realise (although he should have known from his own experience with TTTW) that, far from attracting any criticism or sanction, his French tutor had, by discouraging students and causing them to discontinue their courses, in all likelihood proved himself to be fine managerial material and was about to be promoted managing director.

M's disappointment with JCC became, in a manner of speaking, a turning-point in his 'academic' career, for he at last decided to stop messing around and to register with London University as a candidate for matriculation. With Silversmith now perpetually on the go and a general sense of insecurity pervading No. 12 in the wake of Mrs. Bingley's dread announcement, the conditions for studying – he intended to base his efforts on past examination papers and design his own courses – were, admittedly, not at all good, but M was determined to get to the top of that as yet distant hill, where he too would be the proud possessor of a proper degree and, as a result, a properly educated person, able to hold his head up high in any company.

CHAPTER THIRTY

MISS PRATT and I have had a terrible row, and she has sworn that I shall never see her again. A pity in a way that we had to part in such an undignified manner, but it would certainly be far from the truth if I were to say that I was sorry to see her 'vanish into the sunset', in spite of the fact that in many respects we got on very well indeed and that I undoubtedly owe her a lot. However, bearing in mind the precise circumstances of our long overdue (and hopefully final) separation, it would be more accurate to say that it is I who vanished, for we were at the time at her flat, sipping wine after a candle-lit supper to which she had invited me in order to celebrate my birthday.

It all started innocently enough (that, at any rate, is how some people might judge what happened) with her giving me, by way of a birthday present, a set of white cotton underwear, not realising, of course, that such a present might be perceived by me as yet another in a long and increasingly insufferable series of attempts at burying her claws in the more private domains of my ego.

It is true that I have always felt greatly attracted to 'strong' personalities, especially women, and they to me – at certain periods of my life, for instance during my time at Nuremberg, they used positively to swarm about me like wasps about a jar of honey – but at the same time I have unfailingly resented the way in which they would try to batten on me and do their best to turn me into a kind of zombie. I have never been able to understand the motivation of such people but I suspect that it is this kind of insidious relationship which is at the root of those ancient myths about vampires and the living dead. Myths, of course, are by their very nature simplifying abstractions, and it would therefore be unfair to suggest that in real-life situations the profit-and-loss account can ever be all that one-sided, but one thing is, I believe, certain: unless the relationship be killed stone-dead, it is bound to be revived, with nothing whatsoever achieved. Hence the necessity of driving a stake through the heart of the vampire, which is, of course, a recurrent feature of all stories about Dracula. Be that as it may, ever since our family's escape to Czechoslovakia, when I ceased living at my father's home, my personal freedom has been very important to me, and although up to a point I might go along with strong-minded people, I would never go with them all the way.

A present of any other kind I could have coped with or even welcomed, but underwear! What really started me off, however, so that I behaved in a manner which can only be described as quite ungentlemanly and, generally speaking at least, most uncharacteristic of me, was the girlish giggle with which she neighed at me that the shop at which she had bought the stuff also had a set with a pattern of tiny pink hearts on offer, which would have suited me down to the ground and made me look really 'sweet'. And while I was sitting there smouldering she compounded this offence by suggesting that I might like to try the set on in her bedroom (she promised not to peep!) in order to make quite certain that it really was my size. If it was not, she would be glad to exchange it. Had we not been at her flat and had the atmosphere not been so warm and intimate, I might still have accepted the gift with a modicum of good grace, but now, driven by I know not what demonic force which I could call up but not control, I virtually threw her present back at her, hissing that I was fed up to the back teeth with her incredibly tactless and utterly clumsy approaches, not to mention her domineering, blood-sucking ways, that if she felt in need of a plaything or shadow she had picked the wrong person, etc, etc. As I emitted this torrent of immoderate abuse my real self was sitting back quite comfortably and taking it all in, in the not entirely unfamiliar role of an unconcerned observer.

Miss Pratt's initial protestations of goodwill and my having misunderstood gave way to tears of mortification. Angry, red blotches disfigured her pink-and-white complexion as she launched herself into a virulent counter-attack. She called me vulgar and cheap, a contemptible, ungrateful Romeo, who, having cold-bloodedly taken advantage of her womanly weakness, was now cynically looking for a way to get rid of her. At last she could see me in my true colours, for what I really was. 'At last', I screamed back at her, 'we now know what you really think of me, you man-eating, long-necked hydra.' To which she, totally hysterical by now and positively slavering with rage, responded by screeching that she was lucky to be still alive, that I had not simply done away with her, but how could she ever have been so stupid as to imagine that I was her friend? That was something which she could never forget, never in a thousand years. And so on and so forth.

The quarrel ended as abruptly as it had begun, when, all of a sudden quite formal and with apparently perfect control, Miss Pratt asked me to leave, saying that she never wanted to see me again. Feeling by now rather deflated and ashamed of myself, I tried to explain why I had been so nasty to her, but Miss Pratt, whose self-control was beginning to slip again, merely waved me away, sadly and without another word. If I had gone to her then, put my arm about her shoulders perhaps and comforted her, the evening might well have ended differently, but fearful of the emotional consequences – she would have been bound to misunderstand – and relieved that this ever more irksome relationship had at last come to its desired end, I merely said goodbye and left.

None of this might have happened – although the writing was already on the wall – if Miss Pratt had realised that to present me, of all people, with underwear, however innocuous, was perhaps the most ill-judged thing she could have done, for, on the one hand, it breached a personal tabu which I was absolutely determined to preserve (I did not dare indulge in any of the mother-child intimacy and salacious familiarity which, quite obviously, was what she had in mind) while, on the other hand, a set of underwear given to me on another occasion was in my mind still associated with self-doubt and considerable unease. Miss Pratt, of course, had no idea that she was putting her foot into a veritable hornets' nest, since I had never told her about this unfortunate incident, and, to that extent but to that extent only, it would be unfair to blame her.

It all started a few months before my escape to Poland, at a synagogue in Moravská Ostrava, where my father and I happened to be celebrating the Day of Atonement, the holiest day in the Jewish calendar. Although this was primarily an occasion for fasting, reverence and pure, lofty thoughts (I, for my part, was also much preoccupied with the state of my unhappy stomach and a constant anxiety that I might lose my place in the prayer book), it was also a kind of social event. During the breaks between prayers, it was, therefore, by no means uncommon for total strangers to talk to one another about whatever topic happened to be uppermost in their minds. This being the case, my father and I were not the least bit surprised and indeed rather flattered when the tall, well-dressed gentleman in the row immediately in front of us turned around and inquired what we thought of the service. After the preliminary exchanges, once the conversation had become more personal, he intimated that he had some influence with the board of directors of Bata and might therefore be able to assist me in obtaining an apprenticeship at Zlin, the internationally famous centre of the shoe industry, where Bata had its headquarters.

To understand fully why my father and I reacted to this suggestion as if we had just been offered the keys to paradise, it is necessary to realise that before the war Bata was widely regarded as one of the most progressive commercial organisations in the world, not only in operational respects but, more importantly as far as we were concerned, in matters of training. There was general agreement that an apprenticeship at Zlin was tantamount to an exceedingly good future, full of every good thing and totally secure. The very fact that the country was, at that time, at the edge of an abyss and every Jew, in particular, had reason to fear the shape of things to come, contributed to this view, which under the circumstances was not at all well-founded, but we were sick to death of uncertainty and gloom and only too ready to escape to Utopia.

It would be no exaggeration to say that both my father, whose attitudes in most matters and especially in regard to personal relationships tended to be based on naïve optimism (at least according to his detractors, chief among whom was my Uncle Max), and I, who was equally gullible, equally ready to believe in everybody's good intentions, were infinitely grateful for what Dr. Hahnenschrey – that was the kindly stranger's name – was offering to do for me. Considering the place and the occasion, we even saw in his proposal the benign will of our Creator, with whom I, for my part, had long been on the friendliest of terms. Besides, Dr. Hahnenschrey's very appearance suggested well-heeled respectability, and it was therefore without the slightest hesitation that I agreed to meet him in town at the Automat, that splendid self-service bar, for a bite to eat and a discussion of what should be done for me to gain access to Zlin and my heart's current desire. Having agreed on a date and time suitable to both of us, we returned to our devotions, with my concentration, at least, now under even more severe strain.

The eating part of our meeting was an undoubted success, with me gorging myself on various open sandwiches made succulent with cheese and gherkin, salmon garnished with a slice of lemon, rich, garlicky sausage and marinated herring with lashings of raw onion. Dr. Hahnenschrey, a veritable fairy godfather (to coin a phrase), paid for all this without a murmur, and even insisted that I should try the *Schokoladentorte* and have some of the Automat's delicious coffee with *Schlagobers*. After such delights it would quite clearly have been churlish to refuse his invitation to his flat, which, as he explained, would be a more comfortable, altogether more private place to transact the real business of the afternoon.

His flat, near the top of a modern block nearby, was indeed a revelation. As soon as I entered, I immediately realised (although I would not on any account describe myself as a connoisseur in such matters) that this was truly a place of absolute harmony, even perfection, combining, as it did, elegance and a touch of luxury with an air of uncluttered spaciousness and, at the same time, a sense of cosy intimacy, at least partly due to the sensuously soft, charcoal-grey wall-to-wall carpeting and the fact that all the rooms were centrally heated to a most agreeable temperature. The pictures on the pale-grey walls – only a few and, as I could tell, selected with the utmost care – were evidence of my host's exquisite taste, as indeed were the furniture (mahogany throughout) and the curtains, as well as, of course, the various cushions, rugs and other items without which a place cannot be wholly *comme il faut*.

As Dr. Hahnenschrey took me on a conducted tour of the various rooms I was positively breathless with admiration, quite bowled over by the splendour of it all, and in no state to disagree when he suggested that I too might aspire to a similar or possibly even superior life-style if I played my cards right and took full advantage of such opportunities as happened to come my way. He asked me to call him Gusti – all his other close friends did – and intimated that, in spite of the fact that we hadn't known each other for all that long, he already sensed a deep bond between us. He hoped that I too was aware of this bond, which, in the fullness of time and provided that we always treated each other with perfect, unstinting sincerity, would certainly deepen and mature. As we entered the bathroom – all mirrors and pink and white – he even presented me with a neatly wrapped parcel, a gift, as he put it, which I must not be too proud to accept, seeing that it was meant to seal our new friendship.

In the sitting-room, where we eventually landed up, Dr. Hahnenschrey poured two small glasses of sweet liqueur and proposed, in very civil terms, a toast to my future and our lasting association. Then he was off to the bathroom in order, as he explained, to freshen up and get rid of the grime of the city. 'If you too would like to have a pleasant, invigorating bath, please don't on any account be shy,' he suggested, 'but if you would prefer to look at some books until I return, there are some particularly good ones in the bedroom.'

Browsing through some of the books scattered here and there, even I, who had been trying so hard to avoid the obvious, was finally compelled to face up to the realisation that what my host had in mind were things quite different from everlasting platonic friendship or my glorious future in the shoe industry. This I found quite alarming and fairly distasteful, for what I most fervently desired could only be attained with the willing co-operation of young girls – not so much such as I had known in the past or knew at the time but rather as I fondly imagined them. In any case and whatever the circumstances, I was not in any way ready for emotional and physical abandon, which I dreaded as one might dread jumping into a bottomless abyss and which, dimly aware that reality could never be as good as my dreams and idealised images, I perceived as a kind of self-betrayal, the sort of thing biblical Esau had been guilty of when he sold his birthright to Jacob for a mess of porridge.

Obstinately clinging to my illusions, I nevertheless continued to hope that my misgivings would turn out to have been ill-founded and that we would presently be embarked upon an impeccably practical and businesslike discussion of my prospects and how best to advance them. However, once he had rejoined me it did not take long for Dr. Hahnenschrey – magnificently attired in a dark-green and gold dressing gown with a dragon on its back and fragrant with perfume – to make his intentions absolutely plain. How, after all, could I possibly have misunderstood his attempts at prying into my most private concerns or at touching, under the guise of avuncular benevolence, various parts of my body? Abhorrent as I found all this, I still confined myself to merely warding him off as best I could until, exasperated, no doubt, by what must have seemed to him unreasonable stalling on my part, he at last abandoned his ambiguous approach and told me in so many words that he was getting tired of this 'game' but that he was quite prepared to pay me handsomely if I let him have his way with me.

That finally settled it. Reacting as I usually do when I feel the need to hack my way out of a corner, I shouted at him that he was a disgusting, filthy old man (this made him wince), that his money stank to high heaven, and similar stuff, whereas he, suddenly aware of the fact that I might be overheard by his neighbours, kept, rather incongruously, entreating me to lower my voice, which made me shout even louder. Having had my say, I left, and he made no attempt to stop me. And on the way out I grabbed the parcel which he had given to me earlier, too bloody-minded by now to leave it behind. This eventually proved to contain a set of light-blue underwear of a most unusual kind and, from any practical point of view, useless.

When, several months later, I escaped from Czechoslovakia to Poland, the underwear remained at my landlady's flat, together with various other possessions which I had kept there. As for Dr. Hahnenschrey, I never saw him again. However, my father (whom I had told, in suitably edited form, what had happened) did on one occasion run into him in the street and, wishing to show his disapproval in a forceful manner, attempted to spit in his face. Being much shorter than Dr. Hahnenschrey, he did not quite reach his intended target, but his message, no doubt, came across loud and clear.

Two other approaches of a fundamentally similar, although less blatant, kind have been made to me since, causing me to wonder whether my personality was perhaps flawed in some way or whether, after all, experiences such as this were far more common than was generally assumed and simply one of the hazards of youth. As I see it now, all human beings but especially the young, whose attitudes and preferences are not as yet set in a definite mould, share both male and female characteristics, and in matters of attraction and attractiveness the boundaries are therefore far less clearly drawn than our traditional, pragmatically oriented view of life would suggest. Still, I do not like to think of myself as an object of other people's desires, and I really hate being regarded as the kind of person who would be likely to welcome a gift of underwear.

The preparations for the TTTW Christmas party are now in full swing. I have heard that Dr. Pendlebloom has hired a large hall for this purpose, as he wishes to make this year's party the best ever, a truly memorable and prestigious event. They say that he has engaged a real band and even that the whole event will be organised by the former head of the French department, dear Monsieur Chanteclerc, whose manufacturing venture is in really dire straits. I, for my part, can't see how anyone could possibly know that, seeing that Monsieur C. is not the kind of person who would ever admit such a thing. Still, if Dr. P. has really decided to let bygones be bygones and to entrust Antoine with such an important matter as organising the Christmas party, it would certainly prove that he is really a great softie at heart and even more complex than anyone thought. Be that as it may, I am looking forward to this (as to any) party with very mixed feelings.

CHAPTER THIRTY ONE

WEARING his best suit (to be precise, he did not own any other), M arrived early at the community hall hired for the TTTW Christmas party by Miss Gomberg, and was immediately collared by dear Monsieur Chanteclerc, who, as it appeared, had indeed been put in charge of this important occasion and now asked him, with a most gratifying air of complete trust which made M feel as if he were being sent on a quest for the holy grail, to do something about the chairs, tubular-steel affairs with dirty-looking olive-green fabric seats, stacked in a great heap in one corner of the room. Monsieur Chanteclerc, very much in control of his crew of 'volunteers' – other unfortunates who had not had the good sense to delay their arrival until the revelries were well under way – was charging to and fro, issuing and then countermanding instructions, jollying everyone along, and generally having a whale of a time. Frascatti, his hyperactive dog, was also enjoying himself hugely – especially in the immediate vicinity of the tall Christmas tree now in the process of being decorated – to the great delight of some but to the considerable consternation of others.

Ever positive and helpful but without the slightest inkling of what might be expected of him M, who quite enjoyed busying himself in such a menial but hopefully useful manner, proceeded to place the chairs in equidistant arrangement along the walls. As soon as he had finished, he – ever happy to be of service, a personality trait he shared with Frascatti – went to draw Monsieur Chanteclerc's attention to his contribution, and the latter thanked him profusely, while not unexpectedly pointing out that the chairs could not, of course, stay as they were and that it might in any case be better if anyone wishing to sit down during the party simply fetched a chair from some central but reasonably unobtrusive point, so would M mind stacking them again neatly in the far corner of the room. M did not mind at all but went about this new task with undiminished gusto and contentment. After all, he now had the feel of the chairs and rightly considered himself as rather an expert at chair-handling.

While M was still engaged in this constructive fashion, Dr. Pendlebloom arrived with his entourage, the somewhat conspicuous centre of which was Miss Gomberg. She, resplendent in a long, star-spangled gown and wearing glasses with a matching butterfly frame, clearly dominated the fashion scene throughout much of the evening, at any rate until the rather belated arrival of Madame Bellringer, who, for some unknown reason believing this to be a fancy-dress event, had decided to come as the sugar-plum fairy. A portly old gentleman with irascible features and a very red nose stood next to Dr. Pendlebloom, who introduced him as his good friend Sir Alistair Ladbroke, a member of his club and now a major shareholder and the new President of TTTW. The nobleman's presence and the questions which it implied threw a temporary shadow over the proceedings, but once he had turned his attention, in roughly equal measure, to a bottle of something or other especially provided for his use as well as to the indubitable charms of Miss Jennipet Bitterjug, one of the most talented escorters, of whom it was rumoured that as an 'entertainer' she was second to none, he was soon forgotten. In any case, he did not stay long – nor, incidentally, did Miss Bitterjug, which was, in a way, disappointing, since many had hoped that she might be prepared to demonstrate her art later in the evening, when all the notables would have gone and the atmosphere would have become more relaxed.

It took a little time for the ice to be broken (quite understandably, of course, seeing that folk with similar professional interests do tend to find each other utterly repellent), but thanks mainly to the foresight of Monsieur Chanteclerc, who, by stealth and persuasion, had made quite certain that there would be no shortage of stimulating beverage, the party soon got well and truly under way, and whatever preparations had not as yet been completed were simply abandoned. M too decided that the time had come for him to desist from any further stacking of chairs, however enjoyable, and to join the throng of fellow tutors and members of the administrative staff – smiling, smirking or broadly grinning, shyly appreciative or purposefully grave – who were now in the process of converging upon Dr. Pendlebloom in order to offer him their thanks for having been invited to what, as they all agreed, promised to be a most memorable occasion, while reaffirming, each in his own way, their unswerving loyalty to TTTW. Flashing his golden signet ring as he carved up the air with a wealth of welcoming gestures, and stroking his black moustache (which for this event had been groomed to a point of unbelievable perfection) and but occasionally glancing at his diamond-studded watch, an item acquired by him but recently at a most favourable discount, Dr. Pendlebloom received all this homage with great and highly commendable good humour.

Only when he was confronted by M, who in his eagerness to do the right thing had omitted to wash his hands or even to remove the dust and cobwebs – incidental results of his recent activity – from his suit, did he almost but not in fact twitch his left eyelid in what might well have been an air of disapproving wonderment. Once M had become aware of his somewhat bedraggled state he, quite reasonably, decided that the only course open to him was to pretend that there was nothing whatsoever amiss and to continue with his gesture of extending his right hand for a manly, seasonal handshake. It is, of course, greatly to Dr. Pendlebloom's credit that, even as he gripped M's (at that moment) distinctly unappealing hand firmly and without apparent hesitation, he confined himself to hissing – albeit in a manner so discreet that only those in their immediate proximity and a foot or two beyond could hear him – something to the effect that he found M's appearance rather curious, indeed perplexing, and would advise him to improve it without delay. M responded with a rather sheepish grin and immediate retreat to the gentlemen's washroom.

In his haste to reach his destination in order there to comply with his employer's request, M had quite forgotten to collect his free pocket comb with the text 'TTTW – Tutors To The World' imprinted upon it in eye-catching gold – a gift graciously provided for every member of the organisation – and found upon his return that all the combs had gone, most probably because some greedy person had helped himself to more than one of those useful implements. This, in his present situation, was rather a pity, for since, in the course of his chair-stacking labours, he had been perspiring heavily, his at the best of times unruly hair was, as the mirror in the washroom had told him, not only stickily moist but excessively dishevelled and in dire need of readjustment. To do him justice, he did, in fact, ask several colleagues to lend him their combs but without success, their disingenuous excuses ranging from Galbraith's banal 'My comb? Oh yes, my comb. I wonder where it has got to?' to Jeremiah Claybore's more imaginative 'Why, of course you can, my dear fellow, or, rather, I would have been happy to let you use it. Pity that in this heat its teeth have gone soft and can no longer manage any hair but my own, so I can't let you have it, after all.' Jeremiah was, in fact, as bald as an egg, but it was quite true that the heat in the room was almost unbearable, as evidenced by the excessively steamy atmosphere.

By this stage it was becoming obvious that the party was going to be a definite success. Dr. Pendlebloom, who now appeared to be planning some deep commercial strategy with Mr. Smallgrove, his personal consultant in all matters financial, and Mr. Woodlock of Woodlock, Woodlock and Spring, had already addressed 'the troops', inspiring them with the momentous news that in future TTTW would also provide the services of gentleman escorters, who, in order to distinguish them from the ladies, would be wearing extremely smart olive-green uniforms, and exhorting them, each and every one, to ever greater exertions in the service of TTTW, to which he referred, not quite aptly perhaps, as their common Alma Mater, pronouncing it the English way. As always when he was faced with such unheeding distortions of foreign words and names as the English were prone to perpetrate – due perhaps to an unshakable conviction that they were a race apart, better in every way than those poor slobs not fortunate enough to have been born and bred in their glorious land – M, who knew all about sound-shifts and such matters, winced, for he, in turn, had never doubted that positively the only way to speak Latin was the one taught at the Klappenhorn in Vienna. Whereas very few of those present had the faintest idea what Dr. Pendlebloom was talking about, one or two of the more highly educated such as Dr. McGill and Mme. Brausebrot from reception were, of course, quite familiar with this metaphor and reacted to Dr. Pendlebloom's use thereof with appropriately suppressed amusement, thus demonstrating their indubitable cultural superiority. As for little Jenny Fingerstaff from Accounts, she got hold, as she generally did, of the wrong end of the stick, inasmuch as she thought that her employer must be referring to Mrs. Mather, the fat lady who lived in the big house at the top of her road and whose name, for all she knew, might well be Alma, but couldn't quite work out where she came into the picture.

The music – provided at very reasonable cost by the 'Yodelling Oberunterbergers', who had been prevailed upon to desist, at least during the more formal stages of the evening, from renditions of their speciality and to confine themselves to more conventional fare – constituted a background of very acceptable but above all very suitable noise, as various couples, mainly but by no means exclusively young escorters and their guests, were out 'on the floor' dancing (there had been quite an influx of 'outsiders' as well, including several snooker-players on a mission of seasonal goodwill, members of a local club who had brought their cues – a development of which Dr. Pendlebloom and Miss Gomberg appeared as yet to be mercifully unaware) and Monsieur Chanteclerc and his dog disported themselves among them in what might loosely have been described as a Cossack-type leap dance. The buffet, of course, was in a state of permanent siege – some people's capacity and craving for 'refreshments' of all kinds, but especially of the liquid variety, being indeed quite astonishing – and wherever one looked there were groups of guests roaring with laughter, spiritedly raising their glasses to each other or apparently deep in animated discourse.

In the midst of such jollity a casual observer might therefore well have concluded that everyone, without any exception whatsoever, was having an absolutely stupendous time. Yet, as at any party, there were some so shy, so burdened with a sense of their own social inadequacy that for them this glittering occasion was nothing but a nightmare of protracted boredom and embarrassment. Shunned by most of the other guests, as contact with them tended to be both difficult and quite unrewarding, they, as much out of place as professional mourners at a wedding, stood about clutching generally empty glasses in hot, perspiring hands and counting the seconds until they might decently and unobtrusively depart. However, these solitary folk – mainly 'occasional' members of the TTTW panel of tutors, who did not 'know a soul', including some who were quite unable to communicate in English or any other of the languages represented – were not entirely overlooked, for Mrs. Bashmati, the rather luscious teacher of Hindi – pleasingly effervescent and but slightly unsteady on her sturdy, yet highly appealing undercarriage in spite of the fact that her alcoholic intake had been very much smaller than that of some of her colleagues – kept waddling from one to the other, inviting them to 'enjoy themselves' by getting 'involved'. In her green, gold-embroidered sari and with her dusky, plump cheeks made up to a darkish pinky-red tinge, she looked 'good enough to eat' and like some highly mature exotic fruit 'full of Eastern promise'.

Of course, not all the 'square pegs' belonged to this category, for almost equally out of place were those who, knowing at least some of the other guests, 'circulated' with dogged determination from group to group and generally wherever they might hope to be moderately welcome or at least tolerated. One such wanderer was M, who – too soon deprived of his chair-handling function and, as was his invariable lot at parties, far from the centres of attention – never, throughout the remainder of the evening, allowed his radiant expression indicative of intense interest and equally intense enjoyment, which like some festive garment he had assumed for this very occasion, to slip. As had happened to him so often before at similar events, he suffered a severe facial spasm for his pains.

Besides, he had a special problem which prevented him from enjoying himself to the full, inasmuch as he was being singularly unsuccessful in his chase after that elusive butterfly Catty, who, with her hair brushed upward and back in a sunny wave the colour of ripe corn and wearing her navy-blue dress, an elegant garment bought specially that very afternoon, looked – to M at least – fiendishly appetising. He had long been planning (although not in any definite way) to take advantage of this very occasion, when they might both be less inhibited than they usually were and social taboos might be less stringent, in order to 'enjoy' her, in one way or another. Flitting from pleasure to pleasure, however – sharing a joke here, exchanging smiles there and with, as it seemed to M, total abandonment dancing with one partner or another (M himself did not dance although he had had lessons in Australia) – she did not seem to have any time for him, and, try as he would, he couldn't get anywhere near her. Catty, the party girl, seemed to be quite a different person from the Catty he knew and desired, and there was absolutely nothing he could do about it.

Following the not unwelcome departure of Dr. Pendlebloom and the other VIPs, the atmosphere became more relaxed, somewhat steamy and even slightly mad. As the lights (rigged up by Monsieur Chanteclerc and his minions) flickered on the Christmas tree, Mr. Galbraith, already far beyond the boundaries of discretion, insisted on rendering in his high-piping voice that very popular song about 'Peanuts, crackers and a bottle of rum', for which he was handsomely applauded, young Mr. McBarnaby, at fifteen stone or thereabouts not the lightest of men, agreed to demonstrate the steps of a highland fling on top of a table which, in the event, did not prove equal to the onslaught, and Miss Kalinka Cillilit, who had slipped to the floor, had to be forcibly restrained from removing her undergarments. The Oberunterbergers, happily released by now from previous constraints, gave eardrum-splitting demonstrations of their yodelling skills, and four of them gave a display of their world-famous "Goat-herders' *Schuhplattler*". Even Frascatti joined in, understandably convinced that what they could do, he could do better.

M, half crazy with frustrated lust, was perhaps not on top of the world, but, to judge from the quality of his voice and the way he kept preening himself, Dr. McGill certainly was. 'I make it a point never to send Christmas cards,' he now boomed, intent on making his controversial views known to as wide an audience as possible, 'and such as I do receive I immediately convey to the dustbin.'

'Very wise, if I may say so,' cut in Mr. Daker while helping himself to yet another egg-and-tomato sandwich. 'These sandwiches are really quite tasty, considering ...'

'In our house, let me tell you,' – Dr. McGill, who had not the slightest intention of giving way to anyone and, in particular, to his friend, Mr. Daker, whom he thought of as rather a windbag and a fuddy-duddy, continued regardless – 'unsolicited presents are, as a matter of invariable routine, returned to the donor, for it is my firm and unshakable conviction that waste such as they invariably entail must on no account be encouraged.'

'I know what you mean, sir', said Mr. Lariani, who, having sidled up to them, now hoped to back up Dr. McGill's contention and thus to gain his approval by explaining that since the donor of a present not specifically requested could not, as a rule, know whether or not it would meet the recipient's current requirements and might, in fact, be unwelcome or even harmful, serious waste was indeed inevitable, but he did not get the chance to say any of this, for Dr. McGill was off again.

'Take, for instance, wrapping paper,' he proclaimed. 'If paper is needed to protect an object, well and good! But the paper in which presents are generally wrapped has quite a different function inasmuch as it is intended to add to the appeal of the object in question and thus mislead the recipient about the true value of the gift.'

'And, of course, we must not forget,' added M, who, having temporarily succeeded in putting Catty out of his mind, had joined this group and was now valiantly attempting to enrich the 'conversation' by pointing out that a present which was not the result of some personal sacrifice was as such devoid of any value whatsoever even though it might be very useful to the recipient. He did not, however, manage to complete his sentence, for Dr. McGill, tired no doubt of all this profundity, was moving away from him, and both Mr. Daker and Mr. Lariani had disappeared.

To console himself, M headed for the buffet but found his way barred by Madame Tartagliu, the buxom teacher of Romanian, and Mr. Clematis, whose special subject was Esperanto but who had in fact never been called upon to teach this or any other language. Having welcomed M as an old friend, Madame Tartagliu informed him, at great and pointless length, about her various problems and afflictions and how greatly she adored marvellous Dr. Pendlebloom, dear Miss Gomberg, Mr. Glub, the caretaker, and anyone else she could think of. As for thin and lanky Mr. Clematis, who wore, as he apparently did at every such occasion, a splendidly black-and-cream checkered suit, he, when it was finally his turn (Madame Tartagliu having walked off to talk to another old and cherished friend), explained earnestly why, in his considered opinion – an opinion, he affirmed, which he shared with a number of leading linguists and which was solidly supported by certain quite incontrovertible statistics – the future, such as it might be, belonged to Esperanto. Eventually M did manage to get away after all and make tracks for the buffet, which he did at speed, for he was by then in dire need of nourishment. However, the last sandwich had gone and the coffee was stone-cold, so M made do with the squashed and runny remains of what had once been a chocolate gateau of most sumptuous appearance. While forcing down the sickly stuff, he fell prey to Dr. Norbert, a Dutch colleague, who described to him, in a manner gravely intense, the numerous virtues of soup-on-a-stick, a product somewhat akin to the humble lollipop, which he claimed to be in the process of inventing. 'It will be available in many different varieties,' he explained, 'with chicken taste or mushroom-and-garlic taste or any other taste the public demands. Best of all, two most secret ingredients will ensure that in the mouth of the person sucking – in my patents such persons will be referred to quite simply as the "suckers" – the initially solid soup will liquefy and simultaneously heat up, thus making it eminently suitable for travellers, snackers and indeed anyone in need of hot, liquid soup. Believe me, my dear young colleague, we are here at the threshold of an entirely new era, with our feet firmly on the road to untold riches.'

M, who himself had 'invented' many an ingenious device, thought soup-on-a-stick an excellent idea and readily joined Dr. Norbert in his fantasy of unlimited wealth, in which he, it seemed, might have a share. In fact, he might well have revealed his own very latest creation, a method of communal heating based on controlled exploitation of the energy which small children expend as they run to and fro and jump about in their nurseries – he had even written a poem on this fascinating subject – had Dr. Norbert at this stage not asked him to lend him five pounds, promising to repay this sum with interest as soon as his 'boat came in'. For the miserly sum of fifty pounds, he would indeed be prepared to make M his 'sleeping partner'. Such a request was, of course, bound to make M extremely cautious, particularly as he did not have the slightest wish to become yet another sucker, especially of soup-on-a-stick. Besides, being badly in need of 'hydraulic discharge', he, in turn, pretended to have seen an old, long-lost friend at the other end of the hall and made his escape, again in the by now familiar direction of the gentlemen's washroom.

The weather being exceptionally cold M, who attached great value to his physical well-being, had donned two pairs of long woollen underpants, the openings of which did not precisely coincide – a circumstance which, given the pressure he was under, nearly caused him serious discomfort and major humiliation. Very fortunately, he managed, in a manner of speaking, to beat the clock, and he left the convenience in a state of considerable relief, which, however, far from alleviating his other pressing problem – Catty and what to do about her – actually aggravated it. He was, even in his present mildly inebriated state, too much of a realist to rate his chances at all highly, but, if anything, this very fact contributed to his desire, augmenting and stimulating his fantasies. Nothing, after all, was more likely to heighten the poignancy of his cravings more effectively than if they remained unsatisfied. Ultimate satisfaction was, as he had long suspected, a terminal event, and to that extent constituted a transition from real, pleasurable experience, which he saw as pertaining purely to the realm of sensation, to a state of mind characterised by a total lack of feeling, a kind of partial death, or, what was even worse, depression, disillusionment and anxiety in one form or another. The ancient Romans, who knew a thing or two and whose common sense was simply superb, had it that *post coitum omne animal triste*, an observation of which M was fully aware – as, indeed, he was of his Uncle Moritz's favourite principle 'moderation in all things', which however did not do the latter much good at the gaming tables of Monte Carlo and Baden Baden, where he failed quite singularly to quit while he was still reasonably solvent.

It goes without saying that on his way back from the gentlemen's washroom to the festive hall no such philosophical thoughts intruded into M's consciousness. His return might well have been rather a non-event hardly worth recording, had he not happened to pass by the store-room to the right of the corridor, which was small and dismal with but a single blind window and normally used for storing tables and chairs. In the course of previous visits to the washroom, M, being by nature unobservant of his environment and, for this and numerous other reasons, quite unsuitable for a career in the police-force, had paid absolutely no attention to that room, but on the present occasion he was drawn to it as by a powerful magnet, for he heard familiar but not immediately recognisable voices emanating from inside. As he brought his more efficient ear closer to the door (his ears were not of uniform efficiency), he was further able to make out that the two occupants of the store-room were a man and a girl. The man said something to the girl – it might have been an order although M could not be sure of that – and then started to hum a tune which, mainly during his seafaring days, M had learned to associate with strip-tease, an art also much practised at places of entertainment throughout Soho. No-one could normally have been more discreet and indeed gentlemanly than M, but there are limits to what a man can stand. As he bent down and endeavoured to peer through the mercifully unblocked keyhole, he at first couldn't see anything at all but eventually discerned a broad back covered by a black gown and above it what could only be the black tassle of a mortar-board such as the one worn on ceremonial occasions by his colleague, Dr. McGill. So that was who it was! M had always suspected the good doctor of being a humbug and a bit of a voyeur, and this proved it. At the same time he could not but wish that he himself were now in the shoes of that old swine (that is how he now thought of him, not without a hint of admiration), as indeed he might well have been if he were not always so hypercautious or, to put it more bluntly, such a bloody coward. Then an awful realisation dawned on him. The girl, of course, was none other than Catty, now probably without a stitch of clothing on her lovely body, and quite possibly prone across the sturdy knees of Dr. McGill, her 'fatherly friend'. How could he, M, have been so unbelievably stupid, so absolutely dense, as not to guess what was going on between those two? And to crown it all, McGill was a married man with children, but this, quite clearly, did not bother them in the least – probably even added spice and interest to their relationship. Still, he'd give anything …

Suddenly aware that he was not alone, that someone was watching him, M straightened his back and looked round, only to encounter Catty's ironical gaze as she regarded him with frank amusement and barely concealed disdain. She, far from bare or prone across anybody's knees, was utterly, tantalisingly delectable and as neat and tidy as if she had just come out of a presentation wrapper.

'Having a good time?', she enquired. 'Must be interesting, whatever's going on in there.' And as if this were not enough – as if the joke needed further amplification – there was Dr. McGill coming along the corridor on his way to the gentlemen's washroom. 'So that's where you meet your girlfriend,' he said, 'I had been wondering what had become of you two. Love must indeed be wonderful.'

Too shattered to say a single word in reply, M simply turned and fled.

Mr. Allbright was a small, bespectacled man with greyish, crumpled features and a permanently apologetic smile. Looking at him, or in casual conversation, it was impossible to tell that he was, in fact, a something or other of considerable distinction, well known not only in his own field but also to the general public throughout the world. His determination to master German was due mainly to his love of literature and a quite obsessive desire to read the immortal works of Schiller, Goethe and Thomas Mann in the language in which they had been written. Due most likely to his already considerable age, his powers of concentration and memory were rather poor, and, even after two years of individual tuition, he was still unable to formulate a reasonably intelligible sentence in German, still struggling with the most elementary principles of grammar. In his efforts to reach his goal, he was, to all intents and purposes, like a man without a map or compass stumbling about in dense fog on a mountain, with no idea at all where he has come from or where he is going.

M really liked Mr. Allbright and wished him well, but he dreaded their lessons, for, whereas some of M's other students were only too happy to switch to English and general conversation – after only a few perfunctory and mercifully quite brief attempts at improving their German – which could be quite enjoyable and made time pass, Mr. Allbright always insisted on ploughing through his textbook, a first-year course for grammar schools, as if it were holy writ, over and over again, never permitting himself to be deflected from the purpose at hand. Not that they ever got beyond lesson twelve, by which time he would again have forgotten most of what had gone before and, being a great and unquestioning believer in the value of laying sound foundations, felt that it might be a good idea to go over that all-too-well-trodden ground again. Indeed, it would be true to say that Mr. Allbright regarded sound foundations in general with virtually mystical fervour. Furthermore – and that was the core of the problem – Mr. Allbright had great, even unshakable, confidence in

M's ability as a teacher, in spite of the fact that what they had achieved together had, so far, been hardly worth the investment.

As for M, on the other hand, it was not unusual for him to forget his lesson with Mr. Allbright entirely or, finding himself in some desperately wrong place, not to be able to get to it in good time. On one unforgettable and indeed never forgotten occasion he actually failed to recall where the lesson, which he knew to have been scheduled, was to take place, and, wandering from classroom to classroom, wasted much time before eventually discovering Mr. Allbright's whereabouts, whereupon the latter, not in the least put out by the resultant delay, cut short, with a gesture of perfect forgiveness, M's garbled, breathless explanations and invited him to explain, once more, the vagaries of the indefinite article or some similarly elementary point. It will be readily understood that M's search for his misplaced student – in the course of which he had had to enter quite a few classrooms, most of them occupied and with lessons in progress – gave rise to much frivolity, with one of M's colleagues, a Texan specialist in American English (who, at Dr. Pendlebloom's special request, always wore a complete cowboy's outfit including a 10-gallon hat in class), even going so far as to suggest that he might organise a posse to help him locate his quarry. Embarrassment too could not be avoided and in one case proved to be quite considerable. Indeed, this episode, an ever fertile source of banter, made him feel rather as in those far-off days at the Klappenhorn when, as was so frequently the case, he had missed the starting-bell in the morning. Still, none of this was the fault of Mr. Allbright – that immensely tolerant man who never complained (as well he might have), displayed not the slightest annoyance when M let him down once again, and continued to smile through it all like some benign and benevolent guru – and he, at any rate, should not be blamed for M's difficulties in this regard.

It was the morning after Lipkin's farewell party – he was finally off to rejoin his Rosabelle – and M was feeling out-of-sorts and very much under the weather. Truth to tell, it had not really been a party, for apart from Lipkin only M had been present, but the evening had dragged on endlessly, with Lipkin sipping away at anything alcoholic in sight and becoming increasingly sentimental as the hours wore on. However, true to his resolution never again to miss a lesson with Mr. Allbright and to make special efforts in order to merit his good opinion, M had, for his first lesson of the new year, actually made it to the right classroom before Mr. Allbright himself arrived, a fact which cannot have escaped the attention of the latter and must surely have filled him with a great, overwhelming sense of optimism, although (of course) he, a gentleman through and through, did not exhibit the slightest trace of vulgar surprise or pleasure at this unexpected turn of events.

As the lesson got under way M found it increasingly difficult to keep awake. His eyes kept closing, his head felt unduly heavy and out of control, and even speaking presented untold problems. To give himself some respite, he instructed Mr. Allbright to read a lengthy passage from the book, and thus temporarily released from the necessity of further effort, allowed himself to give in, for a moment only (he thought), to his by now irresistible drowsiness. In his mind he relived again the various stages of his escape to Poland, the way he had cleverly waited until dark and then enquired the way from a pair of lovers too busy with their own concerns to pay much attention to him or hand him over to the authorities, how, on his long trek to Michailovce, he had avoided any unwelcome curiosity on the part of such border-guards as he came across by wishing them, in rudimentary Polish, a good evening and then asking them the time, and how, eventually, he had approached a woman in traditionally Jewish black garb on her way to a cottage on the outskirts of the village, as his instinct told him that she was the right person to ask for assistance. This is where his recollections and his dream definitely parted company, for she, beckoning him to follow, now appeared to be growing ever larger and increasingly less distinct until she faded entirely into the blackness of the night.

Suddenly, M found himself in a crowded stable lit dimly by one sputtering candle, surrounded on all sides by a multitude of unbelievably noisy domestic animals – horses neighing, cows mooing, dogs barking, donkeys braying and chickens clucking. Wherever he looked there were goats and sheep, and he saw a large black cat sitting on a rafter. The woman too had reappeared, and now he could see that it was indeed his stepmother, brandishing a fearsome stick and hectically swaying to and fro in a rocking-chair. M, in dire panic, was desperately looking for a way out, when the scene changed again and he was facing, across a table, a single grey sheep, the other animals and the woman in black having, at least for the time being, vanished. M and the sheep – a monstrously large sheep it was, with a permanent, irritating twinkle in its eye – were locked in an excruciatingly tedious game which involved the picking-up of various figures (close inspection revealed them to be rigidified, tiny effigies of the stable folk that had previously given M such a rowdy reception) and depositing them in various areas of the table, the only rule apparently being that whenever M picked up the figure of the woman in black, as indeed he was bound to do from time to time, the sheep, its twinkle broadening to a grin such as its kind is known for, would rise wheezing on its shaggy, disgustingly soiled hindlegs and, thus rampant, start pounding his chest violently with its front hooves, while M in much torment and fearing for his life, begged it to desist.

The first sight that met M's eyes when he – not without some effort and reluctance – opened them, was Mr. Allbright, who was tapping him gently on the shoulder in order to wake him up. Mr. Allbright was still smiling benignly as he explained that the bell had rung, signalling the end of the lesson. It took M a little while to grasp the full significance of what had happened, but once he, not by any means a fool, had understood, he at last realised that teaching was not for him after all and that he had better change his 'profession' forthwith.